# The Life and Times

# of Nobody Worth A Damn

# by

# Robert Rogers

Also by Robert G. Rogers

Tale of Two Sisters
Murder in the Pine Belt
Killing in Oil
Jennifer's Dream
The Pinebelt Chicken War
The La Jolla Shores Murders
Murder at the La Jolla Apogee,
No Morning Dew
Brother James and the Second
Comng
All Bishop Bone Murder Mysteries.

The Christian Detective,
That La Jolla Lawyer, murder mysteries

Runt Wade, Suspense/Thriller and,
The End is Near

Jodie Mae, Historical Fiction

French Quarter Affair, Contemporary Drama

Juvenile Adventures: Lost Indian Gold, Taylor's Wish,
Swamp Ghost Mystery, Armageddon Ritual,

Children's Picture book: Fancy Fairy

# Chapter 1

The blue greyhound bus squeaked to a stop on the gravel road and after the orange dust plume following it had drifted past and settled, the uniformed driver pushed a button and the bus door opened with a loud "swoosh." A man with a frown on his face adjusted his backpack and moved quickly down the aisle, glancing through the bus windows to check the outside as he did. His name was Caleb Stanley. Moments before, he had pulled the bus's cord signaling it to stop at the lower end of Marshall Park, a few miles outside the small town in south Mississippi where he was born, Marshalltown.

It was Sunday, the weekend before Memorial Day. He knew the park would be full, even as much as it would be the next weekend, the holiday weekend. It was always full on weekends, well it always had been. It had been years since he was there. He knew that people fled their cramped homes during weekends with energetic children to relax and enjoy the wilderness expanse and freedom of the park. He doubted that had changed.

When Caleb was at the steps, the driver touched the dark bill of his gray hat and with the smile remembered from the orientation lecture mouthed words that sounded like, "Watch your step, Sir."

But, Caleb wasn't paying attention. He trudged wearily down the steps without a reply, staring blankly into the woods facing the bus. The worn brown leather-canvass backpack wobbled between his shoulders, evidence that it held very little.

No breeze greeted him as he stepped from the bus steps onto the gravel road with a crunch. He immediately felt the early afternoon sun bearing down. He stepped away to let the door close and the bus continue to Marshalltown, its next scheduled stop.

Caleb wore a short sleeved khaki shirt which matched his pants, both worn and frayed. No belt held his pants in place, but he had one in his backpack. He'd taken it off during the trip. His old tennis shoes, once white, had loosely tied laces so he could easily take them off during the long ride and put them back on without a hindrance.

With a sigh, he pushed his plastic rimmed glasses back onto his nose and headed for the path directly ahead. It led into the woods.

*****

About fifty years had passed since he'd been on the path and from where he stood, it didn't look to have changed much in all that time. The last time he was there was for an outing with his mother and father and brothers and sisters. He was eleven years old then and not very tall. Now, he had just turned sixty and stood a shade under six feet tall.

Having spent much of his career bent over a work bench, he stood with a slight stoop. His hair, though thinning, was light brown with gray streaks. He hadn't had a haircut in a long time so the hair stuck out here and there and partially covered his ears. Likewise he hadn't seen fit to shave during the same period so a thick brown beard covered his face and stuck out in patches. Not that he cared about either, a haircut or a shave.

His face was gaunt with no hint of a smile; prominent cheek bones, a nose with a slight bow; his eyes bright green but bloodshot. He was reasonably fit, with good shoulders and no extra weight, not that he worked at it. It just happened that way.

Caleb had never been considered handsome or even attractive, certainly not enough that would stop anyone for a second look and few ever did, not that he cared in the slightest. His face was plain. He knew it and accepted it as part of his persona, the way he was. Why waste time trying to change what he couldn't change. Life was simpler that way. Besides, he'd come to accept that people looked at what he did or what he could do for them, not what he looked like or even how he went about doing what he did. For much of his working life, he had been content to be, what he called himself, an invisible man.

His dad, in his sixties, had begun suffering small strokes while Caleb was in high school and was forced to take it easy. He had become the manager of the local hard board plant, but still worked their farm when he could until his health forced him to retire. When that happened and he could no longer do the things he had been doing, he became depressed and never recovered. Caleb's mother, who had worked side-by-side with him on the farm, also went into a depression. They figured her depression and ultimate health decline was probably related to their dad's poor health.

Before his mom's and dad's health went bad, they had been a happy family. They couldn't wait for the weekends when his dad and mom always had something planned for the family to do together. Sometimes it was just working the farm but on other times, they went places. But whatever it was that they did, they always had fun and they always enjoyed being together.

That all changed when their health deteriorated. His mom and dad barely spoke to each other let alone the children. And, they never went out together again. The children kept the farm up and tried to cheer up their mom and dad but they didn't succeed. It was like they had given up on life. And, eventually, their depressions wore on the children to the point that they couldn't wait to leave home. Though never expressed, they felt they were no longer a family, certainly not the family they had all loved.

On the money side of the change, his dad had enough money coming in to cover their expenses, but not enough to pay anything for anything the children might want to do, like go to college. As a result, his younger brother and sister moved to Alabama and found jobs as soon as they could. His older brother joined the Marines and became a career soldier. Caleb enlisted in the Army to get the GI Bill for college. Even with that, he had to work part time, in the department's testing lab, to cover everything. He graduated as an electrical engineer with a specialty in automotive electronics.

He had married right out of college at age twenty four, the oldest in his class. He often wondered how it had happened, the marriage. But, his focus at the time was undertaking the job he'd been offered and handling the responsibilities in a way that would please his employer and make his family proud. Although he wasn't sure how much they cared or even understood what he was doing by that time. When he visited, it was like they barely recognized him, like he was a stranger. The last time he came home, he cried at the despair he had felt trying to carry on conversations with them. Looking back, after that day, he quit caring about anything but his work.

His wife, an attractive woman, had actually asked him to marry her within a month or so of coming to California and beginning work. They'd met at a community gathering he'd inadvertently attended at the request of his boss, one of the organizers. Her boldness was something of a surprise, but not much of one. It was the age of the liberated women and they assumed rights previously owned exclusively by men. Besides, he hadn't had that much experience with women and, just then, he was still absorbing the responsibilities of his first real job.

He had taken a job with an automotive design company in California and never left it. His dad had also been an engineer when he went to work at the hardwood plant. He once told Caleb that he'd never met an electrical problem he couldn't solve. Caleb was proud to follow in his footsteps and liked to say the same thing about his abilities.

So, it came to pass, the marriage. At her request, they bought a house, her selection, which they never left.

They had two children, a boy and a girl. Both left home when they went to college and never came back, not even for holidays. He wasn't surprised about that. Most of the time, well, practically all of the time, it seemed that four strangers shared the house without bothering to get to know the others. It reminded him of how things were at his family home after his mom and dad had lapsed irretrievably into depression.

Now and then, he discussed his feelings, or lack of feelings, with his wife. She passed them off as "looking for problems where none existed. You're the only one worrying." So, as he did with situations that involved feelings, he took the easy way out and accepted her comments at face value. No need to rock the boat, he decided.

He wasn't sure where the children worked or lived after their graduation. He got the impression that they were in contact with his mother but she rarely spoke of them and when he asked, she gave him an "all is okay" answer.

Caleb had outlived his parents, his brothers and sisters and all his relatives. When they were alive, before the "depressions" he felt he was somebody, the "son of" or "the brother of" and felt pride, but when they were gone, he felt like he was nobody and somehow accepted that.

Being an engineer, even the responsible one he'd become, never took him to the level of being part of a happy family. The job always seemed something he'd agreed to do for enough money to take care of the responsibilities life had handed him, not anything that carried the feelings he had felt during the happy times with his family.

He knew it was normal for people to die, including parents and siblings, but it seemed strange to him. They had always been there, always with a kind word, always loving, and always supportive when they were healthy. Then, they slipped away and he eventually accepted that fact but it came at a price. Part of him died in the process.

His wife had told him many times that he was unfeeling and not well liked by the people they knew. He didn't argue with her assessment. Reactions on the faces of the people at work and people he met in everyday life had already told him he was not well liked. As far as feelings, well, he didn't care about people any more than they cared about him. That's not to say he actively disliked anyone. It was more that he didn't actively like anyone.

He knew that's how people saw him as well, just a person they had to deal with now and then. They were as nice and cordial as they had to be to get done what had to be done before moving on. Most, he found, only wanted to hear things that made them feel better. Very few wanted to take the time to make anybody else feel better.

One morning, he got out of bed, looked in the mirror and said, "I'm tired of all the damned one way verbal feel-goods that I lay on every Tom, Dick and Harry, maybe a Jane or two, that I run into." He called his approach to everyday life an "adjective, adverb" personality, a way to get a job done or to ease past an encounter without conflict and if lucky, perhaps leave a good impression that'd make the next encounter easier.

So, he quit his "adjective, adverb" personality and, all those who had occasionally detoured past for one of his "feel-good" pats on the back quit pretending to care about anything but whatever job he was doing. That reaction was all Caleb needed to build a wall between him and a society churning with built-in rules, some spoken, some unspoken, that controlled those who submitted to the mindless churn. Besides, he had long since grown tired of people offering the "most wonderful" "the greatest" "the cure for all ills" and on and on and all with ever increasing prices. It was an easy jump from that hypocrisy to turning away from what was happening in the rest of the world, hypocrisy on a grand scale, and often deadly.

What he never took time to consider was the impact the wall would have on him, not that he cared. In effect, it separated him even more from people and the normal feelings that all had, the joy, anger, concern, likes and dislikes. And, so, he quit learning about that part of life and without realizing it, he became more remote than he'd been; he quit smiling or even pretending to smile. And, when his parents and siblings were gone, he quit all feelings and was content to be what he called a special purpose machine, taking care of his job and his family.

Besides, he thought, there has never been a damn thing I could do about anything, anywhere, other than my job. And, doing that let him eat, pay his bills and take care of his wife and children which he deemed his primary responsibility.

He ceased voting for whoever was claiming to do something but when elected always found an excuse for not doing it and always pointed at someone else who prevented it. He quit reading the newspapers, quit watching the news and quit becoming aggravated or frustrated by things always beyond his control. Besides, nothing ever seemed to change for the better no matter who did or didn't do it and the media devolved into a medium that only seemed to air excuses for failure.

As far as he was concerned, he lived in a culture of smoke and mirrors controlled by people he never met or saw but who always seemed to want something from him, usually money. Resigning from the organized part of the world relieved him of those burdens as well. And, all of that made life simple for him. Except for his work, everything else was nothing and that, in the final analysis, completed his transfer into invisibility. And, being invisible, he told himself, means I don't have to jump when the guys with the smoke and mirrors say I should.

Over time, people abandoned all pretenses when dealing with Caleb, they just did what had to be done to get the benefit of whatever job he was doing and he preferred life that way. To succeed, he had always depended on his wits and the discipline to use them. That much did not change. He never asked for help from anyone nor had he ever needed any. If a job couldn't be done by him, it couldn't be done. He inherited that confidence from his father.

And, when that came to an end, he had nothing left, no friends and no family, only the depression he'd probably had since the last time he'd visited his mom and dad. So, he caught a greyhound bus to return to the only place he had ever been truly happy. He came to Marshall Park where his family had come, as they often did – the happy times - for an overnight campout when he was a teenager. The last time they ended up staying three nights, fishing, swimming, cooking out, singing and playing games. His father played the guitar and his mother sang. It was the most fun he'd ever had or ever had since that time. He and his two brothers and sister explored wherever the trails in the park led and found adventures along each.

# Chapter 2

For a moment, Caleb held up to stare into the shadows of the narrow, dirt path which visitors used to access the lower part of the park. Branches of the pines and oaks lining the path formed a canopy to cover the trail in shadows but sun light found openings and broke the shadows into irregular patches and streaks that moved with the wind through the trees, back and forth, like live things playing over the black dirt.

Before continuing, he took note of the thorny wild plum trees flanking both sides of the path's opening. They sprouted out of the red clay belt that swept through South Mississippi from plum pits dropped by birds in the scant top soil over the clay. Rain and sunlight had done the rest. Just then, the limbs were laden with red and yellow plums, just beginning to ripen.

The trees were far enough off the gravel road to avoid the slashing blades of grading equipment used by the county crews to keep the road in usable condition. And, far enough back for the road dust to settle before covering the juicy, sweet plums that would ripen in the summer which was right around the corner.

In fact, eighty degree temperatures had already begun to fill the days with heat and humidity. Mercifully, rains came frequently to provide relief to those who had to be outside.

Beads of sweat had begun to form on his forehead. After a moment's hesitation, he reached back, yanked a cap out of his backpack and pulled it onto his head to shade it from the bright sunlight. It was an instinctive move. Afterwards, he questioned why he had chosen to avoid a bit of aggravation from the sun when he had something far more important to confront than the glare of the sun. But, the hat was on so he left it there. Too much trouble to take off and shove back into his pack. It was his way; minimum effort yielded minimum aggravation.

There was no parking in that area so park goers had to park across the road in someone's pasture and walk the few hundred yards to the path to get into the park. Most visitors preferred to park their cars and trucks, even campers, up the road in the designated parking area. They felt more secure leaving their vehicles there. Also, most of the camp sites were near the parking area and also closer to Marshall River which bordered the park and provided the park's main attraction. But heartier campers, those preferring to be more alone, liked the private end of the park, the part Caleb remembered.

He had never given much thought as to whether the town was named after the river or the river named after the town.

He hurried along the shaded path that would take him into the park. Scents of wild flowers mingled with other scents from the woods and followed him as he hurried along. They were the smells he remembered from years before.

After a few minutes' walk, he reached the end of the path that opened into a flat clearing overlooking the river. That was where his parents had raised their tent when they came to the park and where they had dug a little hole for a campfire. From below the clearing, where he stood, came the gentle flowing sounds of the river. Birds sang in the trees around the opening adding music to the river's gentle flow.

He dropped his backpack on the ground and walked to the edge of the tree covered slope to view the river. The water, slightly green then, would take the color of clay from the ground it passed through when the heavy rains came. And, the river's currents would become more turbulent then.

Birds in the tree's branches took flight when he came close but soon returned when they decided he meant them no harm. Two squirrels chattered on a high branch and watched.

From someplace down the river, he heard voices, the voices of a family, maybe more than one, having fun as he and his family had once had. He turned in that direction but could see nothing.

Having finished his look at the river, he reached inside one of the pouches of his backpack for a camping knife. With the knife, he dug a small opening in the center of the area for a fire pit. When it was about a foot deep, he tore a newspaper, also from the backpack, into shreds and put it in the bottom of the pit. The shredded newspaper, he covered with dead leaves and pine straw. On top of all that, he placed several small stones in a circle, leaned back for a look and nodded. The job was half done.

He reached into the backpack again and pulled out an empty fruit juice can. Inside the can was a plastic bag filled with leaves, flower buds and washed roots. All he needed to finish the job was water.

Behind him towered a huge rock, like a miniature mountain standing sentinel over the slope down to the river. He stood and walked toward it. When he had last been there, he and his brothers discovered that the rock housed a cave accessible by a narrow sand stone path that ran parallel to the river. Over the years since, briars and vines had grown and covered every opening of the rock.

It would have been almost impossible for anyone to know there was a cave inside, waiting to be re-discovered. However, Caleb knew the cave was there, and armed with that knowledge and his knife, he cut through enough briars and vines to open the sand stone path that ended at the mouth of the cave. He was after the cool water that flowed from inside the cave into the river.

Years before, he and his brothers proclaimed the water to be the best they'd ever tasted. His father had first discovered it but let them discover it for themselves with a few hints. The water was why the father had picked that spot for their camp out.

I hope it's still there, Caleb thought.

He was not disappointed. As he grew close to the cave's small opening, he saw the crystalline sparkle of clear water flowing from the mouth of the cave down the sandstone slope to the river. Remembering it from the last time he was there, almost made him smile, but he let it go. It wasn't a smiling day.

He dipped the can he'd brought into the stream until it was about half full and walked back to the small hole he'd dug. He cut the leaves and stems and small roots from the plastic bag into bite sized pieces on his handkerchief before crushing it together with flower buds from the plastic bag. Once that was done, he sat the can with the water on the circle of rocks he'd placed in the fire pit and he took matches from the backpack to lite it. That's when he heard a voice saying something he couldn't catch.

Except for the sounds of campers coming from someplace down the river, he hadn't seen anyone and hadn't heard anyone. He searched the clearing but could see no one. He shrugged it off and again directed his attention to the fire pit.

There, he heard it again! Was it the voice of a man or a woman? He couldn't tell, but he did understand what was said, "Good afternoon, Caleb."

*Someone knew his name? How could that be?*

Was it coming from inside the cave? It sounded like it was and yet, he was just at the mouth of the cave and had seen nothing, had heard nothing. Besides, the mouth was still covered in briars. No one could have gotten inside.

"I'm going nuts," he said. "It figures."

"Looks like water hemlock on your handkerchief. You've brought it here to end it all, to the place you remember from your childhood. A touch of wistfulness, I'd say, to leave your troubles behind in a place where you had truly felt peace and happiness. I'd say the last place you had been happy. That was before your dad began having his strokes."

"What? How do you know? You know my name. How'd you know about my dad? Who are you? I suppose you're going to give me the story about not doing it. People need me so I should stick around. Well, I'll tell you, nobody needs me. Nobody will miss me. I'm an invisible man in this world. That's why I'm here."

"No indeed. I'm not going to try and stop you. I applaud your decision. When you've done all you came to do, you should leave. Otherwise, you're just a burden on everybody else. I support your freedom to do that, an exercise of your free will. More people should do the same when they look ahead and see nothing, as you have. They should apply that discipline to other burdens they face. The world might be a better place," the voice said.

"I'm only concerned with me, my wasted life, not the world's. I resigned from the world years ago."

"Well, waste no more, Caleb. Light your fire."

"How do you know me?"

"I know everything I want to know and it just so happens that I picked you to know you in your final hours. You became my project."

"Your project?"

"Sure. Remember school, when the teacher gave everyone projects to teach you how to think, how to discipline your thoughts and how to put them under your control instead of under the control of one instinct or another? I don't need to do that, but I thought in my last days here, I'd make you my project since you had a beginning, middle and now your end," the voice explained.

Caleb still couldn't see anything. "I don't see you. Where in the hell are you hiding?"

"I'm not hiding. You can hear me can't you?"

"Yeah."

"Would seeing me make what you're hearing anything clearer?" it asked.

Caleb shook his head. "I guess not."

"Well, then talking should be all we need for our conversation."

Caleb shrugged. "Yeah. Well, if you'll excuse me, I have to finish my job. I didn't come here to talk to strange voices."

"I'm not strange, but please do proceed. Make your stew. That water hemlock will most certainly kill you, Caleb. Painfully, but I don't suppose a bit of pain would matter to a man like you."

"A bit of pain, as you say, will pale beside what I've already suffered," Caleb said.

"The pain you brought on yourself when you ... as you say, resigned from the world, quit being a human, you could say."

Caleb looked around. He frowned at the comment. "Hmm. You may be right. But, it's too late to change that now."

He struck a match against a stone. It burst into a flame which he stuck into the torn newspaper. It caught fire immediately. He re-positioned his can of water on top of the circle of rocks in the hole and leaned back to watch it warm. The handkerchief with the mix of hemlock lay on the ground next to the pit.

"Since you're going to die, Caleb, there's one thing you might want to do before you go. I'd like it for my project."

Caleb turned to face the rock, where the voice seemed to come from. "What thing? There's nothing else for me to do. You want me to pray?" He scoffed. "Hell of a lot of good that's ever done anybody. I don't think there's been a miracle lately. I haven't seen one unless it's a miracle that you're talking to me. I haven't had a personal conversation in ... well, I can't remember the last one I did have."

The voice laughed. "No doubt, since you elected to become invisible. I agree however, praying won't do you any good. No, I was thinking about a little boy a couple of hundred yards from here. Can't be more than six. Drifted away from his family and their friends. They're busy joking and carrying on ... drinking beer. The problem is, he's about to wander into a marshy spot to pick wild blueberries. You know how kids are. Maybe adults too, when you get down to it. They just see what they're after and don't look for things that might interfere with getting them."

Caleb looked down at the fire. Steam had begun to twist out of the can of hot water. "Get on with it. The water is ready for my mix. Your project is about to end, prematurely."

"Not prematurely, but I understand your thinking. Projects end when they end. I'm sorry to take so long. Thoughtless of me. My point is this. There are three large cotton mouth moccasins sunning around the blueberry bushes. Water fills the area when it rains and the snakes move in, looking for something that shows up in the water. The thing is, Caleb, the snakes have heard the boy and are on alert. Coiled up, ready to strike. They consider him an intruder and will bite him before he ever reaches the blueberries. He'll be dead before his family even knows he's gone."

"Nothing to do with me."

"I know, since everything to you is nothing, but you could stop him, the poor innocent boy. Just for the hell of it. He never did anything to anybody. He's just like you were years and years ago, young and innocent. It'll only take ten minutes and you can still make your hemlock stew. It'll still kill you within hours after you eat it or drink it, whatever. What's ten minutes? You could do one good thing before you die, though. Save that little boy. I don't think you've done anything good lately, have you?"

Caleb rubbed the top of his head as if considering the voice's question. "Never stopped to think about it. If I did it was accidental."

"Head downstream. You'll get to the pool just as he's about to step into it. Better hurry though or you'll be too late."

Caleb stared hard at his can of water. Flames curled around it. He touched the crumbled pile of hemlock on his handkerchief with a frown. "The boy's not my problem."

"He's going to be dead," the voice said. "Kind of selfish, don't you think. Only take a couple of minutes to save him."

Caleb shook his head. Not my damned problem.

"It's on your plate to solve. And, you're the only one who can."

Caleb shifted his look from the can of boiling water toward where the voice seemed to be coming from and frowned.

"The can's not going anywhere."

Caleb cursed, stood and after a last glance back at the can of water on the fire, began jogging in the direction the voice had sent him. A few seconds later, he saw the small boy, standing at the edge of a marshy depression and saw the green blueberry bushes growing from small mounds of earth at the far edge. He couldn't see the snakes, but had no doubt they were there. The boy took a step into the edge of the pool.

"Wait," he called to the boy who looked around to see who had spoken. When he saw Caleb, he stopped and began backing away.

"Snakes," Caleb said.

By then, he was beside the boy and pointing at the black, coiled snakes partly concealed under rotting debris. "See."

Relief couldn't have been more obvious on the boy's face when he saw the huge snakes curling around. He stuck his fingers in his mouth and nodded. "Mama said …"

"She was right."

Caleb took the boy by the hand and walked him downstream toward where, he correctly assumed, their camp was located. Soon, he saw men women and children huddled in a nervous gathering. The boy pulled free of Caleb's hand and ran toward them.

"Mama … Daddy …" he shouted with arms outstretched.

Everyone turned. Smiles of relief replaced the concerned frowns on their faces.

One of the men, somewhat short and overweight, dropped to one knee and held his arms out for the boy to run into. One hand held a can of beer. A woman kneeled beside them and pulled the boy into her arms. She hugged him and kissed his face. The little boy began crying.

As Caleb turned to leave, he heard the boy say, "A man –" His arm pointed toward Caleb. The rest was lost.

Caleb saw everyone staring at him. He didn't stop. However, he did pick up the pace as he began jogging back to the can of water he'd left on the camp fire, and the crumbled handful of hemlock next to it. He hated being interrupted and finishing that was what he'd come to do.

Behind him, he heard a man's voice call, "Wade … Leroy …" The man sounded frantic.

The tone of the call hastened Caleb's hurried jog away. Soon he was beside his fire pit. Spirals of steam curled up from the water in the can. He felt some relief.

"Should be just right for your mix," the voice said. "Put it in. Your troubles will soon be over. By the way, I think the little boy was grateful. Scared, but grateful. Too bad you couldn't hang around. Good thing though."

Caleb nodded, got to his knees and reached for the hemlock.

"I'm not so sure about his family. Knowing human nature as I do, especially when it's drained of will power by canned spirits, the beer they were drinking, I bet they're going to assume you abducted that little boy with mal-intent but changed your mind. Well, maybe you didn't change your mind, they'll be thinking, just finished what you intended."

Caleb looked in the direction of the voice then back in the direction of where he'd left the boy. He heard angry, frantic voices. And, they were headed in his direction.

"Hell," he said.

"'Fraid so," the voice said. "They're coming after you, Caleb. The beer they've been drinking all day will give them all the courage they need to track you down. I doubt you'll have time to finish your brew before they get here. And, I seriously doubt they'd let you finish anything after they find you. In fact, I imagine you'll spend the night in a jail cell, with a few bruises, until that little boy gets a doctor's examination to see what awful things you did to him."

"I saved his life. You …" More angry voices coming from downstream interrupted him.

"I think you did the right thing, don't you? How could you know how his parents would react? If I were you, though, I'd gather my stuff including your hemlock and get out of here. I'd leave the can. I'd say you only have a couple of minutes. There's the junk yard over the bridge. Good place to hide for the night." The bridge spanned the river.

Caleb had seen it from the bus window as it drove past, before he pulled the cord to be let out. He grabbed his backpack in one hand, shoved his hemlock back into the plastic bag and put it into the backpack. He kicked the can over. The water hissed and spewed steam as it flowed over the fire.

Within seconds, he was running down the dirt path toward the gravel road and the safety of the automotive junk yard a few hundred yards away. He was gone by the time the boy's parents and their friends reached his fire pit.

*****

Someone called. "Billy Ray! You find the bastard?"

"I'm here! The son of a bitch is gone."

The others spread out in a circle but found no trace of Caleb. A few made it to the gravel road but Caleb was already over the bridge by then, standing in front of the fenced junk yard ready to find a hiding place to spend the night.

# Chapter 3

He spotted a small animal trail that led into the junk yard. Ignoring the "No Trespassing" sign, he ducked under the barbed wire fence, got onto the trail and was soon swallowed up by rusting cars and trucks. Over the years, seeds brought by the wind and birds had sprouted into trees that found places to grow in the open spots of the junk yard and had begun to retake what man had cleared. It was dusk dark by that time. The rush of the river rolled up the gentle slope on his left as he walked through the rusted remains of abandoned vehicles.

The little trail soon played out so he wandered between the vehicles piled against one another until he found an opening surrounded by decaying cars and trucks. It looked to have been used at one time by someone as a camp site but from the weeds and debris, it had been a very long time since it had. Someone had dragged out enough car seats and cushions from the abandoned vehicles to make a sleeping bench under an old oak tree which had found enough nourishment to survive. There were also the ash remains of a fire in a fire pit, rusted cans and the rotting remnants of paper wrappers.

He propped his backpack against the trunk of the tree and took a deep breath. No angry voices could be heard behind him, only the calm, sweeping sounds of the river. He had escaped.

He regretted leaving his can behind, but if he had any luck at all, it'd still be there tomorrow. He'd get it then. Nothing really had changed. He could finished what he'd come to do tomorrow. One more day's not going to change anything.

"There's time to get another fire going, Caleb. No need to wait until tomorrow. There are probably plenty of cans around here. In fact, there's one right over there. To your right. May have to scoot down to the river for your water. It'll be dirty, but that shouldn't be a problem for your purpose. What's a little dirty water to a dead man?"

"Yeah," Caleb said without thinking and glanced to his right for the can. Sure enough, there was a can a few feet away, one with very little rust on it. He picked it up and looked for a place to dig a new fire pit.

"You can get out of here tonight," the voice said. "Reminds me of an old folk song. All your troubles, Lord, soon be over. I may have messed up a couple of words, but that's the gist."

As if suddenly realizing he was talking to someone, he twisted this way and that but could see nothing. "What the hell! You followed me! What are you? Who are you? "

"Well, if you insist, I'll give you a brief glance." With that, a blur appeared in the mist of the late afternoon a few feet from where he stood. At first it looked like a man in a dark suit, but that image changed to that of a woman also in a dark suit. Then, the images vanished, leaving a small orange Glow, no larger than the tip of the match Caleb had stuck earlier.

Caleb thought, it finally happened. I've gone completely crazy. I always suspected I had. Now, I have proof. Or, maybe it's Alzheimer's. Probably that. I'm glad I'm getting out of here.

As if hearing his thoughts, the voice said, "No, none of the above. I tried to tell you but, being human, you wanted to see something you understood. Now you have but do you know any more than you did? You don't. I'm still nothing to you. Well, kind of like you, the invisible nobody, but I'm really nothing, really invisible. I could be a man or a woman, but I'm not. I'm the glow you see. I don't expect you to comprehend. Why would you want to? You're about to die. I'll record your death as the final chapter of my project.

You began as somebody but then became nobody who eventually became invisible and then died. Nobody will ever know or care. Because you've been dead for years haven't you? And, nobody has cared. Well except for the little boy. He was glad you weren't dead."

"You're a cold bloodied thing, whatever you are."

"Aren't you? Do you care about anything ... or anybody? Isn't that what got you here? Of course you cared enough to rescue that little boy. Who knows, maybe he'll grow up to be president or develop something that'll cure cancers, one dose cures all."

Caleb grimaced and turned his head to face the river and to recall what he'd just done. He nodded. "I didn't have an axe to grind with the boy."

"But, I have to say it showed you are still a human. Unlike me. I don't have the capacity to care. I am logical but I have no feelings. You do, apparently. I do the right thing, well if I do, because it is the correct thing to do in order to solve one problem or another. It's my nature, yours too when you get right down to it. Well it was when you were in California and had a job and a few minutes ago, you solved another one. Made you feel good, didn't it? Rescuing that boy."

Caleb didn't answer. Instead, he stared pensively at the orange Glow, which looked brighter in the darkness that had suddenly covered everything. From someplace in the distance, a night owl hooted. Another answered.

"Maybe you should ... should have gotten a pet, a dog or cat, something that'd love you. Give you something to think about beside your hemlock stew."

Caleb stared at the glow and said. "Right now, when I go, I won't have anybody or anything to feel sad or morn me. If I had a pet, I'd feel guilty about leaving. But, of course, you knew that didn't you. You smart ass."

"Ah, well I wouldn't have picked you as a project if you hadn't been smart. Not as smart as I am, but smart enough to withdraw from the human race when you realized you couldn't do anything about anything."

"Yeah. Thanks, I guess."

"However, since you - I'll take the liberty to say - enjoyed your good deed, the saving of the boy, maybe I should tell you about some other rescue work, more good deeds, you could do before you hemlock-away your final minutes. No need to rush anything as permanent as that, wouldn't you say?"

"Getting it out of the way as soon as possible seems to me to be the right way to proceed."

The voice made a suggestion. "Say you decided to put it off. Think about this. There are a number of old people up and down the road you came in on. Some of them can hardly get out of bed, let alone do the things that need doing to stay alive. They have some help, but not nearly enough. You could see how helping them out hits you. Who knows, you might even like it. I imagine they'd welcome your help if you offered. Well, perhaps not all of them, but a bunch would. You might pick up a few things."

*What could I pick up? I have all I need. My hemlock.*

Caleb glanced at the can in his hand without speaking. It was covered in the orange Glow that seemed to have spread over everything around him.

*What the hell is that? Am I going crazy?*

"Right. Who cares about them?" the voice asked. "Dig a pit and start your fire? Actually, there's a pit already," the voice said. "You could see better with a fire. There's paper and enough twigs scattered about to make a decent fire. That'll keep away the mosquitoes. They grow 'em big around here. I'm sure you remember."

"I guess." He gathered up the scraps of paper, old hamburger wrappings and put them into the old fire pit with several hands full of twigs and lit the pile with a match. Within seconds, a yellow-orange flame spread its reach into the area around Caleb. Indeed, the mosquitoes which had been buzzing about retreated.

"Now, you can see enough to finish the poison stew you were about to cook up. Nobody will find your body here for ... who knows when. Maybe never. Especially if you climb into the back of one of the old cars after you've finished it off. Well, if you still want to?"

"You think you're pretty smart don't you? You tricked me into saving that little boy. Then you tell me about some old people who need my help. You think I'll jump at the chance to help them and give up leaving my misery behind."

"I don't know what you're going to do. It's your free will, not mine. But, I am pretty smart. Smarter than you for sure. I just said that. And, I don't have feelings to overcome before I make a decision. No greed, no selfishness, no anger, no need to dominate anyone to get my ego boosted, none of what you're burdened with. I just flow into problems with logic as my weapon and come up with a solution. The question is, what are you going to do? Finish off your stew and wait for your final darkness or help the old people I told you about?"

"Yeah. What am I going to do?" Caleb asked. "I don't know just now. I have to admit, saving that boy did get rid of the depression that's been hanging over me for months, maybe years. Probably an adrenalin rush. I've had 'em before. They never last very long. I'll wait it out. Once my depression comes back, I'll finish my hemlock stew. That's what I came to do."

"I know. So, while you're waiting, tell me about it, your depression. Of course, I know, but I'd like to hear it from you, in your own words ... for my project. That's a quote from somebody ... in your own words. If I were human, I might manage a nervous laugh but I'm not."

# Chapter 4

Caleb began to tell the orange glow about his life and, he felt pretty damn stupid doing it. Was the thing real or something his crazy mind hatched up, his Alzheimer's. But, having nothing better to do while he waited for his adrenalin rush to ebb away, he did it.

"A couple of years ago, our firm began to ship work overseas, China mostly. They told us by doing that our company could expand into more complex projects. Mostly, we designed systems for old cars to keep 'em going or to improve performance or just to correct for factory defects. Mine were electrical for the most part. Anyway, we got down to less than a dozen employees. Some were let go. Others found other jobs when they saw what was happening. I should have, but I had blinders on. My problems kept me coming in. Our techs soon left as well so the survivors had to not only design but build test units as well. Then, they cut us down to six. It was pretty clear we were not going to expand.

"I was working ten hours a day. Never at home. My wife didn't seem to mind so I kept working. We needed the money and, as I said, I was blind to practically everything. I don't think I was human."

"You were, just not an expressive one. Unfeeling, I think your wife said you were."

"Yeah. My wife. She worked - a teacher - but we never seemed to have enough. Working ten hours a day helped that. She always took care of everything, managed the money, remembered birthdays, paid bills, everything. We'd taken out a reverse mortgage on the house to get the kids through college and into new cars so our monthly overhead had gotten pretty high.

Finally, only me and the president of the firm were left. I still thought we'd get through it. As I said, I had blinders on. A one track mind. Finally, one Friday, he came by, handed me a check and the keys. 'That's your severance,' he told me. 'Put the keys in the mail slot when you leave. We're out of business.'"

"Rough," Glow said.

"It was. I'd been expecting it, but the president kept saying we were going to open a new product line and start hiring again. It never happened."

"So, you went home to tell your wife."

"I did, but when I got there, Myrna was dressed and waiting at the kitchen table, half a glass of wine sat in front of her. Her eyes were red, like she'd been crying. All her things, clothes, furniture and furnishing had been moved out of the house. I didn't understand what was going on until after she'd told me why she was leaving, the real story of our marriage. What a sham it had been and how sorry she was that I'd been a pawn in it. I couldn't believe it and yet, I should have."

Myrna told him she had been in love with a married man when she met Caleb. The man's wife had all the money so he couldn't leave her. So Myrna and the man she really loved, made the best of things; had a "love nest" and saw each other when they could. When Caleb came along, she proposed and he accepted.

Nine months after the marriage, maybe a few days earlier, they had a son.

On that last day, Myrna told him that the boy he had thought was his was instead the married man's child. Later they had a girl, which, she said, was also the married man's child. She said she was sorry she and Caleb didn't have children, but her lover didn't want her to do that so she didn't.

"It was a shock to hear all that, but with everything that had happened that day, it didn't knock me dead. Maybe she had told the kids," Caleb said. "Maybe they'd met their real father. Maybe not. Looking back, that may be why we had such a cold household. There was never any laughter or joy in the house. The whole thing was a charade, including my life. Like she said, I was a pawn, something to be sacrificed and I was."

"Maybe you should have turned your questions loose sooner. Should have done a little thinking, instead of keeping your head stuck in the sand of the failing business where you worked."

"I should have. Could be I used work as a crutch to get by, avoid thinking … avoid caring. Most likely I did. I took everything else for granted and was glad to do it. The company had shrunk and I was doing two jobs, at least, mine and a tech's. I hardly had time to go to the bathroom let alone think about anything. I had been letting my wife handle all our business affairs, personal ones too for years. She was good at things like that and I signed what she shoved in front of me. I've probably been depressed for years and just assumed it was normal."

"You have been, Caleb. Clearly. You never adjusted to what happened to your parents. Instead, you just shut all joy out of your life. And, all feelings too. You survived, but that's about all. So, your wife walked out the front door. Took your car, I imagine."

"Yeah. We only had the one by then. She had me sign the divorce papers. I guess that's why she waited. She did tell me she felt sorry for me; sorry she had deceived me all those years. I had no feelings left to care one way or the other. Hadn't had for years, thinking back. She left me a pile of mail to sort through. She had been doing it for years. I threw it all away before I left. Didn't figure to need it coming here with my hemlock."

"True," Glow said.

"Yeah. Her lover's wife had died so they were finally free to get married, she said. Our house had no equity over the mortgage. She'd checked that out with the realtors. When I left, I mailed the keys to the bank."

"So your depression turned terminal at that point?"

"It did. I did some research on the Internet and asked a nursery to order some water hemlock for me. I put it in my back pack and came down here to wrap things up."

"But now, you're having second thoughts?"

"I feel better. I guess that means I'm having second thoughts at the moment. More like, as long as the adrenalin in my system, I'll be on a high. When it's gone, I'll be ready for my hemlock."

"Good. I suppose, in your culture. Get on with it."

"That's right. When it's over, it's over. However, saving the boy's life – thanks to you – gave me a look at what I'd been missing for most of my life. Avoiding is a more accurate description of it. I've avoided caring about anything … or anybody, except my next work assignment. I think I completely quit caring when my family died, even before that. I just let life push me along without stopping to push back."

"Well, you still have your pot of poison waiting. In the meantime, I guess you'd better do something about food. You're going to get hungry."

"You're right. I guess you knew."

"As I said, I know everything I want to know," Glow said.

"Well, I am hungry." He reached into his back pack and pulled out a candy bar, one of three he'd packed for the trip. He'd eaten one. He devoured both within seconds.

"So, I've told you my story. What's yours?" Caleb asked the glowing light and immediately felt colossally stupid.

"Ah, well, you may have trouble understanding what I'm going to tell you, but I'll try to make it simple. I'm part of a unique energy system. Pockets of energy with interconnecting links for communicating back and forth and the power to reach out and cause things to happen in our world. Our world never dies, never expands, never shrinks."

"How'd you come into being?"

"I don't know and never cared. I just know that we exist and we manipulate parts of our system to make things happen. It's what we do. Then, we destroy most of what we have done and do something else. Some of what we create, we think is worth saving. Those things, we study and watch."

"Like us?"

"That's right. For example, one day, a few seconds of our time, millions of years of yours, we put an energy burst into a chamber with some contaminates we'd made up to see what would happen. Something did happen and soon we noticed little particles floating around the chamber with things happening on them," Glow explained.

"Our universe?"

"Yep. That's how you got started. One of our experiments. So, in order to study the growth of the particles, we divided part of our energy system into Glows, like mine, little investigative energy blips, and dispatched them to all the particles showing activity. I've been here since your planet popped up in our chamber, studying and sending back reports to the energy grid to see what intelligence we can get from it. You've discovered many things about your universe, and have theorized many more. Some of the developments on other particles, beyond your reach at the moment, have discovered more. The growths - like humans on yours - on those other particles are building engines to harness elements you think exist and will use the elements as fuel to go from particle to particle to investigate."

"That sounds like bullshit, if you'll pardon me for saying. They have people in white coats looking for people like you."

"Say what you will, Caleb. I've learned about all I can learn. My conclusions are sound and logical. Now, I'm just waiting to be picked up. Doing you as a project is the last thing on my list of things to do. You're keeping me from getting … your word, bored."

"Bored! And, I'm your project! What bullshit?" Caleb laughed. "So, what have you learned? I can't believe I'm doing this."

"About you or your little particle, your earth?

"Earth. Hell, there's nothing to learn about me. I am nothing."

"Well, Your culture had a promising beginning. I was impressed. Your ancestors came out of the trees, put on clothes, made tools and began to dominate their hostile environment. As they did, they went forth and multiplied, like one of your ancestors told them to do."

"That's out of the Old Testament, the Christian Bible."

"Until that pronouncement, your instinct to procreate, your dominant instinct, hadn't been made official."

"Hunger is –"

Glow interrupted to say, "Satisfying your hunger is what you do to have strength enough to satisfy your instinct to procreate, Caleb. Don't get the cart before the horse. The horse has the strength, but it's the cart that does the job." Usually, as it did then, when Glow interrupted, the orb intensified.

Caleb grunted. He didn't agree, but didn't figure he was going to change the glow's mind, whatever the hell it was.

"The consequences of domination, whether in the realm of moving a mountain or killing some germ, was looked upon as progress, which it was. Until now, your culture has rewarded humans who have made progress by doing something useful or beneficial to other humans. And rewards have motivated humans to make more progress, to produce even more beneficial things. But, now, your culture seems to be satisfied with what you've done, your past accomplishments. You have lost the motivation to make the decisions needed to expand the domination of your environment."

Caleb wanted to object, "I don't _"

"Don't interrupt. I'm telling you truths you may not know. You've become lazy and permissive, satisfied to sit back and enjoy what you have done. As a result, it seems to me, logically anyway, that you are headed down the road to self-destruction. You are procreating faster than you are producing what you need to support all that you have created along the way."

Caleb said, "You're saying we're like mindless pests on a bush, eating and procreating until nothing is left. Then we all die of starvation? That's Easter Island!"

"Easter Island is one example. There are others but that one hits home. Humans there used up all the resources their environment had made available for them. When there was nothing left to keep them going, like your pests on a bush, they more or less died."

"That's more bull shit! Maybe we have gotten lazy. Hell, I don't know. But, I know that our elected officials are looking out for us. They won't let that something like Easter Island happen."

"Unfortunately, your elected officials are not looking out for you. They once were, but over time, some of the rewards given to humans for making progress, have been given to those officials. The producing humans want an advantage in their struggles for more rewards. Greed has driven them to take short cuts along the way. And, your officials have become greedy for more of the rewards they have been given to give the producing humans their short cuts.

From what I've seen, the democracies of the world, those elected officials you're talking about as your saviors, have evolved, maybe I should say devolved, into little more than figureheads being manipulated by a handful of humans driven by greed.

And, the other humans, thinking like you that the elected officials will protect them, eat fast food, drink beer, watch mindless television, procreate and take on mountains of debt that they've been told are good for them by the greedy humans. That makes them …, kind of like slaves."

"Slaves or not, we have checks and balances to stop greedy behavior by our officials."

"I imagine it's been awhile since anybody looked to see if the checks and balances still work. I didn't expect you to understand. So, are you going to eat your hemlock stew or get up in the morning and head down the road to work for food? I found that expression of yours, about working for food, to be fetching."

Caleb didn't answer right away but after considering Glow's question, said, "Unless I wake up depressed, I think I will. Right now, eating my last meal doesn't look as satisfying as it did when I got off the bus. My depression is gone, for now, but I'll keep my hemlock in case it returns."

"Up to you, Caleb. It's your free will."

"I'm probably ape shit crazy but let me ask you a question."

"Ask and you will receive."

"Why in the hell should I believe a damn thing you said. A Chamber experiment! That sounds like total bullshit!"

"No doubt it does. I don't have any proof to back up anything I've said. But, let me turn it back to you. For all you know, you may be some kind of being with the ability to create everything you think or see or do. In other words, can you prove you haven't day dreamed your entire life?"

Caleb opened his mouth as if to speak, but he had no answer.

"I didn't think so. I will give you something else to think about. When you came down from the trees and put on clothes and set out to do the things you have done, dominating your environment, did it ever occur to you that the discoveries you've made are all imbued with unyielding logic. For example, all the constants your scientists have discovered over the years to explain your physical world were here even before you climbed out of the trees. We put them there, when we planned the experiment that created you.

For example, without Planck's discovery of his constant, with some help from Einstein, scientists would not know the relationship between electrons, protons and light. Without an understanding of light, humans wouldn't have been able to understand how life could exist. Plank's constant opened the door for more progress … and more rewards for those making it. I just slipped that in, about the rewards."

Caleb didn't know enough to disagree and falling back into his hidden personality, didn't say anything.

The voice continued. "Let me hit you with pi, that crazy number 3.141 that seems to go on forever, the odd constant that students and technical people all over the world have to use to calculate the distance around a circle. You probably know that pi multiplied by the diameter gives you the distance around every circle of every size."

"I know pi. I've used it. I'm an engineer."

"Well, how about all those other little formulas your teachers made you learn, for example, the one for all triangles, a squared plus b squared equals c squared. All that logic, all those relationships, were part of the energy burst we injected into that chamber, a few of our minutes ago. What'd you think? Somehow it just happened. You had primitive origins, but our logic has always been part of your world, waiting for you to discover it. And, you have discovered much, but there is still much that you haven't discovered or done."

"Frankly, I quit giving a rat's ass about any of that a long time ago. But, you may have a point. I'll give you that much."

"You don't have to give me anything. I've been here a long time, I know I'm right. In the past, you, the people of your world, have enjoyed the gains that came from your hard work … your drive to dominate the environment. But now, you are content to enjoy those gains without continuing the hard work that got them. You have become permissive and lazy.

To avoid your drift toward self-destruction, humans must overcome the decay that comes from the permissive acceptance of the non-producing elements in your culture. Your awareness of the benefits those elements enjoy from your hard work, may very well have encouraged you to become lazy. And your laziness has most likely undercut your discipline and motivation to continue your discoveries … to make more gains.

So, you have a choice, stop the decay that comes from the permissive acceptance of laziness or accept the destruction of the culture you have created through your hard work and sacrifices over the centuries. Get ready for your Easter Island."

"Just touching that hemlock must have pushed me over the edge of sanity. I think that long before we reach self-destruction, somebody will do what is necessary to stop it. People are still going to make babies and babies are still going to need food. Somebody will do something to stop their crying."

"I don't think anybody did anything on Easter Island. Babies must have cried there."

"This is not Easter Island. And, this is a new age. People will do something"

"And that … shall I call it false optimism, somehow gives you hope so you don't have to worry?" Glow asked.

Caleb fell asleep without answering but, he did think for a while before he did. It was puzzling but for some reason he couldn't put his finger on, he had enjoyed his conversation with Glow. Although he suspected he was talking to himself, he hadn't been doing even that much lately.

Though too faint for him to grasp completely, in his sleepy state, came the words, "I know, Caleb. But, you're alive for one more day."

The next morning, as the first spread of the sun's rays brought light into the junk yard, Caleb got up and considered his situation. He was still not depressed. What he was though, was desperately hungry. Glow wasn't around to bother him, only the growl in his stomach.

He got on the gravel road and headed toward Marshalltown but he wasn't going there. His goal were the small homes between the park and the town where he hoped he could indeed, work for food, like the glow had said.

Only his hunger drove him. It had been a long time since he'd had to have direct contact with anyone. That was one of the things he'd given up when he became invisible. He wondered if he'd remember how to act, what to say.

He remembered one thing. Keep smiling and nodding.

# Chapter 5

A few minutes' walk brought him to a small, wood frame house on stilts three feet off the ground. Some were made of bricks, some, the originals, were made of hickory rounds. The house looked balanced though, not leaning one way or the other.

Somebody did a good job. Roof looks fairly new, he thought, shoving hunger out of his mind as much as he could. His stomach had been growling since he woke up and hadn't stopped.

The roof, like many country houses, was asphalt shingled. The house was what people called a "shotgun shack," in Mississippi. The kind where someone could shoot a shotgun through the front door and the pellets would pass out the back door without hitting anything. It had been freshly painted too, Caleb figured, about the same time as the old roof had been replaced.

The garden along the road brought him down the dirt driveway to the wood steps which he hurried up. It needed weeding, something he would gladly do in exchange for food.

On the right side of the front porch, a gray wooden swing hung from the ceiling. A single cushion lay against an arm rest. On the left were a couple of straight back chairs with cane bottoms. No dog, he observed before taking a step onto the porch.

He knocked on the screen door. It was latched and the door behind it was closed. There was no answer so he knocked again and said, loudly, "Hello. Anybody home?"

A shrill woman's voice answered from inside. "Git! I don't want any. I ain't got no money and I ain't buying if I did. So git!"

"I'm not selling. I don't want your money. I just want to weed your corn patch for whatever food you can spare."

Seconds later, the front door swung open. A thin, elderly woman stared at him through the rusted screen of the screen door. "Who are you? You look like a tramp. I ain't having no tramps on my property. Git on!"

"I'm just looking for work, Ma'am. I saw your corn patch as I walked up. Got some weeds in it. I could clean 'em out for a little food. No money."

"Ain't needin' no help. Hoe and file out yonder but I ain't promising nothing. Ain't needin' nothin." She pointed in the direction of a small shed on the side of the house.

Caleb thanked her, picked up the hoe from the shed and began to hoe. It took the better part of an hour. The exercise pushed away his hunger. He knew he was still hungry but the urge had abated.

He then did the same for several rows of vegetables. With the hoe back to the shed, he returned to the porch to tell the lady what he'd done, in case she wanted to inspect his work.

The front door was still open. He knocked on the door frame. Seconds later, the screen door flew open. In it stood the old lady, her glasses clinging to the crown of her nose. But, that wasn't what really got Caleb's attention. What did get his attention was the double barreled shotgun in her hands.

"Now, I tole you to git and you ain't done it. I'm gonna fill you with buckshot if you ain't off my porch 'fore I count to ten. Onlyest thang my old man ever done was teach me how to shot this damn shotgun. I'm already on five 'n countin'."

She raised the shotgun. The weight of it shook in the old woman's arms but she managed to point it in Caleb's general direction. He turned, jumped off the porch and ran back to the road.

He heard the old lady laughing behind him. "Tole 'im to git! I reckon I showed 'im. Ain't puttin' up with no-goods out to take from me."

Caleb looked back to make sure she wasn't coming after him. She wasn't. The screen door slammed shut. The front door slammed behind it.

Damn, he thought. That must have been one of the people Glow said might not welcome me. If I had picked up anything from her, it would have been a butt full of buckshot.

As soon as he was down the road a bit, the hunger he'd shoved aside while working in the woman's corn and vegetable patches, reemerged with a vengeance. His stomach once again began to growl and turn the middle of his body into a streak of sharp pain. He felt light headed and dizzy, like he was going to pass out.

He shook his head as if that would help. It didn't. "Looks like hunger's going to finish off what my hemlock stew never got a chance to. So be it."

An old car rumbled along the road and passed, trailing a tail of yellow clay dust. Before it reached him, he'd hopped off the road to the other side of the drainage ditch alongside. He wished for a plum tree, even one with green plums, but saw none.

He was about to sit down and see if he could wait it out, but up ahead, he saw another old farm house. That renewed his strength. Instead of walking and fighting off hunger, he began to run to distract his body. It worked.

A few minutes of running brought him to the driveway of the farm house. The house was old, like the first he'd come to – the shotgun woman's – but bigger and on the opposite side of the road. It had a tin roof, wood siding, porches; the front porch with a swing suspended to the ceiling by chains. An elderly man and woman sat rocking back and forth. She was in the swing and he was in a chair, drinking from coffee mugs and talking. Four wooden rocking chairs, separated by small tables, sat at the other side of the porch. As he approached, he saw enough of the back porch to know it was about the same as the front.

One porch was for sitting in the morning, the other in the afternoon when the sun's headed for the sunset, he thought as he left the road and walked toward them. He forced a smile he didn't feel as he drew close. He looked at them and said, "Hello, how're you getting along this fine morning."

How in the hell can I get food out of them? What the hell, I have to try. I'm as hungry as a starving dog.

They stopped talking and drinking coffee and gave him a studied, suspicious look. Then, the man nodded with a smile and said, "We're fine, Sir. What you be looking for?"

He gestured with his head at the woman sitting in the swing next to him and added, "Mama can't hear so good so if you want to talk to her you'll have to speak up."

Caleb opened his mouth to ask if they had any work for him, but the woman gave him a concerned look, smiled and told her husband, "Git this man a cup of coffee, Earnest. And a biscuit. Looks to me like he could use a cup. He 'peers to be a mite hungry."

She got that right, Caleb thought and gave her an agreeing nod.

Earnest struggled to his feet and asked Caleb, "You want a little jam in that biscuit?"

"Yes sir, if it wouldn't be much trouble." He renewed his smile. Both looked fragile, he thought.

While he was gone, Caleb noticed the woman staring at him. After a bit, she cleared her throat and said, "You know, they's talk about a wild man running 'round in Marshall Park scaring people. Something in the paper 'bout it. Radio too. That be you?"

Caleb opened his mouth to reply, but about that time, Earnest had hobbled back with a cup of coffee in one hand and a small plate with a huge biscuit filled with jelly in the other. The biscuit threatened to fall off the plate but somehow managed to hang on.

He handed it to Caleb who thanked him and took a drink of the coffee immediately. It felt like he was drinking from the fountain of youth. He also managed a bite of the biscuit off the plate. He remembered the jelly as mayhaw from when he was a kid. The trees grew wild along creek branches. Fathers and mothers assigned the picking of the small red berries that grew on them to the kids and made jelly out of them.

He took another bite and another drink of coffee. "Delicious!" he said, loud enough for the woman to hear.

She smiled and nodded.

The man pulled over a rocking chair and motioned for him to sit down. Caleb did.

The woman pointed to him and repeated her question, "That be you? The wild man ... a' scaring folks."

Caleb said, "I reckon it might be me. I look kind of wild with this hair and all, but I didn't think I scared anybody."

Earnest picked up the conversation. "The paper didn't say he scared anybody, Mama. It just said people were scared that there might be a wild man running loose in the park. That little boy said the man saved him from gittin' snake bit."

"That's right, Earnest. Shore 'nuff. I just got it mixed up, like I do now and again. 'N the doctor said nothin' had happened to that boy. That boy's mama said she was grateful that man brought him back, like he did."

"I'd like to read that story if you still have it," Caleb said without much of a pause from eating the biscuit and drinking the coffee. I might just live.

"It's right chere," the woman said with a heavy accent as she reached over, picked the newspaper off the swing beside her and handed it to him.

The story was front page with a picture of the boy and his parents. Caleb recognized the man as the one kneeling and reaching out for the boy with a beer in one hand. He didn't remember the woman. The story said the father was a deputy sheriff. He was quoted as saying they wanted to see what "that man" was doing out there. "... what he might be up to."

Caleb finished the coffee and jelly biscuit while he pondered the deputy's quote. He didn't want to be dragged into town by the sheriff for anything, let alone to be questioned for no good reason. He just wanted to be left alone.

His stomach no longer growled and he didn't feel dizzy. Thought I was going to die, he thought. Glad I still have my hemlock. That's my real ticket out of here. Save a boy's life and next thing I know they want to drag me into town to see what I'm up to. So much for Glow's recommendations. And, the old woman down the road, the shotgun woman, had in mind killing me.

Earnest looked at Caleb then at his wife. He said, "Mama, you think you could cut this man's hair and that awful lookin' beard some, Make him look more civilized. Maybe people wouldn't be so scared if you did."

The woman looked Caleb over for a minute and said, "Brang me them scissors and comb, Earnest. I'm fixin' to give this man a haircut. You know where they are?"

Caleb had in mind objecting but knew he needed a haircut in the worst way so he said nothing.

Earnest shook his head and left to retrieve them. A minute or so later, he returned and handed them to the woman.

"You drag yore chair over here close to me. I'll cut that hair. I cut Earnest's all the time, arthritis 'n all. Don't I, Daddy?"

Caleb noted their informal use of names, left over when they had small children and wanted to teach them what to call their parents.

"And you do a good job, Mama." He reached over and patted her knee with a smile.

"Bring him another cup of coffee and a biscuit, Daddy. He still looks a little peaked," she said before starting on his hair.

Caleb managed to eat his biscuit and drink his coffee while she clipped away. She used what looked like a razor blade in a holder with a comb to cut his beard. The comb let her keep the length of the beard the same. "Beards 're the hardest," she said as she labored on.

"Yes ma'am," Caleb agreed.

About thirty minutes later, Earnest brought a mirror for him to see how he looked.

"I do look like a human again," he said. "Not a wild man." And, I feel a hell of a lot better, he thought. Thanks to the biscuits and coffee.

Earnest laughed. "I tole you. Mama can make anybody look good."

"Well, you must have some work around here I can do to pay for all this." He waved his empty coffee cup in front of him.

Earnest said, "Well, sir, Mama's brother's boys come by now and then to clean the stalls. That's the hardest thang to do. All that cow manure. Has to be cleaned out so the cows don't have to stand in it. Red helps out when he can. He's a nice lookin' man. He has that truck stop up the road. He can do jes 'bout anything. Usually though, he sends Hugo to help us. Used to, I should say."

The woman spoke up, saying, "Hugo was cleaning the house for us. It'd take him most of the morning. I don't think he liked it much, but he sure did a good job, didn't he Daddy?"

"He did when he wasn't talking about Red. He couldn't say enough about Red," Earnest said.

"We reckon he's put Red on a pedestal, don't we Daddy? The way he went on about him."

"He shore acts like he did. But, Hugo's quit coming. Red said he got busy at the service station," Earnest said.

The woman scoffed loudly. "Busy at the service station, my foot! He quit coming when he heard you talking 'bout him, Daddy."

Earnest shook his head and looked into the yard as if he was trying to remember what the woman was talking about. After a second or two, he looked at her and said, "I reckon you're right, Mama. I remember now."

He looked at Caleb and explained. "One time – well, it was the last time he was here – he'd been cleaning the house and doing a real good job, like always. I came out here and told Mama, 'Mama,' I said, "That Hugo cleans house like a woman. Everything is spic and span. Not a lick of dust anywhere.'"

"'N just as Daddy was saying that, Hugo had come to the door. He just stood there while Earnest was telling what a good job he was doing. That was the last time he came to help. Now a church woman helps with the cleaning."

Earnest half smiled and said, "I kind 'a think Hugo was upset 'bout what I'd said. 'Bout cleaning house like a woman. For the life of me, I can't understand why but for sure when he came out of the door, he looked at me like he was real mad. 'N he didn't speak to me when he left."

"Yes sir, I remember that. He gave you a dirty look, Daddy, 'n he left without saying goodbye or anything."

"And, he never came back," Earnest said.

"Red said he got busy at the service station! I jes think he just didn't want to come back, that's what I think."

"Don't be hard on him, Mama. They have to keep that place open twenty four hours a day. When them truckers want gas, they want gas. Red fixed him a place to stay over the station so he can get down there in a hurry if somebody rolls up late and needs something."

"You mos' likely right," the woman said. "May the Lord forgive me for making a judgment like I did."

"I'm sure he will," Caleb said.

She shook her head.

Earnest stopped talking and rocked back and forth in his chair as if considering what he wanted to say next.

While he considered, the woman looked at Caleb and said, "Red's always been good to us though. He fixed our electrics and our plumbing when they went bad. Says all we have to do is call him. The boy's come out and clean the stalls. Now that's a hard job. Cleaning out that cow manure." He explained that the "boys" were Mama's kin folks then added, "Them boys've got busy workin' and ain't been able to come by lately. They're both carpenters and this time of year, they stay on the job from day light to dark. They're good boys, but they have to make a livin'."

"I imagine it is a hard job," Caleb said.

Earnest shook his head in agreement. "'Specially when it's wet. Smells some too."

Caleb agreed.

Mama chimed in, "Church people come by and do the milkin' for us. Rheumatism got so bad in Daddy's hands, he can't do it anymore. 'N I give it up a long time ago. Couldn't squeeze the teets."

"Mama was a good milker though. Cows loved her. We just …" He shrugged and let the thought drop.

"Why don't I clean the stalls," Caleb said. "If you need it. I can't do the milking, but I can  clean. I know how to work a shovel but I never learned how to milk."

"Uh huh," Earnest said. "If you wouldn't mind." He walked to the edge of the porch and looked at an old building at the back. "Don't need the milkin' just now anyway. But them stalls could shore use a good cleaning."

Caleb stood and said, "Point me to where everything is."

Earnest pointed to their barn and said, "Well, they's a wheel barrow and a shovel and pitch fork just inside the barn. You'll need that, I expect. You can spread the manure in the pasture. Good for the grass. I do appreciate you help'n out 'n all."

Caleb shook his head, jumped off the porch and hurried out to the barn. He opened the barn gates and went inside. The cows were outside in a fenced area. There were three of them, two older milk cows and one yearling. Caleb found the hay and pitchforked a couple of piles into the yard for them. He also took a bucket and filled their water troughs. He found a well at the back of the house. Somebody had put a pump inside so all he had to do was turn on a spigot.

With that warm up, he took the wheel barrow inside and began cleaning the cow manure from the stalls. Had to be at least almost a month's accumulation, he figured. Piles of it, mostly wet and all smelly.

Nevertheless, he dug into it, shoveling it into the wheelbarrow and pushing it out into the pasture where he dumped it into little depressions here and there, the likely remains of rotted tree stumps, he figured. After three hours of exhausting work, he had cleaned four stalls. He stood back for a long look then began to spread fresh straw about.

Leaving the barn, he looked down. His tennis shoes were black with manure as were his pants. He sighed and looked around until he spotted a wash tub on a bench. A scrub board sat inside the tub. He didn't figure "Mama or Earnest" did any washing, so, either the church people did it or they had a washing machine someplace. He didn't see one so he took off his shoes, rinsed them as best he could before washing them in the cold water he poured into the tub. That done, he took off his pants and did the same thing. Nobody was looking. He squeezed them as dry as he could and put them back on.

He walked back to the front of the house. Earnest and Mama were still sitting on the front porch staring across the road as if waiting for something interesting to happen.

"I finished," Caleb announced. "Want to take a look?"

"I reckon I trust you done a good job," Earnest said. He looked at his wife and said, "I tole you he'us a good 'un."

"You did. But, my, my, Earnest, looka there at 'im. He's done got all wet."

"No problem," Caleb said and explained about washing his clothes after cleaning the stalls.

The woman said to her husband, "Daddy, you go on in yonder and get him some of your old clothes out of the trunk."

Caleb began to protest but the woman shushed him, saying, "Earnest outgrowed them old clothes years ago. Don't know why we don't throw 'em away. Not worth foolin' with, I reckon."

By then, Earnest had gone inside and was already back, holding a shirt and pair of pants.

Caleb thanked them and went to the barn to change. The pants were a bit large in the waist but his belt took care of the excess. The dry clothes felt good. His shoes were still wet but he figured they'd dry long before he got back to the junk yard.

At the woman's biding, Earnest went inside and got Caleb some left over biscuits, a piece of fried chicken, half a dozen eggs, a slab of bacon and a pint jar of "sweet" milk.

Caleb protested enough to be polite but was glad to get the food.

"Wish we had a coffee pot we could lend you. If you get one, we'll give you some coffee," she said as she handed him the food. "Seems like anybody dropping by here always brings coffee. We got plenty."

He thanked them both and hurried down the road toward the river. He figured he'd done his day's work for that day. And, he wasn't hungry anymore.

# Chapter 6

Reading that newspaper triggered some thoughts he had to deal with. Mostly, he had some thinking to do about seeing the sheriff. He didn't want to, but kind of figured they weren't going to just walk away without talking to the "wild man in the swamp." The thought of having the sheriff after him pushed him toward the depression he'd left behind the day before. He wondered if the glow was going to haunt him about the sheriff. The absurdity of that thought caused him to scoff.

"Damn, I was feeling better," he said as he trudged along the road. He was relieved that no cars or trucks came along to cover him in dust. Soon, he could see the river bridge ahead … and the trail to the park's camp sites along the river; in particular his cave camp site.

He tried to shrug off the threat from the sheriff, tried to put it behind him by thinking of what he'd done to help Earnest and … Mama. Surprisingly, by the time he'd reached the wild plum trees and the trail between them, he didn't feel the dark cloud of despair a depression usually brought when it was hanging over his head. He felt relieved. For years, it seemed a depression had become part of his life. It had always flooded in when things went wrong in his life, which was often.

He turned onto the trail holding the little bag of "groceries" Earnest and Mama had given him. The beauty and tranquility of the umbrella of green over the trail and singing of birds in the trees, made it easier to push the "sheriff" problem out of his mind. It still nagged at his thoughts, but other things became more important. Like where was he going to make his camp. He favored the cave over the junk yard. The junk yard was too open and too exposed if the sheriff sent out a "posse."

"I'd be a dead duck."

On the other hand, nobody was ever likely to find him in the cave. He hoped.

That decision made, he left his bag of groceries behind a bush and hurried to the junk yard for his backpack. He returned, retrieved his groceries and continued on the trail. When he reached the end of the trail, he held up and stayed in the shadows to check the outside and to listen. He was worried that indeed, they might be searching for him, looking for the "wild man of the swamps." But, there were no people in sight and he didn't hear any voices.

That's a relief.

The fire pit hadn't been disturbed. The extra twigs and leaves he'd left in a pile beside them when he began boiling the water for his hemlock stew hadn't been moved. He imagined the remains of the fire he'd started were probably still sizzling when the family of the boy he'd saved came searching for him.

"Wonder what they made of that? Wild man with a camp fire!"

He placed his bag beside it and turned his attention to the cave which he wanted to use as his camp. The first afternoon, he'd cut his way to the mouth of the cave to get water for his hemlock stew, but hadn't tried to cut through the dense growth of briars and vines to get inside. Was the cave still there? He hadn't able to see and hadn't cared. He was only after water. Now, though, he was interested in a place to sleep until he could decide what to do with his life.

*Ruefully*, he thought, *I've got more problems than I came here with.*

"I'm damned glad I didn't throw away my hemlock."

He looked at the towering rock that once concealed the cave he and his brothers had explored and made their hideout. He wondered if it was still there. Even if it is, will it be big enough for me now?

He stared apprehensively at the narrow sandstone trail along the outside of the rocky outcropping, barely a foot wide. One slip and he'd tumble down the bank into the river. It hadn't seemed important when all he wanted was water for his hemlock stew. And, if he'd slipped and tumbled into the river, so what? But, things had changed … a bit anyway.

"Been a long time since I was inside the cave," he said. "Hell, the roof might have caved in since then. Well, only one way to find out."

He sighed, took his knife and edged his way along the trail to the mouth of the cave. Water still poured out the mouth to fall into the river, he noted.

He got to his knees, braced himself and began cutting the formidable layer of vines and briars from the cave's opening. After half an hour, he had cut through enough to poke his head inside. To his relief, the cave was still there, and looked plenty big enough to accommodate him. However, still more briars and vines needed to be cut. So, he proceeded to hack away the rest of the thorny entanglements that had snaked through the openings in the rocky walls to clog the inside.

"Plenty of room," he said. There were good sized ledges on both sides of the small stream of water that flowed through the cave. And, the rocky ceiling of the cave was high enough for him to sit comfortably on them, even stand in places.

By that time, the water was looking cool and inviting and he was thirsty. So, he scooped some into his cupped hand and drank his fill. Then, he went outside and wolfed down one of the biscuits he'd been given and drank some of the milk from the jar in his bag. That assuaged his hunger. And, so far he'd heard no voice.

"Maybe I'm going sane," he mumbled.

Afterwards, he took his grocery bag inside and put the food next to a small eddy in the stream to keep it cool.

"Well, I have a safe place to sleep, water to drink and a place for any food I get," he said. He remembered his encounter with the shotgun lady.

"Hmm, I guess I'll need a bed," he said, looking at the wider of the ledges that bordered the stream. He thought about the cushions he'd slept on in the junk yard, the night before, but rejected the idea. Too much trouble to bring them over and he wasn't sure they'd fit anyway. He decided to pile straw on the ledge and cover it with something. That'd be his bed.

Finding the straw was easy. Pine trees grew all around, like weeds, and dropped pine straw on the ground when it turned brown. He brought in enough to make a bed and lay down. The ends of the straw stuck through his clothes like needles. That sent him into the park, searching through garbage cans for blankets or covers or sheets campers may have discarded. An hour's digging in the cans yielded a decent blanket. Brown and stained some, but dry and in relatively good shape. He spread the blanket over his thick layer of pine straw and lay on top. It was comfortable.

His problems had shrunk. There was the thing about a coffee pot. The cup Earnest had given him tasted damn good and, if he hung around, he knew he'd want more. "No coffee as yet, but I'll need a pot if and when I get any."

He'd just dug into half a dozen garbage cans in the park and hadn't seen anything that might serve the purpose. But, he bet he could find an old pot or bucket someplace in the junk yard that would work. He'd seen a couple of wrecked campers and vans that might have one. "Maybe even a frying pan for the bacon and eggs they gave me."

He jogged across the bridge to search for what he could find. If Glow was about, it didn't show itself or say anything. That made Caleb figure his Alzheimer's was taking a break, resting up from all the work he'd done that morning.

*Maybe I should do more work. Get rid of the glow for good.*

After half an hour of tearing about, he found an old coffee pot, a blue enamel thing, chipped with a rusted handle, but otherwise usable. No holes. The frying pan search was easy. He ran across two in a camper and took the smaller one.

An extra were the old books he'd found in the camper, a couple by Dick Francis and a couple more by Tony Hillerman, both of which he'd probably already read. He wasn't sure if either man was still alive since he hadn't seen anything by either in a long while, but knew he'd enjoy re-reading their books.

The sun was still relatively high by the time he'd gotten back to his camp. "Can't be more than two o'clock," he said looking up.

He lugged everything back to his campsite. Thankfully, there were no people in the park, either having an outing or searching for him. And, there was no voice talking to him. That was a relief. *Maybe I'm not completely insane.*

He stowed his finds and his backpack inside the cave. "Now, all I need is coffee for the pot."

Something else had been nagging at him and he finally figured out what it was. *Not much light in here, but if I'm going to be staying here for any time, it's be nice to be able to read a newspaper or one of the books I found.*

In his prior life, as he called his time in California, he often read books to stave off an attack of depression. Getting lost in somebody's fictional adventure was as good as a vacation, which he never took, opting instead for money he gave to his wife. As he had always done, he let his mind tackle the problem of getting a light inside the cave. After a few minutes of thinking, he had a possible solution. The solution required tools, but he'd seen a large tool kit in the back of a wrecked truck and bet there were enough tools inside it to do what he planned to do.

"Still got over five hours of daylight left. Thanks to daylight saving's time." In the early days of his career, he'd done harder jobs in less time. But first, he had one thing to look at and judge, without that, his solution was worthless.

He walked to the mouth of the cave and bent down where the ceiling was low to evaluate the fall of the little stream as it left the mouth of the cave and flowed down the slope to the river. After half a minute's study, he decided that fall of the little stream was enough to do what was needed.

"Plenty of speed," he said of the stream. "Now, all I need is a generator and a way to turn the rotor."

An old car was what he wanted; something built before the computer age took over and digitized everything. Once computers took over, the weekenders could no longer easily work on their cars. One problem he had, however, was rigging blades to the generator so the running water in the stream could turn it. His solution was to remove the fan that cooled the car's radiator and attach it to the generator. Ordinarily a belt driven by the car's motor turned it, but since he could not do that, he had to have an alternative way to drive the generator. The car's radiator fan was the answer.

The rest of his plan called for cannibalizing the regulator and generator's control circuitry from a car along with its interior lights. Two lights, he figured, should work. Hanging low, the lights should be bright enough to see and to read by, no more than he would be doing. They didn't have to look good, just give light. And, he'd need a switch to turn them off.

He hurried back across the bridge into the junk yard. His first stop was the truck where he'd seen the tool kit. It was heavy, but manageable and filled with tools of all kinds. Next, he found an old Chevrolet that had a generator that looked in decent condition, no rust or damage. The regulator and circuitry connected to the generator looked good as well.

He opened the tool kit, pulled out the tools he needed and began the dismantling process. After a couple of hours of work, he had removed the generator, its regulator system and two light fixtures from two cars. He took the car's radiator fan and rigged it to the generator's pulley. It took an hour to attach the fan to the generator and test it by hand to see if the generator would turn. It seemed okay.

He carried the generator and the rest of the system back to his cave. Since he could only generate electricity if the radiator fan turned the generator's rotor fast enough, he mounted it to the sandstone layer on the left side of the cave's mouth. That required hand drilling holes in the sandstone and securing the generator, which was heavy, to the sandstone.

A left side mount would not be visible to anyone standing outside for a look down at the river. And, there was sufficient room for him to slip in and out of the cave's mouth on the right side.

Surprisingly, driven by the force of the stream the fan easily turned the rotor and even gave off a pleasant hum. Satisfied with that, he connected the rest of the system including two hanging lights. It was past dark when he'd twisted the last two wires together. If there hadn't been a full moon filling the cave with silver shafts of light, he could not have finished.

He reached over and flipped on the switch he'd inserted into the circuit. The lights came on and filled the cave with yellow light, bright enough to read by but not so bright as to attract attention.

"Be damn," he said. "It works."

"And, He said let there be light and behold, there was light," Glow suddenly appeared and was speaking. "Forgive me for quoting from your good Book. I couldn't resist."

"I thought I'd lost you. Thought I was having a lucid interval."

"Hang onto your fantasies. Could be a sign of intelligence. Might come in handy down the road."

"Babble on. I'm surprised a lightning bolt hasn't struck you dead already. Quoting the Bible sacrilegiously is frowned on, most likely a high sin, I've forgotten. Maybe I'm glad it hasn't, particularly if I'm the one doing the quoting,"

"Congratulations on the lights. Now, you can read at night. Have a little entertainment while you're deciding what to do with your hemlock. Right?"

"Yeah." He'd forgotten all about his hemlock.

Caleb went outside and checked for light coming from openings and crevices in the cave's rocky exterior. There were a few spots here and there which he plugged by shoving straw and leaves into them.

"All I need is for somebody, like sheriff's deputies searching for a wild man, to wander by and see my light."

To be on the safe side though, the next evening Caleb would mix mud with the straw and leaves and re-do the plugging. The mouth of the cave was a problem. He had to live with it that night, but he'd eventually nail pieces of wood from the junkyard together to make a kind of door which he could wedge into place at night.

"You have come a long way, Caleb. From being ready to cook a hemlock stew and leave all this behind to bringing light into your cave. Maybe not altogether your cave," Glow spoke to him from someplace in the recesses of the cave. "I didn't tell you, but this cave is where I have been living while I'm waiting to be transported home. What you'd call home, anyway."

"I must be going nuts. Too much pressure over the years. It finally got to me."

"I figured you'd think something like that. Isn't that something humans call rationalization? By the way, how'd you get along with the shotgun lady?"

"Why didn't you tell me about her?" Caleb asked.

"I didn't want to spoil your fun. Made you hop around though didn't she? I figured it'd be a test to see if your new found outlook was strong enough to survive a confrontation of that scale."

"I wouldn't want to test it every day." He had to admit that the day, even with the shotgun threat, was a welcome relief from the ones he'd been waking up to for months, maybe even years. It was what – the day he just had - he once called "touching earth."

Meaning it renewed his touch with reality and gave him strength to carry on. Glow faded to nothing and Caleb accepted it with a shake of his head.

For his supper, he dragged up a log round and sat on it watching a fire in his fire pit while he ate a biscuit and the fried chicken from Earnest and Mama. He wished he knew her name. He drank the last of the milk to wash it down.

"A change," Glow reappeared and said, "from your California life. Eating around a camp fire."

"Yeah. It's relaxing to sit here and look at a fire burning and listen to the river without having some job to go to"

"You did have a couple of jobs, the barn cleaning and rigging the lights, but you seen your duty and you done it clear. Another one of your quaint sayings I picked up along the way. Anyway, solving problems is what you've done all your life, except solving your own - your wife and children. You always avoided even looking at yours. And, look what it got you, a handful of hemlock."

Caleb grimaced at the last thing Glow said. "Yeah. Probably some kind of emotional hang up, but you're right. Except for my own problems, my fatal flaw, I see a problem and my brain starts looking for ways to solve it. Today's were kind of simple. Well, cleaning up the cow shit was. The lights were more difficult and more fun to solve."

"Your depression is gone. That's why you haven't thought about your hemlock. Haven't needed it. I'd say doing things has been good therapy for you. Helping the old people. Making your little nest in the cave better. And, you should add your talks with me to that list."

"Talks with you?"

"Sure. I've been your father confessor and your Doctor Freud. I let you tell me your problems. So, they flowed from you to me. You got rid of them. Modern psycho-therapy. Wouldn't you say? Talked them away."

"I don't know. I've never been to a shrink."

"You haven't missed much. Just getting out like you've been doing, finding out that you still have some worth as a human being is a lot cheaper than paying somebody to listen to your problems and give you platitudes or a bottle of drugs."

Caleb nodded. "Well, I have to say I've enjoyed doing something useful. Helping those old folks gave me a new perspective. Visiting with them, seeing how they live, was a trip back in time. I doubt anything's changed along that road in decades. Kids have moved out and left their mamas and papas living in what amounts to a state of suspended animation. But, everything works, suspended animation or not, and they're as comfortable as ever… if you take away their rheumatism." He half laughed but it was true. Their arthritis probably kept them in pain much of the time.

"Having lived most of your life in state-of-the-art California, I thought you might enjoy a look back at the way things were. Like when you were a kid, Caleb," Glow told him.

Caleb shrugged with a grimace. "I guess you were right, Glow, sending me down the road. The sheriff thing nags at me though, threatening to drag me back into a depression. I saved the boy and the sheriff wants to question me about it like I did something wrong."

"That's one of those human problems where self-interest over-rules common sense. The deputy, Billy Ray Johnson, has a chip on his shoulder. He wants to be sheriff and he figures free publicity will get him there. He's going to ride the wild man story for all it's worth."

"How do you know all that shit? Even know the asshole's name."

"Well, I ignore lots of, what'd you call it, shit, but I take it all in. My memory banks never get saturated. There is also a police department in Marshalltown. If you told them your story that might get you around the deputy's quest for free publicity at your expense."

"Hmm, yeah. Good idea. I suppose I could go there, act dumb, like I heard they wanted to talk to me, not the sheriff."

"The police chief is a decent enough guy. Doesn't have an axe to grind like the deputy. I can't say I'd trust the deputy. You're just a rung up the ladder he needs to climb."

"Maybe I'd better walk to town tomorrow and see the police. The woman down the road gave me a haircut and trimmed my beard today. Plus, she gave me some clean clothes. I look half-way decent."

"Better than you've looked in a long time, Caleb."

Caleb pulled his backpack open and reached inside for his wallet. He counted his money. He still had $297 dollars left from his severance check.

That should be enough to keep them from claiming I'm a vagrant. Also, I've been working. What the hell, common labor is work. That's where all work begins, at the common level, using my hands and my back. It's all uphill from there.

"I believe you have a handle on it," Glow said. "And, you have bacon and eggs and biscuits and, what did they call it up the road, sweet milk, for breakfast. A ploughman's meal."

Caleb climbed on top of his straw mattress, opened a Dick Francis book and read for an hour before switching off his home made light. Glow didn't interrupt.

# Chapter 7

The next morning, Caleb scrubbed his cast iron frying pan in the stream to clean it enough to fry the bacon and the eggs he'd earned shoveling cow manure. That, with a remaining biscuit was his breakfast. As a friendly gesture, he offered some to Glow, who had briefly greeted him as he got up, but was turned down.

"We don't eat," was Glow's reply. "Our renewal comes from all the little particles of energy you can't see, zipping through the air. We also get energy from the sun but it's so bright, it's more of a bother than a benefit. Makes me jumpy."

Caleb responded with a kind of half laugh and said, "Glad to hear it." More for me. He shook his head in disbelief. Am I making this up?

Caleb cleaned up after breakfast and wished for a cup of coffee.

"Guess you'll have to hit the road again, Caleb. If you want to work enough to earn a cup or two of coffee," Glow said.

The sun was still on the rise behind the trees on the other side of the rocky tower that housed his cave.

"Yeah. Early enough for me to do some work, I guess, if anybody wants help. I can see the police chief in the afternoon."

Having to see the police chief was not something he wanted to do. It was a problem but one, to quote Glow, that depended on the free will of the police chief for a solution. *Damnit to hell. I saved the little boy's life! Now, I have to explain it.*

*****

He left his camp and hurried down the road. As he approached the shotgun lady's home, he saw her in the garden, examining the early ears of corn on the stalks. He hesitated to see if the shotgun was in sight. He breathed a sigh of relief when he saw she was unarmed except for the stick she used to brace herself.

He moved to the other side of the road and picked up his pace to get past as quickly as possible. As he did, he heard the woman calling out urgently, "Man, man! Wait!"

Damn! He dared a look in her direction. With the aid of the hickory stick he held, she was hobbling toward him as fast as she could. At first, he wanted to ignore her and to get past before she could reach the road. But, seeing that she was mostly unarmed, he turned into her driveway to meet her half way.

"Mister," she said, breathlessly. "Did you come by here yesterday morning?"

His first instinct was to give her a flippant response but seeing the earnest look on her face, decided to play it straight and say, "Yes. I did."

"My pastor come by with his Christian Soldiers in the afternoon wantin' to weed the garden. They said it had already been weeded. They wanted to know who done it. I had to thank on it. Hard. As best I could recollect, it seemed like somebody might 've done it, but I couldn't rightly get it into my head who. Well sir, later on, I kind of remembered. That was you, warn't it? You weeded my corn patch and my peas?"

*Is she going to run into her house for the shotgun?* Caleb thought about what he should say for a couple of seconds before answering but he was ready to leave in a hurry if she even looked like she was going for the shotgun.

"Yes, I did. I don't think you liked it much however. You told me to leave."

The woman bowed her head and let it shake back and forth three or four times. "I'm so sorry, Mister. I ain't all here some of the time. If you know what I mean?" She patted the top of her head. "I forget a lot, these days."

Caleb sighed and shook his head. "It's okay."

"No, I don't reckon it is. People say I go a mite crazy now and again and I don't even know I'm doing it. Can I make it up?"

Caleb shook his head. "Not a problem. I forget things myself now and then. Talk to myself too." He thought of how he talked to Glow.

"The pastor said you done a good job. He said you must be a good man to work that hard."

Caleb was stuck for an answer but managed a "Thank you."

I did a "good job" for years and look how I ended up, no wife, no family, no house and no job. Talking to an orange Glow in the dark and guarding my hemlock.

"You stay here, mister. I'm going to the house to git you a mess of fried chicken."

Before he could protest, she'd turned and began hobbling toward her front door. To make things easier, he followed so she wouldn't have so far to walk. He met her at the front door. In her hand was a bag. "Got some fried chicken and cornbread for you." She handed him the bag. "Left over from last night."

He thanked her.

"Next time, if I commence to act crazy, you just keep on walking."

Caleb agreed. Count on it.

He hurried away with the bag, leaving the woman staring after him.

*****

Soon Earnest's and Mama's house came into view. In the drive way sat two pickup trucks. The door of one was open. He saw four men working around the barn and in the garden he didn't get to the day before. He figured they were the "kinfolks" – her brother's boys - who had been too busy to do the work he'd done.

Earnest and his wife sat on the front porch in the swing. It looked like each held a mug in their hands.

*Coffee? Wish I had a cup.*

He made a decision not to stop. They couldn't possibly need his help.

They saw him as he hurried along and called out. He couldn't hear what they were saying, but knew they were calling out and waving for him to come to the porch. He did.

"I saw that you had help today," he said. "So, I was headed to the next house."

"You jes come on up here and have a cup of coffee with us and one of Mama's biscuits," Earnest said.

Mama shook her head. "You set down. Earnest'll get you a cup."

He did and within seconds, he was sitting in one of their rocking chairs drinking a cup of coffee and eating a biscuit filled with mayhaw jelly.

He thanked them and gave them high praise for the coffee and the jelly biscuit.

Mama said, "We called the sheriff yesterday and told him you'd come by and done work for us. I told him you were no more a wild man than Earnest."

"Yes, sir, she did," Earnest said with a big grin. "That deputy, Billy Ray, drove out in the afternoon and talked to us. He told us you were dangerous and we shouldn't let you on our property."

Mama jumped in at that point and said, "We told him that was a lot of hooey. You were a good man. He said they was about to organize a party to find you. They was intending to track you down!"

Earnest said, "I told him that was a waste of time and money."

The deputy left after that, Earnest told him.

Caleb thanked them for sticking up for him and finished his coffee and the biscuit. But, the deputy's zeal to track him down and accuse him of doing something wrong bothered the hell out of him.

As he left, one of the men working came back to one of the trucks for a tool or something and said hello with a long look at Caleb.

Caleb returned the greeting and offered his hand.

The man laughed. "You must be the wild man ever body's talkin' about. I don't reckon you look all that wild to me. Earnest said you helped out yesterday. We appreciate it. Them stalls were as clean as I've ever seen."

Caleb thanked him and turned to wave goodbye to Earnest and his wife on the porch. They smiled and waved.

He hurried on down the road to the next house. It was about fifteen minutes further along. He stopped at the driveway to check for dogs. There was one. A mixed breed of some sort, he figured, with a loud bark and bared teeth. A junk yard dog. Fortunately it was chained to an oak tree in the front yard, far enough away from the front porch to let him continue without getting bit.

Like most country houses, he'd seen, it had porches, front and back. He could see the swing on the front porch but not the back. An older Chevrolet truck sat on the grass beside the house.

The roof was metal, with some rust showing but not much. The pine siding hadn't seen paint in a very long time, he decided in a glance, but it looked in good shape. The house was suspended off the ground by four foot high stilts, some brick, some block. The windows were the old fashioned kind with small panes, all covered with white lace curtains.

As he began the walk down the drive to the house, the golden sheen of corn silks from the sizable corn patch on his right caught his eye. The rows ran parallel to the road. Like the vibrantly green corn stalks in Earnest's patch, the golden tassels at the tops of the stalks were in full bloom, silks drooped over budding ears of corn in protective green shucks.

Caleb knew the ears were edible even then, but they still had some growing left to do.

At that moment, a realization popped into his thoughts. The colors at his grade school were green and gold, just like the corn stalk. I wonder if way back when, they grabbed at the colors of a corn stalk to use for the school colors. This is corn country.

The thought was interrupted by a mockingbird that fluttered to the ground beside a stalk. After a nervous look around, it began pecking furiously. Within seconds, two more joined the first, evidently to see if they could get some of what the first bird had discovered.

Caleb remembered how his family always had a corn patch, partly for eating, partly for feeding to chickens and a cow they had. It was often his job to pull the ears of corn when they became big enough to eat and later, at harvest time, for the livestock.

Nearing the end of the driveway, he noted an open garage with a woman working over a table inside. A fluorescent light hung over it.

He climbed the stairs and knocked on the door frame. The dog continued to bark and pulled at the chain like he was ready to take on a pack of lions. The front door was open, but the screen was latched. From inside he heard the sounds of country western music.

Within seconds of his knock, an older lady appeared. She lifted the latch, pushed the door open a crack and said, "Yes. What do you want?" The dress she wore might have fit at one time but looking at it then, Caleb thought it seemed to be struggling to hang onto her shoulders. Whatever pattern and color it might have had at one time, had been washed away years before. Must 've lost weight and wore the thing out, he thought.

"I uh, do field work," Caleb said with some hesitancy, recalling his last encounter. "I was wondering if you had any work for me? I work for food. You decide how much and what. I'm not proud. Do you have any?"

He glanced at the dog, still straining to break free.

The woman also looked. "That's Red's dog. He loaned him to us. We had a prowler so we chain him to the side of the house at night. Haven't had a prowler since. He's coming for him today or tomorrow. Makes a lot of racket."

Caleb agreed and repeated his earlier question.

The woman switched her dark eyes past his face to look behind him, like, Caleb thought to himself with a chuckle, she was preparing herself for the hordes he must have brought with him, waiting to overwhelm her.

Finally, she said, "My daughter handles the work outside. I cook 'n clean and help out inside." She pointed toward the garage where Caleb had seen the woman working.

She closed the screen door and disappeared into the darkness of the house.

Caleb wandered toward the garage where she'd pointed. The woman he seen working, *probably in her early forties*, he figured, was putting something together on the table.

In pretty good shape, he thought and immediately realized that was the first woman he'd taken the time to look at in … well, since he got married.

*Looks like she's fitting twigs together. Gluing 'em. Making something. What?*

When she heard him approach, she stopped her task and looked up. In a glance, he decided she might be a few years older, but could easily claim forty. Her face was without lines. Her hair, brown, hadn't been arranged in a beauty parlor, but was neatly combed and styled without flair. Her eyes were a bright blue. The dress she wore, off color white and long and casual, was a better fit than the one the lady at the door had been wearing. A pink sash looped around her midsection was basically the dress's only color. Tennis shoes covered her feet.

"What do you want?" she asked, getting right to the point.

Caleb told her his name and gave her his story, glancing around as he did for shotguns. He saw none. Instead, he noticed small objects sitting on wood shelves along the garage walls. Most looked no larger than four or five inches wide and tall, all fashioned from twigs, some painted in muted earth tones, some the color of the twigs. *Some have a shellac coating*, he thought after a closer look.

"My name's Julie," she told him. "I reckon I could use a little help 'bout now. I make these little things, art objects if you want to be kind, for the craft store, Red's, at the edge of town. The store is right off the interstate and a state highway. Great location. And, you have to walk past to get to town from here on the park road. " She gestured at the wooden shelves in the garage. "I promised Jefferson – he prefers to be called Red - I'd have him a dozen more before the weekend. Holiday coming up, you know."

Caleb nodded like he knew, but he'd totally forgotten.

"I'm running behind," she said. "He sells out to tourists on Saturdays. Usually. I make 'em out of twigs from the woods. I try to stay with a Mississippi theme. Tourists like that. Pay decent money too. Me and mama don't get rich, but we make enough to pay our taxes and the light bill."

*Red's the guy Earnest and Mama were talking about. So, he's got more than a truck stop and he loans out his dog.*

He looked over her shoulder and took a step forward to get a better look at what she'd pointed to on the shelves. Most were circular in shape with a loop for hanging them from something. Some held miniature birds, blue and red. A few were like boxed picture frames. They held butterflies. All things the woman had made by hand.

And, she'd carved pieces of wood into the creatures that inhabited the land with her. Faces of little pigs were on some. Birds appeared anchored to others. The faces of dogs, cats, even horses and cows had been carved on others. Some, she'd left natural, others she'd coated with a stain or shellac.

"Beautiful," he said with a gesture. "Works of art. Impressive."

She accepted the compliment with a nod. "Well, just now, I need you to take that basket." She pointed to a straw basket beside the table. "And go into the woods back of the house. There are lots of dead vines and crooked limbs and roots lying around. I'll need what you can find so I can finish up what I have to do. Get me a basket full?"

He glanced at the vines and pieces of wood on her table to gain an understanding of her needs and nodded.

With the hand clippers she'd offered and an axe for the roots, he picked up the basket and hurried into the woods to see what he could find. He had no problem. Muscadine grape vines grew all over. He even saw a few muscadine grapes left over from somebody's picking and took one. It was sweet enough but he didn't care for the seeds and let one be enough.

Enough dried, dead vines were around to give him plenty to pick from. He gathered the ones with the most curves and turns to make her job of fashioning rounded cages easier. And, there were other vines. He cut them as well, along with small, twisted and gnarled branches that had some artistic merit, he deduced. A few dried roots caught his attention. He cut them free with the axe. She can use them for carving, he thought.

While he worked, his thoughts kept returning to what Earnest and his wife had said about the deputy, "gonna track him down."

Damnit to hell, I just came down here to die. Damn Glow … hell no. I needed to save that little boy no matter what. Glow was right. Besides, it snapped me right out of my depression. Still, I hope seeing the police chief will get the son of a bitching deputy off my back.

All the time he cursed the deputy sheriff, he worked to fill his basket with the vines and roots Julie had sent him to collect. When it was done, he quick walked back to where she was still working in her garage workshop and gave her the basket.

She thanked him and looked at the clock hanging from the garage wall. "You got time to feed the chickens and pick up the eggs?"

He did.

"Watch out for the old rooster. He doesn't know you and might take you for an intruder. He has sharp spurs."

Like the dog, looking for something … or somebody he doesn't know, to bite.

He said he'd be on high alert with the rooster. She told him where the dried corn was and the egg basket. It hung on a peg on the back porch. Minutes later, he was spreading corn in the chicken yard. He deliberately threw a handful away from the red rooster to draw him toward the yard's fence where he stayed. Chickens, mostly white, some gray and white, sang as they hurried from kernel to kernel of the corn, pecking at each until it all disappeared.

He also filled the water bowls and drank his fill as he did. The hens went from pecking to drinking to get the kernels down. And, there were a number of young pullets scratching around, attesting to the rooster's work. He closed the gate behind him and walked past the barn as he headed back to the garage.

A cow and calf were in separate, open stalls behind the barn. He stopped long enough to throw fresh straw into both stalls.

By the time he made it back to the garage, the woman, Julie, was finishing up.

"I'll get you something," she said and hurried away. She came out the back door with a couple of jars of canned vegetables, half a dozen biscuits, two eggs, a slab of bacon and a pint of fresh milk, all in a bag.

"That's too much," Caleb said but she insisted.

"Drop by again. There's always work to be done around here. And, we generally have something we can give you to eat. Some of its leftovers but still good."

He wanted to ask if she had any extra coffee but thought that'd be pushy so he didn't. Instead, he thanked her and headed toward the road.

# Chapter 8

The milk she'd given him caused him to change the plan to walk into town and see the police chief. He needed to put the milk into the cold water before it soured.

*I'll have time to walk into town after I do that*, he thought. He looked at the sun. *Plenty of time. Besides, I need to stop at a store for coffee and some other things.*

He hadn't brought a toothbrush. Didn't figure he'd need one. But, now, he was thinking he did.

He went inside the cave and put the little jar of milk into the eddy of the stream to keep it cold. He'd placed small rocks from around the camp site at the edge of the eddy to secure the cold things he'd put into the water. Earlier, the pint jar he'd put in the stream had begun to drift before he could drink it all. That triggered his thinking about the rocks.

He put the rest of what Julie and the shotgun lady had given him on a ledge in the cave.

Glow hadn't manifested itself. Caleb took the absence as a sign he might still be sane, at least part of the time. He was premature.

Just then, Glow said from someplace back in the cave, "The twig lady was nice, wasn't she?"

For some strange reason, it pleased him that Glow decided to speak. It also troubled him that he might be talking to himself somehow and was indeed going nuts. Delusional, he figured, somehow related to Alzheimer's. Well, so be it. Serves me right for shutting out life all these years.

He realized just then that he'd never had a friend he could talk to … well, no friend at all.

Before he could answer Glow's question, it said, "Even if I were a manifestation of your Alzheimer's talking back, you're still enjoying it, aren't you?"

"I guess so. Being nuts isn't as bad as I've imagined it would be."

"Some humans enjoy being … nuts. Saves having to take responsibility."

"Yeah," he said. "Okay, what about the twig lady? Julie's her name. I figure you already know her life history."

"Of course I do, but I'm not going to tell you that much about her. That'd be like telling you a book's ending before you read it. I will tell you that she'll have work for you. Oh, and, she's married. I'm telling you that in case you get any ideas."

"I didn't see a husband. She didn't say anything about one either. Anyway, I don't get ideas in that direction. I'm still dead, remember. Have been for years. That's still why I came here, to finish the job."

"I know. I'm waiting for you to do just that so I can move on. Well, she wouldn't have said anything about being married unless she felt threatened by you … and, wanted to warn you off."

"So, I'm not a threat. What else?"

"I'm not going to write the story for you, Caleb. Besides, your story is a function of free will, remember. You're on your own. And, there are more houses up and down the road for you to visit, people to help. And, you need to see the police chief in town. If you don't deal with that problem, you'll likely end up cooking your hemlock stew."

"Yeah. Go back to sleep."

"By now, Caleb, you must know we never sleep. I have other things to do, things you could never understand. You're still a project until you cook your hemlock stew, but my assignment is worldwide."

"Yeah."

He shrugged with a sigh of resignation and began his walk back to the gravel road that would take him to Marshalltown to see the police chief. It was a task he dreaded and wished he could avoid but so far no way had presented itself.

The shotgun lady was nowhere in sight when he walked by her house. And, no shotgun.

Likewise, Earnest and his wife were missing from their front porch. And the two pickups that had been in the front yard that morning were also gone.

*Earnest and Mama are probably having their afternoon nap. Wish I were.*

One pickup passed him and slowed like he was going to stop and offer him a ride. Instead, the man in overalls driving took a long look and kept going. Caleb laughed.

He saw the twig lady, Julie, loading a box into the back of her truck as he passed her house. From the way she moved, fast and nervously, he figured she was getting the twig art objects she'd been working on to the craft's store for tourists to buy over the upcoming Memorial Day weekend.

He almost waved but decided against it. It didn't matter anyway. She'd already turned to go back into her garage work area for another box. He looked toward the house for any sign of her husband but saw none. Her mother either.

As he walked past her house, a bothered thought popped into his mind. *What if the police want to know where I'm sleeping? I'll have to tell them something and I don't want to tell them about the cave.*

He almost turned around to pick up some things from the cave to leave at the junk yard. He could tell them he was sleeping in the junk yard if they asked. He didn't stop walking. It had to be done, talking to the police.

*The cushions I slept on are still there. The ashes from my fire are there. The fast food wrappers are some evidence that somebody has been camping there at one time. I'll rely on that. Hell, I don't want to be lugging crap back and forth.*

He was also worried that the police chief might very well march him right over to the sheriff's deputy and leave him there. The sheriff, or that crazy deputy, would likely jump at the chance to throw him into a cell and invite in the local newspaper and television station to watch him question the "pervert who'd molested his son."

Twice along the way, he thought about his bag of hemlock and abandoning the walk into town in favor of returning to his cave to cook and eat his hemlock. He'd die and nobody would ever find his body and his troubles would be over. The problem was, he wasn't sure he wanted to die anymore. He was living for the first time since he was a kid. He'd spent most of his adult life avoiding living. He couldn't say why, but it had made him feel good to do something for somebody who truly needed it, the three families along the road, including the shotgun woman. And, all three actually thanked him. And, there was Glow, talking to Glow. A strange thing but it gave him comfort somehow.

He picked up his pace.

Passing a group of businesses near the Interstate, he slowed for a look. One building was clearly a truck stop and convenience store. It was a two story building. The upper floor looked to be an apartment with a covered stairway on the side. Hugo's place to live, he remembered Earnest saying.

The gas pumps could accommodate large trucks, freight haulers as well as small trucks and autos. From the number of trucks parked at the rear, it appeared to Caleb that some drivers pulled in for a rest break. He also saw what he assumed was a small, prefabbed log cabin with a front porch at the rear of the property. He wondered if Red rented out the cabin to people who were too tired to drive another mile.

Separated from the first building some distance away, was another building. Caleb's eye first caught the sign on the end second of the building. It read, "Red Neck Crafts and Art Objects."

*Must be where Julie sells her arts and crafts*, he surmised.

The other section of that building was a restaurant with the name, "Southern Eats and Drinks." Below the main sign were the words, "come and eat if you can stand it." It was still lunch time – called dinner time around Marshalltown - and the parking spaces were filled.

It looked like things had begun with the truck stop and expanded over the years into the other two businesses. Caleb didn't recognize the gasoline sign and figured the station was an independent.

An energetic man in his fifties, Caleb deduced, hurried authoritatively toward an 18 wheeler with a man fidgeting nervously beside the open cab door. He was a few inches under six feet, had a medium build with hair cut neatly short. He was already gesturing toward a location for the truck as he grew close. The driver acknowledged and began to climb back into the truck.

*Ex-military*, Caleb thought. *Must be Hugo, Red's right hand man. I can see why he might feel put out having to shovel cow shit. Hell, he's managerial material. I wish I had that option.*

As he hurried on past, the store's door opened and a beefy man came out walking fast. From the distance, Caleb figured he was about his height, maybe an inch or so shorter. Younger for sure. No stomach flopped over his belt. His red hair gleamed in the sun.

Red, he thought. Be damned. The man who sells Julie's arts and crafts … in that store. How about that? Gotta be some Irish in his ancestry.

He remembered somebody saying that the Scotts and Irish were settlers in south Mississippi.

Red's face was one of those people would call square and ruggedly handsome. He wore a short sleeved shirt and matching pants that Caleb took for a uniform.

"Red" hurried to an old truck beside one of the pump stations and leaned in to say something to the elderly lady inside. He smiled and retreated to the pump to put in whatever she'd said.

Service with a smile, Caleb thought and walked on.

# Chapter 9

Thirty minutes later, Caleb was standing in front of City Hall which sat on a small hill in the middle of town. That's where somebody told him the police chief had his office. As he looked up at it from the bottom of the steps, he considered one last time whether to abandon the confrontation. For some perhaps silly reason, something out of Shakespeare floated across his mind like a ticker tape, a modified version of Hamlet's soliloquy. *To be or not to be, that is the question. Has it been nobler to suffer the slings and arrows of outrageous fortune that life handed me or should I take arms against my ocean of troubles.*

He decided that taking arms against his troubles was nobler and walked up the steep steps of the ancient City Hall building. Inside, he went to the door, the upper half of which was clouded glass showing the name – "Marshalltown Police Department" – and went inside.

"Can I help you sir," a middle aged woman asked as he came into the room. He could see someone he took to be the police chief in an office to the left of the receptionist. The man, in his sixties and partially bald, wore a white shirt so bright, Caleb thought he might need sun glasses for the interview.

"I'd like to see the police chief," Caleb told her.

She wanted to know why.

"I'm the guy the newspaper called a wild man. I think somebody around here wants to interview me."

She took a hard look. Apparently satisfied that he wasn't going to kill anyone immediately, she got up and went inside the chief's office, closing the door behind her. Seconds later, the door opened and she reappeared.

"Go inside, sir. Chief Bush will see you," she said with a gesture and looked him up and down as she said it.

The chief stood as Caleb walked in. He had a policeman's gut, Caleb noticed. It hung over his belt. *Too many free lunches and free beers. Shorter than me. A square face, hard and lined. Seen a few miles.* But, otherwise he looked friendly enough. No gun in hand.

"Come in and take a chair. I go by the name of Andy or Chief if you're in a hurry or Chief Bush if you've been arrested or afraid you might be," he said, motioning Caleb toward the chair facing his desk. Caleb sat down.

"Thank you. I'm Caleb Stanley," Caleb said.

"Okay, Lurline says you're the wild man the sheriff's been looking for. Have to say, you don't look all that wild to me, but who knows? Have you been eating raw rabbits or squirrels, bashing children over the head?" He added a forced smile and rubbed a hand over his hair. It had turned mostly gray over the years. Caleb put his age at about his, early sixties.

He decided not to tell him about his haircut. "No sir. I just got to town a few days ago. I saw a little boy about to step into a kind of bog. I'd seen some snakes in it before and was afraid he'd get bit so I stopped him and took him back to, I assumed, his parents. Looked like a bunch of people having a camp out and he ran to them when we got close."

"That squares with what I've heard, but Billy Ray – he's the deputy sheriff – thinks you're some kind of child molester just come to town. What are you doing here … in Marshalltown? If you don't mind me asking."

"I don't." Caleb told him how his job had been shipped to the Far East and how his wife had left him the same day. All his kin folks were dead so he decided to come "home," to Marshalltown, where he was born, to live out his days.

"Sounds like you've had some bad times. Where you been sleeping?"

Caleb agreed about the bad times and told him he was sleeping in "the junk yard" just past the park. "Haven't had time to find a place. Even if I did, I don't know if I have enough money to pay rent. I'm working for food right now. Glad to get the work."

"You say you come from 'round here? Where 'bouts would that be?" The chief eyed him suspiciously.

"Shady Oaks, just north of town. My folks lived there until they died in a car accident. About fifteen or so years ago as far as I can remember. Something like that, anyway. My dad wasn't supposed to be driving with his health problems, but he was as stubborn as a mule. My mother lived on for a few years but she was never the same. I figure she died with my dad. I think she felt the same way."

The Chief shook his head with understanding sympathy.

Caleb continued, "Jerry and Jennifer, my younger brother and sister also died in the accident. They were visiting from Atlanta. They wanted to be married in our church and asked dad and mom to help make it happen. My wife handled things for my folks after they … passed away, the funerals and their affairs. Spared me. I was trying to survive, work wise. I think I know where they were all buried. My older brother, Aaron, died in Afghanistan a long time ago. Special Forces. I'm the last Stanley alive as far as I know."

The chief's face softened. Caleb was practically kin folk. "All that happened before my time. I moved here from Meridian seven years ago. I assume you don't own the house now. Else you wouldn't be sleeping rough like you are."

"No, I don't. As I said, my wife took care of everything after they died, including the sale of the house and furnishings, I assume. She handled all our business affairs. I signed what she shoved at me to sign. I just worked and brought in the money."

"I can understand that. I kind of fall into the same category. I make it and my wife spends it."

Caleb laughed.

"Any cousins or other relatives left behind? I guess not, but thought I'd ask."

"No. Aaron was career military and apparently had no interest in getting married. Jerry and Jennifer were visiting to discuss their upcoming marriages. Fortunately they left their fiancées in Atlanta or they'd be dead too. They wanted to have a joint ceremony here in Marshalltown. They'd been living with their fiancées for years. Living in sin, some around here might say. All had careers and, I understand, were reluctant to give them up … not to mention the money, to get married and have families but time was running out so they made a decision to get married. Unfortunately, it did run out for them. My dad, who was driving, may have had a heart attack or fatal stroke."

"Too bad. Where're you working? Maybe I should ask, are you?"

"I am, kind of. So far I'm helping the folks along Park Road. Earnest and his wife and some others. I don't know their last names."

"Earnest and Bessie Walters. Nice people. Getting a little old. Down with arthritis. Kind of hard for them to get around. People drop by and give 'em a hand. Got two girls. Both married. Live out of state. They come back and visit when they can. Nice of you to help 'em out."

"They give me food."

He gave an approving grunt.

"They called me about you. Said you were good people. I believed them."

"I thank them. I haven't met better myself."

"I called the sheriff and told him. They'd already called him."

Caleb nodded. "Glad to hear somebody's talking with good sense. I also did some work for a lady by the name of Julie. Makes art objects out of twigs and things. Does carvings too. Apparently does very well at it. I didn't ask for a last name. Didn't figure I needed to know."

"Julie Howard. Married. No children. Artistic, everybody says. Sells everything she makes in Red's craft store. Her husband, Charlie, shot and killed a gambler he owed five thousand dollars. Never went to trial. The DA said there was provocation. He might have gotten off with a light sentence or no sentence at all, but he left town. The gambler, Scooter he was called, has family. Scooter shot first but missed. Charlie didn't. The DA might not have even prosecuted. It looked like self-defense. Took place in front of Charlie's house."

"Must have made the news," Caleb said.

"It did. The DA's not that concerned about Charlie so he's not chasing after him. I think he's up north someplace. But Billy Ray's got a bug up his ass to find him. Most around the country call him BR or Billy. I understand he'd got the hots for Julie. Figures if he gets rid of Charlie, he could get into her pants. From what I hear, hell would have to freeze over before she'd climb into the sack with an asshole like Billy. But he ain't the brightest light in the pack and hasn't got sense enough to quit. 'Sides, he's married. We all wonder how he managed that."

"I think I saw him at the park when I took his boy back. By the way, I ran into a woman on the road, kind of neighbors to Earnest and Bessie. I call her shotgun lady 'cause she threatened me with a double barrel shotgun. First house after you cross the river bridge.

Her husband taught her how to shoot, she told me. I never got her name. I felt lucky she didn't shoot me. I'd weeded her corn patch and garden. She may have a touch of Alzheimer's. Kind of admitted it yesterday when she caught me at the road. She didn't have her shotgun."

The chief laughed and slapped the top of his desk with the palm of his hand. "Be damned! That'd be Alma Cochran. She's never been married. Just wishes she had been. I think she has spells, maybe it is Alzheimer's. She lived with a man for a while. Promised to marry her. Nice enough guy, but it didn't work out. One morning she woke up and he was gone. Hasn't been heard from since. They did have a girl. She got educated and moved to New York. Works for an advertising agency. Sends money back to the church to look in on her mama now and then. She visits a couple of times a year, brings her family."

He looked at the clock on his desk. "Well, I guess we'd better take you over to see the sheriff. I know you're looking forward to that."

Caleb's heart sank. He was hoping against reality that it'd end with the chief. *I should'a known better.*

"Yeah."

"He won't bite."

The chief continued, "His office is in the annex attached to the jail we all use to house our desperados. Just across the street behind us. Old Billy would have the newspaper and radio and television all over me if I turned you loose, which I'd prefer to do. But, that'd send him running off at the mouth about how there's no law and order in Marshalltown. Of course, he'd also be saying that would change when he becomes sheriff." He smiled. "Let's go, Mr. Wild Man."

He slapped his official hat on his head, motioned for Caleb to follow and headed out the door. "Be back in a jiffy, Lurline." He told her where he'd be.

She said something Caleb didn't catch.

A short walk brought them to a white, non-descript building behind City Hall. Half of which had barred windows.

The jailhouse, Caleb thought. Hope to hell I don't end up sleeping there tonight.

Chief Bush pushed through the main door, nodded at a young woman at a desk and headed for the sheriff's office on the right, which he entered without knocking. The door was opened. A big man in a grayish uniform sat behind the desk. He looked to be in his fifties with a long, narrow face, lots of lines, and white hair creeping into the black he'd been born with. He hadn't yet developed a stomach.

*May not have been in office long enough*, Caleb thought.

"Sheriff," the chief said with a wave back at Caleb. "This here's the wild man of the swamps, Billy Ray's been running on about. Caleb Stanley. Doesn't look all that wild to me. Had family here. Way back. All dead now. Caleb came back home to spend his last years here. As far as I'm concerned, he's no threat to anybody."

The sheriff got out of his chair and reached out for Caleb's hand. Caleb figured he was a couple of inches over six feet tall.

"Sheriff Tolar," he said, forcing a smile. His voice sounded like it came off the gravel road Caleb had traveled to get into town, rough and deep.

The smile didn't look to Caleb like it came naturally. "Glad to meet you. Friend of the Chief's is a friend of mine." He picked up the phone, punched in some numbers and said firmly. "Get in here, BR! I got your damn wild man."

He gave the Chief and Caleb a knowing smile. "Might as well sit a spell. Billy Ray's gonna keep us waiting. Let me know who's boss 'round here."

"They say he's gonna give you a run for the money, next election," Chief Bush said.

"He might, but the election hasn't started yet. I know a few things about Billy that he won't like getting out. Give the voters something to think about. He's got lots of kin and they got lots of friends, but there's still lots of voters in the County they don't know."

While they waited, Caleb gave the sheriff the same story he'd given the Chief, about camping at a place in the junk yard the other side of the river. The sheriff made notes.

"Better make a report," the sheriff said when he'd finished. "I imagine that property's posted. Could get into trouble sleeping there if the owner catches you. Old man Andrews, I think, owns it. I'll call the constable for that area and let him know. See what he says. If he says move, you have to move. The constable's a good man. He'll keep an eye out for you. I doubt old man Andrews gives a rat's ass about somebody sleeping out there."

"Thank you. I appreciate it. If he says move, I'll move," Caleb promised.

The sheriff finished writing and called out, "Ruby, can you type this up."

The young woman they'd walked past earlier came in, took his handwritten sheet with a nod and walked toward the door.

The sheriff called after her. "And make a file. One more thing, call Billy Ray on his mobile – I called his cell and left a message. You'll probably have better luck. When he comes in, have him sign the bottom of the report. I want proof that he knows this man is not under suspicion of any kind."

"Yes sir, I will," Ruby told him.

She closed the sheriff's door behind her. They heard her talking to someone on the phone. Billy Ray, Caleb thought.

The chief looked over his shoulder with a sly grin and asked the sheriff. "That Ruby's got a pair of jugs on her, ain't she? How do you get any work done?"

The sheriff laughed. "A man's gotta have some motivation to come to work."

"I reckon," the chief replied. "I'm gonna have to re-think my hiring policy."

Caleb nodded, more to himself than to the others. He'd noticed her endowments as well. The second time he'd actually taken note of a woman. The lady called Julie was the first one. Somebody nice he enjoyed talking to. He didn't know whether to curse himself about it or just relax and figure he'd rejoined the human race, the male part of it anyway.

About ten or so minutes later, the man Caleb had seen at the park with a beer in one hand, Billy Ray, hustled into the Sheriff's office, wild eyed. Another deputy followed. He was introduced as Leroy something. Too quick for Caleb to hear.

"This is bullshit, Sheriff!" He said, waving the paper Caleb assumed to be the sheriff's report in front of him. "Is this him, the pervert?" Billy Ray asked, pointing at Caleb.

The sheriff stood and stepped in front of Billy Ray.

Deliberately, Caleb thought, intimidate his deputy with his size.

"Yep," the sheriff said, in a tone even rougher and deeper than before. He poked Billy Ray in the chest with his index finger and added, "And, you're to leave him the hell alone, Billy Ray. The man's done nothing but save your boy's life. The doctor said as much. The Walters said he was okay, a good man. So far you're the only one saying different. Have you ever heard the saying about the only one being out of step, accusing everybody else? That'd be you! Now, shut your mouth about this man!"

Billy Ray ignored the sheriff's admonishment, stepped back and shouted at Caleb. "You pulled my boy's pants down didn't you?"

"What! I didn't touch your boy's pants. I just stopped him from getting snake bit. Just like he said in the newspaper."

"You're a lying pervert! I'm gonna see your ass in jail. They'll love you in Parchman. You'll spend yore days and nights bent over." Parchman was the state's penitentiary in the northern part of the state.

"Billy Ray, shut your damn fool mouth or you'll end up at Whitfield," the sheriff said, pointing his finger at the deputy. "And I'll be glad to drive the ambulance that takes you out there."

Mississippi had a string of institutions around the state to treat the mentally ill. Easier to get into than out, some said.

The sheriff gave a wave toward Caleb and continued, "This man was born and raised here. Had family here too, till they all died. Brother killed in Afghanistan. You managed to dodge that war didn't you? You're making a damn fool of yourself. Like always. This man's free to go. I've filed a report and I guess you've read it … and signed it." He waged a finger at his deputy.

The deputy scoffed, and took a step back and glared at Caleb. "Right now, I don't have enough evidence to charge you, but if you step out of line, I'm gonna be waiting for you."

Before leaving the sheriff's office, he turned to his boss and said, "That's what's wrong with you, Sheriff. You lettin' criminals go free. Should be locking 'em up. We'd have less crime." With that, he stalked out. The other deputy followed closely.

"If old Billy Ray turned in a hurry, Leroy would get a broke nose," the sheriff said with a grin, implying that Leroy had his nose stuck up so far in Billy Ray's behind a quick turn would surely break it.

The sheriff looked at the chief and Caleb and said, "As I said, you're free to go. I hate to say it, but that Billy Ray is a bad 'un. I'd fire him if he wasn't running for my job. If I fired him, he'd be all over it. But, watch what you do for a while till this blows over. You may have to move if Andrews kicks up a fuss about you trespassing."

Caleb nodded and thanked him.

The Chief patted him on the back outside the jail and offered to help him find a place to live when he got ready. He talked a bit about places where Caleb might find a job.

"Thank you, Chief. I'll sure look you up as soon as this Billy Ray shit passes over," Caleb said. "I need that aggravation like I need another hole in my head."

"I hear you. Well, get on about your business, Mr. Stanley." he said as they parted company. "Remember what the Sheriff said. Billy Ray makes his own law when it suits him."

Caleb promised to be careful.

Hell, all I do is do day labor for food. Cleaning cow shit out of stalls. How careful can I be?

Walking away, a wave of depression hit him. It was hard to accept that somebody would be gunning for him just because he wanted another man's job. *He's got it into his head that I'm the path to the sheriff's office. Son of a bitch!*

A few minutes along, he saw a bench along the sidewalk and sat down to collect his thoughts. Staring down, he wondered if he'd made a mistake holding up on cooking his hemlock. *My going out of business plan.*

*Thank God I still have it. I must have been crazy to think my life would get better. I was a fool.*

He had intended picking up a toothbrush and pound of coffee, maybe a few other things, from the local Wal-Mart but had second thoughts. *Why in hell should I waste my money?*

He let a few minutes pass. Then, with a sigh, he stood and pointed himself in the direction of the river and his cave. He'd made a decision. It was time. Past time.

As he walked, staring down at the pavement, he hoped Glow wouldn't be around. Glow hadn't said not to eat and drink the hemlock stew, but he got the feeling it was trying to trick him into changing his mind. Lately, though, it had been missing now and then. All he needed was about fifteen minutes alone. After a few blocks, he heard a car engine behind him. The toot of a horn caused him to turn around. It was Julie Howard in her truck.

"Mr. Stanley," she called from the truck's open window.

How'd she get my name? I didn't tell her.

"I'm going to Wal-Mart. Then, I'm going home. Let me give you a ride. I won't be in Wal-Mart long." The frown on her face puzzled him but he had other things on his mind. Before he could say no to her offer of a ride, she'd opened the door for him to climb in. He shrugged and did.

"How'd you know my name?"

"Oh. Yes, your name. I'm furious," she said. "Billy Ray Owens was just at the house. I drove off and left him standing in my front yard. I felt like running over him. He said he had come to warn me that no matter what the sheriff was saying, you were a pervert and a thug. I should watch you every minute and never let you on my property. He told me your name and where you're from. Said you were born around here."

Caleb sighed and let out a loud breath. He told her the same story he'd told the Chief and the Sheriff then added, "I've been to see the police chief and the sheriff. The folks down the road, the Walters, said the Sheriff wanted to talk to me. I decided to see the chief first. He walked me over to the sheriff's office, I assume, to protect me from the deputy, Billy Ray. The sheriff called him in and told him, in effect, to leave me alone. It didn't set well with Billy Ray who stormed out. I guess he went to your place."

"I guess. He told me to warn everybody on the road about you. I'm going to complain to the sheriff. He's harassing people. You know what else?"

"No."

"I'm married. He's married but he keeps asking me to go out with him. Someplace out of town, he says. Ha. I absolutely detest the guy. I'd never go anyplace with him. He's been after my husband since he got into a shootout with a guy he owed money. Do you know about that?"

Caleb nodded. "A little."

"My husband got out of town before the guy's brother could kill him. He sends me a letter now and then via one of his cousins. He won't ever come back here. Billy Ray wants to catch him so he'll have something to wave about at the next election."

"He wants to be sheriff."

"That'd be a disaster. He's no better than the thugs he tries to arrest. My husband shot a guy who had a gun on him, about to shoot, and Billy Ray's been all over it. The sheriff's letting criminals go free. The man's brother was telling it all over town that he was going to kill my husband. My husband didn't have a choice. He had to run or get shot in the back."

"I'm sorry you've had so much trouble."

She shook her head. "Me too. Last letter I got from Charlie, that's my husband's name, said he'd met somebody else and was trying to put his life back together. He told me I could get a divorce, but I'm not going to. No reason to."

"They're hard on you. Divorces. My wife got one." He didn't know how hard it was on her however. He suspected hers was easy. He'd heard divorces were hard from people he'd worked with. Lots of them got divorces. Most had married young.

At Wal-Mart, she parked to go inside. He stayed in the truck. He didn't figure to need anything anymore. He had all he needed in the cave at the park. Listening to her troubles didn't help him at all. Just more evidence that everything in his life still boiled down to nothing.

A few minutes passed and she was back with a bag of what he assumed were groceries, which she put behind her seat.

Driving home, she said, "Listen, me and Mama 're cooking a stew for dinner. Been stewing in a pressure cooker for over an hour now. It's always good. Why don't you join us? We always have a little left over for people dropping in."

Caleb was already shaking his head, no and thinking, *I have my own stew waiting for me.*

He said, "I have some things I'm working on but thanks."

But, Julie wouldn't take no for an answer. "Come on Caleb. This isn't California where being busy is a way of life. I've read about California living where everybody's got goals they work at all the time. You have to come. Mama said she wants to talk to you and I do too. It'll be ready about the time the sun goes down. I'll drop you off at the junk yard where Billy Ray says you're camping out. You'll have time to do what you're doing and walk back. Okay?"

She looked at him with a sparkle in her eye and a big smile on her face, like she really wanted him to come to dinner.

Caleb sighed. *Damnit! Every time I get ready to get out of here, something happens. Well, I guess going out with a full stomach won't be so bad.*

"Okay," he told her, smiling and nodding. "I'll be there. I'm looking forward to it. I bet you and your mother can cook up a storm."

"Some people think so."

She dropped him off at the junk yard drive and waved goodbye. Also adding a smile which looked genuine to him.

When she had driven out of sight, he walked back across the bridge and went to his cave hideout where he took a quick, cold bath with a piece of soap he'd found in one of the garbage cans and dressed in the clothes he'd worn to the park the first day. He'd washed them after his encounter with the cow shit and mud from the Walters' barn. Then, he waited until the sun was poised minutes above the horizon before he began his walk back to Julie's house. From his prior trips up and down the road, he knew it'd take about thirty minutes to get there.

Ordinarily, he might have allowed himself to get excited about a home cooked dinner by an attractive lady and her mother, but his confrontation with Billy Ray had changed that. But, there was no doubting that he was hungry.

# Chapter 10

Caleb hesitated as the turned into Julie's driveway as people do when they see something different. Up the road, the headlights of a car pulling off the road caught his eye. It was too far away and that, plus the car's lights, kept him from seeing any more. The lights went off so he assumed it had somehow quit running and its owner would have to go for help or call someone. Not uncommon even when Caleb was young.

He was walking up front steps as the sun was just slipping below the horizon. He could still see its orange glow through the trees behind her house. His knock brought her mother to the door for a warm welcoming hug. The dress she wore, something simple but smart, fit perfectly. A southern tradition, he knew. Julie wasn't far behind with her hug. She had also put on a stylish outfit. Both acted if they were glad to see him.

That almost lifted the despair that had been hanging over his head since he left the sheriff's office. The greeting embraces they met him with, kind of pushed it away. Nevertheless, his decision hadn't changed. All he wanted to do was eat his damn hemlock stew and get on with it. I'm tired of being here, tired of taking crap from anybody who wants to crap on somebody else for their own good.

He didn't say that however, forced a smile and stayed with the usual greetings he had used when going to someone's house for dinner. It had been a long time since he had. For the last few years of his past life, his ex-wife did all the dinner going, made excuses about why he couldn't go. A project on his desk or workbench was much more welcome than a plate of something all would proclaim as "delicious" on a dinner table surrounded by the phony smiles and competing conversations of well-dressed guests.

"I'm so glad you invited me," he said, adding enthusiasm he didn't feel. "A hot meal! Wow! You don't know how much I've looked forward to it." He hoped that came out sounding unrehearsed. However, he wasn't sure it was forced because he'd caught the dinner smell from the kitchen and enjoyed it.

*Damned if that's not about the best smell that's come my way in a long time.* He found himself remembering the dinners his mother cooked. His ex-wife didn't cook that much. If the box in the supermarket looked good, she bought it and cooked it in the microwave.

They said how glad they were he could make it and appeared to be sincere. They sat in the living room for the usual small talk before dinner. One or the other of them made trips back and forth to the kitchen to keep dinner on track. Julie said they were having roast beef and vegetables. Caleb didn't catch the names, but thought she'd said potatoes and green beans.

He found himself smiling and felt like a simpleton but they were smiling too, so he accepted it as normal social behavior. Something he'd been ignoring for longer than he cared to remember. *I guess I've been ignoring life,* he remembered. *Avoiding it.*

He asked how Julie got into arts and crafts. That came about after her husband left and they had to do something for money. Her mother had moved in with her after Charlie had to leave in a hurry. They had been pleasantly surprised at how well Julie had been doing, selling her crafts.

They tip toed around his situation. He was glad but explained some of his history, the company closing its doors and his wife deciding to get a divorce.

"I didn't blame her, all things considered. Our life together had reached an end point. The children were educated and had moved away to begin their lives. She wanted to get on with hers. I wasn't much of a husband or father. I decided to come home, Marshalltown, and see if I could start over."

That wasn't true, but he sure as hell didn't want to get into the real reason he'd come, to cook his hemlock stew and take a last sleep, a long one, something he planned to do after dinner that night.

Julie's mother, Bonnie Fae, offered him a little whiskey and coke. He hesitated but then said he'd love one. It had been a long time since he'd had anything strong. His wife ordinarily had wine at dinner and he didn't take issue, just drank the dry, paint stripping red she sat before him.

"We don't normally drink," Bonnie Fae said, "but we do keep a little on hand for friends." She smiled and looked him in the eyes as though she was enjoying having him as a guest. His wife's friends sometimes forced a smile, but it never came with a sincere look in their eyes. And, he never had anybody he called a friend, over.

It tasted good. He counseled himself to drink it slowly to avoid a reaction. So, he sipped it with Julie while Bonnie Fae finished getting dinner on the table. Julie drank something with a brown color in a glass to be hospitable but he never doubted for a moment that it was anything but a soft drink. Neither lady struck him as leaning toward alcohol as a way to relax. That was quite a departure from the California culture where no dinner party would begin or end without something alcoholic.

*I don't think I'll have to get used to it.* However, that thought didn't come nearly so forcefully as it had earlier.

He didn't hesitate when they called "dinner." He was ready. The table was covered in a white linen cloth, place mats for each of them, with the silver was correctly placed besides the plates. He felt like he was eating in an exclusive restaurant but on this occasion, he could be relaxed instead of sitting in his chair making up things to say to others his wife, usually the case, had invited.

And, the dinner was everything the smells had promised. Somehow the magic of a pressure cooker had blended the tastes of all the vegetables, meat and spices together and the results were fantastic. And, he was generous in his praise, without having to make up what to say. That was also a first for him in a long time.

Julie served coffee with dinner instead of wine. It was decaffeinated, freshly perked and good. Cream was offered. He accepted.

And, for desert, Bonnie Fae had made a lemon ice box pie, a southern delight, served with milk. He'd never tasted better. Not even from his mother.

He had only sincere compliments for both women during dinner. What's more, every time he looked over the table, they were looking at him and smiling. In particular, Julie was not only smiling with her lips, but also with her crystal blue eyes. Well, that was how he saw it.

Hell, she's married and I'm going to my cave to go out of business. Besides, I don't know how to treat a woman. Ruining her life would be enough to send me to hell.

But the notion of cooking his hemlock wasn't looming nearly as large in his thoughts as it had been when he left his cave to walk there. He chided himself for being indecisive.

*Was it the dinner? Was it just talking to the ladies? Hmm, was it the way Julie smiled at me? When was the last time anybody smiled at me like that?* He chanced a look at her. She was looking at him. *Smiling with happiness and a twinkle in her eyes*, he thought. He remembered the warmth of her body close to his when she hugged him. A sense of regret swept over him that he'd wasted most of his life without really feeling that close to anybody.

The only other person who even came close was a technician at the company. She helped him with the test projects he built from his designs. She was always smiling at him, rubbing his back and standing as close as possible, close enough for him to feel the warmth of her body.

He finally realized that she was interested in him. A couple of times, she hinted that they should go out, even asked him to lunch a number of times, but he always refused. It wasn't a deliberate refusal. He didn't even acknowledge what she had been doing until after she was married and quit doing it. They became friends until she quit to have her first child and didn't return.

But, now and then, he remembered her smiling face and encouraging words. He wondered how many other people had actually liked him, how many others he'd ignored, as he shut out the world. Once more, he thought about the life he'd wasted, his.

Dinner was over. They talked over the table a bit longer. He offered to wash the dishes, his job when his wife entertained. Well, rinsing them anyway. He'd rinse and put them in the dishwasher while she and their guests drank after dinner wine in the family room. But, Julie and her mother steadfastly refused his offer.

"No," Julie said. "We do our dishes. Don't we mother? We have our own way of doing things, Caleb."

"I wish I could help," he said. "It'd make me feel better."

She told him he could come by and help with chores now and then, if he wanted to. He agreed and stood to leave.

"If I can't help, I guess I'd better get going and let you ladies get to it."

Bonnie Fae told him good night, gave him another warm southern hug and went into the kitchen to get started.

Julie walked him to the door and did the same thing, hugged him like she meant it and added a kiss on his cheek. She whispered in his ear, "Don't let 'em wear you down, Caleb. You're a good man, better than the likes of Billy Ray and his buddies. They're out for what they can get and don't care who they step on getting it."

He thanked her and bounded off the porch, much happier than he'd been in a long time. The hemlock stew he'd planed for that night had left his thoughts.

*Real, honest to God people*, he thought. *I didn't think they existed anymore. Coming back here has been like a trip back in time, when things were simpler and people were real.*

He hurried to the road, paused and turned back to wave. Julie was at her front door. She smiled and waved back before going inside.

He let himself see her for real the first time. She had light brown hair cut to hang above her shoulders. She was on the slim side, not skinny but certainly not heavy. In fact, Caleb decided, she was just about right for her height, five feet six inches, maybe a bit more. Her blue eyes had captivated him. But, one of the more striking things about her, other than her smile, was the way she moved. She walked easily, with the grace of a dancer though he doubted she had ever been a dancer.

He cursed himself for even thinking such things about a married woman.

The car he'd seen pulling off the road as he came up, was still sitting off the road. The front side of the car was visible in the twilight. There looked to be something on top of the car, but partially behind the bushes the way it was parked, he couldn't tell what it was.

Still waiting for its owner to come back with help. Somebody has to find a part or somebody has to be found who can fix it, he supposed. He was wrong on both as he would soon find out.

He was almost skipping as he hurried along the gravel road. When he realized what he was doing, he felt like a fool but smiled at himself. It was one of the few times he could remember that he just let go and let his feelings be his guide.

He laughed to himself, unlike my new friend, Glow. All logic, not feelings.

As he walked along, he became aware of a noise on the road behind him. A car? He turned to see it easing along slowly, way behind him, with its lights still off.

*What the hell? That was the car parked off the road down from Julie's house? And, there is something on top! Lights? Damn, that's a police ... no that's a sheriff's car. Billy Ray or one of his buddies, watching to see what I'm doing and where I'm going. Well, I guess I'll be walking to the junk yard.*

It was good dark when he passed the footpath to his cave hideout. He glanced at it and wished he could take it, but the car was still following, slowly with it lights out. He kept walking. He hurried across the river bridge, heard the rushing waters below, until he reached the junk yard turn off.

As he had done before, he lifted the strands of barbed wire and crawled through. The car suddenly turned on its light, reeved its motor and drove on down the road. He turned but couldn't see the driver.

With the car no longer following him, he could sleep in his cave. So, he got back on the road and felt good enough to jog back across the bridge. At the far end, just before he reached the trail to the cave, he heard Glow's familiar voice. "I think you enjoyed yourself tonight, Caleb."

Caleb grudgingly acknowledged that he had, all the time having to accept the fact that he could be talking to himself. He shook his head as if to clear it of the thought. It didn't.

*I guess I've made up a friend I can talk to, even if the friend is me. Odd though. Glow seems real but how could that be? Dr. Freud,* he laughed to himself.

"I hate to disturb your tranquility but I thought you ought to know that your good friend, Billy Ray is going to pick up his buddy, Leroy, and head back to Julie's house. He wants Leroy there as a witness if things go like he wants or as a scapegoat if the shit hits the fan like it usually does with his schemes."

"Thanks," Caleb said, wondering if he'd gone off the tracks, talking to himself.

"He's on the warpath so be watchful," Glow continued. "The constable saw you getting out of her truck when she gave you a ride from town and called him. Billy Ray was fit to be tied and began watching her house when you showed up for dinner. A pervert like you, going into his wanna-be-girlfriend's house for who knows what. Something with romantic leanings, he figured, and he sure as hell wasn't going to stand still for that."

"Damn," Caleb cursed. "No choice but to go back."

"Kind of what I thought you'd say. That's why I told you. You're my project after all and I want you in as many precarious situations as possible while I'm here. It'll make my report more interesting."

Caleb picked up his jog to get to Julie's as soon as he could. With the moon as bright as it was, he had no trouble seeing the road.

Ten minutes down the road, Glow chimed in, "I think you'd better get into the woods while Billy Ray gets past you. His car is about half a mile behind you."

Caleb began to hear it about that time and barely made it off the road before the car came roaring past. He was back on the road as soon as the car's taillights were past, jogging as fast as he could.

Out of breath and sweating profusely, he came to Julie's corn patch and ducked off the road between the rows of green stalks until he got close enough to her house to see what was happening.

The official sheriff's car that passed him was parked in her driveway. A uniformed Billy Ray stood at the bottom of her front steps talking to Julie non-stop, shaking his head and waving his arms as he did. Leroy stood a step back, listening with hands on his hips. Her mother was not on the porch.

Caleb dropped down behind the last clump of corn stalks at her driveway and listened to Billy Ray's diatribe.

"I can't believe you'd let that pervert in your house with your dear sweet mother. And, to let him eat at your table. Have you taken leave of yore senses, woman?"

Julie shouted back. "I've had enough of your stupid remarks, Billy Ray! You don't own me. You're just a deputy sheriff. If I need help, I'll call. I don't need any. How can I make that any clearer? Caleb Stanley is not a pervert. He's a decent man. I wish there were more like him."

"That's a load of cow manure! I'm going in there to make sure your doors have locks that work. I'm not gonna be responsible for any harm comin' to you, Julie. You know how I care –"

"If you say that one more time, Billy Ray, I'm going to call the sheriff and tell him what a total failure you are. You are married. I'm married. Even if I weren't married, and even if you were the last man on earth, I still wouldn't let you through my front door. Do I make myself clear?"

With that, Billy Ray began stomping his way up the steps.

What the hell, Caleb thought and reached over to the edge of the drive way to pick up a large piece of gravel. He had no thought that he could hit Billy Ray, but hoped the rock would come close enough to make him think about the fool he was making of himself.

Caleb stepped back and let the rock fly. By then, Billy Ray was one step from the porch. The sound Caleb made when he threw the rock caused the deputy to hold up and turn toward the corn patch. That was when the rock got there … and hit Billy Ray squarely in the forehead.

"Son of a bitch!" he shouted and staggered back down the steps pawing at the cut in his forehead. He cursed again, yanked his automatic from its holster and began firing into the corn patch where he'd seen movement.

Leroy did the same.

When Caleb saw them grab for the guns, he turned and ran away, in a crouch. When he heard the first shot, which didn't come close to him, he dropped to his knees and crawled until he reached the end of the row. There, he turned left and crawled into the woods bordering the corn patch.

By that time, Billy Ray had recovered his senses and got into the car. It had a spot light. With Leroy driving slowly, Billy Ray moved the spot light about the corn stalks and into the woods where Caleb was lying flat and not moving. Both men continued firing into the patch and into the woods. The bullets sailed well over Caleb's head.

Then, suddenly, Billy Ray's car accelerated, throwing gravel from behind the back tires.

Caleb knew what was happening. They were going to race back to the junk yard and get there before he could. They'd wait and when he showed up, he'd be arrested after "he'd resisted and had to be forcibly restrained."

He cursed, got to his feet, made it through the corn patch to the road and began running as fast as he could. His only hope was that somehow, Billy Ray would get held up or couldn't find his junk yard camp site. He knew that was almost impossible but he ran anyway.

An old baseball quip came into his thoughts. It ain't over till it's over.

Billy Ray's car lights were ahead and growing dimmer. He knew he'd never make it but he ran on anyway. After ten or so yards, he felt a kind of dizziness come over him. Like he was about to pass out.

I'd be safe if I went to the cave, but if they don't find me at the junk yard, they'll know I threw the rock. But, I can't get to the junk yard in time. I'm not even sure I can get to the cave. It's over for me, he thought. I might as well die right here in the road. The dizziness he'd felt swept over him. He felt himself falling.

Next thing he knew, he felt the car seats in his junk yard camp under him, the worn blanket on top. What the hell! Did I make it? Have I been dreaming the whole damn thing? Dinner with Julie and her mother. It didn't happen. I guess this is what it feels like to lose your mind. I've lost mine. I'm even sweating. Son of a bitch. Well, it is what it is. They'll have to put me away someplace. A fruit cake.

He pulled the cover around him and tried to go to asleep.

# Chapter 11

Billy Ray and Leroy reached the junk yard and pulled into the bushes across the road. Both got out.

Billy Ray took out his cell phone and called the constable. "Wade, you seen him yet?"

Wade replied. "I just saw you and Leroy drive up but I ain't seen that man. I reckon you got here first. I'm parked just down the road out of sight. You can't see me but I can see the bridge. Nobody's crossed it in the last twenty minutes since I've been watching."

Billy Ray told him to keep watching but if he saw the man, he was to drive down. "As a witness," he added.

Wade promised.

Billy Ray turned to Leroy and said, "Go down to where he told the sheriff he was making camp and see what you can find. I'll keep watch up here. If that sucker comes across that bridge, I'm going to have his ass. If he even looks at me cross eyed, I'll shoot him. Another case solved by Billy Ray, your next sheriff."

"Might outta be careful, Billy Ray. Sheriff said we was to leave him be. He ain't done nothin' wrong. What the sheriff said."

Billy Ray touched the cut on his forehead, still bleeding but less than it was. "The sheriff's half senile, Leroy. You know that. That's why I'm going to beat his ass next election. Now, by God, I got me some evidence that the man is up to no good. He hit me with a damn rock. Could'a killed me. I reckon that's enough evidence to take him in, don't you?'

Leroy swallowed his rebuttal to Billy Ray's comment and reluctantly agreed. He hurried away, flashlight in hand, down the little animal trail Caleb had followed when he first came to the junk yard. Billy Ray stepped into the shadows of the bushes along the road to watch and wait, his right hand resting on the butt of his automatic. He took the time to click off the safety. He had already made his decision. He'd shoot the bastard and make up a story to back it up. To hell with the sheriff and police chief. They ain't here.

\*\*\*\*\*

Leroy found the opening spot between the junkers where Caleb had told the Sheriff and Police Chief he had his junk yard camp site. He saw Caleb's form under a cover on his car seat bed. How the hell can he be here? Nevertheless, he turned off his flashlight and carefully approached. When he was a couple of feet away, he turned on his flashlight and said, "You! On your feet!"

Caleb, who had heard him approaching, even watched him out of the corner of his eye, rolled over and pretended to be just waking up. "What? Who are you? What do you want?"

He rolled off his bed and stood. Leroy could see that Caleb didn't have a weapon of any kind.

Caleb stared at Leroy and said. "You're the law. You have a uniform on. Did I do something wrong? I thought it was okay for me to sleep here. I'm doing handyman work for folks along the road."

"You threw a rock and hit the deputy sheriff 'n I'm bringing you in." He was still puzzled. How in the hell could the man have beaten them to the junk yard? No way in hell, was his conclusion.

Not my problem, he told himself. Billy's.

"I didn't throw a rock," Caleb said. "I haven't seen a deputy sheriff till you woke me."

"Shut the fuck up. Move it." He ordered Caleb to walk ahead of him toward the gravel road. Once there, the man would be Billy's responsibility. *If he shoots him, well, I'd back him up. Have to.*

When they pushed through the barbed wire strands at the road, Billy Ray heard the noise and came from behind his hiding place in the bushes.

"What the hell!" he said when he saw both Leroy and Caleb. "Where'd he come from?"

Leroy told Caleb to stop where he was. "Billy Ray, I gotta tell you, this man was asleep. No way on God's earth could he be the one that chunked that rock at you. No way in hell could he 'uv beat us back here."

Billy Ray put his automatic back into its holster and stared at Leroy and Caleb, frowning. "Son of a bitch," he mumbled and rubbed his chin as if that might give him an answer to his question. As he did, the constable having seen the commotion, drove down and parked in the road. He got out and walked to where the three men stood.

"Wade," Billy Ray said to the man. "We got 'im. We caught the son of a bitch."

"He can't be the one, BR," Wade said. "I been watchin' that bridge from up yonder since I got chere. Ain't nobody come over that bridge 'cept you and Leroy."

"He did it somehow," Billy Ray said. "I ain't worryin' how."

Wade was shaking his head, disagreeing. "You better be. Gotta be somebody else chucked that rock at you, BR. Wasn't this man."

"No matter what else he's done, he's trespassing," Billy Ray said, pointing at the sign on the fence post.

"Uh, not really. I called old man Andrews like they tole me. He said he didn't care if the man slept in there. Ain't no trespassing and this man didn't chunk no rock at you."

Billy Ray shouted, "He did it! You hear me. You saw him come over that bridge before we got here. Never mind how. You saw him. I'm tellin' you. You got it!"

"Now, hold on, BR. Hold on. You know I'm supporting you for sheriff. I think it's time we got a new sheriff and I'm backing you, but I ain't gonna lie for you. I don't think that's right. I answer to a bigger man than you, Jesus, every Sunday. That man tells me I ain't to lie and I ain't lying!"

Billy Ray stared at the constable, his face twisted into a grimace. He decided that Wade was not likely to change his mind and said, "How about this, Wade. You can say you drove up just as me and Leroy was arresting this man, right chere."

Wade thought about that a second or two. "I reckon I can say that. Yeah. Okay. I can say that. Just don't ask me to lie."

"I ain't liking to lie neither, Billy Ray," Leroy said. "Damnit to hell. I don't think this man chunked that rock. He was asleep when I got back there. He couldn't 've got here before us. The man chunkin' that rock was still in that corn field when we drove off."

"I reckon you gonna have to get to where you'll like it, Leroy. If you want to be my chief deputy when I'm sheriff," Billy Ray said.

Leroy hung his head without replying.

Caleb decided it was time to speak up. "I didn't throw any rocks at anybody. I never have. I told … Leroy already. What are you talking about? I ate at a meal with Mrs. Howard and her mother tonight and walked back here. I was tired so I went to bed. This is the first I've heard about any rock throwing." He held his arms out as if to add a plea to what he'd just said.

"Bull shit!  Shut the fuck up!" Billy Ray shouted and shoved Caleb in the chest, forcing him back. Without holding up, he grabbed his automatic from its holster and pointed it at him. His finger squeezed down.

"Hold up, BR," Wade shouted and grabbed the deputy's arm before he could shoot. "This man ain't threatenin' you. You pushed him! Put that damn gun away. I'll report you, as God is my witness, if you shoot 'im. I'll, by God, report you."

Billy Ray turned and gave the man a cold stare, then reluctantly shoved the weapon back into its holster.

"We're takin' him in. We'll file a complaint and let the sheriff decide what to do. If he lets him go, I'll talk to the newspaper. If he doesn't, so be it. I'll take the credit. We'll let the court decide and that ain't likely to happen till after the election. I'll be the sheriff then. I'll make the damn law and they ain't gonna be no room in this town for perverts." He poked a finger into Caleb's chest. "Put the cuffs on 'im, Leroy. He's a criminal. Treat him like one."

Wade stood to one side, shaking his head in disagreement. He was also wondering about his decision to support Billy Ray for sheriff. He'd known Billy Ray practically all his life. They'd fished together, chased girls - never caught any - but now he was wondering if he had ever really known the man. Acts like he's outta control.

"I ain't likin' this, Billy Ray," he told him. "Not one bit 'n I ain't having no part of it. You hear?"

"No guts, Wade. That's you. Never had any. Ain't never gonna have any. Takes guts to be a leader. That's why I'll make a good sheriff. I ain't afraid to call a spade a spade. This man's a pervert and he tried to kill me. Me and Leroy saw him throwing that rock. We're taking 'im in."

Leroy began edging back, shaking his head, "no" as he did. The look on his face made clear what he was thinking. He hadn't seen Caleb do anything and hoped he wouldn't have to say he had. Even so, he put the cuffs on Caleb and shoved him into the back of their car for the trip to jail where he would spend at least one night.

*****

Billy Ray booked Caleb into Jail charged with assault with a deadly weapon, a rock. Leroy signed the booking sheet. Wade didn't come with them.

"Put 'im in the drunk tank," Billy Ray told the booking guy. "They can get rowdy in there. This man will fit right in."

"Don't look drunk to me, Billy Ray," the man told him, eyeing Caleb up and down.

"I said he was drunk. You questioning me?"

"Uh, no. I was just saying ... just talkin' 's all. I'll put him in the tank if that's what you're sayin'."

"That's what I'm sayin'."

So, Caleb went into the drunk tank with some others, one old guy high on vanilla extract, two young men in their twenties picked up after a liquid night out, a black guy wearing the half of a shirt that hadn't been torn off. He'd been picked up after getting drunk and knocking heads in a bar.

Caleb sat down in one corner of the cell and looked at the bunch he would be with the rest of the night. The black guy occupying one end of the single bunk bed, seemed mellow enough, probably still under the influence. The old guy, on the other end of the bed, looked like he was praying – his lips were moving. *He'll likely be praying in the morning. Thanking the Lord he's still alive.*

The two young men beside the old man were subdued, half in a drug or alcohol induced stupor ... at least for the moment. Who could say what they'd be doing after they've sobered up and start looking around for somebody to blame for being there.

*Probably be crying for their mamas,* Caleb quipped to himself.

Except for the black guy, Caleb figured he could handle himself with the rest. In the morning more deputies would be in the jail and available to break up a fight or a beating ... if all four got after him. All he had to do was survive until the morning, which he did.

The morning came. Breakfast of grits and a biscuit was served with a luke-warm liquid the inmates called coffee. A few minutes after the trays were picked up, Billy Ray showed up with the sheriff, big grin on his face. Leroy trailed a step or two behind. They looked into the cell where Caleb sat on a bunk, staring at the floor. He looked in their direction, primarily at the sheriff who grimaced and looked away.

"Son of a bitch hit me in the head with a rock," Billy Ray was telling him. "Mrs. Howard had invited him to supper. Big assed mistake. I heard about it and tried to warn her to be careful with people like him. I was nice about it. Man ain't had no cause to hit me with a rock. Ask Leroy."

The sheriff glanced at Leroy who looked at his feet and shook his head showing his agreement with Billy Ray. The sheriff frowned to indicate how he felt about Leroy's agreement.

"I think you boys were off the reservation, going out there. None of your business who Mrs. Howard cooks for."

"I agree, sheriff, but I felt it was our duty to warn her –"

"Warn her! About what? I told you that man had done nothing wrong. You were to leave him alone but you don't listen too good do you Billy Ray?" He let out a loud breath of air, shook his head in disgust and added with colloquial bias, "Sometimes, Billy Ray, you ain't got the sense God give a billy goat."

"You gonna turn him lose?"

The sheriff laughed. "And have you run down to the newspaper telling the whole damn country that I'm soft on crime? No, Billy Ray, I'm going to investigate this arrest by my chief deputy who acts to me like he needs his head looked into. Then, I'm going to turn him loose. Got it, Billy Ray?" he asked, the last while looking at Caleb. Caleb nodded.

Billy Ray turned and walked away without answering. Leroy, lagging his customary one pace behind, followed.

The sheriff went back to his office. He wasn't a happy man. Billy Ray was pushing him around and he didn't like it one bit. He picked up his phone and called Julie Howard.

"Mrs. Howard," he said, introducing himself. "Billy Ray arrested Caleb Stanley last night. Charged him with assault and battery. Said Mr. Stanley hit Billy Ray with a rock. What can you tell me?"

Julie told the sheriff how Billy Ray stood at the bottom of her steps raising cane about how she'd invited Caleb for supper. "There's not one thing wrong with Caleb Stanley, sheriff. Me and mother enjoyed his company. He worked for me when I needed help and he does good work. I didn't see who hit Billy Ray. It looked like the rock came from the corn patch, a long way off. But I didn't see who threw it. I didn't see anybody in the corn patch and I don't see how Billy Ray or Leroy could have.

Caleb had left long before Billy Ray got here, about an hour before. Billy Ray said he was coming into my house to check my doors. Make sure they were locked or could be locked. That was none of his business. When I refused, he stormed up the steps. Scared me. It was like he was going to knock me down if he had to, to get into the house."

"Was that when he was hit with a rock?"

"Yes. Mother was in the door behind me. She heard everything. You want to talk to her?"

"Not just now. I may have to later."

"Billy Ray and Leroy starting shooting into my corn patch. Knocked off a bunch of ears of corn. They got in that car they drive and shined the spot light all over. When they didn't see anything, I guess, they drove off in a hurry headed toward the park."

"Most likely to the junk yard where Stanley's been sleeping."

*****

The sheriff had Caleb transferred from the drunk-tank to a separate cell. The men in the cell with Caleb had already sobered up and were pacing up and down, scowling and ready to lash out at anybody for any reason. It was like they were daring anybody to even look at them.

After Caleb was re-situated, the sheriff said, "I figure you'll be more comfortable in there. Now and then, some of our drunks start sobering up and start looking for heads to bang. Now, suppose you tell me your side of the story."

Caleb told him about his supper invitation from Julie and her mother. How much he enjoyed it.

"I got on the road after dinner and walked to the junk yard where I'm sleeping till I can find a place to stay. Takes me at least thirty minutes, maybe forty, to walk that far. It was still daylight when I got to the junk yard. I was tired and sleepy after the big dinner so I went right to sleep."

The sheriff mumbled an agreement.

Caleb continued. "Next thing I know, somebody's shining a flashlight in my face telling me to get up and head to the road for attacking a sheriff's deputy. I tried to reason with him and the deputy, Billy Ray. He was waiting at the road. I think he's the man whose son I saved from the snake bite. They weren't having any of what I was saying."

"Yeah."

"Another guy drove up while we were talking, a constable I think, and they started arguing. The deputy called him Wade." He recited the exchange between Billy Ray and Wade.

The sheriff said, "Hmm. Well sir, you sit back and rest. Looks like you're gonna' get a free lunch. I've got some work to do. I 'pect you'll be out of here t'reckly."

*****

The sheriff had Ruby call Wade to come in.

"I'll be there in a bit," Wade told her. *What the hell am I gonna say? Billy Ray acted like a damn fool arresting that man. Well, I tole 'im I wasn't gonna lie for him and I ain't. I want to see my mama again 'n I won't get there if I start lying. Maybe I can dodge the questions. Would it be a lie if I didn't exactly give a straight answer?*

The sheriff returned to his office to wait for Wade who strolled in with a worried look on his face.

"Come on in Wade," he called when he saw the constable outside. "We got some serious talking to do."

Wade shook his head. After the usual meaningless exchanges that passed for a greeting, the sheriff asked him to sit down.

"Now Wade, I want to tell you what I've heard about what happened last night at Andrew's old junk yard. That's so you won't start forgetting stuff or making stuff up. You follow me?"

Wade shook his head.

"Who you been talkin' to?" Wade asked, looking to find a way to avoid saying anything worthwhile.

"I'll tell you what I've been told so you'll know what I know." Without attributing anything to Caleb, the sheriff recited what Caleb said as though it had been handed down from on high.

"I can't see any way we can hold a law abiding citizen for something he couldn't possibly have done. You were watching that bridge for twenty minutes before Billy Ray and Leroy pulled up. Well, if somebody hit Billy with a rock, it'd take at least thirty minutes to get from Mrs. Howard's place to that junk yard. A car could make it in probably ten or so. Do you agree?"

*Damned if he doesn't know everything*, Wade thought and said, "Uh, yes, sir. Sounds 'bout right to me."

"So, how would that man, Caleb Stanley, the man Leroy found sleeping in the junk yard, have been able to get from Mrs. Howard's to the junk yard before Billy Ray and Leroy got there. You didn't see Mr. Stanley come across the bridge, did you?"

Wade shook his head.

"Well, tell me what you did see." He extended his open palms toward the man and sat back in his chair to see what he was going to say.

At first Wade wanted to say he didn't remember anything but knew it'd sound like the lie it was and he'd be running for election and the good Lord 'ud be listening. So, he took a deep breath, let it out loudly, and told the sheriff all that had been said and all that he had seen, specifically that he had not seen Caleb Stanley come across the river bridge during the time he'd been watching.

"Unless the man can fly," Wade said. "I don't see how he could have hit Billy Ray and got back to that junk yard before they did. He'd have to walk, even run and they were driving."

The sheriff nodded and said, "I agree with you, Wade. By the way, I've heard you're supporting Billy for sheriff. You're making a mistake, but it's yours to make. I'll be lettin' folks in your district know what I think 'bout that. Am I makin' myself clear?"

Wade looked away for a second or two then said, "Yes, sir. Sheriff, I've known him all my life, but frankly just now I don't know what to make of him. He's let this Stanley man get under his skin. Actin' plum crazy. Hell, I was at the park with them the day they started drinking and let their boy wander off. I was damn glad when the boy got brought back. The doctor said wasn't a thing done to him. Not a blamed thing. I told BR to let it go, but he's fixated on it. Like I said, the Lord knows there's no way that man could 've hit BR with a rock and hightailed it to that junk yard before I got there and for sure before they got there. Had to be somebody else, sheriff, throwing that rock."

"Thank you for telling me, Wade."

"Who told you?"

"Gonna have to keep that under my hat for now. I was asked not to tell. Billy Ray's got lots of kin folks in the county. All of 'em got squirrel shooters."

Wade understood that.

After Wade had gone, the sheriff had Ruby call the local newspaper and television station to arrange a conference. He asked Billy Ray to join him in front of the jail at three that afternoon.

"Got an announcement I want to make. I want you there to get your share of the credit," the sheriff told Billy Ray, tongue in cheek. Of course, Billy Ray didn't suspect anything. He figured he'd arrested a criminal and wanted some credit.

# Chapter 12

Promptly at three, the sheriff showed up with Caleb in tow. Billy Ray had arrived early and was kibitzing back and forth with the media people, patting himself on the back for having arrested a man who'd attacked him and most likely had either molested or tried to molest his son.

The sheriff mounted the platform set up for the media event, patted the microphone to get a sound. Having gotten one, he looked out at the four media representatives who had shown up, smiled and said, "Well, I guess we'd better get on with it."

He looked toward Billy Ray, then toward Caleb. "You all know my chief deputy Billy Ray Johnson. He's a good man. Probably the most experienced deputy on my staff. And, I bet you all know that Billy's gonna run against me, next election. He figures I'm getting soft."

The news and television people laughed politely.

"This man on my right is Caleb Stanley. Mr. Stanley has had some bad problems lately." He told the listeners about Caleb's job being shipped to the Orient and alluded to his marital problems. He went on to talk about Caleb's connections with Marshalltown, his mother and father and the auto accident that killed his father and two of Caleb's siblings.

"His older brother died in Afghanistan, serving his country."

By that time, Billy Ray began to fidget nervously, staring at the sheriff with a frown. Clearly, the news conference wasn't going in the direction he'd anticipated.

"Mr. Stanley came home, Marshalltown, to live out his days. He didn't have a job so he walked, that's right walked, up and down the park road working for those good folks for whatever food they could spare. He didn't go on welfare, he went to work. But, let me go back. Before Mr. Stanley could even do that, he rescued Billy Ray's little boy from getting snake bit. That's why I wanted Billy Ray up here."

Billy Ray waved lamely at the four representatives who were already bored and glancing at their watches and cell phones.

"To make a long story short, I want to confess that now and then, even our office makes a mistake. We made one last night. My deputy, Billy Ray, arrested Mr. Stanley thinking he'd hit him with a rock at Mrs. Howard's place. Hit 'im square in the head. We talked to all the witnesses and found out that Mr. Stanley was at the junk yard where he's camping out when somebody threw that rock and hit my deputy in the head. We're all sorry as hell he got hit but when you get right down do it though, I'm afraid my young deputy didn't stop to consider that unless Mr. Stanley could fly, there was no way he had time to throw that rock and get back to the junk yard before they did. But, Mr. Stanley can't fly. Can you Mr. Stanley?"

Caleb smiled and shook his head. But, just then, he kind of had the idea he might have has some help. Glow. I might have been flying.

"But my deputy arrested him and told me to work out the details. Funny thing about that. When you get right down to it, Billy Ray wanted me to fix his mistake. Made me wonder what he would have done had he been sheriff. Who would he have asked to clean up after him, then? Be his mother."

The four laughed with more vigor that time. Billy Ray turned red and looked as if he wanted to bolt from the platform and run for his life.

"Well, I think my deputy is a good man but I reckon he needs to get a few more miles under his belt and a few more years on the job before he has the judgment to head up a law enforcement department. Come over here Billy Ray and apologize to this man, Caleb Stanley, and maybe he won't sue us for unlawful arrest. What do you think? Do you have anybody else you can ask about it?"

Billy Ray moved to the microphone, reluctantly, glanced in the sheriff's direction and mumbled, "Sorry." He immediately walked away.

The sheriff asked Caleb if he was satisfied. Caleb stood behind the microphone and said as far as he was concerned, he'd already put it behind him. "I thank the sheriff for the hot meal they served for lunch. The breakfast, whatever it was, needs work." He grinned and the four media reps did also.

The reps asked Caleb questions about his past and present life, what he was going to do. How long did he figure he'd have to sleep rough in the junk yard? Caleb gave them pretty much the same story he'd given the chief of police and the sheriff.

Someone re-asked the question about how long he expected to sleep in the junk yard.

Caleb answered with a little more detail. "Not too long. Right now it's summer. I'll have to find a place to stay before fall, before it gets cold. As for what I'm going to do, I'd like to get back into automotive, the electrical side, but I haven't had time to see what might be available around Marshalltown."

He was about to get a break in that department.

Another asked if he intended filing a law suit.

"No. I understand Mr. Johnson. He's a knee jerk kind of guy. Shoots first and asks questions later. I'd say he's needs to learn patience if he's going to stay in law enforcement."

"Do you think he'll be a good sheriff?"

"From what I've seen, you have a good sheriff. Somebody once said, if it ain't broke, don't fix it. Well, I don't think your sheriff is broke."

The sheriff took the microphone and thanked them for coming. And, he thanked Caleb for his understanding and for his generous comments about him.

Billy Ray didn't fare well in the next newspaper edition. And, he didn't do well in the television story either. Caleb was sure Billy Ray would blame his humiliation by the sheriff on him, but there wasn't anything he could do about it. For certain, the man's quest to be sheriff had taken a big hit.

Caleb detoured past Wal-Mart for a tooth brush and a pound of coffee before trudging down Park Road out of town.

*****

When Leroy came by Billy Ray's house later that afternoon, Billy was in the back yard, half a six-pack of beer into a depression.

"He's got a beer for you," Billy's wife, Earnestine, told Leroy and pointed him to the back. "Been at it since he got home. Moping around, drinking beer. I'm sick and tired of it, Leroy. See if you can talk some sense into him."

Leroy wasn't sure anybody could do that.

Leroy walked to where Billy Ray sat staring at the pond behind his double wide, holding his next beer, his shirt opened. Buttons lay around the chair where they fell after he'd yanked it open. Empties also lay all around his chair. An empty bag of chips was on the table beside him. He barely acknowledged Leroy's arrival but did throw him a can of beer.

"Sorry I missed your big do with the newspaper and television. Had to sort out the Satcher's. squabble. She was tearing her husband another one. She caught him in the barn with the widow woman up the road and took a hickory stick to him. I saved his ass. So, what happened at the news conference?"

"What happened is that the sheriff whipped my ass in public. Like I was a shirt tailed young'un. He made a fool outta me, Leroy. A complete fool. I went there thinkin' I'd done some good and he made everybody laugh at me. I didn't look at the television news, but I don't see how I can show my face in public anytime soon."

"How'd he do that?"

Billy Ray gave the gist of what had happened. "I had to apologize to a pervert who hit me with a rock. Shut the hell up, now," he said when he saw Leroy open his mouth to object. "Don't you start telling me he couldn't 'a done it. He did. And the sheriff let him go. Can you believe that? The sheriff fuckin' let him go!"

"Damn. When you called and told me about the news conference, I just knew the sheriff was gonna resign and let you be the sheriff for bringin' that man in."

Billy Ray laughed. It was a hollow laugh. "The sheriff's a stupid bastard, but he's got some street smarts. I just have to figure out something to get back at 'im. And at that bastard fruit cake from California. I'm gonna get him good, the queer son of a bitch. That's all they have out there. Land of the fruits and nuts."

Leroy shook his head but didn't agree. *Where does he git that shit?* That's what he thought as he drew down on the can of beer Billy Ray had thrown him. Instead, he burped and said, "Why don't you just pull back and let folks forget some. Something'll come up, Billy Ray. Always does, don't it. You'll get another chance to show your stuff."

"I'm thinking, Leroy. I'm thinking." He reached over and popped the top of another beer. "Old lady says she's gonna leave me if I don't straighten up. Gonna take the boy and go live with her old mama."

"Better listen to her, Billy Ray. Earnestine's a good woman."

"Yeah." He shot a look toward the house as if to see where she was. He didn't see her. "I'm gonna get in the Howard woman's pants. She likes me. I can tell."

"I ain't so sure of that. Seems to me like she don't."

"That's the way they are. Play hard to get so you'll chase 'em."

Leroy wasn't buying that, but didn't argue. He'd learned that Billy Ray wasn't to be argued with.

Leroy finished his beer and went home, leaving Billy Ray staring at his pond. His thoughts were in shambles. Billy Ray's gonna sure get into trouble If he don't get hold of himself. Ain't no good gonna come from chasing that Howard woman. Her old man's already shot one man. I don't think he'd stop at another. I guess I don't know squat 'bout women but she sure don't look like she likes old Billy Ray.

\*\*\*\*\*

Caleb was so relieved to be out of jail and out of the clutches of Billy Ray, he forgot all about the deep depression he'd nursed the night before in the drunk-tank. His thoughts were on Julie and her mother. He wanted to see how they were doing.

He stopped at their house on his walk from town. The "junk yard" dog they had chained to a tree was gone. Good, he thought. All he needed was for the chain to break.

He was headed up the porch steps when he heard Julie's agitated voice from the back part of the house. In fact, he was certain he'd heard her utter a couple of curse words.

Has to be something serious. Billy Ray?

He jumped off the porch and hurried to the back. As he did, he saw the problem. Julie was wrestling with the battery of her old truck, trying to get it back into its holder under the hood.

"Hold up, Julie," he called and ran the rest of the way. He grabbed the battery from her and positioned it in the holder behind the radiator and fastened the cables to its terminals.

Julie let out a noisy breath of air and said. "Thank you, Caleb. This has been one of those days when everything wants to slip out of my hand or slide sideways."

"Sorry. I've had them too."

"The guy at the shop seems to think there's a short in the system someplace. I've been charging it every week or so." She gestured at the battery charger on the back porch.

"Might as well get in and give it a try. See if the charge worked."

She slid in and turned the key. The old engine turned over the first time and fired and ran smoothly.

"The guy's probably right, must be a short someplace. Turn it off. I'll see what I can find."

He explained that in older cars, wires sometimes pulled away from their harness and wore against the engine block until the insulation was gone and the wires were exposed. And when the bare wire contacted the metal engine block, enough of the battery was drained to cause it to go dead after a while.

Fortunately, there was enough sunlight left for Caleb to see everything under the hood. He picked up every electrical wire he could touch and followed it to a terminal point. Finally he pulled a little green one out and turned it over for a look. "Here it is, I bet. Take a look." A copper wire showed through the insulation.

"Probably contacting the engine block and draining the battery over time."

"I never would have guessed," she said. "Charlie could fix cars a little. In these parts, most men grow up with their heads under a car hood. More than I did or wanted to."

"Charlie? Your husband?"

She agreed. "He's … well, I don't know where he is right now. Up north, I think. He got into some trouble and had to leave. I'm not sure he's ever coming back. I get a letter from him now and then."

"I think I understand. The sheriff told me something about it, but it's none of my business." Caleb said, then asked, "Do you have any black insulation tape? If I put a little tape around this wire, you should get a lot more miles out your charge this time. "

She found a roll of black tape in Charlie's tool chest. Caleb cut a couple of pieces to wrap around the wire then shoved the wire back into its slot.

"Thank you," she said. "I'd give you a hug, but wrestling with the battery left me covered in grime."

"No problem. I'm glad I could help. It has been awhile since I did anything productive. As simple as that was, it was a step up from shoveling cow manure." He smiled.

"I could tell Odom you know about a car's electrical system. Odom has a shop in town that does electrical work on cars. Maybe he could use you in his shop when he runs into a hard problem."

Caleb was sure his face lit up at the thought of doing something he understood. "That'd be great. If he … well, I just remembered something. I don't have a cell phone. My wife took hers and mine. Actually, I gave her mine. I didn't figure I'd need it."
*Hell, I didn't need a phone to go out of business.*

She stared at him blank faced for a moment or two then said, "Uh, Charlie didn't take his cell phone here when he left. I could let you use it, if … well, I'd have to charge you for anything extra on my bill. Would that be okay? I'm kind of on a tight budget. Mother gets a little social security and I sell my crafts, but we're not swimming in money."

"That'll be okay. I'd only use it if somebody wanted me for work … that Odom guy. Don't give it a second thought. I'll pay you for anything I add to your bill." *How might be a problem but I'll promise first and figure out how when the time comes.* "Will you tell Odom to call me if he has a hard electrical problem? Anybody can take care of the easy stuff."

She said she would.

He told her it was time to get back to his camp, but she invited him in for a piece of pie and cup of coffee. He didn't refuse.

"Meant to tell you," she said. "You can borrow Charlie's old bike. It's leaning against wall of the garage. It'll save you time gettin' back and forth."

"Thanks. That's great." A bike would save time and make getting around in the heat a lot easier.

Bonnie Fae had already cut the ice box pie and had the decaf perking when they walked in the back door. "I was just fixin' to call y'all in," she said.

Caleb sat down and enjoyed both. He wished they'd offered seconds, but they didn't and he was afraid to ask. Maybe what they'd eaten was the last of it. While they were eating, Caleb asked Julie to recount the night Billy Ray threatened to tear into the house on the pretext of checking the locks on their doors.

"If that rock hadn't hit him square in the forehead, I guess he would have," she said. "Lord knows what he was really after. I hate to think."

Bonnie Fae said, "I kind of figure I know what he had in mind. That kind thinks from, pardon my French, their smaller head."

Caleb laughed.

"Was it you who chunked that rock?" Bonnie Fae asked.

Caleb nodded. "I didn't think it'd hit him but I sure was glad it did."

"I don't see how you did it," Julie said.

"I just let it fly." He also figured he had Glow to thank for his accuracy. He laughed to himself.

He told them about his meeting with the sheriff and the sheriff's press conference with him and Billy Ray. "He put Billy Ray in his place. I never saw anybody squirm as much as deputy Billy did. I figure his plans to run for sheriff went backward."

"He's way too immature to be sheriff," Julie said.

"The sheriff said as much. The reporters laughed. Billy had to apologize. He didn't hang around afterwards. However, I've been around enough like Billy to know he's not going to forget what the sheriff did to him."

"That sheriff can take care of himself," Bonnie Fae said and with a puzzled look on her face asked, "By the way, we've been wondering how you got to the junk yard before they did? They were shooting at you in the corn patch and then they drove off. I don't see how you could possibly beat them."

He remembered his fainting spell. That had to be Glow, flying me back to the junk yard ahead of Billy and Leroy. Well, I'm in Glow's debt. I wonder if he exceeded his mandate to observe the happenings and report, not to participate. Well, if he did, I'm glad. Otherwise, I'd still be in jail. Maybe mandate restrictions didn't apply to special projects, like me.

He looked at her, searching his thoughts for a believable answer. He sure wasn't going to tell them about Glow. Finally, he said, "They got there ahead of me, but they didn't know where my camp was and while Leroy was searching around, I slipped past Billy Ray and got to my camp before they did."

"You were lucky," Julie said. "Me and mother were praying for you."

"Must have worked," he said and stood to leave. "At least this time, Billy Ray and Leroy won't be waiting."

"We'd let you sleep in one of our rooms," Julie said, following him to the front door. "But, lots of folks around here think like Billy Ray. Lord knows, I don't need tongues wagging and cutting down on my sales. Things are tight enough as they are," Julie said.

"I wouldn't think of it," Caleb said. "I understand the ways of a close community like Marshalltown. It's part of the culture. I respect that."

He promised to stop by from time to time to see if there was anything he could do to help. Julie thanked him and assured him there was always something he could do, especially when she was beginning a craft project.

Bonnie Fae brought him a bag of food. He thanked her.

"I'll tell Odom about you. He may call," Julie promised, smiled and gave him a hug goodbye.

He didn't tell her, but thought, I'm not going to hold my breath. However, he wasn't thinking about his hemlock stew. He felt relieved but knew not to get too excited. He was still a long way from having anything that approached a normal life. Still, just knowing Julie makes me happy. I like her.

The warmth from her body as she hugged him and her warm smile when she drew close sent a surge through his body. He hadn't felt anything like it since he could remember. His eyes met hers and locked on. It was an experience he'd never had. It was mesmerizing, like he was suddenly bonded to her, like they were one. He released her, but reluctantly. He had wanted to hold on and would have sworn she felt the same way.

He left her in the door and walked away. He glanced back once and tried to push the feeling he'd had out seconds before of his mind. People around here are naturally friendly, he told himself. It's part of the culture. Don't get carried away. They don't even think twice about it.

But he did, think twice about it.

# Chapter 13

Caleb picked up Charlie's rickety old bike and began pedaling down the road to his cave. As he did, his thoughts played an old tune he hadn't heard in years. Blue Skies, a Bing Crosby song. Smiling at me. Nothing but blue skies.

He laughed at himself being so juvenile and forced the tune out of his thoughts. And, with each easy turn of the wheels, he thanked them both. The bike that made the journey so much easier and quicker, that and the blue skies. He laughed again.

Assuming Glow hadn't been picked up, he wanted to thank him for his help. The assumption that Glow had helped appealed to him more than the explanation he feared was closer to the truth, his Alzheimer's. However, clinging to the possibility that Glow was somehow real, as absolutely bizarre as that was, enabled him to think he wasn't suffering from Alzheimer's after all.

But, Glow doesn't make any sense at all. Hell, maybe it was like I told Julie. I was so stressed out, I quit thinking and did exactly like I said, got to the junk yard before Leroy could find my camp site. Could have been that under stress, I blacked out, but kept running, maybe even faster, till I got to the junk yard. Then, I got lucky. Makes more sense than talking to an orange glow like it was real or accepting Alzheimer's as my fate. I'll go with that. That's the only damn thing that makes sense. Now, if the glow is gone when I get back, maybe I can start trying to put my life into perspective. Do I finish off my hemlock stew or wait awhile.

His next thought was of Julie, the feeling he had when he looked into her eyes. Following that was a thought about Charlie and that killed his thought about Julie. But, he did quit thinking about his hemlock stew.

Caleb rolled off the road, hid the bike in the bushes and hurried into his cave. By then, the afternoon twilight had been replaced by darkness.

He flipped on the light switch he'd installed to fill the cave with light. He still needed to put the door he'd fashioned over the mouth of the cave but would do that later. He glanced around the inside of the cave, into the darkest crevices. There was no Glow to talk to. He felt disappointed but was relieved that no could hear his thoughts. If anyone could hear his conversations with his imaginary companion, he'd likely be hauled off to the looney bin without question.

He sat on his makeshift bed and opened a Hillerman Indian adventure book, and read about a murder investigation by Leaphorn and Chee until his eyes began to close. He'd read it before but could only remember flashes so it never got boring.

He fell asleep with Julie in his thoughts, her smiling face, her beautiful blue eyes. He knew she was a forbidden fantasy but wished she wasn't. He pushed his thoughts aside but tears ran down the sides of his face. He wiped them away with the back of his hand but Julie stayed in his thoughts.

The next morning, he fried bacon and eggs and made coffee in the pot he'd found. Julie was in his thoughts as though she was sitting beside him, real. He warmed one of the stale biscuits in the frying pan he'd used for the eggs. He made the coffee, campground style – boiled the water and threw in a handful of grounds until it bubbled up in the pot. And, he ate it all and didn't think twice about how it tasted. As far as he was concerned, it was okay.

He finished and washed up his frying pan and other utensils and thought about his day. His day at the jail had thrown his thoughts into turmoil and his dinner with Julie and Bonnie Fay kept them there. The night's sleep helped but now he had to address the day. Hunger would return by the evening and certainly in the morning. He needed food and that meant more work.

As he readied himself for the new day, he heard Glow say, "good morning."

*I thought it was gone.*

Half of him was glad – he'd have somebody to talk to even if the somebody, he suspected, might be him. The other half was not so glad. That meant he was likely still suffering from delusions.

"Good morning. I figured you had been picked up to go home or that I was going sane and you were no longer in my head."

"I am here and you are sane, Caleb. I had to go to the middle-east to look at a developing situation. I could have looked at it from here, but I wanted a closer look. The leader of a radical religious sect had directed the killing of everyone who didn't aspire to his sect's beliefs. It was a blood bath. It was yet another demonstration of the human path to self-destruction. The instinct to dominate led to the conclusion that failure to submit to domination should be punished by death."

"That's been going on forever," Caleb replied. "Most religion sects I've read about do the same thing. Kill anybody who disagrees. If not kill, certainly ostracize."

"Even religions not considered sects can get pretty brutal. Christian religions sponsored crusades with killings as part of their mandate to spread the Word."

"They don't do that anymore," Caleb said.

"These days, your laws have adopted the tenants of your Bible. So, you don't have to follow the good Book so much as just obey the law. In fact, some philosophers think the process of replacing the teachings of the good Book with codified laws, is having the effect of minimizing the Christian religion, squeezing it out."

Caleb shook his head. "I don't know what you're talking about."

"Surely, you do. It was a sin to look upon a woman's nakedness, unless it was your wife. A violation of your God's law. I think you know what I'm talking about now," Glow told him.

"Yeah. No nudity."

"Well, your man-made laws say it's okay to look at all the nakedness you want. You have nude bars on every corner of some down-towns. Unrestricted sex is for sale on the internet. If you don't want to buy it, you can certainly see it. And, the list of plastic surgeons has exploded. Now, women have outstanding boobs for men to look at and go straight to hell," Glow said.

Caleb heard what he assumed was a Glow chuckle at the boob quip.

"So, the carnal flood gates have been opened, Caleb. Your biblical sins have been codified away. Man's law has squeezed out God's law. That's the process I'm talking about, your drift into undisciplined permissiveness. Throw in your drug culture and the drift is picking up speed. Now, you can buy drugs legally."

"Yeah. Well, maybe so. Not my problem and nothing I can do about it. I resigned from all that years ago. I obey the law. If that's the same as obeying the teachings of the Bible, I guess I'll go to heaven."

"Maybe that's why I picked you as a project. To see how you fared or would fare in a world still filled with religious strife and headed for -" What Glow was going to say, was interrupted by Caleb.

"I've heard all that. It doesn't mean shit to me so why waste your time telling me? I want to tell you about what does mean something to me. Thanks to you," Caleb said.

"I'm waiting. Tell away," Glow said.

Caleb then talked about Julie's offer to help him get work trouble shooting automotive electrical systems for her mechanic. He didn't mention his mesmerizing experience.

"People act like they care. Like they want to help. I hardly know what to make of it, but I have to say it touches me. Julie didn't have to offer –"

That time Glow interrupted him, saying, "I know about that and about your mesmerizing experience so save your breath telling me or trying to talk around it. You'll get a call today, in fact. I won't tell you what the problem is, but you'll find it in less than thirty minutes and pick up a few dollars, some of which you'll spend at Wal-Mart."

*At least I didn't get embarrassed having to explain how I acted like a teenager in love when I looked into Julie's eye,* Caleb thought.

"You have to follow your free will dealing with Julie. She'll follow hers. Who knows what's going to happen?" With that unanswered question, Glow vanished in an orange streak.

"What the hell does that mean? It's gone. Who knows what the hell he's talking about?"

Caleb had been on the verge of asking how he knew but just shook his head instead. It said it knew everything. I'm beginning to believe it. Was it real somehow or was he again playing fantasy games with himself? Where did it come from, if it is real? It must be, but how?

He cleaned up his camp site, got his bike from behind the blueberry bushes and headed down the road. Until and unless he did get a call, he still had to work for his food.

*****

The shotgun lady was standing at the edge of her garden looking over it so he assumed she was having a lucid interval and stopped to see if he could help. He could. She wanted some "roastin' ears" of corn and pointed him to the stalks she'd already picked out. Caleb went into the corn patch and pulled half a dozen of the newest ears of corn, the ones she'd pointed to. He took them to her kitchen and put them beside her sink.

"You want me to shuck 'em and clean 'em?" he asked.

"If you wouldn't mind?"

He recalled from his youth that shucking and cleaning the "silks" from the ears were the most onerous parts of getting corn ready for the pot. Kids usually got the job and most always hated it. Afterwards, he picked up her eggs, put out hay for her cows and made sure their water troughs were full.

When it was time to say goodbye, she offered him a couple of ears of the corn he'd picked. He turned her down. Too much trouble for him to cook it. So she added a couple of eggs for his trouble plus a quarter of a loaf of cornbread. And, she invited him to sit down for a cup of coffee and another biscuit with fig jam. They talked about nothing in particular. Mostly, he let her do the talking.

After a while, she asked, "Would you take some turnip greens?" she asked. "Cooked 'em yesterday. I could put some pepper sauce on 'em. All you'd have to do is warm 'em up some."

He told her he'd be delighted to have them. She put them in a plastic container for him and added a pint of milk. All of a sudden, he had supper.

She told him to come back. She enjoyed his company. He was relieved she hadn't gone for her shotgun when he walked up.

He had too much food to carry up the road to the Walters so he pedaled back to his cave to store it. All but the milk went into a cool corner of the cave. The milk went into the stream, securely contained within the eddy he'd made.

Glow was not around. He had decided to accept whatever it was without trying to explain it. It was either dementia creeping in or a consequence of the pressure he had been under for years without fully realizing it, or something from another world. He was reluctant to even think it could be the latter, it was so bizarre. But, a lot of the things Glow had said weren't things he normally thought about so he couldn't just dismiss it as a drift into Alzheimer's, even though it was looking more and more like that was where he was headed.

He had finished putting away his "groceries" when the phone Julie had given him, rang. Be damned, just like Glow said. "What the hell," he said.

He punched the button and said, "Hello."

It was Odom and he had an electrical job on a truck he couldn't handle. "It ain't the batt'ry," the man said. "Or the generator or anything else I usually check." He gave Caleb directions to his shop.

An hour later, Caleb was listening to what Odom had already tried to do to fix the problem. Caleb asked for a schematic diagram of the car's electrical system. With a volt meter, he checked nodes for signals and signal strengths. After thirty minutes of probing and measuring he'd found the problem. A lead had come loose from its connection to another lead inside a plastic router box. Caleb soldered the two leads back together and asked Odom to try it. The old truck's engine turned over right away, coughed out blue smoke from non-combusted gas and ran smoothly.

Odom thanked him and gave him four fives for his trouble.

On his way home, Caleb stopped by Julie's. She was still gone but Bonnie Fae answered the door. She offered coffee, but Caleb turned her down. It was late in the day and he wanted to see about rigging a shower in one corner of his cave. Even though cold, a shower seemed preferable to the hand bathing he'd been doing before he went out. He'd have to go to the junk yard and look into one of the campers he'd been in to get what he needed. He'd also need a pump to lift the water from the stream to the shower head, a little work, but nothing he couldn't handle.

Before leaving, he gave Bonnie Fae the five dollar bill he owed Julie and explained what had happened. She promised to tell Julie.

As he began his turn onto the gravel road, a car roared up the road behind him. He looked over his shoulder. It was a sheriff's car. He didn't have to think too hard to guess who was driving, Billy Ray, and, he was flying. He pointed the car at Caleb but turned away as he closed, sending a plume of clay dust and gravel all over. As he passed, he held down his horn and then, stuck his arm in the air to give Caleb the third finger.

Leroy sat in the passenger seat, shaking his head and saying something to Billy Ray. Whatever it was, it was ignored. Billy Ray shouted, "Ass hole!" out the window and something about taking a bus and words lost in the noise. Caleb assumed it was an order to get out of town.

Bonnie Fae witnessed the commotion from the porch and saw the police car flash by. She shook her head in disbelief.

Caleb held up and shouted back, "No harm done."

She waved.

*****

In the car, Billy Ray practically screamed at Leroy. "Did you see that son of a bitch? He was on Julie's old man's bicycle! She gave him the bicycle! That bastard … hit me with a rock and now he's sleeping with her! Damn him!"

Leroy tried to calm him down but nothing worked. Billy Ray continued cursing and accusing. "I'm gonna kill that pervert! You wait and see, Leroy. One step out of line and he's a dead man."

"Yeah, and if you don't come to yore senses, BR, I'll be visiting you at the crazy house or behind bars."

That back and forth exchange continued until they reached town.

*****

Caleb stopped by his cave for the tools he'd need to take a shower head and rubber tubing from a wrecked camper. After he had that, he removed a pump and enough wiring to connect it to his generator. He assembled it over a flat rock in the back of the cave using a roll of tape from an old tool chest. He worried that the tape didn't have enough glue to secure the connections. And, for sure the connections did leak, but only a bit.

When he had finished, he took a cold water shower and dried himself with worn towels taken from the same camper. They were in fairly good condition as far as being relatively clean. He dressed in his other set of clothes.

If I get more money, I'll buy something from Wal-Mart, he thought.

Also found in the camper were three plastic plates and a number of eating utensils. He'd been making do with his camper knife and a forked stick.

It was time for supper. He warmed the shotgun lady's turnips and threw a handful of coffee in the pot. With that done, he sat down on an oak log he'd dragged from the woods, facing his fire pit and ate supper. The coffee washed everything down.

It was good dark by the time he'd finished and washed his newly found dishes. He turned on the cave lights and put everything away.

The amount of light the two fixtures gave out was plenty adequate for the cave. In fact, he went outside to make sure none of it was escaping for people like Billy Ray to see should they be walking around the park with their squirrel shooters looking for a target. He couldn't see a spot of light.

With his new tooth brush, he brushed his teeth over the stream.

Damn, that felt good. I hate to think how many teeth I'd have left if I hadn't bought a tooth brush. Hell, I didn't think I'd need one. I had my hemlock stew.

He glanced around to check. The bag was still where he'd left it, against the cave wall. Without a doubt, he wasn't going to throw it away. As far as he was concerned, his life was still day to day. When he got right down to what he faced, he had to admit he still had no real reason to live. I really still have no life. Working for food hardly qualifies.

Julie's face popped into his thoughts, the way she smile and the cheerful lift in her words but he dismissed her immediately. Even if she weren't married, why in the hell would she ever look twice at me. I'm a nobody. But, the feeling he had when he held her close pushed back into his thoughts and stayed there for a while. Damn.

What did Glow say about non-productive humans? Humans should have the discipline and will to do something about them. Well, when the time comes, I'll do just that.

He heard a voice, one he recognized.

"You are not non-productive, Caleb. You're helping the folks along the road, especially Julie and her mother. They've certainly responded to your kindness. If you want to call it that? They know somebody cares. In today's world, that's hard to find. Nobody has the time to care anymore. And your kindness and caring saved them from who knows what when you plunked Billy Ray on the head with that rock."

"Yeah. With your help."

Glow didn't respond to that, saying instead, "Just say you got lucky again. And, you helped Odom get that old farmer's truck going. With a start like that, you'll probably get more calls, at least for a short time."

"What do you mean by … short time?"

But, the Glow disappeared without answering.

What the hell. Must have had an emergency to investigate someplace in the world. Damn, I sound like it's real. Maybe it is. Maybe it is.

Caleb picked up the book he'd started, sat on his pallet and began to read. Night birds in the trees outside sang and carried on as they had been doing for decades, he decided. He enjoyed their company.

Soon, he felt his eye lids grow heavy. He turned off his lights and fell asleep.

Dogs barking in the night woke him briefly, but the barking went in the other direction, away from his cave. And, he'd heard no human voices with it. That relieved him enough to fall back asleep immediately.

# Chapter 14

Birds got Caleb up early the next morning. He went outside to start his breakfast fire. Half a dozen small deer were passing as he poked his head around the rocky outcropping that concealed his cave. They paused as if to check his intent. He made no threatening moves so they continued their easy pace down the slope to the river where they'd drink their morning fill before disappearing into the woods to gaze.

When his fire got going, he put two pieces of bacon in his pan to fry. When it was crisp, he broke two eggs in the pan to fry in the bacon drippings. At the same time, he warmed the last of his biscuits and slipped in a slice of butter to melt. His coffee was boiling and ready to drink by the time his eggs were done.

He enjoyed breakfast with birds singing, a couple of early butterflies searching late blooms for nectar and the relaxing sounds of the river flowing along at the bottom of the slope his camp site looked over. No Glow. Strangely, he missed having somebody to talk to. Maybe if I start talking to myself, Glow will come back, he thought with a suppressed laugh. And, just maybe, the stress is lightening up to the extent that I'm getting back to normal and don't need Glow to talk to.

He shrugged it off and shifted his attention to "working for food." As he stood to bike down the trail to the road, the cell phone Julie had given him rang. It was Odom and he needed help. His electrical man was out with a bad back and he had three cars in the shop, well two cars and a truck. A carpenter needed the truck for work.

Caleb told him he'd be there within thirty minutes. Odom said he had a shelf full of meters and a book of schematic diagrams that would help.

\*\*\*\*\*

The truck's battery wouldn't stay charged, Odom had said. Almost without checking, Caleb knew it was most likely the alternator. It was and he had the truck up and running within the hour, even with the battery recharge. The two cars were a little more of a problem. One had a crack in the alternator belt requiring a new belt. That one took about thirty minutes to track down. The last one was a little tricky. It was a bad solenoid. The car had to be towed into Odom's shop.

Caleb was finished with all three a few minutes after noon. The carpenter showed up almost as soon as he was called for the truck. So, Odom paid him for the truck work, sixty dollars. Payment for the cars would have to wait until they were picked up that afternoon.

"Uh," Odom said as Caleb mounted his bike to leave. "You got time to go by another shop? Old buddy of mine has a problem he can't solve. He's called the manufacturer but they haven't called back."

Caleb said he'd look at it. Odom let him use an old junker to drive to the shop. The car with the problem also had to be towed in. It wouldn't start.

"May be in the crankshaft sensor circuit," Caleb told Odom's friend and began testing the relay unit that completed the magnetic circuit after the car's ignition key was turned on. He jumped the four-wire relay he figured might be bad to complete the circuit. The jumper by-pass worked so he replaced the relay and had the car running within the hour. That job was the one the auto shops talked about afterwards. Not so much that he found it but the speed and ease with which he did.

The owner gave him a pat on the back. Years of experience, Caleb thought. Odd how things pay off now and then.

While he was there, he helped the man's electrical guy diagnose a busted ignition switch and find one of those hidden fuses manufacturers seem to hide when they want to protect a valuable car part.

Before he left Odom's shop, he did a quick tune of the junker Odom had let him use. He cleaned and tightened the spark plugs as well as the battery cables and the corroded terminals. It ran a lot smoother after that. He hoped Odom would offer him the use of the car, but he didn't. He did promise to call if he had more work.

Caleb took the sixty dollars and bought a pair of work clothes and new tennis shoes from Wal-Mart before biking to his cave hideout. He rolled in around six that afternoon. No sooner than he'd hidden his bike, his phone rang. It was Odom.

He didn't have any more work just then, but he'd gotten a couple of calls from other shops who could use his help.  The regular guy in one repair shot was fishing in the gulf for a week and somebody had just brought in a car with a couple of problems. Also, another shop in town had a car with maybe a bad generator or alternator or maybe both. Caleb wrote down the numbers to call the next morning.

"Hell, just show up in the morning. They'll be happy to see you," Odom said. "Call 'em now if you want to. I reckon they're still working. They don't quit if somebody's waitin' on a car."

Caleb called both and promised to be there the next morning. Both shop owners expressed grateful sighs of relief. That'd mean getting up a little earlier. He'd use the phone alarm to get him up, if the birds didn't do it first.

*****

Caleb spent the next few weeks subbing for electrical technicians who were out for one reason or another, usually some kind of injury or vacations but just as often off to "tend to" members of the family who were sick.

Now and then, a shop owner wanted him to diagnosis a problem his man couldn't find. Some of those involved finding lose hidden ground connections that drained batteries, broken harness wires that more often than not required running replacement wires. And, some were more difficult but Caleb had no problem diagnosing them. They were busy times for Caleb and he enjoyed them.

He kept his contacts with the elderly along the road, stopping by in the early morning to see if there was anything he could do. He also expanded the number he helped by continuing down the road in the direction of the junkyard.

The rest of the time, Odom and some of the other shops had begun to call about the more difficult electrical problems they'd run into with the old cars they were servicing. Caleb jumped at the opportunity to tackle those, and enjoyed the challenge. He solved a problem that manifested itself with a sulfur smell. That one was the most challenging. He finally tracked it down as the alternator overcharging the battery and had to replace the alternator. That happened with many of the defective parts he found in the old cars. They were too old to be repaired but in a town like Marshalltown, where old cars and trucks were the rule, old parts were stocked by the parts shops.

He also fixed a starter motor, a water pump, a voltage regulator, and replaced old wiring, some of which he had to practically get under the hood to track down. He was spending almost four hours a day solving electrical problems. His hands were dirtier than they were when he was doing design work, but he was back doing, at least in the neighborhood of, what he'd been trained to do and what he had enjoyed for almost thirty years. It felt good.

Productive, he thought with a suppressed laughed, giving Glow credit for the thought.

He was getting paid in cash and he was still getting food from the folks along park road. Also, Julie and Bonnie Fae regularly invited him to supper at least twice a week and he regularly enjoyed hugging Julia goodbye at the front door and always looked into her blue eyes as he did. And, she was always smiling as he left.

The food was always good, mostly fresh vegetables with meat of some sort, usually chicken. They had plenty and Bonnie Fae didn't mind grabbing one up from the chicken yard and wringing its neck for an evening meal. Caleb didn't mind plucking feathers, even cleaning 'em though that took some fortitude, but he could never wring their necks.

Bonnie Fae laughed at his reluctance and didn't mind at all. "The good Lord sent them chickens to us and He expects us to do what we have to do to eat them."

Caleb didn't argue, but he likewise didn't wring any necks.

Over their dinners together, Julie and Bonnie Fae talked about the problems they'd had with their husbands. Bonnie Fae's husband left her shortly after Julie was born, never to be seen or heard from again. Julie's husband, Charlie, wrote once in a while. He'd told her he was seeing someone else and told her she should do the same. It wasn't likely he'd ever return to Marshalltown.

In a relaxed moment, Caleb told them about his wife's deception. Both women gasped as he did.

"At first, it laid me low," he said, "but I'm over it now." He wasn't too sure of that, but figured it was the thing to say.

*****

During one of their later suppers together, Julie told Caleb, "I got a letter from Charlie a couple of days ago. It had divorce papers he wanted me to sign and mail back. The letter had a check for two thousand dollars. He said it was all he could afford. He was sorry for all the trouble he'd caused. He prayed I'd get over him and have a good life."

Caleb said, "I'd say that's probably the last time you'll hear from him." He wondered what, if anything, that might mean to him but dared not tease himself about it. He was afraid the rejection she'd give him might trigger a search for his bag of hemlock and a can full of water.

"That's what Mother said. I signed the papers and mailed them back. I put the check in the bank. It went through."

"Well, what are you going to do now?"

She shook her head. "About the … well, … I'll keep doing what I have been doing, making crafts for the Craft Store at the Interstate stop."

"Some women never get over being left. I think you handled yours very well."

"I suppose." She thanked him. "One odd thing. It looked to me like the letter had been opened."

Bonnie Fae said, "Most likely he forgot to put the check in first time he sealed it."

Julie shook her head.

Julie's goodbye hug that night felt even warmer to Caleb. And, he caught the scent of something pleasant, her perfume? It had been a long time since he'd enjoyed the smell of a woman's perfume. He didn't dare let himself think there could ever be anything between them but for a few moments while she was in his arms and he was enjoying the hint of her perfume, he wished there could be.

It bothered him that Billy Ray thought there may be something already. He had drawn that conclusion after Billy Ray had roared past him on the road near her house a couple of times, cursing and honking his horn, and giving him the third finger. And, he always swerved like he was going to knock him off the road, only to right the car at the last second. The times Caleb was able to look, he saw Leroy saying something and if his face was any indicator, he wasn't approving.

*****

Caleb counted the money he'd earned working in the shops and was surprised at how much he had. Almost a thousand dollars. Hell, that's enough to start looking for a room in somebody's garage apartment in town.

"I'm used to my cave, even like it," he told himself, "But it's going to get cold one of these days and I'll need someplace warmer to sleep."

So, the next day, he picked up the town's throw away paper that contained some news, but mostly advertisement. What he was looking for were rentals. From what he remembered, widows in small towns most always had a room or garage apartment to rent. It helped with their budgets.

He found half a dozen he decided he could afford and drove past them. Two were in a rough part of town. The bicycle wouldn't last one night, he thought. Two others looked okay. Both were garage walk-ups. He called for the rental rate. Both were within his budget. He'd call the next day.

But, he still had time to stop by houses along the road to see if they needed any work done. The food they gave him kept his grocery budget very low. Mostly all he had to buy extra was a pound of coffee.

*****

One afternoon, after doing a couple of jobs for Odom, he pedaled his borrowed bike down the road past the junk yard. He'd passed a number of old houses down that way on his bus ride in and wanted to see if the folks living in them needed help. He'd come to get a sense of worth when he helped the older folks along the road.

The first house he came to was an old craftsman with a front porch, swing, rockers and all. It sat back from the road but was visible. A middle aged lady answered his knock, hair frazzled, no makeup so she wasn't expecting anybody and wasn't going anyplace. He gave her his pitch about "working for food."

She looked at him suspiciously for a few seconds, but apparently decided he was an honest man.

"Well, my husband does most of the chores 'round here but he's been busy. He drives a truck. So, if you want to, you can cut that tree over yonder." She pointed to a tree that had fallen or blown down. It was obviously dead. The top had fallen off long before, Caleb figured. Only the lower trunk was left. The saw and axe were in her husband's workshop at the rear of the house.

He grabbed both with a pair of gloves and began cutting. First, he cut the trunk into rounds the size of her fireplace. She'd told him how long. That done, he put the rounds into a wagon and took them to a covered area beside the workshop. But, first, he split the rounds so they'd burn easier.

She gave him some left over fried chicken, a piece of cornbread and a slice of peach pie. They had a number of fruit trees in an orchard at the rear of the house.

He thanked her and rolled on to the next house, less than a quarter of a mile on down. A man answered that door. He was on the short side, and about as wide as he was tall and smelled of beer.

Not that old, Caleb thought. Still got all his hair too. Won't be any work for me here. Even so, he introduced himself and was about to give his pitch about working for food but the man interrupted him.

"I know you. Billy Ray's my boy. You the one molested my grandbaby! I don't want you 'round here, you hear!"

Caleb heard alright. "I didn't molest anybody. I have two children of my own. I don't molest children." Caleb said. He turned to leave without waiting for an answer.

"My boy says you do!" the man shouted. "You come back here, I'll be waitin'."

"You do that," Caleb turned and shouted back.

That's it for this day, Caleb thought. Billy Ray's daddy has the same level of intelligence as his son. Ignorance must be bliss. Sure beats the hell out of thinking.

He was recalling how the deputy recently sprayed him with road dust in front of Julie's house, topping it off with a third finger and          calling          him          as          ass-hole.

Sheriff material, without a doubt, Caleb thought cynically.

\*\*\*\*\*

Caleb built a fire and warmed up what he had in his larder for supper. He washed it down with the last of his milk. He hadn't been getting as much food for work as before because of the electrical jobs he'd been doing.

"Guess I'll have to start buying food," he said.

"Success breeds its own list of problems, Caleb," Glow chimed in.

"You're back."

"I am. You've met Billy Ray's main ancestor. I believe you found out the apple didn't fall far from the tree."

"I believe I did. I don't think I'll work for food in that direction anymore."

"Turning your back on him might not be a good idea either."

"What do you mean?"

"You're always asking me that."

"And you're always telling me about free will."

"So true." Glow faded to nothing.

Caleb finished his supper and went to bed.

# Chapter 15

About dark that same day, Billy Ray dropped by his folks' house and heard about Caleb's visit. When he got back into his car, he was red faced and cursing that "son of a bitch. Damn pervert's been by the house."

"So what! Did he do anything? Hell no!" Leroy asked and it wasn't a friendly question. "You run around with a fuckin' chip on your shoulder, Billy Ray. One of these days, somebody's gonna knock it off."

Billy Ray stopped the car and stared at Leroy. "You want to do it! If you do, now's as good a time as any."

"I wasn't saying I was gonna do it Billy Ray. But, hey, don't fuckin' push it okay. I'm getting sick and tired of you carrying on about that man. He ain't done a damn thing 'cept save your boy from getting snake bit. And, you won't let it go. You just got a cob up your ass 'cause he talks to the Howard woman 'n she won't let you in her front door!"

"Sleeps with her, you mean."

"I ain't saying that 'cause I don't know. All we seen is him with a bicycle that probably belonged to Charlie Howard. And, he helps out. That's fuckin' all, Billy Ray!"

Billy Ray didn't answer that, just twirled the car around and headed back to the junk yard. By then, it was dark. He parked, grabbed a flash light from the glove compartment and ran down the trail to Caleb's junk yard camp site. When he got here, Caleb was nowhere in sight.

"Fuckin' ass hole ain't here!" he said, twirling first one way then another to see if he might be hiding someplace, darting frantically in and out between the abandoned wrecks searching. Leroy stood at the edge of the opening and watched, his face a frown.

Finally, Leroy decided to needle him and said, "I reckon it's the God's truth, Billy Ray, whut you been going on about, the man must be staying at the Howard's woman house. You got the hots for a married woman who won't let you in her front door and she's sleeping with a pervert! Be damned, Billy Ray, this jes ain't yore day! And -"

"Ain't gonna be married forever ..." Billy Ray interrupted with a look in the direction of Julie's house, thinking ... wondering if Leroy was right. Without another word, he began running and didn't stop until he was in the car. Leroy hurried to catch up or risk being left behind.

"I hope you ain't 'bout to cause trouble, Billy Ray, 'cause I ain't gonna stand for it. I'm tellin' you, I'm sick and tired of the crazy way you carrin' on. I was just ... joking with you 'bout the man sleeping with her."

"Shut the fuck up!" Billy Ray shouted.

He came to a squealing halt in front of Julie's house and jumped out. He bounded up the steps and hammered on the door. Leroy caught up with him as Julie opened the door.

"He's in 'nare, ain't he?" Billy Ray shouted and leaned right to see into the house. He shouted something about the bicycle she'd given Caleb. How he was always hanging around.

"Who? There's no one here but me and mother. What are you going on about? The bicycle I loaned Mr. Stanley, Caleb. You're acting ... crazy, Billy Ray. He just helps out around here."

"Let's get out of here, Billy Ray," Leroy said and pulled at his arm, half to restrain him from pushing past Julie as he seemed ready to do and half to get him back into the car.

"Yeah, you're sleeping with a pervert and I'm crazy! Too good to ... have anything to do with me, I'm crazy! But okay to sleep with a no good pervert. He's gonna git his and if you're with him, so will you. Mark my words, Julie Howard." He pointed his index finger into her face.

She turned around and told her mother, "Mama you'd better call the sheriff. Tell him what's going on. Now!"

"You gonna catch it now!" Leroy said and jerked Billy Ray around and pulled him off the porch.

Billy Ray knocked his hand loose and drew back to hit him before he came to his senses. "Okay," he said. "Okay. Jes makin' sure … jes makin' sure … trying to …."

"Sorry, Mrs. Howard," Leroy said over his shoulder. "He ain't himself jes now. Uh, … family trouble's upset him."

Leroy put his hand on Billy Ray's back and urged him to the car, into the passenger's seat. He didn't figure his friend was in a fit state to drive.

In fact, Billy Ray rolled down the window as they drove away and shouted, "I ain't forgettin'! You bitch! I ain't forgettin'!"

Leroy cursed and said, "When the sheriff hears about what you been doin', Billy Ray, yore ass is gonna be grass. Hell, you gonna have a hard time keeping your job. Ain't no way in hell you ever gonna be sheriff, the way you goin'."

"What the fuck do you know about anything? You got shit for brains! You damn near flunked out of school. Would 've if I hadn't gave you answers."

Thank God you didn't give me that many. Every damn one you did was wrong.

Billy Ray bitched about Julie sleeping with Caleb all the way to Leroy's house. Leroy said nothing, just tried to figure out what he should do. He decided to let it stand. So far, it was not his problem, as shitty as it was to have to put up with Billy Ray's craziness.

*****

The next morning, with no calls for electrical work from town, Caleb decided to make his bike rounds along the road. He threw the canvas bag he'd found in a park garbage can into the bike's basket for any food he picked up along the way.

No one was out at the shotgun lady's house, he was glad for that. Otherwise, he'd have been compelled to stop there first and who knows what mood she'd have been in. Also, he didn't see Earnest and Bessie on their front porch so he drove on to Julie's house.

She was working in her garage studio, presumably to get another delivery ready. She wore a faded wraparound print dress. He didn't see Bonnie Fae.

She looks pretty, Caleb thought. Get the damn thought out of your head, old buddy. She's taken. But, she's getting a divorce. May be anyway. Damn. Will that matter? Forget it. She's not that dumb.

Seeing Caleb brought a smile to her face. "It's good to see you, Caleb. Mother and I always enjoy your company."

He smiled back and told her how much he enjoyed theirs. He couldn't help but wonder if she liked him.

She stopped what she was doing and said, "We had some excitement last night. Billy Ray and the deputy who hangs around with him, Leroy, stopped by. I thought Billy Ray was going to attack me. He was carrying on like a mad dog. I had Mama call the sheriff. She had to leave a message but when Leroy heard me tell her, he got Billy Ray into the car and they drove off."

Julie took the time to tell Caleb the gist of what the deputy was upset about, the bike she'd loaned him and the assumption he'd made of that.

Caleb's jaw dropped. "What? He said that! I'm glad you called the sheriff. I think the guy's gone off his rocker."

They kicked that around a bit longer before she looked at her work table. He knew she had work to do and asked, "Getting more art and crafts ready?"

She shook her head. "It's an everyday thing now," she said. "Red is working on an Internet catalogue. He's going to offer my things on the Internet!"

"Great," Caleb said.

"I'm so excited," Julie continued. "He already is selling some on a small scale. He wants to go big. If that takes off, I'll have to get some help. As it is, I'm working pretty much full time getting enough craft items for the store. He says other dealers are buying from him for their stores. He's coming over tonight for dinner to talk about the details. Mama's cooking his favorite, meat loaf."

"It sounds very good," Caleb said. "You will need help to keep up with that level of demand. That's great! Good luck."

That's what he said. His thoughts were a little different. When she said Red was coming to dinner, he felt a twinge of jealousy. It sounded like he ate there often ... his favorite, meat loaf.

*You jerk. What do you expect? They work together. They have common interest. She's known him for years, most likely. He's a success. I'm nothing. Now and always have been. Forget it.*

He asked her if he could do anything to help otherwise. She sent him to the barn and chicken coops. And, when he'd finished, she gave him food, which he put in his bag. It wasn't anything that would melt or spoil before he got it back to the cave.

Thoughts of Red coming to dinner stayed with him as he trudged along the road to his cave retreat. Red was a disappointment but his thoughts about Julie had been unrealistic at best, he told himself. *She most likely felt sorry for me and I grabbed that like a hungry dog with a bone.*

*I wonder if this is how love feels. Ironic, he thought. I married the first time without knowing what love was or even caring. I just got married and stayed married until she left me. Now, I might be in love with a married woman that I couldn't possibly marry. She's married and I don't have a pot to piss in as far as supporting her if she wasn't.*

"That equation doesn't balance," he said out loud and vowed to put his thoughts about Julie out of his mind. That was easier said than done, however. They continued to gnaw at his thoughts and sent him into a mild depression.

\*\*\*\*\*

The sheriff and Billy Ray were having a talk about the visit to Julie's house the night before. The deputy sat in a chair in front of the sheriff's desk.

"Billy Ray," the sheriff said, his face red, his deep voice loud and angry leaving no doubt about his feelings. Billy Ray knew he was in for an ass chewing. He sat staring at the floor, wishing he could leave.

*The son of a bitch. After the election, he'll be kissing my ass like the rest of the shit faces around here.*

The sheriff's tirade slowed but stayed with its biting edge. "I'd fire your ass right now 'cept I know you'd run down to the newspaper and scream your ass off 'bout how I did it 'cause I was afraid you were going to run against me and win. Well, I ain't gonna give you that satisfaction. Besides, I want you to run. I'm gonna whip your ass so bad, you won' be able to sit down for a month. Then, I'm gonna fire your ass! Got that?"

His young deputy looked up and said, "Yeah. I'm gonna kick your sorry ass out of here, Sheriff. The people want me."

"Boy, you don't know shit from Shinola. I know you got all them kin folk running around – I didn't know folks could have so many cousins they could marry, but your kin found 'em. Anyway, there're lots of people around the county who think above the waist and they'll be voting too."

"People want somebody's gonna get tough on criminals –"

"Yeah boy, you tough awright 'n you talk tough, but once you get past that bullshit, you don't have a damn thing to show anybody. You remind me of something the boys I was in the Army with used to say. The best part of you ran down your pa's leg. 'N I'm looking at the disgusting part that was left."

Billy Ray opened his mouth to say something but the sheriff waved him off and continued, "Boy, I've told you, you ain't got the brains God gave a billy goat. 'N I'm not wrong. I guess that's why they named you after one. You don't know how to pour piss out of a boot. Jes stick your foot in and blame somebody else for the smell."

"I –"

"Shut the fuck up, I'm talking. I got a call about how you scared Julie and her mother half to death last night. Those poor women. They pay us to protect 'em, not scare 'em, you dumb son of a bitch. When you gonna get it through that thick skull of yours that that man, Caleb Stanley is a better man than you'll ever be. You're the only man in the county stupid enough to keep harping about him. If you say one more fucking word, I may just kick you out before the election. That'd give you something to bitch about but you'll still lose."

"That bitch call –"

"You call that fine lady a bitch and I may shoot you on the spot. God, I'd enjoy that! Ain't a soul with half a brain would complain. In fact, the mayor might declare a holiday."

The sheriff then gave Billy the middle finger. "Dose of your own medicine. A man of the law acting like a kid. I inherited you from my predecessor, one of your inbred cousins, I believe. I should have kicked you out then," He shook his head in disgust. "You are a waste of tax payer's money."

Billy Ray stormed out.

\*\*\*\*\*

Leroy, who had waited in the car for the meeting, caught the brunt of Billy Ray's bitching on the way home. Finally he said, "Hey, I'm getting sick and tired of being your dog, Billy. Quit kicking me when you get called down and get the fuck off my back."

"I'll remember you said that when I'm sheriff. You ain't gonna be my chief deputy."

"Big deal. Don't hold your breath about being sheriff, Billy boy. Hell ain't froze over yet."

The next day, Billy Ray would think better of what he'd said and offer Leroy a lame apology. And, Leroy, knowing he had to work with him at least awhile longer would accept. They shook hands but neither man believed there was anything more to it than a bit of exercise, one of conveniently avoiding facing the real facts. Billy Ray had no respect for Leroy and Leroy had lost respect for Billy Ray. In fact, it crossed Leroy's mind to wash his hand as soon as he could.

Billy Ray thought about apologizing to Julie and Bonnie Fae, but couldn't bring himself to do it.

*****

Back along the road, Caleb saw an old man in front of a shotgun shack he'd passed before and thought abandoned. Some of the wooden siding had split and fallen to the ground. One corner of the porch had collapsed. The screen on the door was rusted, leaving more holes than screen.

He was glad. The man gave him something to think about besides Julie.

The man didn't look as if he'd had a haircut in some time and his face was covered with gray stubble. He wore a pair of glasses, both lenses scuffed up to obscurity.

The yard was filled with dead weeds and the field behind the house was also overgrown with weeds, sapling trees and bushes. An old truck sat at the rear of the house, also surrounded by weeds.

The man stared down at the weeds, as if bewildered. He appeared to be wearing little more than pajamas and slippers. His pot belly pushed against the seam of his pajamas.

Caleb rolled Charlie's old bike into the yard and spoke to the man. He stared at Caleb with the same blank stare he'd had looking at his neglected yard. As if unable to see, he moved close to Caleb.

"Do I know you?" he asked. "Can't see much anymore."

"Caleb Stanley," Caleb answered. "I don't think you know me."

"Rankin's mine. Rankin Owens." He waved over the yard. "My roses," he mumbled. "'Bout dead now."

Caleb didn't see any roses or any kind of flowers, only weeds. He looked at the man and said, "I know. I've come from the church to cut your weeds. That'll help your roses." He fabricated the story, but figured the man could relate to the church better than his usual pitch about working for food.

The man gestured toward a little shed away from the house. It held the lawnmower which looked like it may work. Caleb found a can with gasoline, filled the lawnmower's tank and, after a number of pulls, got it going. He cut the yard, front and back. He didn't bother to pick up the cut weeds. There was no grass under the clippings to worry about saving.

The old man retreated to the porch, sat down in a rocker and stared into the yard where Caleb worked. After Caleb had finished, the man thanked him and said he'd say a prayer for him. He stuck out a hand for Caleb to shake. It completely bypassed him. Caleb took it anyway for a quick shake before driving on.

Earnest and Bessie were still not on the front porch. He noticed that their front door was open and wondered if it had been that way when he passed earlier. Their coffee mugs were also on the little table between their rockers like they'd been drinking coffee but had strangely stopped and abandoned their cups.

Puzzled, Caleb drove into the yard and got off the bike. He walked to the porch and called, "Earnest!" There was no answer. He called again. Still no answer. He also called "Bessie" and got no response.

Could be one or the other got sick and had to be taken to the hospital. Last time I was here, Bessie talked about her arthritis. It was getting worse. Most likely went to the emergency room for treatment , Caleb thought. Wish I knew somebody to call.

With nothing else to do, he turned and biked back toward his camp. Odom had called about a job the next morning. That pleased him. He'd be there.

That afternoon, he took a cold shower to wash away the road dust. Every car and truck that passed sprayed him even though most slowed as much as they could. All the while the cold water was sending shivers up and down his body, he kept thinking about Earnest and Bessie. And, as soon as he'd finished his shower, he called Julie.

"Hello," she answered.

He told her what he'd seen, the Walters' front door open and their coffee cups on the table. And, what he surmised had happened.

"You are probably right but most likely they just went inside for a nap and forgot their cups and the door," she said.

"I called," Caleb told her.

"You should have knocked on the door. They wouldn't have minded. Even if they were taking a nap. They always like company and they liked yours."

"I should have, I suppose. Problem is, I don't like to intrude on anybody. I didn't even want to call in case they were napping."

"Tell you what, Caleb. I'll be done here in an hour or so. I'll drive by on my way home and check on them. If they're not there, I'll call the health care group that looks after them. If they had medical problems, they'd have called the health care right away. By the way, we had a great dinner with Red. He loved the meat loaf. Mama gave him some to take home. I think his Internet idea is going to take off. He's working with some guy out of New York on a catalogue."

"Congratulations! Your stuff is really impressive. I can see why you sell it as fast as you do." *Well, great. And that pretty well does it for me. Stupid of me to think there might be anything between us anyway.*

"Thanks, Caleb. I'll check on the Walters and let you know."

He thanked her. It made him feel better knowing somebody was going to check on them. At their age, anything could have happened. Odd that they would have left their cups on the front porch. That worried him but he dismissed it. Probably a reasonable explanation for it.

He told himself to accept the inevitable and forget about any relationship with Julie. *I don't have a damn thing to offer her. Not a damn thing. I let what's left of my ego overload my common sense. She and Red will make a good team anyway. I'm happy for her.* Nevertheless, he cursed.

# Chapter 16

It was after dark when Julie called. "I'm sorry to be so late, but I've been trying to find out something. I stopped by their house on my way home. I knocked on the front and back doors and called their names. I didn't get an answer. So, I called their health group and got nothing. I asked them to call the children and see if they knew anything. They're probably okay."

"I hope so." He thanked her. It was odd that neither one answered. It would have been understandable if one had gotten ill and had to be taken to the hospital. In that case, the health group would probably have been called. And, if they had gone out, they wouldn't have left the front door open. He lay down to read but couldn't. His thoughts were a scramble.

Julie called back at ten. "The health group contacted the girls. They didn't know anything either. Finally, I called the sheriff's emergency number. He said he'd check around with the hospital and doctors. If they don't know anything, he'll send somebody out to investigate."

"If they were sick or something dire, I guess by now it'd be too late. However, I'd prefer that he send somebody out tonight."

"That's what I said. I think he will."

Caleb didn't sleep much that night. His thoughts were on Earnest and Bessie. What had happened to them? He had begun to put any notion of a relationship with Julia behind him. It was easier than he thought it would be. Once he looked at the stupidity of it, he wondered how he could have let himself even think such a thing. It was impossible.

The next morning, the birds got Caleb up early. He was awake anyway, hoping Julie would have called with a reasonable explanation for why Earnest and Bessie appeared to be missing. She hadn't.

He fried a couple of eggs in bacon drippings, warmed a left over biscuit and washed it down with a cup of coffee, without tasting it. His thoughts were still on Earnest and Bessie. After a quick clean up, he hurried toward town, thankful for the bike.

I'm going to stop by their house this time and go inside. To hell with bothering them. I have to know.

He soon found out that wouldn't be necessary. As he approached their house, he saw an ambulance going down the road ahead of him. Its lights were not on. He took that to be a bad sign. Three cars with Lawton sheriff insignia on the doors and lights on top sat is the yard. One uniformed deputy stood in their driveway, arms folded across this stomach. Just then, Caleb saw another deputy come from the house. He wore a white mask which he removed at the door. It was Billy Ray. Leroy followed him out and did the same.

Caleb rolled down the driveway and stopped in front of the deputy with folded arms. The deputy extended an arm and hand indicating that Caleb was to stop. He did and said, "I'm a friend of the Walters. Julie Howard and I have been trying to find out if anything happened to them. I assume something did from all the activity. I saw an ambulance leaving."

The deputy shook his head and said, "Yes sir. They're both dead. Probably been dead awhile. The coroner will run some tests to find out more. Billy Ray called the forensics people to come out and check for prints and anything that might tell us who did it. How and why?"

Billy Ray looked out and saw Caleb on the bike. He shouted, "Fred, don't let that bastard get anywhere near this house. He probably did it!"

"That's ridiculous," Caleb said. However, he turned the bike around to head for Marshalltown. He still had work to do even if Earnest and Bessie would be in his thoughts. *What a tragedy. What a damn tragedy! Damn. They were such good people.*

\*\*\*\*\*

Caleb called Odom to see if he had any jobs for him. First though, he told him the news about Earnest and Bessie. Odom didn't know them but expressed regret as though he did. In a small town, the death of anybody was considered by most as the death of a family member.

The jobs were relatively simple and Caleb had them all fixed within two hours. Afterward, he used the junker, the old Ford truck, he'd tuned up, to drive to Odom's friend's shop to look at the more complex problem, the questionable generator. It turned out to be a little known fuse which Caleb changed within twenty minutes after he looked under the hood. However, the generator had produced a high voltage spike to cause the fuse to blow so he had to do a little cleaning and make adjustments to the generator to prevent it from happening again. The adjustment took another twenty minutes. The friend was impressed and gave Caleb thirty dollars.

Caleb had an extra five to give to Julie, her share, as he had promised.

He asked Odom if anything else had come in. There was a headlight Caleb could change, a fifteen minute job. Afterward, Odom calculated what he owed Caleb for his work that day. "Comes to about thirty five dollars, I reckon. I could give you a five if you're short."

Caleb said he could wait. Money was far from his thoughts. He was troubled by the deaths of his friends, the Walters.

Why them?

He hurried away. It was a mid-afternoon by the time he reached Julie's house. He leaned the bike against the front porch and knocked on the front door. Might as well leave her the five, he thought.

*****

Julie was at the craft shop delivering art objects, Bonnie Fae said. They knew about Earnest and Bessie being found dead.

Bonnie Fae said, "We heard they'd been bashed over the head. It was a robbery. I don't know what all was taken, money and some other stuff, they're saying."

"Hard to believe," Caleb said. "I don't think I've ever met better folks than the Walters. It's a damn shame. Hell, whoever it was should'a killed me." There was a time when he'd have welcomed it. Not so much just then however.

She looked at him with a question on her face and a frown. "They shouldn't a killed nobody."

He handed her the five he'd gotten from Odom. She tried to refuse it, but he insisted. "It's my agreement with her. If it hadn't been for her, I wouldn't have made it."

She shoved it into her apron pocket with a sigh.

"Tell Julie I dropped by. And how sorry I am about the Walters. Maybe they'll catch whoever did it. Guess I'll go on back to my camp," he said and turned to leave.

"Wait, Caleb, I'm not lettin' you go till we have a cup of coffee … and a piece of pie. I just put a pot on. It won't bring Bessie and Earnest back, but a good piece of pie will take the bad taste out of my mouth. Maybe yours too. Would you have a piece with me?"

He agreed. Caleb had two cups of coffee and with his pie, a dish of peach cobbler with a scoop of ice cream on top. Neither said much, just drank their coffee and ate the pie. It had been a long time since he'd had peach cobbler. His mother had made the last.

When the last sip of coffee was gone, he stood and said, "I don't think pie could taste any better. I just wish I was having it at a better time. I hate it about the Walters."

"Me too. No better people than Earnest and Bessie. I'll tell Julie you dropped by. She put the pie in to bake this morning 'fore she left for the craft store. She's talking to a group of ladies about making crafts. Red set it up. They all want to do what she's doing."

*Right. Red set it up. I wonder if he's married. Julia hasn't said. How could he ask without sounding jealous?* He didn't have an answer. And, he wouldn't ask.

Caleb had heard the song before, about ladies wanting to do something somebody else was doing. People were mesmerized by what somebody else could do and most wanted to emulate it but they rarely could or did.

At the front door, he thanked her again, got on the bike and pedaled off toward his camp. Depression had settled in. Strangely though, it hadn't come with thoughts about his hemlock bag. He would think about that later.

After hiding the bike, he pulled his log seat to the slope and sat there watching the peaceful river flowing along below. Now and then, a big fish made a big splash as it tried to catch its dinner. Birds swooped down for a drink of the water and thankfully didn't become a fish's dinner. One more tragedy would be more than he could stand.

Glow said, "I believe you've gone from bad to worse. You come down here to put your troubles behind you and all you've done is get into more."

Caleb's head jerked around. "What? All my troubles down here are your fault."

"My, my. Are we refusing to take responsibility for our free will?"

"You told me to rescue the boy. Look where that got me?"

"Would you rather he died? Besides, I think that rescue sent you along a new road, helping people out. And, I do believe you've enjoyed it. It gave you a life, a new life. Made you forget your hemlock stew. Drew you out of the shell you'd been in for years. And, what about the calls you've been getting to do electrical work. I'd say you've been having fun for once in your life. I'm including Julie Howard in that equation. Even though she's married. Nevertheless, you have enjoyed looking at her, being around her. Have I said anything wrong?"

Caleb stared at the tiny orange glow for a second or two then replied. "I guess you're right. I know you are. You kicked it all in motion, but you're right. For the most part, I've put my hemlock stew behind me for the time being. I feel like I have a new life." Julie came into his thoughts.

"With Julie in the middle of it."

"I wish," Caleb said and immediately regretted saying it even to his imaginary friend. She was a wish, but to even think she could be more could lead to more frustrations than he could handle. "She's tied in with the guy helping her sell her crafts, Red. I can't compete with him."

"Well, you're facing up to your free will, Caleb. I'll put that in my project report. Caleb has decided he can't compete."

"Yeah," Caleb answered.

"Speaking of free will, what are you going to do about the murder of your new friends, Earnest and Bessie?" the Glow asked.

"What can I do? I didn't do it. I suppose I'll continue doing what I'm doing and let the sheriff find who killed them. It's his job," Caleb said with a shrug.

"Would that it'd be that simple. Free will does muddy the waters, doesn't it? Yours and everybody else's."

"Wait a minute! You're not saying I'm going to get involved?" Caleb asked. "My free will? I don't see that. What could I possibly do?"

"Not deliberately, but your friend Billy Ray has you lined up for killing them. Remember, you're his ticket to the sheriff's office. If he can arrest you for the murder, it'll certainly look good on his political resume. If he pushes, you'll push back, don't you think?"

Caleb shook his head. "My free will huh? I assume you somehow know something's about to happen."

"Billy Ray has free will too and ambition pushing it. I'd say he figures - if he takes the time to figure - that your free will wouldn't make a decent meal for his," Glow said.

"Yeah. An ambitious jerk with limited intelligence but lots of kin folks to make up for it."

"At least. And right about now, I imagine, Billy Ray has Leroy out combing the junk yard for the club used to bash in the heads of your friends. He'll find it and some worthless jewelry the Walters owned that the killer or killers left behind. And, since that's where you have said you're sleeping, Billy Ray will proudly claim to put two and two together and get … Caleb Stanley, as the murderer."

"Are you're saying they did it?"

"I'm not saying. I don't write the story. What I said is that they'll find evidence that points to you. I doubt they care who did it."

"And, there's not a damn thing I can do about it, is there?"

"There's always your hemlock stew."

Caleb nodded. "Yes, my hemlock. Problem is, I'd be letting Billy Ray push me into it. I don't think I can do that. Goes against my nature."

"I figured it might."

"So, what do you recommend?"

"It's your free will, Caleb, not mine. Yours against Billy Ray's. And, who knows how that will play out."

He was right.

*****

Billy Ray sat in front of the sheriff's desk laying out his case against Caleb. Leroy was in the chair next to him.

He leaned forward and said, with a grin, "Leroy found a bloodied club under an old car where the man sleeps in the junk yard. And, under the cushions he sleeps on, was a bag of the Walters' jewelry. We cracked it! We've got their murderer! You said he was innocent of everything. Voters ain't gonna like that, are they?"

The sheriff ignored Billy Ray's comment and asked Leroy, "That the club?" He had pointed at the hickory club inside a plastic bag by Leroy's side. Leroy nodded. He looked back at Billy Ray for him to continue.

Billy Ray gladly did. "Rankin Owens said the man drove by his house, probably the day the Walters were killed. He had a canvas bag in the bike's basket and …. listen to this, he had a club tied to the handle bars."

The sheriff frowned, "No shit?"

"No shit."

"How in the hell could I have been so wrong about the man?" He shook his head back and forth.

"Just like you've been wrong about lots of the thugs you've turned loose, sheriff."

"Yeah. So you've said. You didn't find their gold coins? Had to be worth some big bucks." It was well known around town that Earnest had been collecting gold coins for as long as anyone could remember. It was his inheritance to their girls.

"So far we haven't. We're still looking."

The sheriff sighed. "That club … and the jewelry been looked at by the lab? Finger prints? Blood? All the usual things?"

Billy Ray said, "We just brought the stuff in."

The sheriff looked at Leroy and said, "Get it over to the lab now. I don't want some shyster lawyer arguing we somehow broke the evidence chain."

Billy Ray said, "I'll take it over when we're finished. It's my _"

The sheriff interrupted. "No. Leroy, you take it over. Tell them it's priority. I know they're loaded with work, but tell them I said get on it. Now!"

Billy Ray said, "I want to be there when they look at it."

"Busy as they are, you'll make it. I'll be finished in a minute or two. I want to talk to you some more about the case." With a wave, he sent Leroy out the door with the plastic bag.

"Okay," the sheriff said, "when you walked in, you wanted a search warrant for Julie Howard's house. You think the man's been sleeping there."

Billy Ray turned to face the sheriff. He had been looking at the door behind him.

"We seen him leaving her house on the bike she gave him. He's been eating there too. Stands to reason, he's been sleeping there. I want to bring her in for questioning. She probably knows what's been going on. He may 've hidden the rest of the stuff in her house."

"Don't jump the gun, Billy Ray."

"I ain't."

"I agree she should be questioned but I want the DA involved in that. He can send somebody out to pick her up. I don't trust you to do it. I know you've been acting like a fool, trying to get her to sleep with you. It ain't gonna happen. If Stanley's guilty, I want a conviction. With your attitude … and your history, you could screw it up."

"Shit! My attitude. Hell, if you hadn't interfered, the son of a bitch would've been in jail and the Walters would still be alive."

"That gonna be your campaign slogan?" He waved a finger at the deputy.

"Damn right!"

"Okay, I'll get a warrant to search her house, but you have to wait until the DA is ready to bring her in for questioning. And, I want him to have somebody there when you search. Understand that, Billy Ray? Somebody who doesn't have an axe to grind!"

The deputy shook his head without answering. He got up and hurried out the door muttering "bullshit" as he did.

After he was gone, the sheriff sat at his desk and stared into space, thinking. *I just don't think Stanley did it, but damn, it looks like Billy Ray has him dead to rights. And looks like Stanley is the way the little shit's gonna kick me out of my office. How did I get that so damn wrong?*

He picked up his phone to call the DA. Billy Ray needed a warrant and the DA needed to question Julie Howard and her mother. Like it or not, it was his job to do it. The DA agreed.

*****

About mid-morning the next day, Julie called Caleb. He was on his bike headed into town to see if Odom or any of the other shops had any work for him. He stopped to take her call.

"Caleb," she said with an obvious strain in her voice. "I've just come from the DA's office. Me and Mama. He asked us questions about you. Wanted to know if you'd slept here. All sorts of things. Mostly to do with Earnest and Bessie's murder. They think you did it. They asked Mama if you had a club on Charlie's bike the last time you were here. I guess that was when you and Mama had the peach cobbler I'd baked."

"I didn't."

"She told them she didn't see one. They said they had a witness who had seen the club attached to your handle bars." She cried in the phone.

Caleb waited a few seconds until she'd stopped. "Don't cry, Julie. Somebody's lying or blind. Why would I kill those good people?"

"That's what we said. But, they're out looking for you. They're going to arrest you." More crying. "I'm so sorry. I don't know what to say. We told them we knew you didn't do it. You loved them too much. They also said they'd found some of their jewelry where you slept in the junk yard."

"That's a lie too. I'm not sleeping there anymore. Sounds like Billy Ray's work."

"They searched the house. Turned it upside down, even the garage. Didn't find a thing. The DA sent some people to help."

"There was nothing to find."

"We told them that but they ignored us."

"Billy Ray's got his key to being sheriff."

"I guess. By the way, Odom just called me. He says somebody's been calling all the auto repair shops about you. Telling everybody not to hire you to do anything. Not only are you a pervert, you're also a murderer."

"It figures," Caleb said.

"I cried when he told me. I can't stop. I told him it was a lie. He said he didn't think you'd do anything like that, but he had a business to run and for now, he wasn't going to give you any more work."

Caleb told her he'd leave the bike in the garage where he'd found it and the cell phone in the basket. She protested, but he didn't back down. "For now, you should not have any visible ties to me. It can only cause you trouble until I can put the thing behind me. Tell Odom I understand."

She reluctantly agreed then asked, "Are you going to leave town?"

He wasn't sure. He had to think about it. "I don't want to. I like being here. I like you and Bonnie Fae but I hate being accused of something I didn't do."

He punched off and stared into space. *What the hell am I going to do? No need to go to town or even to Julie's.*

He turned the bike around and returned to the park. He needed to think. Needed to decide what to do.

# Chapter 17

Caleb leaned the bike against the tree and sat down on the log round he'd been using as a seat.

"What am I going to do now?" he said to the river below.

"Good question," Glow asked "What are you going to do? Leave town? Assuming you could, which, by the way, you can't."

He looked around for the glow but couldn't see it. He supposed it was inside the cave. "You're still around, listening to my thoughts."

"You're still my project."

"You picked a loser."

"I'd rather call it one with complications. Unpredictable free will. You're not boring Caleb. That's a fact. And, now you have to make a decision. What's it going to be?"

"My free will?"

"Yep. Your free will."

"I know I didn't do it. I'll start with that charge and attack it head on. I'm going to fight. I'm tired of being kicked around by a jerk."

"Well said. I'll be watching. I love a good fight especially when I'm not the one getting the shit kicked out of them."

"Yeah. I can imagine. I've had experience on that end."

With diminishing sound, Glow said, "Experience is a good thing in a situation like you're in."

Caleb frowned. What the hell does that mean? I guess I'll find out.

Anticipating some snooping around as things heated up, Caleb moved enough of stuff out of the cave to make it appear that he'd been making his camp around the fire pit. He covered the mouth of the cave and the trail with a tangle of briars. That done, he got on the bike and drove it to Julie's and left it and the phone.

Julie's truck was not in its usual place. *At Red's, I guess.*
Bonnie Fae was also not around. Actually, he was glad to get in and
out without having to explain himself again. What more could he
say? He walked the rest of the way to town.

At city hall, he went straight to the police Chief's office. His
door was open and there was no lady out front so he walked in.

"Chief Bush," he said. "I understand the sheriff thinks I
killed the Walters. I didn't but figured the sooner I faced the
problem, the sooner it'd go away."

"Ah, Mr. Stanley. Indeed. There is talk around town that you
bashed those folks head in with a club you carried around on Charlie
Howard's old bike." He didn't smile when he said it. "Sheriff Tolar
says they have a pretty good case."

"Well, there has to be a flaw in it someplace."

"Ben, that's the sheriff's name, and I agree. We don't see it,
but Billy Ray is riding high. Has a witness statement that says you
had the club. They found the club where you sleep, with some of the
jewelry taken from the Walters' home."

Caleb explained how he'd moved to the park to sleep several
weeks ago. "Whoever left the club and jewelry didn't know that."

The chief shook his head. "I dare say. Madison McNally's a
pretty sharp attorney. Kind of a friend. We fish together. Have a beer
now and then. I've asked him to look at the case."

Caleb thanked him.

"Glad to," he said. "You'll be arrested for certain and hauled
in front of the judge for arraignment and bail. Not likely to get bail if
what they're saying holds up but Madison will represent you. We
won't see you railroaded by Billy Ray just because he wants to be
sheriff. Madison will make sure they don't look at the evidence with
blinders on."

A wave of relief swept over Caleb. He was almost overcome
to tears. During his lifetime, hardly anybody had ever done anything
for him and he hadn't asked for anything, but just then, he was at his
wits  end  and  he  was  glad  to  any  help  he  could  get.

The Chief walked him over to the sheriff's office to officially turn him in. The sheriff seemed reluctant and looked weary, but nevertheless told him he was under arrest, suspected of killing and robbing the Walters. Caleb protested but didn't make a big scene. He knew the process was inevitable. The arrest was the first step.

He was given prisoner garb and put into a cell by himself. He sat on the bunk to wait for the next step. He'd be in the cell until was taken before a judge for arraignment and a bail hearing.

That night, Caleb sat on his bunk and stared at the blank wall in front of him. Depression lay over him like a heavy blanket.

"This is my project in which I'm well pleased," the familiar voice said. Glow.

"What do you mean?"

"I mean you exercised your free will and turned yourself in. That took discipline and a decision to do the right thing. You didn't kill those people and you want it known."

"That much is true. One of these days, the Lord's going to strike you dead for taking liberties with his words."

"How do you know I'm not the Lord?"

Caleb looked at the window where he could see the glow. "I don't.  How about Jesus? Was he one of you?"

"Not one of us, Caleb. He had human form unlike me. However, I don't know our origins. There may be a Lord out there someplace. If so, he's never appeared either in person or through a Jesus. However, the Jesus guy said one thing that has stuck with me since I first heard him say it. He said, 'In my father's house are many dwellings.' Well, in our energy sphere there are many data receptors and more are made as needed. I've often wondered if your Jesus might have been pointing at us."

"Yeah. That doesn't do me a hell of a lot of good right now. Billy Ray's going to try to railroad me into the electric chair or whatever they use here these days."

"No doubt. If you die, his political career lives."

"Too bad you can't help me."

"You know my limitations, Caleb. I can't mess with free will. Yours or Billy Ray's. But, at least you'll get a fair trial before you're condemned."

Caleb scoffed. "That's what bothers me."

Just then, the midnight freight approached the town, its lonely whistle blowing long and hard, its wheels rattling over the rails.

"Ah, if only you could be on that train," Glow said.

"Yeah. You heard my thoughts. And, let that whistle chase my blues away. I think that's how the song goes."

"I remember it. Get some rest. You have a big day tomorrow. You get to see how the people who give in to their urges and instincts end up."

With that, the glow diminished to a pin head and vanished.

A deputy wandered by shortly afterward. "I hear you talking?" he asked Caleb.

"Just praying," Caleb said.

"Probably a good idea."

"I thought so too."

That satisfied the deputy.

Caleb spent the rest of the night sitting up, dozing in place. He had breakfast, scrambled eggs, half cooked bacon, cold grits and toast with a tin can filled with coffee.

*****

The sheriff showed up around ten, just before the arraignment and scheduled bail hearing. "We're going to take you to the court room," he said, his voice as full of gravel as ever. "Have to put you in cuffs. Have to follow our rules. We'll take 'em off when we get there. Billy Ray and Leroy will take you over. It's their case."

Caleb said he understood.

Within minutes, the two deputies came with the cuffs and led him to the court. The sheriff led the column.

Outside the courtroom were reporters from the local television station and the two newspapers, one weekly and one local. All had cameras at the ready and shouted questions at the sheriff since he was first in the door to the ante-chamber.

"Will he get bail?" the television reporter asked, the camera running, full lights.

"Has he confessed?" one of the newspaper reporters called out.

The sheriff stopped with a wave toward Billy Ray, Leroy and Caleb. "This is Billy Ray's case. He put it all together. I think y'all should put all your questions to him."

Caleb thought his face showed a slight smile when he said that, nothing big, just a kind of knowing smile. That made him wonder, but it didn't dispel his concerns or his fears. He was facing a murder charge and Billy Ray was determined to prove that he'd killed the Walters. And the sheriff, slight smile notwithstanding, seemed agreeable to let him do just that.

Billy Ray held up long enough to say, "Talk to me after the hearing. This man is guilty and he won't get bail. He bashed in the heads of two of the sweetest people I've ever met."

With that proclamation and a hard yank, Caleb was urged into the courtroom. He saw Julie and Bonnie Fae in chairs, watching as they brought him in. He nodded. If they nodded back, he couldn't see. Billy Ray was pushing him toward the front. Once there, he removed the cuffs.

"Jes so you know, I've got a gun and so does Leroy. Try anything and there won't be a trial," Billy Ray said.

Caleb didn't answer. He was busy rubbing his wrists.

His attorney, McNally, was also present and talked to him briefly – mostly gave him a lawyer's words of encouragement.

McNally was one of those attorneys, Caleb decided, who had cultivated a laid-back, casual look. Shabby was what people around town called McNally's look, Caleb heard later. He wore an old gray suit coat with leather patches where his elbows had worn almost through. His baggy pants didn't match the coat and didn't show a crease. He stood about five foot seven, was overweight and his hair, light brown, lay where the wind blew it. Also, he wore glasses, a pair he'd bought from Wal-Mart. A man of the people, he liked to describe himself. And, the people liked it. He was always booked with cases.

McNally was smiling and seemed confident as he talked to Caleb and afterward when he exchanged words with the sheriff and the DA. Caleb wished he was confident.

Caleb guessed his age at around fifty.

The DA, Sam Washburn, had walked in a few minutes after Caleb was seated. He stood out, slim, about six foot two, and dressed impeccably in a freshly pressed, dark suit with vest. His tie showed the colors of Ole Miss, where he'd gone to law school.

His face had a serious trial look and showed no emotion. And, he also seemed confident. That bothered Caleb. So far, only the sheriff's half smile had given Caleb any hope and he was afraid that hope was the product of wishful thinking.

The judge, in his flowing black robes, took his chair asked McNally for a plea. He stood, pleaded Caleb not guilty and asked for a bail hearing.

Billy Ray stood and said, "No bail for a murderer!"

The judge rapped his gavel and admonished him to remain quiet unless asked to speak. He looked at the DA who nodded. Bail hearings were the norm in a murder case. Usually bail was not granted but a hearing was part of the process. He looked at McNally and asked him to state his case.

McNally hitched at his pants with his elbows. Had to do it twice. The first time apparently didn't do the trick. With that behind him, he wagged his head as he said, "Lots of little things just don't add up in this case, your Honor. They puzzle me and I bet you they'll puzzle you. Maybe even the DA." He glanced at the DA with a smile. "Now and again, when things get put together in a hurry, a horse turns out lookin' like an elephant. And, we all know an elephant won't fit in a horse's stall." He glanced at the DA with a big grin.

The DA, if he saw, didn't respond.

Caleb noticed the sheriff's face. It took on the same smile he'd seen as they'd entered the court house. Caleb hoped he knew something he didn't.

The judge nodded for McNally to continue.

"Glad to, your Honor. Glad to. First of all, forensics found fabrics on the handle of the club suggesting the killer wore gloves. No gloves were found with the club. Now, I agree that if Mr. Stanley had worn gloves, he might have thrown them away, and likely would have, but if he did that why didn't he throw away the club as well? Mr. Stanley looks to me like he's got pretty good sense. So, I think that's very odd and puzzling. And, anything that odd makes me think the club was planted by the real killer, knowing where Mr. Stanley had said he was making camp. In fact, Mr. Stanley has been camping in the park for several weeks. I personally checked and found his camp. So, the club thing's looking a little shaky to me."

The DA stood and said, "Your honor, I'd like to request that my colleague stick to the facts, not his speculative imagination. There's no jury here."

McNally gave a face and laughed.

The judge admonished McNally to do just that, but no one felt he was going to be that strict at a bail hearing.

McNally waited while the judge finished making a note.

"Let me move on to the next odd thing, your Honor. That's the signed witness statement by Mr. Rankin Owens. Mr. Owens says he saw that club tied to Mr. Stanley's bicycle handle bars. That sounds pretty bad for my client. With a statement like that, I don't know why I should even try to defend Mr. Stanley. Notwithstanding my speculative imagination, Sam." He waved in the direction of the DA as if to answer the DA's his earlier comment about his use of 'speculative imagination.'

"Now, I'm going to stipulate that Mr. Owens is a fine man. Most likely goes to church every Sunday. However, I have to ask the court to look hard at his statement. I'm thinking his statement came after some heavvvvy coaching."

Billy Ray jumped out of his seat again. "There wasn't any damn coaching. That's what he said!"

"You speak again and I'll throw you out of this court room," the judge said. "The DA will have an opportunity to speak after Mr. McNally is finished. You're a witness. You speak when spoken to."

The DA stood and thanked the judge.

"The reason I said that about the coaching is this. You see, this may surprise the deputy who took Mr. Owens's statement, but …" McNally turned to look at Billy Ray and Leroy before continuing. "You know what? Mr. Owens is legally blind! I checked around and found his eye doctor, Wilma Beasley. Wilma told me that man couldn't see much beyond two feet." He handed the bailiff a sworn statement from the doctor with a copy to the DA. The bailiff gave it to the judge who quickly read it.

The judge shook his head. "The doctor's statement kind of knocks Owen's statement in the head. You agree counselor?" He asked the DA with raised eyebrows.

"On the face of it, yes. However, we have other evidence. Clear and convincing, your Honor. Finger prints."

The judged uttered what sounded like an "uh huh."

Billy Ray twisted and turned in his seat but kept quiet.

"I'm throwing the statement out," the judge said.

McNally shook his head. "I agree with that. Now, there's the thing with the jewelry." He paused to hitch his pants again. "That's odd too, the jewelry. Everybody in the county knew about Earnest's box of gold coins. Well, everybody except Mr. Stanley. He hasn't been around long enough to know. His fingerprints were not found inside the house. When we heard Earnest had been killed, we figured it was for those coins. Worth some money, folks tell me. Well now, why would Mr. Stanley keep a few items of worthless jewelry and not the coins? And, what would he do with the coins? You'd have to take them someplace where there was a buyer. I don't think anybody in Marshalltown would be a buyer."

The judge raised his eyebrows and nodded.

"And, I can bring in witnesses to testify that Mr. Stanley only had a bike to get around on. No car, your Honor. You want me to bring in a witness?" He gestured at the DA.

"I'll stipulate to that," the DA said.

Billy Ray jumped out of his seat again and shouted. "She has a truck. Julie … Howard has a truck. They could'a been in it together."

The judge rapped his gavel and pointed a finger at Billy Ray. "You keep your mouth shut. Do you understand? This is the last time I'm warning you. For the record, Julie Howard has not been charged with anything in this matter."

The DA said, "Your Honor, may I?" He gestured in the direction of Billy Ray. The judge nodded.

The DA strolled back casually and had a brief conference with the deputy. Afterward, he returned to his table and nodded for McNally to continue who said, "All that jumping up and down like that. Uh, uh, makin' it hard for me to get due process for my client. I don't want that of record just yet though. I'm not nearly 'bout through."

He stared down at the tablet in front of him, sighed and looked both at the DA and at Billy Ray. Caleb figured he was at a loss as to what to say next.

# Chapter 18

Caleb felt like jumping up and running. Everytime his attorney said something, the DA had an answer. And, just then, his attorney looked like he was at a loss for words.

Finally though, he looked toward the judge, shrugged and said, "Okay, let's take a look at the club we've been hearing so much about, the finger prints. I gotta say that when I start thinking about that club, those finger prints jump right to the top of my list. Hard to get around, eh?"

The DA nodded.

"So, let me see if I've got this right, Sam," he said with a brief look at the DA. "I understand that before Mr. Stanley turned himself in, that club was checked for prints. None were found. I can understand that. My client hadn't touched the club. And, from the fabrics the lab found, I'd have been surprised if there had been prints, anybody's. Then a strange –"

"He missed them!" Billy Ray said. "Clarence flat out missed them!" Clarence Tucker was in charge of the forensics' lab.

"That's it!" the judge said and ordered him out.

"I kind of figured the deputy would be jumping up and down about that so I asked Clarence to join us," McNally said. "He's in the back of the court room, ready to tell us if he missed anything. Can I ask him a couple of questions, your Honor? We'll just put him on the stand. Might save us some time."

The judge agreed. "By all means. You've piqued my curiosity, Mr. McNally."

*Mine too,* Caleb thought. *I wonder if all this odd shit had anything to do with the sheriff's mysterious smile. He must have known about it. Billy Ray's case indeed. He was letting Billy Ray shoot          himself          in          the          foot.*

Clarence Tucker took the stand. McNally asked him to describe the sequence of events from the time he was given the club until the present time. He said that the club, inside a plastic bag, was handed to him by Leroy with instruction to check it out immediately. He found the fibers, likely from a glove and blood that matched the blood of the Walters but no prints.

"We didn't see a single fingerprint," he said.

He went on to say that he prepared a report of his findings and sent it to the sheriff. The club in the bag went into the evidence room which was locked up until yesterday afternoon, when Billy Ray and Leroy took the club from the evidence room to examine it.

Sounds suspicious as hell to me, Caleb thought.

"Billy Ray was certain we'd missed fingerprints. An hour or so later, they brought it back and showed me some smudges that looked like fingerprints. I hadn't seen the smudges before. Hard to see how we could have missed them, so, I rechecked the club and found, what I'll call, faint fingerprints, smudged but fingerprints nevertheless. I got my equipment and checked them against the defendants. Although the match wasn't as good as I would have liked, there was enough of a match for me to put in my report that they belonged to the defendant. "

He also testified that fingerprints could not be faked or forged as far as he knew.

The judge looked at McNally. "Well now, your client must have had that club in his hand, Mr. McNally. Looks clear and convincing to me. What have you got to say about that?"

That pronouncement hit Caleb like a ton of bricks. Until then, it looked like he had a chance.

"That's what anybody would think, your Honor. Clear and convincing. No need for a trial, just drag my client out and hang him in the square. Odd though, your Honor. Before my client was arrested, the club showed no fingerprints. Now, Mr. Tucker is a competent man, as we all know. Been on the job for ten years and to my knowledge has never missed fingerprints before." He looked at the man in the chair and asked, "Have you, Mr. Tucker? Ever missed fingerprints?"

Tucker said, "Never. And I don't see how I could have missed them this time. The smudges were pretty visible."

"Thank you, Mr. Tucker," McNally said and continued. "Let me move on a little. After Mr. Stanley was arrested, he was fingerprinted, twice by the way, just to let you know. The fingerprints, my client's, kind of showed up on the club after the first inspection didn't reveal any fingerprints. And, the fingerprints that did show up ... on that second look ... showed up smudged. Like they had fingerprint ink on them. Is that right, Mr. Tucker?"

"Yes, sir."

"Maybe odd, Mr. McNally," the Judge said, "but if Mr. Stanley's fingerprints are on the club, he must have held it. As I understand it, nobody can transfer fingerprints. I'm going to rule against bail."

Caleb was thinking about the lonely hours he was going to spend in his jail cell waiting for trial, not to mention the lonely hours he'd spend waiting for the death sentence to be carried out. *Why in the hell didn't I cook my hemlock and drink it? That's why I came here. Damn Glow. Hell, damn me. How in the hell can there be a Glow? Boot strap rationalization, that's what Glow is. I made it up to put off the inevitable. Big mistake.*

But, McNally wasn't ready to throw in his towel. "I agree with you, your Honor. That sounds pretty danged conclusive. Prints is prints! However, I'd appreciate it if you'd let me finish my presentation. I'm into it and I'd sure like to finish it before you rule."

The judge stared down at him sternly but said nothing.

McNally shrugged, smiled and continued. "So, your Honor, let's see where this due process, the constitution talks about, leads us. There's a little more I can squeeze out of it and to tell you the truth, I'm enjoying it. First thing is this: I reckon I'm gonna have to take issue with your conclusion about my client's fingerprints."

McNally handed the judge two documents and talked about both as he did. The first one was a report by a known forensic expert who had documented proof of 57 cases of fingerprint fraud by police officers in Cape Town. In at least one those cases, fingerprints had been lifted from one object and planted on a murder weapon.

The judge read the report, shaking his head as he did. He looked up for McNally to continue.

The next report was an article in the Journal of Criminal Law and Criminology by a reporter considered something of an expert in the field of fingerprint forgery including transferring prints from one object to another.

The judge quickly glanced at the article. He nodded for McNally to wrap it up.

"Also, your Honor, let me add this. I understand that last year in New Orleans, a legal seminar was held that dealt with fingerprint forgery."

"Are you suggesting that someone in Marshalltown law enforcement committed fingerprint forgery?"

"No, Sir, I'm not because I don't know and that's beyond the scope of my presentation. What I am suggesting however, is that it is possible for … some kind of contamination or, shall I say forgery, to have occurred between the time Mr. Tucker first checked the club for prints and the time he re-checked the club at the request of the two deputies. And, that possibility is supported by the two reports I've given you have and the New Orleans seminar. Uh, let me ask Mr. Tucker another question."

The judge nodded.

"Correct me if I'm wrong, but didn't one set of my client's fingerprints go missing?"

Tucker twisted nervously in the chair and said, "We uh, haven't been able to find the second set."

"Isn't that odd. Smudged fingerprints found on the club and the second fingerprint card with my client's smudged prints on it goes missing. Hmm. Does that sound like an odd coincidence or what?"

"I'm going to object to my colleague's wild goose expedition. Totally beyond the scope of this hearing," the DA stood and said.

The judge agreed, but from the look on his face, he wasn't convinced that something odd had indeed happened.

The DA remained standing and said, "I want it known that I am objecting strenuously to allowing those reports admitted as evidence. And, the New Orleans seminar is not relevant without tying it to this hearing, the murders."

"I agree," the judge said, "but this is a bail hearing and I let almost anything come in. You can object at trial and if Mr. McNally can't lay a proper foundation and tie them to the case, I won't let it in. Do you have anything else, Mr. McNally."

Before McNally could answer, the sheriff stood and asked to address the judge. The judge gave him the okay. "I attended the seminar in New Orleans as did a number of deputies and a number of policemen including our police chief. The seminar relied on the Cape Town report and the Criminology journal article. However, it was made clear that a forgery could be detected with a careful analysis of the forgery."

"Interesting," the judge said. He straightened up and looked into the court room.

Then, he looked down at the attorneys and said, "I have to say that I don't much like what I'm hearing, gentlemen. Mr. McNally makes a persuasive case. There are too many odd things that don't match up. Not to mention a witness statement from a man who's legally blind. And, I most certainly don't like the fact that Mr. Tucker's lab found no fingerprints when they first tested the club. I'd have to say that when the deputies removed the club to examine it, it could have been contaminated somehow. Certainly the evidentiary chain was broken at that point. If this were a trial, I'd be inclined to rule against the admission of the newly found prints."

He looked at Leroy and asked, "Did you or anybody else plant fingerprints on that club? That would be a serious offense."

Leroy stood, red faced, with his mouth opened and tried to look at the judge but couldn't. Finally, he mustered up enough courage to say, "No, sir. We just took a magnifying glass and looked all over the club until we found what looked like fingerprints. We immediately took it back to Clarence and asked him to recheck it."

"Sam, you have anything to add?"

The DA stood. "We relied on the statements of the deputies, your Honor. They claimed to have conducted a thorough investigation. We'll take another look, but frankly I can't see anyway Mr. Stanley can be charged with anything right now. I'm embarrassed, Judge."

"Hmm. Yes. You have anything else, Mr. McNally?"

"Considering the break in the evidence chain, your Honor, and the rest of my presentation, I move that Mr. Stanley be released and that the charge against him dismissed."

The judge rapped his gavel and said, "I'm vacating his plea and ordering him released. This hearing was a travesty, Sheriff Tolar. A blind man's affidavit? Fingerprints mysteriously appearing on a club? Sheriff, I think you should take those deputies out behind the woodshed, if you get my meaning."

"I do." The sheriff smiled.

He looked at Caleb and said, "Mr. Stanley, you're free to go. You can still be charged, but if you are, it had better be with credible evidence!" With that, he twirled around in his chair and left the court room shaking his head as if disgusted. Leroy and Clarence Tucker left as well.

Julie and Bonnie Fay stood and clapped lightly. Caleb smiled and waved.

The sheriff patted Caleb on the back and said, "We'll release you from the jail."

"Okay."

Caleb watched Julie and her mother leave the court room. *Well, I knew I didn't do it. Now, Billy Ray and Leroy will have to conduct an investigation with open eyes instead of blinders. As McNally said, everybody in the county, except me, knew about Earnest's coin collection. How in hell did my prints get on that club? I'm sure glad McNally was on the ball. I hate to think what would have happened if he hadn't been. Somebody's sure gonna catch hell about how my fingerprints got on that club.*

The DA asked McNally, "How in the hell did you learn so much about fingerprint forgery. Damn, when did you get appointed to represent Stanley?"

McNally laughed. "To tell you the truth, I got a call yesterday from some guy with a deep voice. He told me everything I talked about just now. I downloaded the reports from the Internet. He had to be an insider to know all he knew. He also said – I didn't talk about it because it would have been speculation – but he said that Billy Ray had access to the evidence room. You might want somebody to check who signed in between the first time and second times Billy Ray and Leroy signed in. Considering Billy Ray's ambition to become sheriff, he could have planted the prints before he and Leroy signed the club out for a second look."

"That'd be a criminal offense."

"Yep."

"Damn. Well, I guess you earned your fee today," the DA said.

"No fee on this one. I owed the Chief one. "

Caleb smiled to himself when he heard the DA and McNally talking. *Glow's been at it again. Looking after his project. Be damned. Couldn't have been me talking to myself that time.*

He thanked McNally for an excellent presentation and shook his hand. He turned to the sheriff and asked, "I wonder how this will play in your deputy's political plan to be the sheriff?"

"He'll do what the media calls, spinning it, to make it sound like the judge turned loose a dangerous criminal and I let 'im. Good luck to you." He shook Caleb's hand and gave him a pat on the back. "Better get on out there." He gestured to the door out of the courtroom where the reporters waited. "They're waiting for you. Wanting to hear your side of things. I imagine by now Billy Ray has told them how corrupt our judicial system is for turning you lose." He and McNally laughed.

"I'll go with you," McNally said.

So, they walked out to encounter the hungry reporters. Indeed, they had finished with Billy Ray and Leroy who were walking away. Out of the corner of his eyes, Caleb saw the sheriff slip past as the reporters gathered around them.

"Sir, the sheriff's chief deputy claims you were let go on a technicality. Did you kill those people?" a reporter asked.

He told them no with a rebuttal of the allegation. Afterward, he let McNally carry the rest of the interview. He explained how there was no evidence to support the charge against Caleb in the first place, the mostly blind witness, the worthless jewelry and fingerprints that somehow got onto the club after Caleb had been arrested and fingerprinted two times, one set of which were still missing. If the missing set had been transferred to the club, they would have looked smudged.

"Legally there was simply no case against Mr. Stanley and the judge vacated his plea. Let's face it, the deputy sheriff, Billy Ray Owens, did a sloppy job putting the case together. Not surprising because there was no case against Mr. Stanley in the first place. Billy Ray doesn't want to admit that, but that's the bottom line. There was no technicality. There was simply no evidence. Big difference."

McNally also hinted that somehow the missing set of prints ended up on the club. When asked who might have done it, he declined to answer. "I have no idea. That's the job of the sheriff's department to track that down."

They asked Caleb more about his background in Marshalltown and his time in CA. They got into the electrical work he'd been doing for shops around town; his camp by the river and his work for people along the road into town.

The interview took almost an hour. Then, it was over. McNally went back to his office and Caleb signed his release at the sheriff's office and headed out of town.

# Chapter 19

As Caleb walked along the park road out of town, he decided that Billy Ray most likely did transfer his fingerprints from the set he'd given when arrested, to the club or at least tried to. Smudged prints were the result. Maybe he killed the Walters. He immediately admonished himself.

*You're doing what the judge accused McNally of doing, engaging in speculative imagination. Would Billy Ray have been so aggressive if he had killed them? Looks like he would have been afraid of getting found out. On the other hand, he wanted publicity for bringing in the killer. Who knows? I'm free and I doubt he'll come up with anything new that'd tie me to the murders. The gold coins are the only things that'd do it and whoever has those won't want to give them up to help Billy Ray's political career, assuming he knows who has them. Hmm, assuming he doesn't have them himself.*

His thoughts drifted to Julie and Bonnie Fae and another dish of their peach cobbler. A cup of coffee would top it off. *I guess I can stop at their house. They were at the hearing. I'll thank them for supporting me. Maybe they'll take pity on me and offer me a slice of pie and a cup of coffee.*

*Damn, I feel good. Like somebody's stopped beating me.* He never once thought about his hemlock stew.

He passed Red's conglomerate of stores. Lots of traffic. The man has a gold mine.

Soon, he came to Julie's home. She was in the garage workshop, slaving away over her workbench. The shelves behind her brimmed with her art and crafts. He had turned into the driveway, but hesitated.

She's probably getting an order ready. Better if I go on.

As he turned, he heard her call, "Caleb."

He stopped and saw that she'd removed her apron, had walked out of the garage and was walking toward him. He turned to meet her.

"I'm glad you stopped," she said. "Your bike is ready." She gestured toward the garage where it leaned against one wall. "Phone too. It's in the house. Come on in, I'll get it for you."

With that, she hurried inside. He followed her in. Bonnie Fae was at work in the dining room, completing the table settings. A pie sat on a platter on a side board. He couldn't see what kind but knew it'd be delicious and wished he could have a piece.

"Caleb," Bonnie Fae called to him and came out of the dining room. "We were so happy the judge let you go. We knew it couldn't have been you."

He thanked her. They exchanged thoughts about the fiasco while waiting for Julie with the phone. She asked what he thought about the fingerprints that suddenly appeared on the club.

"I don't know, but if I had to guess, I'd say Billy Ray and Leroy were up to their eyeballs in it. Another thing that bothered me but nobody brought it up was the club itself. They found it in the junk yard where they assumed I had been camping. I wonder where they actually found it."

That puzzled Bonnie Fae as well. "That might have been important."

"I'd say, unless they found it in the Walter's front yard. The real killer could have thrown it down there. Even then, they should have disclosed that."

Bonnie Fae agreed.

Julia appeared. "Here," she said and handed Caleb the cell phone.

"I'll resume paying you for the use," he said.

She pointed into the dining room. "Hasn't Mama done a great job? Red is bringing the New York guy, Louie, to dinner tonight. He's acting as Red's representative. The catalogue is ready and Red is ready to launch our Internet campaign. Well Louie is ready. He's running things for us. We're listing with Amazon.com. I've lined up half a dozen ladies to help with orders. They were in my class at Red's."

"I'm impressed. I think you will be a big success," Caleb said. "And, the dining room looks splendid. I wish you a great evening."

No coffee and cobbler today, he thought.

He said his goodbyes and got the bike from the garage. As he rolled down the driveway, he suddenly remembered that he had no food in the cave. He'd thrown everything away before he turned himself in. So, instead of biking to the cave, he went the other direction, toward town. However, Red's convenience store came up first so he stopped there for what he needed.

He was thankful Red was not in sight. He had nothing against the man. He just didn't want to see the guy who had apparently beat him out. *Come on, there was never a competition. I was only a spectator.*

Driving back, with Red on his mind, he tried not to dwell on the party Julie was having that evening but when he did, he always ended up congratulating all of them in his thoughts for doing what they were doing. And, if Julie and Red ended up in a relationship – hell, they may already be in one – so be it.

*Just another one of my stupid errors of judgment. Proves I was right to come here with my hemlock.*

He hid the bike in the woods and went inside the cave. It was cool, unlike the hot and humid outside. After stowing the food he'd bought, he checked his bag of hemlock. *It's about time*, he thought. *Hell, I don't know why I bought food.*

But, he was hungry. He made himself a cheese sandwich, popped the cap of the bottle of beer he'd bought and sat down on his campfire log to eat and drink. It was still cool and tasted great. It was the first he'd had since he got there.

He interrupted his dinner long enough to turn on the radio he'd rigged up to a classical station. It was loud enough to hear outside. Shostakovich's Second Waltz was filling the air with beautiful sounds. He always liked the melody of the waltz. It was calming.

Glow wasn't around. That pleased him as well. Even though it was his free will that got him into the messes he'd gotten into, he couldn't help but think that Glow might have been an influencing factor.

"Even so," he said out loud, "I've had an adventure or two. First excitement I've had in years. Not to mention, the thought of being with Julie, as stupid as it was. It made me feel like a man. Good way to end it all."

He went back inside the cave for the bag of hemlock and to fill the can sitting beside it with water.  He turned off the radio. That done, he lit a camp fire and put the can of water on it. Then, he sat on his log to watch for the curl of steam that would come as the water heated up.

"Always glad to see a man with the courage of his convictions," Glow suddenly said.

Caleb didn't bother to look around. "I thought you had gone back to your energy family."

"No, just flitting about the world, checking on things. Not much has changed. Certainly not for the better."

"I'm not in jail."

"Well, Caleb, I knew you wouldn't be. Billy Ray and his faithful sidekick, Leroy, aren't smart enough to put together a convincing frame. Trying to transfer your fingerprints from the fingerprint card to the club like they did had to be stupid. Maybe they could have done it if they'd had practice, but not on their first attempt. That's why they were smudged."

"You might have told me."

"I wasn't sure about the free wills of the other participants. I had to let things unfold as they would."

Caleb poked at his fire. "Yeah. Well, I'm out of jail and I'm not going back. I don't have any electrical work as far as I know. And, the Walters are dead. So, the number of folks I was working for has dropped. In reality, that only leaves Julie and her mother and who knows what they'll be needing? Couple of others but they never had much work. For certain, I can't count on the shotgun lady for anything but buckshot."

"Good one Caleb. I understand Julie is about to expand her business. She'll be able to hire a handy man to help with her chores. Maybe you could apply."

"Yep." He poked at the fire again and saw the first curls of steam floating out of the can of water. "I doubt it. I do have to figure out what to do however. With Red in the picture, I imagine my days of helping Julie and her mother will be numbered."

"I think I'll tell you about Red," Glow said. "Red is the oldest of three children. His father and mother are dead ... like yours. His father started the convenience store and service station. He was a kind of small town go-getter, always busy, always doing something. He and his wife owned over two hundred acres about three miles from here. When catfish became popular, he put in catfish ponds. When processors wanted more chicken, he build chicken houses. And, he always had a herd of cattle on his pastures."

"Damn," Caleb interrupted. "He's got what it takes. Hell, Julia would be smart if she tied up with him."

"Not for me to say, Caleb. Anyway, his wife tended to the farm when he got busy with the store. Then, she died. Red worked at the store to help out. He had managed to get a degree from the local junior college which was all he needed.

"His brother and sister got married out of high school and moved away to work but Red stayed behind. He liked working at the store and liked Marshalltown, just like you do."

"Did." Caleb wasn't so sure after the hassling he'd been getting from Billy Ray.

"Right. Did."

"After the old man died, they got together and divided things up. Red got the store, some money and the catfish ponds. His brother got the chicken barns. The sister ended up with the old house and the cattle. All are doing well. Red expanded the store as you probably figured out. Added the restaurant and craft store."

"Yeah. A real success story, all of them."

"Don't be grumpy, Caleb."

"You're right." He looked around. "Hell, I'm right. Probably talking to myself again." He shrugged and said, "Julie was never there for me anyway. First, she was married. May still be for all I know. Now, Red pops up. Well, he has always been there. I just didn't know about him. I think my misguided expectations fall into the category of ignorance is bliss."

"Could be."

"What is that supposed to mean? Could be."

"As one of the colorful characters from years ago once said, 'it ain't over till the fat lady sings.' I think another one was, 'it ain't over till it's over.'"

"You're talking about Julie and Red."

"Very perceptive, Caleb. It seems to me you're throwing in the towel – there I've used another one of your colorful sayings – way early. I guess you aren't up to a little competition. In fact, you don't even know if there is competition."

"I assumed. Hell, I'm not that stupid. Two plus two still equals four. I don't need to wait around for somebody to tell me that. What the hell do I have to compete with?"

"Not much. That's true. It just seemed to me that a man of your intelligence and discipline, wouldn't quit early but I guess I was wrong. You'd better put your hemlock in the water and let it simmer some before eating it. I'll write that ending to my project. He gave up without trying."

"Yeah, yeah." Caleb sighed. He poked at the fire again but this time, he shoved the glowing embers to one side of the can. "You know something. Don't you," he said. "I'll sleep on my decision tonight."

"I agree, Caleb. It has little to do with me, but why rush something that can be changed once it's done."

Caleb nodded. He spread the ashes of his fire and turned the can over to extinguish what was left of the embers. He took his bag of hemlock back into the cave. *I don' know why I'm listening to something I can't see, but it makes sense. Maybe I don't want to end it all just yet. Maybe I was looking for an excuse not to.*

He lay down on his bed and closed his eyes. Actually, he was very sleepy. He hadn't slept much in the jail cell and the stress of being in the courtroom, facing being thrown back into the cell, had left him worn out.

*Probably why I got out my hemlock in the first place. I should have waited until I was rested. That's rule number one. Never make important decisions when you're tired unless it's an emergency.*

But, he saw no reason he'd change his mind after a night's sleep and he fell asleep with that thought.

Later, he heard a whisper saying, "I think I hear somebody outside." It was Glow whispering.

Caleb shook his head in disbelief. I can't believe it. I'm waking myself up now. Even so, he got out of bed and peeped through a hole in the cave's wall to look outside.

There was somebody outside. Two men it seemed. Two flashlights cut through the moonlit night occasionally lighting up both men. Billy Ray and Leroy!

"He ain't here, Billy Ray," Leroy complained. "'N he aint at Julie Howard's neither. Red 's at her house, eatin' I reckon. For all you know, she's sleeping with Red. Ain't never slept with the guy from California you got a hard on for."

"Fuck off, Leroy. Keep looking. If he ain't at her house, he's got to be 'round here some 'ers."

"Who knows where he is."

"Sooner or later, he's gonna be here 'n I'll get the bastard."

"What'd he do to you? Hell, he didn't say a word in court. The judge let 'im go."

"They were all in it together. They wanted to let 'im go. The DA didn't say shit and the sheriff, lilly livered bastard, barely opened his mouth. And the fuckin' judge sat there and agreed with everything they said. The shoved my nose in that pervert's shit!"

"You scare me sometimes, Billy Ray."

"Scare you! I know a criminal when I see one. When I'll catch up with 'im, I'm going to kick his ass all the way back to California with the rest of the fruits."

"Shit for brains. That's what your problem is, Billy Ray. You got shit for brains."

"Shut the fuck up and keep looking. He's hiding 'round here someplace. Scared shitless, I reckon."

"He ain't looked scared yet, Billy Ray. And he ain't looked like no fruit to me."

"You don't know how to look."

Leroy cursed.

They spent a few more minutes stalking about with their flashlights before Leroy said, "I'm goin' home Billy Ray. Ain't nobody here. You can wander 'round here all night if you want to. See you tomorrow." He walked toward the trail to the road.

A few seconds later, Billy Ray cursed and followed.

"I thought you'd want to know that," Glow said.

"Yeah. I'm the bastard's obsession."

"And, logic goes out the window with obsessions," Glow replied.

"Yep."

Caleb climbed back in bed. He wondered if they'd be back another night. Billy Ray said he would. *If it's not one thing, it's another. I hope I feel better in the morning.*

He wondered why he thought that. In the past, he often hoped
he wouldn't wake up for the morning. Now I want to wake up
feeling better. What the hell?

*****

As they usually did, birds woke him the next morning, singing in the
trees around the rock that housed his cave. He woke surprisingly
fresh, considering his ordeal and his disappointment of the prior day.
When he went outside, two rabbits sniffed at his camp fire pit as if
searching for any tidbit that may be edible. They hopped away in a
flash when Caleb came in sight. Two squirrels chattered and
watched from a small oak nearby. The cool morning air had a hint of
some bloom in it. The gentle wash of the river rolled up the slope to
his camp site.

He turned on the radio to add to nature's music and cooked
himself a bacon and egg sandwich and that, with two cups of coffee,
was his breakfast.

After clean up, he found himself wondering what he was
going to do that day. There was no thought of hemlock stew. He also
pondered what Billy Ray may do next.

He's obviously slightly deranged. Thinks the world is against
him and I'm leading the charge. I don't see any hope for him. I don't
see how he could be elected to anything. I don't even see how he can
hold the job he has.

With nothing better to do, he cleaned up his camp site and
made sure his cave entrance was well concealed with brush and
briars. Then, he sat down on his log and tried to figure out what to
do next. Nothing came to mind.

# Chapter 20

Caleb's phone rang as he sat there, staring at the river. It was Julie, a surprise because there was no reason to call. Unless she wanted him to do something.

Caleb," she said.

"Yes," he answered. From her tone, Caleb decided she didn't sound happy. He didn't want to think she was calling with bad news. Bad news was all he'd been getting and he didn't want any more. But, she obviously had some.

"Odom called me a while ago. He asked if I'd call you. He said as soon as the judge had made his decision yesterday, Billy Ray and Leroy were running all over town talking about how you were let loose on a technicality even though the club used to kill the Walters had your finger prints on it. For the most part, they talked to every car repair shop in town and threatened to spread the word if anyone of them hired you to do any work."

"He just can't let it go."

"No. He claims the judge and DA were in on it because they were too lazy to prosecute you and the sheriff didn't mind because he was trying to keep his budget low for the County Supervisors."

"The newspaper and television reports should clear that up. McNally did a good job of telling the reporters what really happened. "

"The story was on television news last night. It was a good story. Mama and me watched it on the late news. The reporter said you'd been falsely charged based on poor investigative work. He didn't name anybody."

"I wish I could have seen it. How'd the dinner turn out?"

"Me and Red liked what the guy from New York was saying about sales. He thinks we are going to be busy. I'm so excited. I think selling on Amazon.com is going to be great. Red does too."

He congratulated her. Somehow the sting from the day before had abated. Hearing her talk about Red again didn't send his thoughts into a hemlock spin.

"Maybe the newspaper reports will help. I guess they come out today," he said.

"Probably. He's still going on about you being a pervert, which nobody believes, but Billy Ray's family, as sorry as most of them are, have lots of kin folks in the county. Odom, and the others, are worried that they'll find somebody else to do their work."

"So, Odom doesn't want me coming by. Is that about it? And, Odom asked you to tell me."

She agreed. "But," she said, "Odom doesn't like it. So, what he said was he'll call you if he had a really bad problem. You could work on it on Saturday or Sunday at the shop. The shop is closed those days so if you kept the doors closed, nobody would know you were in there. If anybody knocked, you could ignore it."

Caleb had to laugh. "What a bad joke. Everybody is afraid of a bully who wants to be sheriff."

"Odom is worried he might win. That's what worries them all. If they let you work like you've been doing, and Billy Ray wins, they're afraid he'll make life hell for them."

"What the hell can he do?" Caleb asked.

"Nobody knows, but they're afraid."

"Yeah. I can't say I blame them.  So, it looks like I'm kind of out of business. Have to sneak in through the back door to work." He laughed again. "That's the damnedest thing I've ever run across ... well except for my ex-wife's carryings on. That will always be at the top of my list."

He had let Julie and Bonnie Fae know about Myrna's doings during a weak moment when he was at their house one night.

"I don't doubt it," she said.

"I'll call him. The election will be coming up in a couple of months. When that's over, assuming the folks around here do the right thing, I expect Billy Ray will be out of a job. My feeling is that the sheriff is only keeping him on till the election is over."

"I think you're right. That's what I'm hearing privately from people I know. Except for relatives and friends of relatives, I don't think anybody would pour water on Billy Ray if they came by and he was on fire," Julia said.

"I sure as hell wouldn't. I just wonder what he's planning to do to overcome the sheriff's coup the other week. The sheriff made a fool out of him during that so-called press conference."

"I saw it. It was priceless! Yesterday wasn't bad either. The judge telling the sheriff to take both deputies behind the woodshed. That was on the news last night. We laughed when they reported it."

"I think Billy Ray would have a hard time winning any election right now, no matter how many kin folks he has voting for him," Caleb said.

She agreed. "I feel bad for you Caleb. You've had a lot of trouble. You don't need more. Especially the stuff Billy Ray's throwing at you."

He agreed and thanked her for calling. By then, everybody in town probably knew of his California problems, at least some of them. The only thing he hadn't told anybody was about why he'd really returned to Marshalltown to cook his hemlock stew.

When their phone call ended, he thought about his bag of hemlock, but only in passing and really with a chuckle. Glow had been right, dangling his innuendo to make him think. Just then, his thoughts were primarily focused on Billy Ray. What to do about his scurrilous campaign. No way in hell was he going to let some little disturbed shit like Billy Ray push him around.

*****

So, he decided to call Odom to see how he could work or if he could. If he couldn't, that didn't leave him with many options.

He heard a voice, Glow's. "One step at a time, Caleb."

"Yep. I'm catching on."

When Odom heard Caleb's voice, he began cursing. "I'm telling you, Caleb, we're sick and tired of that little shit. Hell, we watch TV and we read the damn newspapers. Billy Ray's boy said all you did was stop him from getting snake bit. The doctors said nothing had happened to the boy. Why in the hell can't he let it go? We don't mind if he runs for sheriff. Sure as hell, I ain't voting for 'im."

"He seems to think the road to the sheriff's chair runs right through me."

"He's running all over town bitching about a technicality that got you out of jail. That's pure horse shit! The judge ain't no fool. There was no case. The DA agreed. The sheriff agreed. Somebody tried to frame you and most of us kind of figure who that was. He even messed that up. I can put up with a lot of shit but when the shit takes bread off my table, I draw the line. Some of us think it'd be a good idea to do what the judge told the sheriff. Take the little bastard out behind the woodshed and kick some sense into his thick skull."

Caleb agreed. "I'm tired of it. Just when I thought I had something worthwhile to do, he stops that. All I know are electrical systems. It's all I've ever done."

Before his arrest, he had been thinking about getting an apartment in town and becoming a consultant on electrical problems. There were lots of small towns around Marshalltown and some of them had small automotive repair shops. Could have been enough work for him to make a living without shoveling cow shit, he had thought ruefully.

Odom continued, "We know that, Caleb and we're gonna work around Billy Ray for now. The election's coming up. Ain't no way on God's earth he can win. He ain't got that many kin folks. So, I'll tell you what I'm gonna do. It's a pain in the ass, but it'll keep Billy Ray off my back and keep my customers happy. After the election, if there is a God, the sheriff'll kick his ass out and we can have some peace."

Caleb agreed with that.

Odom went on to say that folks around town liked members of law enforcement they knew. Now and then one or the other of them might stumble over the line and want somebody to look the other way, but they were only willing to bend over so far to get somebody like that. Billy Ray crossed the line when he began to interfere with their business.

"Human nature," Caleb said.

Odom told Caleb he'd leave cars with problems in the first and second bays, if he had more than one or if another shop had one. There'd be notes on the car's dash boards, describing the problems.

"I shut my doors around six. You can come by any time after that. Wait till you see my old truck pull out. The key to the door 'll be under the bucket by the back door. I've told the Chief you'll be working here at night so you won't get hassled. None of us believe Billy Ray's thought about you working nights. He doesn't think that far ahead of his next shithouse stop."

And, that's how Caleb kept working. New meaning to the expression, shade tree mechanic, he thought.

During the day, he did his run along the gravel road to see if anybody needed anything done. The shotgun lady was not outside and he didn't knock on her door. Julie wasn't in her garage and her truck was gone so he didn't stop there either. Bonnie Fae had made it clear the first time he'd stopped that Julie was in charge of what needed to be done. Also, he figured if Julie needed help, she could call. People at the two other houses he'd worked for said they were caught up. One house did give him a left over pork chop from the prior night's dinner. He took it and ate it for his supper.

*****

That night, he rolled up on his bike a few minutes before six half a block away and waited until Odom drove away. He parked in back of the shop, out of sight, got the key and went to work.

The truck he opened up first had a bad ignition system and probably should have been replaced but Caleb didn't know where a parts shop was and even if he did, the truck was so old, they'd probably have to order the part anyway. So, he took it apart and repaired it. The other one had an alternator problem that he was also able to repair. He'd finished by a little before nine and was back at his cave by nine thirty.

Billy Ray didn't show up or if he had, he'd come and gone by the time Caleb got back.

The next day was a repeat of the prior day except that Julie was working in her garage so he pulled up and asked if she needed help.

"I probably do, Caleb, but I've been so busy I haven't had time to think. Red's got Mama working in the shop. He's shorthanded. I'm trying to get an order together. I've got women working, making more, but so far what they'd done doesn't satisfy me." She looked behind her as if to check on what needed to be done in the garage. "You could feed and water the chickens. Check for eggs. If you find any, leave them in the basket on the back porch."

She was getting ready to go to the shop and left as Caleb began his task.

There was only one truck in the shop that evening. It had a solenoid problem, an intermittent one that every mechanic dreaded. They were hard to figure out. But, Caleb had seen them all in his time so he knew right away what it was and had it repaired within the hour.

As he finished, he heard the door open behind him. It was the Chief.

"Odom said you'd be working," he said. "Thought I'd stop by on my way home and see how you're getting on."

Caleb said he'd recovered from his night in jail and the trauma of being charged with a crime he didn't do.

"We hated it, me and Ben." Ben was the sheriff's first name, Caleb recalled. "But we had to see it through. With a guy like Billy Ray looking at everything we do, we didn't want to give him anything to go public with. Not with an election coming up."

"Yeah. Any luck finding out who killed them?"

"Ben got a list of most of the coins from their children and sent it out to every coin dealer within two hundred miles of here. Based on the feedback, he figures they were worth in the neighborhood of a hundred thousand dollars."

"That's pretty good."

The chief continued. "Right. He also put notices in the coin quarterly and in a couple of coin newsletters. Just today, he got a call from a NY collector who says he bought one of the stolen coins from a dealer in Mobile."

"I guess he called the dealer."

The chief shook his head, yes. "The dealer said a rough looking woman sold it to him with full documentation but it was definitely one of Earnest's. We figure the killer found the dealer on the Internet and drove it over. He most likely took some of Earnest's papers and modified them to show a new owner."

"Computers make it pretty easy to do these days."

"I think so. One complication. A foreign guy was in the dealer's store haggling over prices when the woman came in. She knew a little about value too. Must have done some Internet research. She had other coins she and the dealer couldn't agree on and when she left, the foreign guy was waiting outside. They haggled some more, but the dealer said it looked like they made a deal."

"No way to trace that."

"No. A dealer in Houston also called. Said a woman tried to sell him some of the coins a couple of days before the Mobile exchange. Sounded like the same woman. They couldn't reach an agreement. Could be the foreign guy bought the lot."

"Damn. End of the investigation, if that happened."

"That's about what Ben said."

Caleb agreed. "What's he going to do?"

"He's sending somebody to Mobile to get a better description. Taking pictures too."

"Rough looking woman. Can't be Billy Ray and Leroy?"

The chief nodded. "Ben said the same thing. Could be a relative, or wife but which one. The guy he sends will take pictures of both wives. We're probably pissing in the wind, but it's the only lead we have. Ben figures Billy Ray might 've needed some campaign money. Figured to kill two birds with one stone. Kill the Walters, frame you and get some money to boot."

"I'd like to see that son of a bitch in jail."

"Lots of us feel that way."

He said goodbye.

Caleb locked up and left. It was dark and he was relieved that the bike's light worked, as small as it was. It let people know he was in the road and gave him just enough light to avoid potholes.

*****

Driving past Red's, he saw Julie's truck parked out front. Through the windows, he saw her inside, talking with Red, both smiling. Bonnie Fae stood watching a few feet away.

Caught up with her shipment, he thought and drove on. May be time for me to give her back her phone. The less I see her, the better off I'll be. I have enough money to buy a cheap phone from Wal-Mart.

He held up at the entrance to the trail, turned off the bike's light and pushed it along the trail. Moon light through the canopy provided enough light. He stopping along the way to listen for voices, Billy Ray's and Leroy's. He didn't hear anything so he hurried along.

At the end of the trail he stopped to check again. Thought I heard something. The camp site was fairly well lit. He couldn't see anything. Probably a wild animal. Even so, he turned on the bicycle light and shinned it around. Not a thing.

He rolled the bicycle into its hiding place in the woods and turned back toward the fire pit and the cave.

# Chapter 21

He was thinking of the beer he had in the cool water of the little stream that poured out of his cave and was headed that way when he heard a click and suddenly a light hit him in the face, half blinding him. He put his hand over his eyes and looked in the direction of the light. He knew before he did who it was. It had to be Billy Ray returning for his pound of flesh.

Sure enough, it was Billy Ray shinning a flash light at him. He wore dungarees and boots. His shirt was tight, showing his muscles which he flexed when talking. "So, you finally made it. I was here before looking for you. I reckon you been shacking up with the Cochran nut case?" Caleb knew he was talking about Alma, the woman he called the shotgun lady.

He opened his mouth to reply but the deputy continued. "Old Red beat you out of Julie's panties, did he? Must have been hard to take. Old Red sleeping with your woman."

"She's not my woman, Billy Ray. Never has been. I just did some work for her ... for food."

"Yeah, and you ate dinner with 'em and slept with her. Maybe both of 'em for all I know. They stuck up for you in court."

"You're full of shit! I think you've got a loose screw. Face facts. Who in the hell would sleep with me. I'm a homeless bum, working for food."

"Doing electrical work now. Well, were doing electrical work. Not anymore. People got wise to you. Thanks to me." He laughed sarcastically.

Caleb decided not to give an answer to that claim. "What do you want? You had your shot in court. The judge ruled against you. And you couldn't get me for hitting you on the head with a rock. Hell, I wasn't there. All I've ever done to you is save your boy from getting bit by some water moccasins. A normal person would be kissing my ass."

"You saying I'm not normal!"

"If the shoe fits, wear it."

With that, Billy Ray snarled and began walking toward Caleb, angling to cut off the trail escape. As he did, he pulled one of those small baseball bats from behind his back and began to wave it about. He turned off the flash light and dropped it on the ground. There was plenty of moonlight.

The son of a bitch plans to kill me with that thing. I need a plan. I could try to outrun the bastard but no way can I get to the trail first. Besides, he may have a gun. An idea flashed into his thoughts, a long shot, but the only shot that might work. He took a step toward the deputy.

"You don't have on your uniform, Billy Ray. That must mean you plan this to be man to man. How do you know I won't kick your ass."

He laughed. "No California fruit's gonna kick my ass." He flexed his muscles. "I plan for this to be your one way ticket out of town … by river. I think you'll leave a note confessing how you killed the Walters. The voters will love that."

"Oh, you can write. Be damned." All the time Caleb talked, he moved but instead of moving toward the deputy, he began an angle more toward the river.

"You slime ball. I'm gonna love watching you squirm when I start breaking your legs. I'm not gonna kill you right away. I want you to suffer and suffer. I want you to beg me to die. You got it? Beg me to die." He moved toward Caleb.

"Well, you're gonna have a long time to wait. You know what they say about people waiting for hell to freeze over?" *He's close now. Damn, I have just one chance. I blow it and I'll be in pain till I die.*

Billy Ray grinned and gave out a grunt and swung the little bat. As he began his swing forward, Caleb jumped up the six inches between his arm reach and the limb of the oak tree beside him, where his angled retreat had taken him. Billy Ray's swing was aimed at Caleb knees but by the time the bat got to where they had been, they weren't there anymore. They were swinging out directly at Billy Ray's head. The bat hit the trunk of the oak and shattered. The impact sent electric waves up the deputy's arms, paralyzing them for a few seconds. As that was happening, Caleb's shoes were hitting the beefy man squarely in the face, knocking him backward.

When Billy Ray hit the ground, the remaining stub of the bat flew out of his hand. Though stunned, the deputy got to his knees and reached behind his back for his automatic. He didn't find it, but unsteady on his feet, he lowered his head and charged Caleb like a water buffalo. Caleb sidestepped most of the charge but Billy Ray's shoulder caught him in the stomach and pushed him to one side.

The deputy twirled around, went into a crouch and began swinging. He unleashed a big right hand that grazed Caleb forehead, then a left that caught him on the shoulder. He dropped back into a crouch and did a little bob and weave as he readied himself for another go but Caleb was ready for him by then. He stepped forward to get inside his wild swings and began jabbing, lefts and rights to the man's face.

When that happened, Billy Ray staggered back and reached back again for his gun, but Caleb stayed close and continued to sting him with lefts and rights, keeping the shorter man off balance. When Billy Ray finally brought his gun around, Caleb hit him as hard as he could with his left fist. The blow knocked the deputy to his knees still clutching his weapon, but by then dangling in his hand. He shook his head but it did no good. Everything was covered in clouds.

Caleb closed in and hit him with a right hand that sent Billy Ray sideways, his jaw hanging. The gun dropped to the ground with the deputy on top of it, unconscious.

"I don't guess I'll be begging," he said over the prone figure.

Just then, Leroy appeared. In his hand was an automatic and it was aimed at Caleb.

*Shit!*

Unlike Billy Ray, Leroy was wearing his uniform. "I can shoot you. It's what he would have wanted." He gestured with his head at Billy Ray. "He'll say you attacked him and I had to back him up."

Caleb looked down at Billy Ray, searching the ground for the man's automatic to see if he had a chance to get it before Leroy could shoot him. It wasn't in sight.

"You know that's a lie," Caleb said. "You must have heard everything he said."

"I did but I forget things. But I'm going to tell you something about Billy Ray."

He proceeded to tell Caleb the reason Billy Ray acted like he did.

When Billy Ray was in high school, he was too short to play basketball and too slow, not to mention small, to play football. He couldn't hit a curve and he backed away from anything inside. So, every time he tried out for anything, he was turned down. The center of the basketball team at the time, witnessed one of his try-outs and said, "Billy Ray is so damned short, all he does is smell my farts."

"Everybody had a good laugh at that. Well everybody except Billy Ray. He was humiliated."

As things went, Leroy went on to say, the quip was shortened to, "Billy Ray is short; he smells farts. The cheerleaders used it when practicing and always got big laughs, as crude as it was. Of course, the principal told them to quit and they did ... while he was around. But it stuck and Billy Ray had to live with it the whole time he was in school. Not only that, no girl would be seen dead with him. He was like something that smelled bad."

"He hasn't improved," Caleb said.

"Maybe. Anyway, I was his only friend. After graduation, which Billy Ray didn't attend, he went to the junior college for one semester. Mostly, he spent his time in the gym, lifting weights."

Caleb shook his head. "I guess he still does, lift weights. He looks muscle bound."

"He does but he won't quit. Anyway, his uncle ran for sheriff and won. Billy Ray's dad asked him to hire his son as a deputy which he did. And, that's where BR has been ever since."

At a party, Leroy told him, where everybody was drinking beer and carrying on, Earnestine, BR's wife, got loaded and let him take her to bed.

"Well, wouldn't you know it, he knocked her up and they had to get married and still are. It's not much of a marriage, but she doesn't have any place to go and BR is still on everybody's to-be-avoided list. The boy they had is the one you rescued. Hell, we all know you didn't do a damn thing to the boy. BR just has a thing for queers. God, he goes crazy when he hears about one."

"I'm not one. Why'd you try to frame me for the Walter's murders?"

"We didn't as far as I know. BR said we should have one more look at the club and we saw the smudged fingerprints."

"Did you plant the club in the junk yard? Had to be you. Few others knew I had slept there."

Leroy's face took on a puzzled look. "Uh, well, we figured if you did it, you'd hide the club where you camped, the junk yard. That's why we looked there for the club."

"Bull shit. You hid it there."

Leroy shook his head and looked sheepish but said nothing.

*They planted it,* Caleb thought, but let it go. Leroy obviously didn't want to admit to anything that could get him fired. *Of course, Billy Ray may have done the fingerprint transfer on his own and possibly planted the club or, as more likely, Leroy is lying to cover his ass.*

Another possibility is that Billy got a club, smeared the Walters blood on it and planted it. Who knows? At least I'm not on the hook anymore for their murders.

"He needs counseling bad," Caleb said. "I don't think he's fit, mentally, to be in any kind of law enforcement. He's too unstable. And sure as hell, he should never be sheriff. I hate to think what shambles he'd make of the office."

Leroy shook his head but didn't say anything. From the look on his face, Caleb figured he agreed.

Caleb pointed at the moaning figure on the ground in front of him and said, "Well, I guess you'd better get your friend home. He'll probably have at least one black eye and maybe a broken jaw, at least cracked. He's not going to be a happy camper."

"Have to call in with a vacation, I reckon."

He picked up the flashlight and put it in his pocket. Then, he bent down and pulled Billy Ray to his feet. The deputy moaned, mumbled curse words and babbled on about "kicking that queer son of a bitches' ass."

Leroy used the flashlight to get him down the lane to his car which he'd parked out of sight. He'd come back for his later. He had told Caleb how he refused to come with Billy Ray, but after he'd gone, he felt he should follow him to the park to make sure he didn't do anything stupid, like shoot Caleb.

Caleb laughed to himself. He would have if I hadn't clobbered him.

When they were well gone, Caleb retreated to the cave and got a beer from the eddy in the stream. He came back to the fire pit, sat on his log bench and drank it to the sounds of something Beethoven composed. The beer tasted good and the music was soothing. And, when the bottle was empty, he climbed in bed.

"Some show, Caleb," Glow said.

"What. I thought you'd gone. Thought maybe I was having a lucid interval. Turning sane."

"Yeah, turning sane. Has a nice ring. No, I was just late getting back. Had to check on the progress of the world, but I got back in time to see you hit your muscular tormentor with that right hand. I'd say you had promise. He'll think twice before he takes you on one-on-one. And Leroy won't be helping. I thought I'd share that with you. He enjoyed seeing you hit him as much as I did."

"Thanks. I'll sleep better. I assume you know about the coins showing up in Mobile."

"Of course."

"Any information you can share with me?"

"Hmm. Looks like the killer needed money. So, he or she killed the Walters to get the coins."

"I figured that!"

"Of course you did. Let me see if … ah, I'll tell you this. All that glitters isn't gold. Run that around your human computer and see what it comes up with."

*What the hell? No need to ask more, it won't tell me. What does that mean? The coins were not real? They were gold, I think. Gold tarnishes over time and doesn't glitter. Is that it? Doesn't make sense. Maybe something else will come to me.*

"That's not much. You could be a little clearer," Caleb said.

"No I can't. I don't get involved in man's free will here or anyplace around your world. I only report on decisions I know will be made, the absolutely logical ones, not the ones left open. Like the world's march toward self-destruction."

"Yeah. Changing the subject are you? You threatened me with that self-destruction thing then left it hanging the last time you threw it at me. Bored me with, I think would be a more accurate assessment," Caleb said.

"Well, you have to admit you have been busy with mundane things, like staying alive."

"And, you bailed me out of a few of those, maybe all. Like your call to my attorney about the two fingerprint articles."

"Well, I had to keep my project going while I was here. In your world, they'd be saying you got lucky," Glow replied.

"Yeah. You keep saying. Good thing for me you weren't recalled while I was midway in one of the mundane things you were talking about. My so called luck would have run out."

"I agree. Else, you'd be getting used to prison drab and gaining weight on prison grub."

"And all the while the rest of the world would be moving on toward self-destruction, right?" Caleb asked sarcastically.

"Ignorance is bliss, Caleb. Isn't that what people say about other people who don't know what they're talking about, like you? Nevertheless, you're actually right. Let me add however that you have the time, and the intellect, to prevent that from happening but to do that, you have to re-harness your discipline. By you, I mean the human race. You'd first have to limit your instinct to procreate or make certain that all humans contribute to the production of whatever you need to support the humans you are creating. And, limiting procreation, I can tell you, will take a stronger will than you have just now."

"No doubt," Caleb agreed.

"Of course, you can have more wars to diminish the numbers who need to be fed. Humans seem to gravitate toward wars and killing each other. I think humans have been taught that there will always be wars and rumors of wars. In other words, wars and the killing that comes with them are part of your history and your future. Wars certainly cut down the number of people who have to be fed. So, humans can keep on procreating."

"After an army goes through, there's not a hell of a lot of decent soil left to grow anything for the survivors. What does that do to your so called theory."

"Not a theory, Caleb. You are right. Even more people die after a war because there's not much to eat for the ones left behind."

"We survive. Humans always come up with something," Caleb said.

"Sure you have. You still kill off millions in the name of one bull shit crusade or another, then find a way to start over. What a waste. Kind of proves my point. Humans don't seem to have to capacity to out think the mistakes of their history. If humans could control their instincts to kill, they wouldn't have to start life over periodically. And that, Caleb, would be an evolutionary step forward for humans. So far I haven't seen it happening. But, who knows, humans may grow too lazy to have more wars. I doubt that will happen, however because your instinct for procreation carries with it the instinct to dominate and, the instinct to dominate inevitably leads to war."

"Come on now, are you saying domination is the fuel for our sex drive?" Caleb scoffed.

"Well, isn't it? Don't you want to dominate the woman you're having sex with?"

Caleb shook his head back and forth as he pondered what he'd just heard. "I ... I don't know. Hell, maybe. Men don't call it domination. We call it possession. Men want to possess the woman. Thinking about it, I guess if we possess a woman, we have to dominate her. Anyway, in my case, I've never given it that much thought. I ... y ... you know, get started and my ... sex part just takes over. By then, it's too late to characterize it as domination or possession. And, it's been a hell of a long time since even that has happened."

"I know. Something you need to remedy by the way. But getting back to the topic on the table, in some of your people that instinct for domination, your so called sex part, spreads from the domination of one woman ... or possession as you prefer to call it, to the domination of lots of people. You must recall enough history to know that. Look at all the men who have gone to go to war to take land that belongs to others and to dominate the people who live on that land. That's a perverse version of your sex drive, the instinct for domination."

"So, our only hope, as you see it is to have wars and kill off people so the rest of us will have enough to eat after we rebuild what the war has destroyed," Caleb said and ended it with a noisy release of air.

"A definite possibility unless wars become too expensive, even for humans giving in to their instinct to dominate. Unfortunately, despots don't think along those lines. Neither do perverse egotists driven to dominate others to prove they're better and stronger. As I said, as things now stand, and most likely will stand, humans are always moving toward self-destruct. After one war ends, there are enough humans on the losing end who live for the opportunity to change the outcome. In effect, they are incubating the next war and the next step toward self-destruction."

"The winners make sure the losers don't get to take that step."

"So far the winners have not been all that successful. That's probably the reason for the phrase out of your Bible about wars and rumors of wars. My logical projection, to give you the result you are hoping for, is that the strong among you, the better armed or the better organized will survive the wars and lead you to a new beginning, a new start. There's always hope that humans will have learned from the mistakes of the last war to avoid those mistakes when they start over. That, Caleb, would also be an evolutionary step forward, one that humans haven't made so far. Only one ever came close to getting that point across and he was killed as you know."

"Yeah. Jesus. People are still waiting for him to come again."

"I know. I don't have an opinion on that coming. I didn't have one on the first. However, I see plenty of pretenders running around, dragging the world toward an unstable future and killing lots of people in the process."

"Our destruction?"

"Yes. The brink of destruction. How does that old song go - you tell me over and over my friend, you don't believe we're on the eve                              of                              destruction."

"I don't. All that stuff's been going on as long as history's been recorded and it hasn't happened yet. Humans are pretty damn quick to make adjustments when their existences are on the line."

"Free will, Caleb. For your sake, I hope you're right. I was sent here to see if I could make a projection. I'm almost ready."

"That means you're almost ready for a recall."

"Yep. I'm already there. Just waiting for the end of my personal project."

"Me?"

"You."

Caleb fell asleep on that.

# Chapter 22

The next morning Caleb turned on the music to compete with the songs the birds sang, made his breakfast and set out for town. Half way along Odom called to tell him he had one truck that needed looking at that evening. Also, he'd been talking to friends in other shops, telling them what he was doing. "They want to join in. I gave them your number."

Caleb thanked him and drove on to town. He bought a cheap cell phone from Wal-Mart so he could give Julie's back, leaving only the bike. He'd offer to buy it when he returned the phone. That way, they'd be completely at arms-length.

While he was in town, one of the shop owners Odom spoke about called him. He had a car for Caleb to look at. "Hell, I don't mind if you come on down now. I ain't afraid of that little squirt. I'd as soon knock him on his ass as look at him."

Caleb had done work for the shop owner before. The guy was scrawny, probably weighed less than 150 but there he was puffing out his chest, ready to take on the deputy who outweighed him by at least fifty pounds and plenty of muscles.

Caleb drove down for a look at the old car, twenty years old. The starter was bad, had worn parts and a wire that separated when the car ran awhile. Rather than try and fix it, he recommended a new starter which the parts shop had in stock.

"I'll call you next time I need help," the owner told him. "Billy Ray can kiss my ass."

*I doubt Billy Ray will be doing much of anything for a few days,* Caleb thought as he mounted his bike for the ride back to his cave.

He'd had stopped by a couple of houses on the way in. Neither had any work for him. Julie was working in the garage and didn't look up when he passed. He figured she was busy and didn't stop. *Push comes to shove, Bonnie Fae can do the chores.*

He did stop on his return. The truck was gone but Bonnie Fae was at home. After they exchanged greetings at the front door, he returned Charlie's cell phone. "Got one from Wal-Mart," he said and showed her.

She didn't protest, just took it for granted, that he would be returning it one day.

"I'd like to buy the bike, if Julie wants to sell it. Ask her when she gets home."

She would.

"You haven't been by in a while," she said.

"I know you all have been busy with Red, getting crafts to him for your catalogue sales, your Internet venture. That has to be a great move. You'll profit from it."

"We have already to a certain extent. It's been hectic. Julie now has three women who can make decent crafts. That takes a load off her. Right now, the store has a surplus but Red thinks sales'll take off and that surplus will disappear in a hurry when the Internet takes hold."

Caleb congratulated them and wished them well. He turned to leave.

"You going without coffee and pie," she said. "Unless you don't like my pie."

He smiled. "I love your pie, but I didn't want to interrupt what you were doing.'

"You're not. What I'm doing is inviting you in." She swung the door open for him.

She had half a coconut custard pie left over. He had a slice with a big cup of coffee.

"Just perked," she said.

He didn't mind telling her that the coffee tasted fresh and the pie was heavenly!

"Julie's having Red over tonight. Why don't you come? Meet the man. Listen to them carry on about the business. He's spending some dollars, from what he's saying. Mostly when he comes over, they do all the talking. I do all the listening and cleaning up. It'd be nice if I had somebody I could talk to."

Caleb hesitated a second before replying. "I'd like to, Bonnie Fae, but I'm working nights, fixing electrical problems for Odom and some of the others in town." He explained how, to get around Billy Ray's campaign, they had asked him to work evenings.

"That's a crying shame," she said. "He ain't been by here in a while, since ... well, I can't remember. I haven't seen him since the judge threw him out of the court room."

"I saw him a couple of times. Tried to settle things but I doubt we did," Caleb said. "We uh, don't exactly see eye to eye."

"Nobody sees eye to eye with him."

*Right now, he's probably having trouble even seeing anything out of his eyes.*

He thanked her for the pie and coffee and biked back to his cave.

With nothing better to do, he cleaned up around his camp site and did some thinking about the future. He also called Odom and the others with his new phone number.

"Winter's coming," he said, talking to himself. "I like the cave. Cold water showers are a pain, but standable. Cooking over a camp fire as well, I never thought I'd be here long enough to reach winter, but now it looks like I will be. I think I'm past my hemlock stage. Ready for a new life. I wish it had been with Julie, but that was not to be. Unrealistic to let myself think it was. She was nice to me when I needed a woman to be nice, but to her, I'm most likely just another worker in her life. I wish her well in her business. And, hell, if Red becomes part of her personal life, so be it. As Glow would say, that's her free will at work. I need to find my own woman. Or do something." The last thing he said ruefully.

"Well said," Glow popped in to say. "Don't get hung up in a past you can't change. That's part of the trouble some humans have, living in the past."

"You're back." Caleb said, turning his head in the direction of the sound. "With more words of wisdom for a man who has already resigned from the human race."

"So you say, Caleb. I had to check on corruption in Africa. Still plenty of natural resources to be exploited. People get elected promising to do that but once they settle into office, they start looking for ways to do the exploiting themselves and keep the money. Let the people die. Theory being, the more that starve, the less problems the leaders have to deal with. I let some people know what's happening. Planted the seeds of enlightenment for their free wills to chew on. Who knows what will happen?"

"Well, if I ever do look at another newspaper, I'll see if anything positive is happening in Africa."

"I doubt you will, Caleb. Besides, you're too far gone to care. And the people affected no longer have the will to object. But, with a new life facing you, who knows? You may change. However, I'm pleased that you've put your hemlock stew behind you. I thought you would. Congratulations."

"You know everything. Thanks."

"A new life is like a new day, full of surprises, not all of them bad."

"Hmm. I guess you're right."

"Of course I am."

Caleb made an agreeing sound.

Glow diminished to nothing.

Gone to parts unknown, he thought. Or, it could be I've flipped a page in my thoughts. Either way was okay with him. He got tired of arguing with the thing. Especially since it was always right.

Though it was too early to look at the truck in Odom's shop, Caleb biked to town anyway. He decided to get a hamburger and fries for dinner, with coffee, decaffeinated. He ordered and as he waited, Leroy walked over. He was eating with his family.

"Mr. Stanley," he said.

Caleb nodded cautiously with a glance around. Billy Ray was not in sight.

"I want to thank you for not calling the sheriff about the other night," Leroy said.

"I kind of figured it was one of those man to man things. Between me and your friend. I was lucky to escape without getting whacked by him. How's he doing?"

"He'll be back at work in a couple of days. He's saying he fell working in his barn."

"He vowing revenge?"

"Not yet. If he starts up, I might just bring him back out to see you and drag his ass home again."

Caleb laughed. "Did you suggest counseling?"

"I hinted at it. He got red in the face and started cursing so I let it drop."

"I'm not surprised."

"He's still running for sheriff. Already filled his papers. The sheriff has to file his, along with a couple of others. They're not serious though, just looking for an excuse to get around town and talk to their friends. It'll be the sheriff and Billy Ray 'fore it's over.

Billy Ray says he's got a plan to get the voters behind him. Says he'll spring it a couple of weeks before the vote. That way the sheriff won't have time to do anything about it."

"I hope it doesn't involve me."

"I kind of doubt it. He'd 'a said. He hasn't said much about you since the other night. I think now that Red's moved in on Julie, you're kind of off the hook."

"Glad to hear it." That's what he said. It was not completely what he meant. He was still struggling to accept the reality of it. And, he didn't trust Billy Ray.

*****

After his fast food dinner, he took care of the truck in Odom's shop. It was an hour job. He had to rebuild a part. A note said Odom didn't have anything the next night. And, he hadn't had any other calls. He felt a letdown but that was the way with business. Busy one day, not so much the next.

He biked to the cave and had, what he'd adopted as a nightly ritual, a bottle of cold beer sitting on his log, listening to the calls of the night birds and owls and the relentless flow of the river. Afterward, he went inside and read until his eyes began to close.

Glow didn't make an appearance that night. And, he fell asleep wondering as he always did, was Glow his imagination, his subconscious or simply his Alzheimer's talking to him? Whatever it was, it seemed to make sense.

He knew he didn't have to worry about Billy Ray making a late night appearance either. With both his eyes still half closed from the fight, he wouldn't be a problem for a while anyway.

*****

The next morning as Caleb was finishing a cup of coffee, sitting on the log in front of his fire-pit, he heard a noise behind and turned, ready for action.

What the hell! Billy Ray? No. it was Julie and she was frowning. Damn, what did I do now?

He stood and with a borrowed smile asked, "What are you doing here?"

"Mama said you brought Charlie's phone back yesterday and asked to buy his bike. You haven't been by much lately so I was wondering if you were cutting us out of your life."

"Not my intent. I go with the flow and it hasn't looked like your life was flowing in my direction. You've been busy with Red getting your Internet sales going. How about a cup of coffee. Not as good as yours, but it is freshly boiled."

She shook her head, yes. Her frown lifted. He went into the cave, got another tin mug and poured her a cup. "No cream or sugar, I recall." She sat on a log across from his. He'd dragged it up to balance the way things looked.

She agreed. "Is that where your camp is, back there?" She pointed at the trail he'd been on.

He said it was without elaborating or offering to show her the cave. Though he felt she wouldn't tell anyone intentionally, she might let something slip.

"So, why have you stopped coming by? Mama said she asked you to eat with us and you said no. You hurt her feelings. She thought you liked her cooking."

"I do. I'm sorry if I hurt her feelings but I had to work." He explained his arrangement with Odom to work evenings. "I think some of the other shops are going to let me work regular hours. Odom will too, eventually. "

He told her about Billy Ray's night time attack and added what he had been thinking. "I felt, with him still stalking about, the fewer ties you had with me, the better. And, you hadn't called me for work lately so I figured we were on the same page."

"Well, we were not. I haven't called because I've been up to my eyeballs getting my catalogue crafts on line. Red has been spearheading the listing through Amazon.com, putting up the money."

He shook his head. He did not dare say anything directly about Red, fearing she'd jump to the conclusion that he was jealous. He was, well, had been, but he didn't want her to know it. His feelings for her were stupid in the first place. He'd already decided that so as it stood, his equation was balanced. He didn't much like it, but he couldn't argue with the logic of it. He had nothing to offer Julie or any woman.

"We had to postpone dinner last night. Red had some business he had to take care of. So, we're doing it tonight and you're invited. About dark. Mama's cooking some Crowder peas with pork chops. Beer to drink if you want something stronger than tea or coffee. Red usually has a beer so we bought a six pack."

"A beer sounds good," he said while he pondered a reply to her invitation.

*Damn. If I tell her I'm working and she talks to Odom, she'll know I'm lying. I'd rather shovel cow manure than have to sit at the table with the guy who damn near pushed me back into the pit I'd been climbing out of. But, what damn choice do I have?*

"Okay. I'll be there. About dark, I assume."

"Yes. And, you can have the bike. I don't need it and Charlie hasn't asked for it back. Our divorce is final – I don't have the final decree yet but he promised it. Otherwise, I don't expect to hear from him again."

He thanked her for the bike and asked, "What do you think about it?" Some women, he'd heard, got depressed when their divorces became final.

"Just another day. We've been separated so long, the divorce is just a dot at the end of the sentence. I expect he'll re-marry right away. He hinted as much. His business is doing well. He's in the security business. He supplies guards to casinos and other businesses."

"Sounds like he landed on his feet. And, I don't suppose the law is after him."

"He thinks not. He called the district attorney and was told there were no outstanding warrants out for him. He could come back, but he has a life up there now and there are no relatives gunning for him."

"I'm sure that was a relief."

"It was." She stood, ready to go and smiled and touched his arm with her hand. "I'm glad you are coming tonight."

He said he was too. Truth was, however, he dreaded having to carry on a conversation with Red. *Could be he and Julie will be talking so much, I won't get dragged into it. I'll talk to Bonnie Fae till I can figure out a way to leave.*

After cleaning up the site, he hopped on the bike, his bike, and drove toward town. The shotgun lady was doing something in her garden as he drove past. He waved and she waved back and called for him to stop. No shotgun was in sight so he did.

"If you got any time, I could use a little help," she told him. "You the one what's hepped me before, ain't you?"

He was.

"My brother and his family are coming by for supper and I need some stuff picked." She rattled off what she needed, pointing into the garden with each name. "I was gonna do it, but this heat done got to my head."

There was a basket and two galvanized buckets at the end of the row where they stood.  He was to use those.

She retreated to the front porch and sat in a rocker while he picked. An hour later, he'd filled all three containers with more than enough for a big dinner. He took the buckets to the porch where she sat. Well, as he drew closer, he could see that she had fallen asleep and breathing regularly.

If I wake her, and she doesn't remember asking me, she'll likely run for her shotgun. I'll just leave the things by her chair and see if I can escape before she wakes. She'll think she picked the things.

As he moved away, no shotgun blast sounded behind him and more to the point, his back didn't feel the sting of hot pellets, so he figured he made it.

He stopped at the other houses he had on his list. One needed the back yard raked. That took less than an hour and earned him four eggs picked from their hen house. The other house needed no help. Their son and daughter in law had been by over the weekend to help clean up and do the outside chores.

*****

Wondering if the sheriff had made any progress with the Mobile coin dealer, he biked to city hall to ask the chief. He figured the less he was seen in the sheriff's office the better.

The chief welcomed him inside. "Have a seat. What can I do for you? I haven't heard of anybody looking for you." He laughed. It seemed that every time Caleb showed up, Billy Ray had a warrant out for him.

He explained how he was looking for an update on the Mobile coin dealer lead.

"Ah, well, the sheriff sent a deputy down there to talk to the guy and show him pictures. As you might expect, he didn't recognize the pictures of Leroy's or Billy Ray's wives. He said the woman was heavily made up, like she was trying to distract anybody from really seeing her. Like all a witness might remember would be her heavy red lipstick and dark mascara. She did have brown hair and brown eyes. The dealer also remembered that. She was, maybe five six or seven. She wore shoes with short heals. He cut a couple of inches off her height for that."

"Doesn't sound like anything one of Billy Ray's bunch would be cunning enough to do."

"Yeah. That was our thought too. Billy Ray's kin aren't that smart," the chief said.

"Does the sheriff have the money to send someone down to make a sketch? He could circulate the sketch around the county. If it's not one of Billy Ray's relatives, it might be a friend of one."

"I forgot to tell you. He's doing that. He'll ask the constables to circulate the sketches. What he's worried about, me too, is the possibility that some of Billy Ray's kind have friends out of state, say in Alabama."

"Then, I'd say he's SOL."

"That's what he says too."

*I wonder if that's what the Glow was talking about with the glitter quip. Someone who isn't who we'd like her to be ... a local relative. Could be my subconscious telling me to think ahead. Who knows? At least I've moved away from the gold coins.*

Nothing else had cropped up in the investigation. Billy Ray was campaigning, putting out campaign posters, getting as many free newspaper interviews as he could. Likewise television interviews.

"Mostly, his campaign slogan is that the sheriff is soft on crime. Elect him and he'll put the criminals in jail where they belong, not on the streets, committing more crime. Now and then, he mentions a pervert 'they' just turned lose and a murderer they let go because they were too lazy to check the facts."

Caleb said, "He didn't mention that he was the one who was supposed to be doing the checking."

Chief Bush laughed. "He forgot that detail. The sheriff is saving his money for the run off. Taking the high road. He figures he'll win the primary and have Billy Ray, most likely, as his opponent in the run offs."

"At one time he said he had something he was going to spring on Billy Ray."

"Don't let it out, but I think Billy Ray worked a deal to avoid a stint in the military. Claimed a disability that was never shown except on paper. Then talked about how he wanted to go fight for his country but couldn't. The disability makes him look like a shirker. Not doing his duty to his country."

"And, a liar."

"Right. Also, the sheriff has one witness who'll say Billy Ray hit his wife a couple of times. Wife beaters don't do well at the polls. Ben also plans to take an excerpt from the press conference where Billy Ray had to apologize for charging you with hitting him with a rock. And, if the media polls show the race is close, he'll put a release together that introduces the bail hearing and has the judge's voice telling him to take Billy Ray behind the wood shed. Ben will come on at the end and say, 'I figure this election is the woodshed and I'll be taking Billy Ray behind it.' He may use McNally and the DA in that one."

"If that doesn't do the trick, nothing will."

The chief concurred.

Caleb said his goodbyes and biked toward home.

# Chapter 23

Passing Red's establishment, he saw both Red and, he assumed, Hugo working outside. Red was helping a truck back into a spot at the rear of the truck stop building. Hugo busied himself empting an overflowing garbage can. He biked on.

Julie's truck was still gone from her house and he didn't see anyone but he stopped anyway. Bonnie Fae answered the door and evidently felt confident enough to let him to feed the chickens and to clean the pen. While doing that, he picked up the freshly laid eggs. The red rooster had seen him often enough to accept him as a bringer of food, not an intruder.

After he'd finished, Bonnie Fae offered coffee and a piece of cake. She wore a cleaning dress but her hair was beautifully styled, like she'd been to the beauty parlor. He knew she hadn't so she or Julie must have done it for the dinner that night. He told her it looked great.

He let her talk during coffee and cake.

"Julie said she drove down to see you this morning."

"She did. Surprised me at breakfast. I was having coffee. Not as good as yours" He chuckled.

"Thank you. She said you were coming to dinner tonight."

He was. "I always enjoy your dinners ... and your desserts." he said to avoid any hint that he disapproved of her cooking.

She beamed a smile and thanked him.

*****

He took a shower in the frigid water he pumped from the cave's stream and dressed in a clean set of work clothes. He'd accumulated three sets by that time. And, just as the sun dropped behind the trees on the other side of the river, he biked to Julie's for a dinner he dreaded.

Red had already arrived. His gray truck sat just off the drive near the porch. Lights were already on in the house. Caleb knocked on the door. Julie let him in with a warm hug and cheerful greeting. She looked great in a pink outfit, slacks and a sleeveless vest over a white ruffled blouse. And, her hair, like her mothers, had been stylishly done. He complimented her.

Red was sitting on the sofa in the living room, nursing a glass of beer. He had pulled on a blazer, white shirt and powder blue pants. His shoes had a polished sheen to them and not a hair was out of place.

Caleb felt drab in his work clothes but shrugged it off. *The best I can do. Besides, it's not a beauty contest.*

Bonnie Fae got Caleb a beer from the kitchen when she saw him come in. She'd changed into a dress with a pattern of colorful flowers and butterflies. He complimented her as well.

"You must be Red," Caleb said and stuck out his hand.

"Right," the red haired man said, standing to grab Caleb's hand in a firm grip. Indeed, he was a bit shorter than Caleb but was much beefier, not fat by any means, just more muscular, like Billy Ray only taller.

Not quite as rough around the edges as I would have thought from seeing him at the station, Caleb thought.

Caleb introduced the Internet business as a conversational topic. Which, from Red's response, they'd already been discussing.

"I was just telling Julia," he said. "The fees charged by the rep go up every time I turn around. I'm beginning to wonder about that."

"You don't trust the guy?" Caleb asked.

Julie said, "We have our catalogue on Amazon and we're selling. I don't see why he keeps charging fees."

"He says it's for advertising and shopping around for other markets for your crafts."

"Maybe he should send you copies of what he's been doing," Caleb offered.

"I've asked," Red replied. "He says no way he can send copies of all the shopping around he's been doing. That's where most of the money goes."

"Has he found any?" Caleb asked.

Red shook his head. "Says they're in the works."

"With all we're having to pay that guy – Red is anyway - and the ladies helping me make the crafts, I'm barely making any money," Julie said. She alluded to their arrangement whereby Red got paid back first so the more he paid out up front, the longer it was before she got much money.

"Me either," Red added. "I'm not making anything either. Not with Louie taking everything."

"Tough," Caleb said.

Bonnie Fae called for dinner.

At the dining room table, Red looked at Caleb and said, "You're the poor guy the sheriff got after for murdering the Walters. They were the nicest people you'd ever want to meet. They said you clubbed them to death and took their coin collection. They found the club where you were sleeping."

"I didn't do it." Caleb said and briefly discussed the chain of events from the time he was arrested and spent the night in jail until the judge threw out Billy Ray's case. He also explained that he was not sleeping where the club was found. The killer or killers or who might be framing him made a mistake on that one.

Red said, "I suppose. He's running around saying where's there's smoke, there's fire. Same thing my grandmother used to say. Says they let you out on a technicality. Says you hid the club there because you'd moved on and didn't figure anybody would look there."

*The guy doesn't read the newspapers or watch TV. No point in trying to educate him.*

Bonnie Fae said, "Well, there was no fire in Caleb's case! And the only smoke was Billy Ray's when the judge said the sheriff should take him behind the woodshed for charging Caleb in the first place. Smoke was coming out of the judge's ears, he was so mad."

Red laughed. "Lots of folks agree with him though. Especially since the sheriff hasn't arrested anybody else."

"He's working on it," Caleb said without disclosing anything about the coin transaction in Mobile and Houston.

While they continued that conversation, Bonnie Fae served their plates, crowder peas with corn bread, pork chops and a salad on the side. Iced tea to drink but Red and Caleb kept their beers.

"He just started his campaign for sheriff," Red said. "He's still mouthing off about how they let you go on a technicality. He's saying the sheriff just didn't do his homework."

"It wasn't the sheriff's case. It was his. The deputy's been on my case since I rescued his son from stepping into a snake pit at the river."

"He wants to be sheriff. He says you molested his boy."

"I can't tell you what that is in front of the ladies. But I can tell you that he'd lying."

Red laughed.

Julie said, "He was coming by here, worrying the heck out of Mama and me. He's married and was pestering the devil out of me. Lately though, he's quit coming by. I think his campaign is keeping him busy."

Red said, "He's been by the store asking if he can put campaign posters around. They tell him only I can approve anything political and I'm always too busy to see him. I still have my catfish farm. I have to manage that. I sell every catfish we raise to local restaurants. In mine too."

"Good. People feel more comfortable if they know they can trust what they eat," Caleb said.

"I hope so."

"Are you going to let Billy Ray put up his posters?"

"I'll turn him down if he ever catches me. No way will I help that guy after the way he's harassed you." He told Julie and reached over to touch her arm, lovingly. She smiled as if she welcomed it.

Caleb didn't like it, but dismissed the thought. *Nothing to do with me. None of my concerns.* But, he wished it were. *Forget it.*

Julie said, "He and Hugo had words one day while I was in the craft store. Hugo practically ordered him off the premises. Billy Ray acted like he was going to arrest Hugo, but he finally left."

"Hugo does not like the guy," Red said. "Says he too pushy."

"That's an understatement," Bonnie Fae said.

Julie agreed. "Not only pushy, obsessed."

Caleb agreed. "I hope he finds something else, besides me, to obsess about. Last time we talked, I got the impression that he had." He remembered standing over Billy Ray's unconscious form at the river.

They congratulated him for making progress. Red wanted to know his secret. Caleb laughed. No way was he going to tell him about the fight.

As the dinner progressed, he asked Caleb about his future plans. "Are you still… working for food?" He smiled faintly, barely letting it show.

Caleb stifled a laugh and explained how he'd been consulting, more or less, with the auto shops around town on their more difficult electrical problems. "If it keeps up, I may open a shop that specializes in electrical problems. I don't know about working for food. I'll have to move into an apartment when it gets cold. I don't know how that will work out. Since the Walters were killed, that doesn't leave me with that many regular houses that need help."

"When I heard about them being killed, it hit me hard. Still bothers me. I don't know why the sheriff hasn't arrested anybody yet. Maybe he is getting lazy." He smiled again, that time it showed.

"I think he's working hard," Caleb countered.

"He'd better or Billy Ray will be sitting in his chair after the election." He looked at Caleb and asked, "I guess you plan on staying here."

He did. As he said that, his packet of hemlock popped into his thoughts. He dismissed it.

"I don't know how you're going to like it, pedaling around on that bike in the winter rains. Sometimes it sleets. Gonna get cold," Red said with a twist of his head and a grin.

"I doubt I'll like it, but I'll get used to it. Easier to do if you have no choice."

"I suppose. Must be … what … kind of embarrassing … grown man riding around on a bicycle."

"You do what you have to do," Caleb said.

"You've had more bad luck than any one man deserves," he continued. "I don't know how you absorbed your wife's infidelity all the way back from when you got married! Wow! And, if that wasn't enough, your … well not yours, children. Another man's. You brought them up and paid for their college educations! Not many men would have stood for that."

Caleb was shocked but nodded his head and forced a slight smile. "I didn't know till the last day we were together."

The only people he'd told that part of the story to were Julie and Bonnie Fae. He'd told the chief and others how his wife had left him, but not the embarrassing history of their marriage. *Not the sort of thing I'd bring up unless I wanted to embarrass somebody. And yet, he doesn't seem to feel any reluctance. I knew I didn't want to come to dinner. Now I know why.*

Julie turned red and gave Red a shocked stare. Bonnie Fae's mouth dropped open. If Red saw either, he ignored them, smiled and looked at Caleb to see what he was going to say.

"You had no idea. You must have had blinders on," Red said.

"Must have. My wife hit me with it the day the company closed when I was having a lot to absorb. I managed to take it all in and decided to come down here, where I was born, to start over. Put the past behind me. Thanks to Julie and some other good people in Marshalltown, I've been able to do that. The deputy's harassment, his obsession, hasn't helped, but I think that's over now."

"From the frying pan into the fire, I'd say. You landed with both feet in the … mud. I was about to call it what it was, but for the ladies." He smiled and gestured at both. "If you didn't have bad luck, I guess you wouldn't have any luck at all." He quoted a cliché that had been kicking around for a while.

"Well said. It has been adventure." Caleb smiled and nodded.

Julie lowered her head as though searching for something on her plate. Bonnie Fae continued to stare as if in shock.

Caleb didn't like what Red had been saying and especially didn't like his revelation about "his children" but all things considered, he did like the fact that Julie and Bonnie Fae didn't seem to like it either.

Red finished his beer. Bonnie Fae asked if he wanted another. He said no.

"Getting back to your rep," Caleb said to change the subject away from him and his troubles. "Why don't you just fire him? You're on Amazon already why keep him on?"

"Uh, well, we signed a one year contract. It has a termination clause but it'd cost us a thousand and a percent of what we make during the year if we did."

"Steep."

"Yeah. But, if he sends one more bill to me for promotional expenses, I think I'll just bite the bullet and cut him off."

"We have to do something," Julie said and Bonnie Fae agreed with her.

Red looked at Caleb and said, "By the way, I understand you hit Billy Ray with a rock. Threw it from the corn patch. That was a hell of a throw. I was impressed. What an arm."

*So, they told him that too. I wish they hadn't. If it gets back to Billy Ray, he'll start up about it all over again.*

"In the heat of the moment," Caleb said. "I didn't think I could throw it that far."

"Amazing what you can do under pressure."

"I suppose." *Also if you have a little help from an Alzheimer friend, like Glow.*

Bonnie Fae cleared the table. Caleb helped while Red and Julie talked business.

For dessert, they had peach cobbler with whipped cream. Bonnie Fae offered decaffeinated coffee which they all accepted.

When they'd finished, Red jumped up and rushed around the table, first hugging Bonnie Fae and praising her for her cooking and everything else he could come up with. Leaving her gushing, he grabbed Julie and held her closer for longer than Caleb felt necessary, and gave her an equal amount of praise, including kisses on both cheeks. That brought a big smile to Julie's face and a red blush.

*A good way to cover up a social faux pau,* Caleb thought. *He must have seen the reactions on their faces. If I didn't know better I'd think he did it deliberately to get a rise out of me or if I wanted to really dig around in the mud, I might think he did it to knock me down a peg or two in front of Bonnie Fae and Julie. Hell, he couldn't knock me down very far.*

He helped Bonnie Fae clear the table. She objected but he did it anyway. Red and Julie retreated to the living room to talk about sales, from what Caleb could hear. Once the dish washer was loaded, Caleb said his goodbyes and left.

Julie hugged him at the front door but didn't look him in the eyes. "I'm so glad you came, Caleb. Please stop by when you can. Whether we have chores or not, me and Mama always love to see you and there's always a piece of cake or pie and coffee waiting. You're like a real person to us." She said it softly, almost a mumble, like she was reluctant or embarrassed.

Caleb didn't know what to make of that so he just thanked her and left. What else would I be but a real person?

\*\*\*\*\*

The bike ride to the cave was uneventful. Mostly he thought about all that had been said, actually all that Red had said. He discovered that none of it bothered him. There was a time that it might have. Well, the fact that Julie and Bonnie Fae had told Red about the problems he'd had with his wife did rub him the wrong way, but he hadn't told them not to repeat it. Of course, he didn't know they'd be talking to anybody who'd be interested, anybody like Red.

A truck passed and honked and somebody waved at him but didn't swerve or curse. Not Billy Ray.

At the cave, he hid the bike as usual though since everyone knew where he was camping out, it didn't make much sense to hide it any more.

"Maybe I'll quit doing it," he said out loud as he sat on the log and had his late night beer. It was his last one. He would have to get more the next day. That meant stopping at Red's because it was close.

*Hope I don't see the rude bastard. The son of a bitch had to be trying to embarrass me in front of Julie and Bonnie Fae.*

"Part of your animal instinct," Glow said. "Kill the weak. All these years and humans still haven't completely overcome it. Those who think they have overcome their animal instinct to kill the weak just haven't confronted themselves yet. Talk's cheap until a price tag is attached."

Caleb twisted around. "Damn, I'm talking to myself again. I wonder when I'll go completely over the edge? But, it's true, or that's how it seems, we want to kill the weak. But, we don't. It's against the law anyway."

"Not officially ... you don't kill them. In fact, some groups spend millions to stop the weak from dying. But, the instinct is still there. That was what Red was showing tonight."

"Unevolved. I agree."

"Maybe he views you as a threat."

"I don't see how. Hell, I'm a bum. He's a successful business man. Younger than I am and handsome. How could I be a threat?"

"Well, you have to think a little, Caleb. Maybe Bonnie Fae and Julie have said good things about you. That'd make a competitor jealous enough to want to put you down."

Caleb laughed. "He'd have to have a loose screw if he thinks I'm a threat."

"Maybe. Maybe not. Could be he's just perceptive. He can't be too dumb. He's a successful businessman."

They left it at that.

# Chapter 24

The next day, Caleb leaned his bike against the wall of Red's convenience store and was headed toward the door for a six pack of beer when sounds of an argument got his attention. He stopped and looked into the parking lot in front of the restaurant. Billy Ray and Red were at it face to face, both red. Billy Ray was in uniform.

Caleb stepped close enough to listen in.

Billy Ray was saying, "You won't let me put up posters, but you don't mind sleeping with a woman who's been sleeping with a pervert and murderer! When I'm sheriff, you may –"

Enraged, Red pushed Billy Ray in the chest with his hands and sent him falling backward.

"You sick, twisted bastard! You apologize for saying that. Julie is a fine woman!" He stepped forward, fists clinched, as if he was going to continue what Caleb had begun at the river, beat the hell out of the deputy.

Billy Ray, flat on his back reached for his Glock automatic and pointed it. "You'd better stop," he shouted. "You're under arrest for assaulting me while I'm on duty. I'll shoot your ass!"

"Bullshit! You're campaigning! I'm going to put an end to that right now!" When he took another step, the deputy put his other hand around the Glock and began to pull the trigger. Suddenly, Hugo flew out from behind a car and threw himself between Billy Ray and Red. The Glock's nine millimeter bullet caught him in the left shoulder. He staggered before falling across the deputy so he couldn't shoot again.

Red jumped in and stomped Billy Ray's hand, sending the automatic sliding away. He picked it up and pointed it at the deputy and from the intense look on his face, intended shooting him.

Though in pain, Hugo saw what was about to happen. He rolled to his feet, jumped up and hugged Red's arms to force them down. "Don't do it, Red! He ain't worth it. Let it go!"

Red stared down at Billy Ray for a second then let his arms drop by his sides and said, "Okay. You got lucky, asshole. But, I'm gonna take your gun to the sheriff and tell him what happened." He looked at Hugo, his face a mask of pain. "I'm calling an ambulance to get you to the hospital."

He hurried inside and did just that. Seeing Billy Ray watching, he walked to where he stood and shouted, "Get your ass off my property and don't come back! If you're not gone before I count to ten, I'll shoot you."

The deputy apparently believed he would so he got into his car and drove away.

Caleb waited until the ambulance came and hauled Hugo away before buying his six pack and biking back to his cave. He'd gotten no calls from Odom or any of the others that day. He didn't know if Billy Ray had scared them or if there was simply no business. It bothered him. He'd run out of money. Then what?

Figuring Julie and Bonnie Fae would want to talk about the dinner and the conversation, he didn't stop at their house on the way back. Give it a couple of days to drift into yesterday's memory. And, the other problem was how he felt about them telling a stranger the problems that brought him to Marshalltown. He told himself he didn't have a good reason to be annoyed, but he was.

Probably just annoyed that they told Red and he rubbed my nose in it.

"Yeah, that's it. And, the son of a bitch seemed to enjoy it," he said out loud and hurried along.

\*\*\*\*\*

In the late afternoon, Billy Ray was called into the sheriff's office. He knew what to expect but dreaded it nonetheless. He opened the door and went inside, then stood behind a chair until the sheriff acknowledged him. He saw what he assumed to be his Glock on the sheriff's desk. After a few seconds, the sheriff looked up, his face an angry frown.

"Billy Ray, you have to be one of the stupidest son of a bitches I've ever run into. When somebody told me you had shit for brains, they were paying you a compliment. Hell, I wish you were that smart. I can tell you that I'm opening an independent investigation into your behavior. Not just the dumb shit stunt you pulled today, but all the dumb shit stunts you've pulled over the years. I don't know if any decision will be reached before the primary or not, but if it is, your ass is out of here. I'm not having you embarrass this department or me another time. Consider yourself suspended as of now. I'm keeping your gun. Hell you might shoot an innocent civilian. Damn, you sure as hell have been trying hard enough."

"Are you going to let me say anything?"

"Say your bit then." The sheriff said with his right palm outstretched.

"I asked the man if he'd mind a political poster on his property. He started ranting and raving about how I'd insulted Julie Howard. I denied it. I told him all I'd done was investigate why she might have been sleeping with that Stanley guy. That's when he pushed me down. He was pissed that I said what I did. Hell, that had nothing to do with him. That was from our prior investigations."

"That's not the story he's telling. He said you accused Ms. Howard of sleeping with a pervert. There's no evidence that Mr. Stanley is a pervert. You know that! And, I've told you that. And yet, you keep harping about it. Sure, Red got pissed about it. He's in business with Ms. Howard. You insulted his business partner. And then, you pulled your Glock to shoot him, an unarmed civilian."

"Hell, sheriff, he was about to attack me. I was on my back and he was coming at me with his fists balled up. He's a hell of a lot bigger than me. I warned him but he kept on a' coming. I didn't have a choice. If he had a beef about what I was saying, he should have filed a complaint with you, not attack me."

"You started it, Billy Ray. You know it! It was all your doing! The moving party pays. You were the moving party."

"Not so, at least not the whole thing. He knocked me down and was about to attack me. Kill me for all I knew. I didn't have a choice. He could have walked away and filed a complaint with you. He had the choice."

The sheriff rapped his fingers on his desk as he pondered what his deputy was saying, evaluating how it would play out in public. To some extent, what he said made sense. Red should have backed away and filed a complaint. With Hugo as a witness, that might have been enough by itself to suspend him. But, he didn't.

*I can still open an investigation and should, but maybe I should wait until a decision has been made to suspend him. That way it won't be my decision and he'll get no political mileage out of it. But, I'm not giving the juvenile bastard his gun back. Lord knows what he might do next.*

*The little bastard's scared, I think. Let me see if I can use that.*

"That's bullshit, Billy Ray. But, I bet you don't want to get suspended before the primary. Might hurt your chances. And I sure as hell want you to have your shot. But, I can tell you this. Even if you get enough votes in the primary to go against me in the final it won't help you one damn bit. I'm gonna whip your ass like it's never been whipped before in the runoff. And, I'm gonna enjoy the hell out of it.

I shouldn't do this, but how about this. I won't suspend you, but in effect, I'll demote you pending the outcome of the investigation. I won't tell anybody however. The investigation will likely take a few weeks to reach a decision. By then, the primary will be over and it won't matter if you've been suspended or not."

Billy Ray looked puzzled. "What kind of demotion?"

"You'll be Leroy's back up. You'll work for him. No gun, just do as he says. He'll know not to say anything to anybody."

*That ought to take the bastard down a peg or two.*

"No gun? What if we get attacked?"

"How many times have you been attacked in the years you've been a deputy?"

Billy Ray shook his head. He knew the answer was none. "I don't like it."

"Well, I could suspend you pending the outcome of the investigation. And for sure, that'd make the papers and the television."

The deputy was already shaking his head. "I don't like it, but if I ain't got a choice, I'll just live with it. Leroy ain't gonna tell me what to do."

"Well, I'll tell Leroy you're his back up. He'll know you're working for him. I imagine he'll get to where he likes that. I imagine he's sick and tired of you bossing him around. You'll get to see how it feels to be on the receiving end. I think I'll enjoy watching him do it."

Billy Ray stood. He looked hard at his gun, shrugged and took a step back. "He's outside. I'll tell him."

"Oh no you won't. I'll tell him but first, I want you to sign a statement to the effect that you agree to the demotion."

He shook his head like he wouldn't.

"Your choice. You're suspended as of –"

"I didn't say I wouldn't. I'll sign the damn thing. And, I'm going to win the election and I'm going to be the sheriff in August. Then, we'll see who's the big shit around here."

"And, it won't be you," the sheriff said and pointed a finger at his deputy.

The sheriff called in Ruby, his secretary, and told her what he needed. While she typed it up, he brought in Leroy and told him with Billy Ray present what had happened.

He then asked Leroy, "Do you think you can handle being in charge of Billy Ray for a few weeks?"

Leroy suppressed a smile and after a look at a shaken Billy Ray said, "I think I can handle it, Sheriff." He looked at his old companion and asked, "How about you, BR, can you adjust to me being in charge?"

Without looking up, Billy Ray shook his head yes and mumbled. "Till I win the damn election. Then, gonna be some changes 'round here. I'll tell you that."

"That'll be when hell freezes over, deputy, or should I say, assistant deputy. That'll be your new title," Sheriff Tolar said.

After Billy Ray was out of the building, the sheriff called Red and read him the riot act.

"You were on the verge of being charged for murder, maybe second degree, but still murder and I don't see how you would have gotten out of it. You just can't damn well go around shooting unarmed people and especially law enforcement officials. Regardless of what you may think of my deputy, he's a sworn law enforcement official. If you have a beef, you have to file a complaint. You don't grab up a gun and start shooting."

"He insulted Julie. And, he was pointing that damn Glock at me."

"But, he didn't shoot did he and you don't know for sure that he would have. Instead, you decided to take the law into your hands and shoot him."

"I guess you're right. I was so mad though, I wasn't thinking straight."

"You sure as hell weren't. You're still down for assault on a sheriff's deputy. You threatened to kill him. I'd guess you could get a couple of years' hard time for that."

"Can you cut me some slack, sheriff? I was out of my head. He'd insulted my friend and shot my manager, also my friend." He told the sheriff he was at the hospital looking out for Hugo who'd been operated on to get the slug out of his shoulder. He was doing okay and would probably be sent home the next day. He'd have to wear a sling for a while.

"I don't know what I can do, Red. If Billy Ray wins and becomes sheriff, it'll be out of my hands. If he loses, I'll see if it goes away."

Red thanked him.

I reckon I can count on him for some campaign contributions, the sheriff thought with a chuckle.

*****

After Billy Ray had signed the paper agreeing to the demotion, he and Leroy left. The sheriff called the Chief and they had a laugh and later a beer to celebrate.

Sheriff Tolar said, "You should have seen the way the little shit squirmed, like he was about to shit in his britches."

"I wish I could 'a been there."

"It was something to see. He knew his tit was in the wringer. And, he was fit to be tied when I told him he wasn't to carry a gun. That gun makes him feel as tall as the big boys."

"I hear it'll be you and Billy Ray in the run offs."

"Yeah, me too. You know Red, don't you?"

"Sure. Pretty good business man. He picked up where his old man left off. Built the business up."

"Yeah. Whether we like it or not, he committed a felony when he threatened to shoot Billy Ray. I'm gonna sit on it awhile. It'll probably go away once I get rid of Billy Ray. Heaven help us all if the little shit wins. If Billy Ray makes something out of it during the campaign, I may have to do something. I don't think he will though. I don't think he'll want his dirty underwear waved about for the public to see."

"I'd think you're right, unless he's completely stupid."

"Hell Andy, if you're gonna introduce his IQ into the mix, I'm gonna be worried."

The chief laughed and asked, "Anything new on the Walters murders?"

"Not a hell of a lot. The constables haven't found anybody who knows the woman in the sketches. Not even close. And, people I know around the county say they haven't heard anybody saying anything incriminating about anybody. By anybody, I mean Billy Ray."

"I figured that out. What's your next move?"

"To tell you the truth, I don't think I have one. Nobody's called about any more coins turning up."

"Maybe they've been sold outside the country."

"That's what worries me. If they have, we may never solve the damn case. Billy Ray's gonna make hay out of that in the run offs."

"Yep. My thinking too."

"Hell Andy, I may just retire. Keep it under your hat, but if I win, I'm going to seriously consider it. I can live off my pension and social security. We don't need much. House's paid for. Kids have jobs."

"Who'd take over for you? Leroy?"

"I don't know. They'd probably hold a special election."

"Well, if you're looking at me, look in another direction. I like it where I am. I only have to kiss one ass to stay employed, the Mayor's. You have to kiss thousands every four years. I don't think I could stand that."

"I'm beginning to think I can't either. It seems to me that everybody wants something."

"I get the same feeling. Mostly, they want me to fix their damn traffic tickets."

"I wish I could get away with anything that easy."

*****

In the hospital, Red shoved his cell phone back into his shirt pocket and looked at his friend, half asleep, half dazed from pain medication.

Hugo blinked and looked at Red. "I'm alive," he said.

"And kicking," Red said. "You're going to be okay, my friend. Have to keep your arm in a sling for a few days, but you'll be okay."

"I can work?"

"Nothing heavy, but no reason you can't do what you've been doing."

"I'd go crazy sitting around."

"Why did you jump in front of the bullet like you did, Hugo? You might have been killed."

Hugo looked hard at Red before answering. "I'd have thought that you would know, Red. I love you. Don't you know?"

Red stared at his manager, shook his head and smiled. "I guess I do." He reached over and put his hand on Hugo's shoulder. "I couldn't ask for better than you, Hugo."

Just so you keep your feelings to yourself, Red thought. He'd suspected Hugo's loyalties went beyond regular employee standards but had ignored his suspicions. And, I'll keep ignoring them. I don't need that complication in my life.

"Thank you, Red. That means a lot to me. I won't let you down."

"You never have."

"How long've you been here?" Hugo asked.

"Since they brought you out of the operating room."

"Who's running the store?"

"Madge and the others. We're okay." Madge was a lady who ran things when Red and Hugo got busy, as they had been just then.

"Yeah, until the truckers start up. They think they can push her around. Better get on back there, Red."

Red looked at his watch. "Yeah. I guess you're right." He stood and stepped toward the door. "Louie called. He wants to do a video of Julie and the others making their crafts. Wants us to pick him up in Nawleens. He's flying in. He'll call and give us his schedule."

"And we're paying for his damn flight. You and Julie, I reckon. First class, most like. The man's ripping us off, Red. Every time we turn around, he wants more money. Hell, a video'll cost bucks. I've had a belly full of that guy holding out his hand and grinning like a like a possum eatin' saw briars."

"Yeah. I think you're right. He's driving a money train through that agreement. I should have had a lawyer look at it. Damn it. He says he can put the video on YouTube. It'll get lots of plays and people will want to buy more of our crafts. I'll have to talk to him. Hell, I'm tapped out. I guess you are too. I appreciate your help. I'll make it up, Hugo."

"I'm not worried, Red. Hell, we've worked together for a long time. I trust you."

"Thanks Hugo. I may end up paying him off. We don't need him anymore. We sure as hell don't need a video for YouTube. I'm gonna cancel the contract. Have to!"

"Damn right! Cancel the damn thing!" Hugo rose out of bed as he said it, winched and dropped back. "Crooked bastard. That's what he is!"

"My fault," Red said, told him goodbye and left. Hugo was still cursing as he closed the door behind him.

"Wop thug's what he is!" Hugo shouted. "What happened to honest people?"

Red asked the nurse to check on Hugo as he passed her in the hall. "He's a bit riled up." She promised.

# Chapter 25

For his dinner that night, Caleb fried a couple of slices of bacon and two eggs. With the pan cleared of both, he fried two slices of bread and ate it on the log in front of his fire pit with a bottle of cold beer from his cave stream. He'd turned on the radio and let the sounds of music blend with the sounds of nature around him. From somewhere in the woods came the scent of something sweet and pleasant. The late afternoon air was cool and pleasing on his face. Birds sang in the trees and looked down at him, waiting for him to leave so they could pick over anything he left.

His passing thought was about Glow. Had Glow finally disappeared from his life? Was it real or a crutch he'd dreamed up to keep from eating the hemlock stew? He never quite felt like it was Alzheimer's although it sure seemed like it was. Hell, it may be.

He recalled the dinner at Julie's and Bonnie Fae's, the ... humiliation, he'd decided, Red had dumped on him. *Maybe I'm wrong. Maybe it's just the guy's way. But, it's not my way and I don't like it and I don't have to like it.*

Oddly enough, his thoughts drifted back to California. Maybe he'd go back. His old company had competitors. He could apply for a job. "Hell, nobody was better than I was," he said. "I have enough to catch the bus back. I've recovered, I think. The humiliation Red dumped on me, straightened me right out. I'm ready to start a new life ... in California. Not a damn thing for me here."

It was twilight. "Hell, I think this is a two beer night," he said and went into his cave for another bottle. When he came out, Julie was standing in front of his fire pit. The sight of her shocked him. He didn't know exactly what to say.

She wore a white blouse that fit her like a glove and slacks with tennis shoes. Damn, she looks good. He'd noticed her attributes before, but just then they seemed to hit him right in the face.

As if she noticed, she smiled. "I decided to drive down to see you. You have enough of that to share with me?" She gestured with her head toward the beer he held in his hand.

"I'll get a glass for you," he said.

"Why don't I come with you," she said. "I'd like to see your hideout. I know you have one someplace. I didn't see a bed roll last time I was here. Do you mind?"

He hesitated then said, "No. Follow me." He was leaving anyway. What difference did it make if she saw the cave? Hell, it'll give her something to tell Red.

As if she'd heard his thoughts, she said, "I won't be telling Red. Me and Mama were mortally embarrassed the way he carried on at dinner. I apologize for him. He's usually so nice and polite. We wished we hadn't told him. It just came out one night when we were having dinner. He asked about you. It was when you were in jail. And, I think he believed you might have killed those two old people."

"I gathered that he might still believe that. The smoke and fire comment he made. I was surprised he rejected Billy Ray's request to put campaign signs on his property. And, he might have if old Billy hadn't said what he did about you sleeping with me. What a joke," Caleb said.

"He told me. Red did."

"It almost got him killed."

"It did! Well, I thought he ought to know about your troubles. You'd worked all your life, supporting your family … till the end … till you found out. You couldn't kill anybody. You were just trying to find a way to survive down here. I'm so sorry. He was so rude. Thoughtless. I couldn't believe it." She reached out and put her arm around his shoulders and rubbed his back with her hand. "I'm just so sorry, Caleb. Can you ever forgive me?"

Damn, her hand warmed him to his toes, well, almost to his toes. He'd never felt that before in all his married days. It reminded him of the life he'd taken for granted. He'd expected nothing from it and had received exactly that. No wonder Myrna took advantage. *Hell, I was ripe for the picking.*

Caleb looked at Julie and realized he'd been lost in thought. He said, "It's okay. It bothered me at the time, but I've gotten over it. If I had to guess, I'd say he was jealous, if you can believe it. Jealous of me. That's kind of a joke." He repeated what he'd said earlier. "Jealous of a homeless man."

She opened her mouth to protest, but he interrupted saying, "Come on, I'll show you where I hang out and get you a glass."

He put the bottle of beer on the stump round he used as a table and motioned for her to follow.

"Be careful. This is a narrow little trail," he said, pausing at the beginning of the sandstone trail that led to the mouth of the cave, where the little stream poured out.

"It is," she said, looking over his shoulder. "I see a little waterfall."

As he urged her along the trail, he explained about the stream that bubbled up from an opening at the back of the cave he was going to show her. "I keep some of my food in it. I made an eddy along one side."

At the mouth of the cave, he stood back and let her enter. When she was inside, he followed. He'd left the light on and the radio so it was pleasant inside. The little stream rippled over its rocky bed past the propellers that generated the electricity for everything.

He explained what he had done to get everything to work, showed her the eddy he'd made.

"I'm impressed," she said, turning this way and that to take it all in. "Really. You ... you are amazing. Wow! How could you do all this?"

He explained how it was basically what he'd done all his professional life. Design, rig-up, repair and re-build electrical systems. "I cannibalized the stuff you see from wrecks in the junk yard."

"You even have a radio … and a bed. All the comforts of home."

He agreed. "Till it gets cold. Then, I'll have to move." Actually, he thought, by then I'll be back in California.

She turned at the same time that he did so they ended up facing each other, her eyes looking into his. It was like he'd suddenly, magically somehow, merged with her, a kind of bond he didn't know existed but he felt it. It overwhelmed him. Without thinking, he reached out with his arms and pulled her close, their eyes still locked together. He kissed her with more passion than he knew he had and she returned it and wrapped her arms around his waist in a tight embrace. He felt her warmth and was lost in it.

"Caleb," she said softly as he slowly unbuttoned her blouse and took off her clothes, like he knew what he was doing. She unbuckled his belt and let his pants fall. He urged her into the bed and neither said a word until their passions were totally spent.

She rolled over. "God, Caleb, it was wonderful. It has been a long time for me. Since Charlie left. I've wanted to … well the first time I saw you in my workshop, you … I don't know, you just have … something unusually sensitive ... maybe feeling is a better word, about you. I was attracted to you. I was afraid you saw the way I looked at you."

"No. I was too busy looking at you," he said and kissed her again. "I've never made love to a woman like that before."

"I've never been made love to by a man like that before."

"I thought you and Red …"

"Goodness no. I think … I thought we were friends … more business friends, if you know what I mean."

He did. He'd had lots of those. Here today, gone tomorrow.

"I love you, Julie. I have, I think, since the first time I saw you in your garage."

She touched his face with her hand. "I love you, Caleb. It's like I'm part of you now. I think of you every night before I fall asleep."

"You've given me a new life, Julie. I was going back to California. I thought it was over for me down here."

"I'm so glad it isn't. I don't know what I'd do if you left."

He took her in his arms, held her tight and kissed her.

"You take my breath away," she said. "I think I'm ready for that beer now."

She got dressed while he rummaged around to find a glass for both of them. He'd been drinking out of the bottle, but it didn't seem appropriate just then.

It was dark when they emerged from the cave. He lit the camp fire and they sat on the log, close, and enjoyed a beer together, listening to the night birds calling, hearing the swirl of the river wash up the slope to them. Insects sang in the darkness around them and competed with the music from the radio.

He put his arm around her shoulders and pulled her close. "I don't think I've ever loved anyone before, Julie. I'm not sure what to do."

"You're doing okay, Caleb." She leaned over so her face touched his.

Her phone rang. "Mama," she said. "I'm sorry. I'm having a beer with Caleb. I know. I should have called. We got to talking. Okay. I'll be there in a few minutes."

She punched off and told Caleb. "Mama has dinner on the table. Would you join us?"

He smiled. "I had what amounts to dinner before you got here. Besides, I just want to sit here and stay mellow."

She laughed. "Me too, if truth be told, but I'd better get home. Mama was worried."

They stood up. He hugged and kissed her again then let her go.

*****

Over the next few weeks, Billy Ray carried on an aggressive campaign, railing on and on about how the sheriff, the DA and judge were soft on crime. "We can't afford to let criminals run free in our God loving communities, threatening our women and children. I'll do something about it. Sheriff Tolar won't. He's proven that, time and time again. It's time for him to retire. Help me help him out. His rocking chair's waitin'."

The property owner next to Red's, let him put up a huge campaign sign saying about the same thing with a statement to the effect that Red was as bad as the others, helping criminals and friends of criminals. "All of us have to join in the war against crime," the bottom line of the sign said.

No one knew if it hurt Red's business or not. When Caleb biked past, the parking lot seemed as full as it ever was.

Billy Ray ran campaign announcements with endorsements from various men and women around the country decrying the lack of enforcement of the criminal laws by the sheriff. He even had one with children crying about how their daddy was killed by a man who was turned loose by the sheriff. He pretty much campaigned full time on full pay and in full deputy's uniform. Leroy didn't complain and nobody made an issue of it. It was kind of understood.

His daddy sobered up and went door to door for his son. And, all the Johnson relatives did the same. It was like an army of Johnsons and in-laws hammering on doors throughout the county.

The sheriff didn't do much direct campaigning. However, he campaigned indirectly by holding press conferences to rebut Billy Ray's announcements which he explained were either false or misleading. "Free advertising," he told the chief.

The polls had them fairly close. The sheriff stayed about four or five points ahead however, no matter what Billy Ray or his kin said or claimed.

The committee to investigate Billy Ray's conduct was convened. Standing members included the Police Chief, the Superintendent of Schools, the President of the Chamber of Commerce, the Chairman of the County Library Board, a retired judge who presided over the meetings, and the sheriff who excused himself from Billy Ray's investigation. A reporter made notes and a recording was made of all meetings.

Over the period of the investigation, they called Billy Ray first to get his side of the stories. After he'd testified, they made a list of witnesses they'd call to rebut or confirm what he claimed was the truth. Leroy and the sheriff were on the list. And, all would take an oath to tell the truth.

The primary was held. As expected, the sheriff came in first. Close behind him was Billy Ray. None of the others captured enough votes to worry about.

Billy Ray held a press conference to thank everybody who'd campaigned on his behalf. He promised to be their next sheriff and he vowed he'd do a better job cleaning up crime in the county than Sheriff Tolar. "At one time, he might have been a good sheriff, but let's face it, he's grown old and lazy. I'm young and ready to get to work. I'll clean up crime in the county. Criminals better watch out. If you're into crime, you'd better be outta this county. I'm not soft on crime, I'm hard. Watch me."

The sheriff also held a press conference to thank his supporters. His size and his gravelly voice made a favorable impression on those who attended, including Caleb. He laughed at Billy Ray's claim.

He said, "You go to Parchman and ask the inmates who's soft on crime. They'll tell you Sheriff Tolar is not. You ask the victims of crime in this county who's soft on crime. They'll tell you Sheriff Tolar is not."

He wound up his press conference by saying that youth was a good thing to have on your side. And, sometimes he wished he had it but experience and good judgment were even better than youth and he had both.

He told the reporters that they'd find out during the run off that Billy Ray was young and inexperienced.

"Too young and Too inexperienced to be sheriff. Plus, he has a bad habit of twisting facts around so he gets more out of them than he should. I'll tell you more as we get into the campaign. As someone once said, don't touch that dial, the best is yet to come," he said.

*****

Caleb ignored the campaign rhetoric including Billy Ray's references to him, about how the sheriff had let him go after he'd developed clear cases against him.

He was as happy as he'd ever been in his life. He hadn't thrown away his bag of hemlock, but he hadn't thought about it either since Julie's twilight visit. And, Glow had quit making an appearance. He'd either been recalled or was busy elsewhere or was just letting Caleb's free will do what it would.

He frequently ate dinner with Julie and Bonnie Fae and enjoyed each one. They never had him and Red for dinner at the same time. And, Julie frequently showed up at his cave for visits and he certainly enjoyed each one.

During the next dinner together, Red was the topic of discussion, that and their business arrangement with Amazon. Both women apologized again for Red's behavior. Caleb excused them and passed off Red's apparent rudeness as a male display of man-to-man enthusiasm and, an assertion of top dog dominance, where rudeness is often the order of the day.

They also discussed the shooting. It was still on everybody's minds. And, the sheriff made references to it when he was out on the stump. How Billy Ray was about to shoot an unarmed man in front of his place of business and would have if the man's manager hadn't jumped in. Because he knew how well liked Red was, he added Red's name when he told the story.

"Poor Hugo," Bonnie Fae added. "He's had some bad luck, getting shot … his sister dying."

"How's he doing?" Caleb asked. "I saw him outside today when I biked by. Arm's in a sling but he looked okay. I'd been in town negotiating with Odom to buy his old Ford truck." He'd agreed to pay a thousand dollars for it with two hundred down. Odom would take money from his earnings to pay the rest. "Will his arm be okay?"

"Red says his arm's going to be as good as it was," Bonnie Fae said. "They have one problem though. The rep from New York, Louie, has gone missing. Hugo went to pick him up and he didn't show. Red called his office and they didn't know where he was. They think he got on the plane to New Orleans. Hugo showed up to pick him up and he never came out. The airline said he was on the flight but he could have gotten off in Atlanta when it stopped. I thought he was a sweet man. I know Julie and Red thought he was charging too much for what he did, but that had nothing to do with me. He was always nice to me, charming."

"He kissed Mama's hand," Julie said with a smile. "She's been in love with him ever since."

Caleb laughed and asked, "Wonder what happened to him?"

"Red thinks he came out and caught a cab into town. Hugo was late picking him up. Got caught in a storm at Slidel and had to stop till it passed over. Hugo reported him missing to the New Orleans police after he checked with the Monteleon where he usually stays when he's in town. He wasn't there. So far they haven't found him. His office is worried. He didn't call in, like he usually does."

"Be damned."

Julia picked up the conversation and said, "That's what Red says. It doesn't hurt us, actually. Red says we don't really need him until we get ready to expand. Red's not having to shell out money every time Louie turns around. He'd been talking about expanding into other markets. Right now though, our sales are picking up. We aren't doing gangbusters on Amazon but okay. And, we're still selling out at Red's craft store," Julia said.

"What happened to Hugo's sister?" Caleb asked. "You said she'd died."

"Cancer," Bonnie Fae told him. "Smoker all her life. Finally caught up with her."

"Too bad."

"Hugo was depressed, especially after he got shot on top of it."

"Bad news comes in bunches, sometimes." Caleb knew that from experience.

"She left him her house in New Orleans and some money which he invested in the business, the craft's business," Julie said.

"So, you have a new partner."

"Well, he's Red's partner but under our agreement, Red and now Hugo, get paid out of catalogue sales before we get very much. I might have told you."

"Somebody did," Caleb said.

He guessed that was reasonably fair, that they got paid first. She wasn't worse off for having listed with Amazon and sooner or later, as soon as Red and Hugo recouped their investments, she'd be better off.

"Hugo looks ex-military."

Julie answered. "He is. He retired after twenty years. He and Red met at a trade show in New Orleans a few years ago when Red was expanding. He was looking for a job and Red needed a manager."

"He got a good one," Bonnie Fae said. "He can do it all."

"He must live in the apartment over the truck stop."

"That's right," Julie said. "Red lives in the log cabin at the rear of the property." She looked at him for a second and added, "I've never been in it, in case you're wondering."

"I wasn't but I had wondered where he was living. The log cabin looked like a good bet," Caleb said. "I'm going to look for an apartment in town as soon as I pay off Odom for the truck."

He and the other shop owners had quit the pretense of bootlegging Caleb's help. He was on call and stayed moderately busy. He'd opened a bank account the balance of which had grown steadily.

"What are you doing about mail?" Bonnie Fae asked.

"Damn, I haven't thought about mail until now. I never worried about it in California. My wife took care of everything. All I did was bring home money to pay the bills. She did the rest. She gave me a stack of mail the day she left. It was in a bag. I threw it away without looking at it She'd always done that. I remember when she handed the sack to me, she said something … like you should look at it. I was too shocked to even care."

"You should put in a change of address. Get a PO box in town first," Julie said. "You may have important mail you've been missing."

"Could be. I don't know what I could have been missing, though." Maybe a job offer? I could use a laugh.

Nevertheless, the next day, Caleb did just that, got a PO Box and put in a change of address. He'd get a few surprises.

# Chapter 26

As the campaign picked up, Billy Ray began to focus more on specifics, notably the murder of the Walters. He'd arrested the main suspect only to have the sheriff let him go on a technicality.

"Won't be no technicalities when I'm sheriff. Only convictions!"

The sheriff brought out McNally to refute that but the public was beginning to listen. Even so, the sheriff stayed ahead a couple of points in the polls.

Then, the sheriff made the announcement about Billy Ray "beating" his wife. And, he had a backup witness. "A man who beats his wife ain't fit to hold a public office!" He shouted at one of his speeches. That went over well and his lead climbed back to three points.

Later the sheriff had someone else disclose how Billy Ray had prevailed on a doctor to declare him unfit to serve in the military and how afterward, he went about the country talking about how he would have joined up to serve his country if he'd been physically able.

People stepped back to think about Billy Ray's character after the sheriff's disclosure made the rounds. The sheriff's lead immediately jumped to four points and Billy Ray got worried.

"When you gonna pull your rabbit out of the hat?" Leroy asked, chiding him really.

"I'm jes 'bout ready to do jes that," Billy Ray replied. "So, don't git your bowels in an uproar. I'm still gonna win this election."

Leroy'd just been called as a witness by the committee investigating Billy Ray. He hemmed and hawed, but when all was said and done, he told the truth. It wouldn't do Billy Ray any good, but if he won the election, it wouldn't hurt him. He'd be sheriff.

Wade, the constable, was also called to give testimony.

Wade's testimony was part of the claim the sheriff made that Billy Ray and Leroy had brought in an innocent man and charged him with hitting Billy Ray with a rock when it was physically impossible for Caleb to have done it. The deputy ignored the facts and charged Caleb anyway. Of course, no one knew about the influence of "Glow."

Caleb was also called by the committee to testify. They asked about the "rock throwing" incident. He said the first he'd heard was after Leroy woke him up. "From what I heard about it, I wouldn't have been able to throw a rock that far even if I had been there." The committee already knew that, but wanted to dot the eyes and cross the tees.

They were more interested in what he was doing when the Walters were killed. He testified that he wasn't exactly sure since he didn't know exactly when they were killed. He gave an account of what he did the day he became suspicious and asked Julie Howard to investigate when they didn't answer when he knocked on their door. He testified that he'd never been inside their house. And, his finger prints were not found inside after they were murdered, not even smudged ones.

*****

A few days after his appearance before the committee, Caleb was called by Chief Bush. "Caleb," he said. "How'd you like to do a little back door campaigning for the sheriff?"

"Tell me what you have in mind. I don't have a pot to piss in as far as money," Caleb answered.

"No money. Here's what I want you to do. Ben agrees." He proceeded to tell him what he had in mind.

Caleb laughed and said. "Sounds like California politics. I'll do it. When?"

The chief told him where to go and when and what to do.

The sheriff was holding his kick-off rally at the town's Civic Center on a Saturday night. Refreshments and food would be available, after the speeches. They didn't want people to crowd in to eat and drink only to leave when the speeches began. For the most part, only the sheriff would speak. He'd have a couple of guys introducing him and what they said would be political.

Caleb was given more specific instructions and some coaching. He showed up on time and stood about where the organizer told him to stand.

The Mayor gave his laudatory introduction and received a loud round of applause.

Chief Bush came next and talked specifically about how the sheriff had reorganized the department, bringing in all the latest in technology to improve the performance of the department to make the jobs of the deputies much more efficient.

"More efficiency leads to an improved rate of apprehension of criminals and an improved rate of solving cases," the Chief said. "That's what Sheriff Tolar did! He didn't sit in his chair and read the newspapers, he got his hands dirty solving crime. He went after the criminals, hard and fast, and he caught them. No one in the state has a better record catching criminals."

Caleb doubted anybody had done the research on that claim but it was a political speech and the sheriff wasn't making it.

Finally, the sheriff got to stand behind the podium and speak. His tall figure was as imposing as his deep, gravelly voice was dominating. He talked about his record as sheriff, all he had done to improve the department and to make it more responsive to crime.

"We get to a crime scene faster and with better equipment than any law enforcement department in this damned state. You can quote me on that. I'm not soft on crime. I'm tough on crime."

The applause took over for several minutes.

Finally, the chairman of the rally got up and waved his hands for quiet so the sheriff could continue.

"I thank you good folks for coming. It means a lot to me. My young and inexperienced challenger says I'm soft. He says I turn lose criminals. He says I'm too lazy to do a good job. Well, I can tell you if there's anything soft in my office, it's Billy Ray's head. The only people I've turned loose were the ones he brought in with sloppy work."

He went on to talk about the man his chief deputy brought in for hitting him on the head with a rock. "Turned out the man couldn't have possibly hit him with the rock."

That was Caleb's cue. He waved and shouted. "That's right. I'm the guy he dragged to the jail and tried to frame."

All eyes turned to the side where he stood.

He went on to tell the story of how someone had indeed hit the deputy in the head at Julie Howard's home. Afterward, the deputy and his assistant shot up a corn field before jumping into their car and racing to the junk yard where he was sleeping.

"Now, I know because I've walked it, it takes a little over thirty minutes to get from the Howard's house to the junk yard. I've been told it takes a car about five minutes to drive there. The assistant deputy woke me and told Billy Ray I was asleep and couldn't possibly have been the one who hit him. The constable watching the junk yard from up the road drove down and told him the same thing. Even with everybody telling him he was wrong, Billy Ray cuffed me and threw me into his back seat and dragged me into a jail cell!" Caleb said, his voice growing louder toward the end.

Curses and "boos" came from the crowd.

"Of course, when the sheriff did his investigation, the same investigation Billy Ray should have done, he concluded that Billy Ray had made a mistake. Billy Ray stood up and told the television people and the newspaper people he'd made a mistake and apologized to me. I still didn't like it and I sure am happy to tell everybody what a sloppy job Billy Ray did. I tell you, if he wins this election, I expect crime to increase and I expect convictions to decrease!"

The applause, right on cue, rattled the windows.

The sheriff continued his speech, naming the criminals he'd charged and brought to justice. His success rate, he said, was better than any of his predecessors. And, nobody challenged that claim.

Somebody shouted out "What about the Walter's murders?"

"I'm glad you brought that up," the sheriff said with a gesture in the direction of the voice.

He talked about the case and how Billy Ray had charged Caleb Stanley for the crime. "He was the same man he had charged with hitting him in the head with a rock." He laughed and said, "From what I've seen of Billy Ray, I'd say if you wanted to hit him where it'd do no good, it'd be in the head. He rarely uses that part of his body."

The sheriff's supporters stomped and clapped and shouted support.

The sheriff went over the case in detail including what McNally said at the arraignment and bail hearing. "Billy Ray was convinced that this man had killed those dear people. Mr. Stanley's finger prints magically appeared on the club after a man with ten years' experience and his entire staff examined it carefully when it was brought in and found nothing. Even the judge was upset. Let me see. What did he say? I remember. He said I should take deputy Billy Ray out behind the wood shed and teach him a lesson he'd remember next time he investigated a murder case." In a loud voice, the sheriff shouted, "He threw the case out! He threw it out and walked off the bench, disgusted. I was embarrassed!"

Caleb shouted, "What about me? I had to spend time in jail. The deputy took an eye witness statement from a legally blind man that said I had the club. The man couldn't see two feet in front of him."

Those attending the rally let out a gasp. Caleb held up for a couple of seconds then continued.

"And, if my prints were on the club, why weren't they in the house? And, if I stole the Walters' coin collection, where were the coins? Last I heard, somebody was trying to sell the coins in Houston and Mobile. I only have a bicycle to get around on. No way could I get to Mobile or Houston to do anything. Fact is, Billy Ray just didn't do his job. He didn't do it then, and he didn't do it when somebody hit him in the head with a rock and he sure as hell won't do it if he's elected. He doesn't have a track record, he has a track wreck."

Again, the applause was deafening. The sheriff's supporters had been briefed.

The sheriff finished up and the food and beverage tables were opened.

The television and newspaper reporters flocked around Caleb to ask questions. Most of which had already been asked and answered after the arraignment but Caleb stood there and patiently repeated what he'd already said.

It'd be on the late evening news and in the next day's newspapers. It didn't do Billy Ray's quest to be sheriff any good and Billy knew it.

*****

Since Leroy was still about his only friend, actually the only non-relative who'd listen to him, he talked it over with him, both holding beers and looking at the pond in Billy Ray's back yard.

"He nailed me good, Leroy. I don't know why I let you talk me into charging the man."

"What! Hell, BR, it wasn't me and you know it."

"You're my deputy. You put the cuffs on the man. You threw him in jail. You found the fingerprints."

"I cuffed him because you told me to. Same reason I threw him in jail. You dragged me to the evidence room to look at the club one more time. Hell, we'd already looked at it after I found it in the junk yard where the man wasn't even sleeping anymore. I didn't see a damn fingerprint on that club until we went back – your idea, in case you forgot - just before the hearing. So, don't try to lay that bullshit on me, assistant deputy." He pointed at Billy Ray, all the while nodding his head.

"Yeah, assistant deputy. You've been demoted. And, after the votes are counted, you ain't gonna be that!"

He stormed away cursing, "Son of a bitch."

Billy Ray tried to stop him but it was too late. He'd try to patch it up later.

# Chapter 27

The polls showed the sheriff in a six point lead, considered insurmountable at that late date in the campaign. He and the chief had a beer in City Hall to celebrate.

"The civic center thing was a wipe out!" the chief said. "Who came up with Stanley shouting out like he did?"

"It came out of a meeting. That got the juices flowing. We got headline stories in the papers and the television."

"I don't know what else he can throw at you," the chief said.

"Me either but he still has that army of relatives and friends of same, out there campaigning. It'll probably be close, but I'm beginning to feel like I can make it."

"Billy Ray screwed up with Stanley. Hell, he should have thanked him for saving his boy and called it a day."

"He wanted something he could dangle in front of the voters and a homeless guy without Marshalltown roots looked like the perfect dangle. No relatives to piss off."

"I guess. The Walters murders must have looked like a gift from heaven. He'd already been harping about Stanley and wham 'o, Stanley turns up with a link to the Walters. It might have worked if Billy Ray hadn't brought in the blind guy as a witness. That was smart. The smudged fingerprints didn't hurt either. That sure as hell looked like somebody on the inside tried to transfer the prints to the club handle."

"I prayed when McNally told that in court. Billy Ray must have done that. Hell, for all I know, he killed the Walters for the coins. He needed money to run for my office. Only problem with that is the woman out trying to sell them. We can't find a connection that makes sense to Billy Ray. Has to be a friend of a friend and has to be somebody who knows a little about coins. I don't see that in Billy Ray's family."

"Yeah. Me either. What are you going to do next?"

"My manager says step back and keep quiet. Don't make mistakes. Unless Billy Ray can pull a rabbit out of a hat, it's over. That's what he says."

"What does he want out of it?"

"I'm paying him a fee, but he wants a job. I'll see what I can find for him. Anything around City Hall you can point me to?"

The chief laughed. "I wish I had a nickel for every time a politician has asked me that. I'll keep my eyes open. The mayor has a job now and then. Do you have anything you can offer him?"

"I know the tax assessor. I saved him a couple of times from drunk driving charges. If he has property, I bet I can get him a lower assessment."

"That might work. I'll talk to him."

\*\*\*\*\*

Caleb had dinner with Julie and Bonnie Fae the night after the Civic Center rally for the sheriff. He had told them what was going to happen.

"We tried to find you but even when you started shouting, we could barely find you and after it was all over, and most everybody went for the drinks and food, you were surrounded by news people. We finally went home," Julie said.

"I looked for you too. They told me to stand by the wall so they could see me," he said. "I didn't stay for the food either. I doubt anything was left by the time the news people finished with me."

"We saw you on television," Bonnie Fae said. "You did a great job. The commentators said they think the election is over."

"Wow!"

"Yeah," Julie said. "Big wow! I think you can relax now."

"I hope so. The guy was just using me to win the election. He had no real campaign. I don't guess he's been bothering you anymore," He asked Julie.

She shook her head, no.

At dinner, they talked mostly about her craft sales. The Amazon listing seemed to be paying off with more sales. She wasn't getting much out of it because Red and Hugo had to be repaid first. But, down the line, she expected a decent return. Julie also told him she'd received the final divorce decree. She had known about it but hadn't actually received a copy.

"Funny thing," she told him. "The envelope had been opened and resealed. Could have been the court, but it was odd. Second time it's happened."

"Probably the court secretary. Sealed it before the decree was in it." He laughed. "Had to reopen it to save a stamp."

She shook her head.

They'd find out later that the secretary wasn't the one who'd opened it.

"I've been wanting to ask. Have you heard anything else about Earnest and Bessie, their murders?" Bonnie Fae asked Caleb.

"I talked a little with the chief about it. They've pretty much hit a dead end. Without the coins to chase, they don't have any leads. They think the coins were sold to a foreign investor and they have no way of tracing that."

They kicked that around a bit.

"I kind of thought it might have been Billy Ray and Leroy or at least Billy Ray," Caleb said.

"To get money for his campaign?" Julie asked.

Caleb shook his head, yes. "Problem is, they can't trace the woman who approached the Mobile dealer. They've been all over the county with sketches. Nobody knows her. Could be a friend or relative out of state. If it is, they may never trace them. And, in that case, they may never catch whoever did it."

Bonnie Fae cursed, unusual for her.

"My sentiments as well," Caleb said.

"Maybe the sheriff should expand his search. Maybe somebody else did it," Julie said.

"I think he has but he hasn't come up with any real suspects," Caleb replied. "One of Billy Ray's relatives built a big house on a river someplace. Cost some money but he apparently borrowed it. There's still some question about that. Billy Ray, the sheriff's contacts say, has been using money from his relatives up till now … and cheap labor, also courtesy of his relatives."

"I don't know anybody else the sheriff could look at," Julie said. "I live pretty close to home and my work."

"Me too."

But, Caleb began thinking. *Only people in the county knew about the coins. Is somebody sitting on the money they got when they sold the coins to the foreign guy? Assuming they did sell them. Could be they're just holding onto them till the smoke clears. The woman is the big fly in the ointment. Problem is, she's the only one seen with a coin from the collection. What was it Glow said … all that glitters is not gold. What did it mean?*

He put his thoughts aside and enjoyed dinner. It was always delicious. After all those years of just eating what his wife put in front of him, it was a unique experience to taste and actually enjoy the food. And, Bonnie Fae never failed to have a truly remarkable dessert.

He was pleased they hadn't served meat loaf, Red's favorite.

And, these days, Caleb didn't have to ride the bike home in the dark, he had Odom's Ford junker and it made the trip in around five minutes. He parked it in the pasture across from the park and walked the rest of the way.

Walking along the trail with his flashlight, he reminded himself to check his post office box the next day. So far all he'd been getting was junk mail.

*****

"Are you here?" he asked after he'd turned on the cave light and popped the top of a beer. He'd been content with tea at dinner.

Seconds later, he saw Glow from the dark recesses of the cave. "Of course I'm here."

"I thought you were out of reach, maybe someplace in the Middle East looking at troubles."

"I was, but I keep a little spec on you, kind of like one of your surveillance cameras. You are still my project. I note that you are no longer thinking of me as your Alzheimer's."

"I've given up. Either you are or you are not. At least I can talk to you about personal matters without worrying if I'm scaring the hell out of you. Do you have any comments on anything that's happened?"

"Are you talking about the dog and pony show at the Civic Center? It was okay for human consumption. Simple minded but effective. I think it knocked Billy Ray for a loop. As I said simple minded. Anything would. He'll try to come up with something to counter it."

"What?"

"You know I won't tell you that. That would be cheating. Free will and all that."

"Yeah. Free will. If there is such a thing?"

"Of course, it's influenced by everything and everybody you come into contact with, but it's there waiting to make something happen, usually some kind of mistake."

"Yeah. The kind I make. By the way, speaking of mistakes, I've been meaning to ask, if you don't mind, what the hell did you mean by 'all that glitters is not gold.' I can't come up with anything."

"Ah, been thinking about that have you? Well, I'm not going to tell you anymore. I think you are intuitive enough to figure it out. Keep at it."

"Keep at it? I didn't know I was … at it."

Glow extinguished its self.

"Damn. Another enigmatic answer. Some project I am. But, he said I was thinking about it. Let me see. What the hell have I been thinking about?"

*All that glitters is not gold. I was thinking in terms of the coins but they were apparently real. Maybe Glow was saying something much broader. What else could that be? Something wasn't what it was supposed to be. What the hell could that be?*

He committed it to his subconscious and went to bed.

The next morning, he cooked breakfast over a camp fire to the music of nature in the trees and coming from the river to blend with the classical music from his radio. And, he ate it with a cup of boiled coffee and enjoyed it all.

Odom called with an electrical problem and said one of his buddies had a car they didn't know what to do with. Would he mind taking a look? He promised to come by within the hour.

*****

Odom's car took about an hour and a half to get running. It was age related. No parts were readily available so Caleb had to rebuild the old one and reinstall it. The car at his buddy's shop was somewhat easier. They had overlooked the obvious. Caleb saw it right away and showed it to the junior electrical man who had it out and replaced within an hour. In the interest of good will and future business, he didn't charge for it.

From that job, he drove to the post office to check on mail. He had a batch with most of it falling into the junk mail category. However, there were two items that surprised the heck out of him, a pleasant surprise. Well, his 401k report should not have and wouldn't have had he not always relied on his wife to check his reports. She never said anything about them so he more or less forgot all about it.

He opened the envelope and took a look. The amount staggered him. He looked again. There it was, he had over half a million dollars in his account. *Son of a bitch. All those years of paying in. I kind of figured she'd taken it all out. Here I am, working for food and I have a pretty good investment I could be living on. I have to do some thinking.*

If the 401k was a staggering surprise, the next envelope he opened was even greater.

"What the hell!" He said even though some people standing around could hear him. He looked again, checked the date to see if maybe it was an old letter. No, it was a current tax bill for the home he grew up in, his mom's and dad's. And, he apparently owned it, the house and over a hundred acres with a pond, a requisite for country homes. Livestock had to be watered and kids wanted a place to swim and frolic in the summer and a place for everybody to fish.

"Have to," he said still staring at the paper in his hand. "This is a tax bill and it shows my name. Damn!"

"Myrna must have had it put in my name after my folks died. I knew the property came to me. I was the only heir, but I just figured she sold it. Shoved the papers at me and I signed them without looking, like I usually did," he said. "Be damned. I guess I owe her an apology ... or thanks. She knew how much it meant to me. I guess that's why she looked a little funny when she handed me the bag of mail I threw away. Could have been a tax bill on the house was one of the letters ... and a 401k report. She must have known. Be damned. I guess she had some empathy for me ... maybe it was hard on her, after all was said and done, living a pretense life with me. I'll write her a letter if I can find her address."

He owed a little over two thousand dollars on the tax bill. "I'll draw on my 401k to pay it."

He drove out to see the place. It had been years since he'd been there and he was shocked to see it. Weeds and scrub trees had grown up all around it. Somebody had nailed boards over the windows to keep out vandals, he supposed.

His dad kept a spare key in the garage. It was still there so he got in the back door. The house smelled musty and dank. It was somewhat dark inside but enough light came in through the cracks to let him see. The furnishings were all gone except for the gas stove. His mother preferred to cook with gas so his dad bought her the best there was. And, it was still there.

"Myrna must have sold everything else or people took it. Maybe she couldn't sell the house. I guess not. It technically belonged to me. Or, hell, maybe she hung onto it knowing she'd leave me one day and I'd need a place to come to die. I don't know if she was that perceptive or not. I'll thank her anyway."

Well, he'd need to get the utilities turned on. Maybe get some insurance. It was odd the place hadn't burned down already. But, the problem of where to go for the winter had just been solved. He could go home. He could have his old room but figured he'd take the master bedroom instead. Bigger.

"I wonder if Julie will mind driving up here? I could drive down there, but Bonnie Fae would be around." He was thinking about their relaxing times together.

He'd work on that later. He had much work to do before the place would be livable.

His next stop was at the county office to pay the taxes. He found that he had enough in his checking account to cover that much. Afterwards, he stopped at the library and wrote the manager of his 401k and asked for a withdrawal of ten thousand dollars. That, he figured, should cover the rest of his expenses. Of course, he'd buy used furniture at junk stores and the Salvation Army warehouse. He had some cooking ware in the cave and knew where he could get more if he needed more, the junk yard.

He'd get insurance for the house after he received the ten thousand dollars.

Hmm, he had a thought about his future. *Why don't I become a traveling electrical-car consultant? He'd thought about it before and it seemed a good idea. No charge for problems I can't fix or diagnose. Hell, I'll find a van I can repair in the junk yard, buy it and get it to running. I'll paint something on the sides to tell people what I do. Put an ad in the local papers a hundred miles around and wait for calls.*

He'd think more about it. See if any bugs popped up.

All of a sudden life began to look better, in fact, very good. Really the first time he'd felt that good since he was a kid living at home.

He went to Wal-Mart and bought enough cleaning supplies to clean the house and spent the rest of the day doing that. The window coverings came off. Surprisingly, the windows were okay, none broken out. A couple with cracks but all worked with a little effort. His dad was a stickler about getting things to work.

I guess I also must have inherited my obsession over problems from him. Hell, maybe too much.

The next day was more of the same except in the yard. He cut the weeds and scrub trees and bushes then stood back for a look. While he worked outside, the utility companies came and connected the electricity and water. His dad had a sprinkler system for the yards so Caleb watered the grass that was left after throwing out fertilizer.

Inside, no pipes leaked, the commodes flushed and all fixtures worked including the gas stove and water heater. He had to turn the water heater on. A miracle, he thought as he took a hot shower at the end of the day.

"Damn, I have a house! My own damned house," he said as he walked from room to room.

# Chapter 28

He asked Julie and Bonnie Fae if they wanted to look at it. They said yes so he took them out to see it, after dinner. It was a three bedroom house with three baths actually. No powder room though one of the bedroom baths did have a door to the hall. His dad figured guests with a need wouldn't mind sharing a bath with a bedroom.

They walked through it with him, room to room, touching the walls, turning on the water in the bathroom, checking the windows, much like a prospective buyer would do. At the end, they proclaimed it to be a "good house."

"You'll like it here," Bonnie Fae said.

He agreed. All he needed was a bed and a few other items to make it livable. He'd pick up those the next day.

The next morning however, he had two jobs to look at, both old trucks. They turned out to have parts that needed to be rebuilt, rewired actually. It took him a couple of hours to finish the jobs. The trucks worked fine afterwards and he got paid on the spot. He'd performed so well that the shop owners trusted his work enough to pay him when he'd finished a job.

He drove from the shop to the Salvation Army warehouse and bought bedding for his house. His purchase also included a table and chairs for eating which required an extra trip. There was a breakfast bar in the kitchen which would be sufficient for him, but he felt he needed something for guests, Bonnie Fae and Julie.

By the end of the day, the house was livable. All he had to do was move his stuff from the cave to the house. And, that he intended doing the following day.

In the meantime, Billy Ray was ready to pull his rabbit out of the hat. He tracked Leroy down to tell him what it was and to enlist his aid.

"What the hell, Billy Ray, that warrant has probably expired," Leroy said when his "assistant deputy" told him he was going to arrest Charlie Howard using the warrant that was in the file. He knew his address in the Mississippi Delta.

"No problem with the warrant. It was extended a year. Charlie has a security firm. We'll pick him at his office," Billy Ray told him.

"Hmm. Well, I guess that's official business then." How in the hell did he get that extended? I bet he has a friend in the record's section. "We'll arrest the guy, Billy Ray. That'll make the headlines and get the friends of the guy Charlie shot on your side. Scooter Todd."

"My thinking too, Leroy. Uh, I'll let you take the credit since you think I set you up on the Stanley arrest."

"Naw. It's okay. We were both hot under the collar last time we talked. You're running for sheriff. You take the credit. You can take care of me after you're elected."

"Great. I'll pick you up in the morning. We have to get a move on. Election's coming up and the polls say I'm behind the big assed bastard who's sitting in my chair. My daddy says he was so ugly when he was born, he was left in the swamps and had to eat saw briars to stay alive. That's why he sounds like he does."

Leroy looked at him for a second or two then said, "Uh huh."

"I'll tell you something else, Leroy, the sheriff ain't the only one who can think. How about this for the Walters murders. Charlie needed money for his business. He knows about the coins and drives down one night and hits those old people over their heads. Takes their coins, dresses like a woman and tries to sell them in Mobile. And, I guess he sold them to some foreign guy who was in the coin shop."

"Yeah, Billy Ray. That'd be something if he did it."

"That'd be getting me a new job, that's what. Sheriff. All we gotta do is get Charlie to confess. Or find some stuff that came from their                                                                                    house."

"Somebody's gonna wonder how he knew about the homeless guy in the junk yard."

"Nobody'll care if he confesses to the killings."

"Yeah." He was wondering just how they were going to get Charlie to confess. He was a shoot first, talk later kind of guy. Billy Ray knows that better than me. He lived close to the guy.

"We're gonna kick some ass tomorrow, Leroy."

*****

The next day, while Caleb worked on his new found house, Billy Ray and Leroy drove to the delta to arrest Charlie Howard for the killings of Earnest and Bessie Walters even though the warrant they carried was to arrest Charlie Howard for the killing of Scooter Todd. Billy Ray hadn't told Leroy about arresting him for the murders of the Walters.

Billy Ray convinced Wilson Ray, a local reporter, to come along. He was happy to come. It would be a big story and he'd have the by line.

To make sure the warrant was still valid, Leroy read it over before they set out. Surely enough, it had been extended a year. That's all he needed. He didn't have to ask how or why. It was in black and white.

Leroy drove. He was armed with his Glock. Billy Ray brought his squirrel shooter, a twenty-two automatic. Leroy wasn't sure that was okay, but he didn't know Billy Ray had it until they were underway. He would have checked with the sheriff but he was speaking at a breakfast meeting of the Kiwanis Club.

*Maybe nothing will happen. Besides it'll be hard to kill anybody with a twenty two. And, I ain't shooting at nobody unless they shoot at me.*

They stopped for lunch about half way there; hamburgers with fries and beers. Leroy only drank part of his since he was driving but Billy Ray killed his to the last drop. Wilson stayed with coke to drink.

Even with the GPS guiding them, they managed to get lost twice before finding the small street on which Charlie had his security service office. It was dusk dark by the time they pulled up on the small street at the driveway into the office parking lot. The office was located in a single wide mobile home on which a porch had been added. Lights were on inside.

A man could be seen moving about. A woman sat working at a desk.

"Nobody else," Billy Ray said. "We got lucky. Should be an easy arrest." He looked over his shoulder at the young man in the back seat, the reporter who'd come along for the story.

"Can you see?"

"Sure. I'll have to get out and get closer to take pictures though."

"I'll get you there, Wilson," Billy Ray replied. "Good newspaper reporter has to get close to get a good story."

"That's right, man."

"Okay, So how do you want to do this, Billy Ray?" Leroy asked. He took a quick look at the man in the back seat. "I think it's crazy bringing a newspaper guy into an arrest. What if he gets shot? Damn crazy, Billy Ray."

"It'd be crazy not to, Leroy. It's my ticket to the sheriff's office. Without newspaper coverage, the whole thing is a waste."

"It'll be good, Leroy," the newspaper guy said, patting Leroy on the back. "I'll be watching my ass."

"You better."

"I'd like to get Charlie outside. Be easier to make an arrest, I think. Can you tell if he's carrying a gun?" Billy Ray asked.

Leroy peered through the window. "Hell, from here, I can barely tell he's a man."

"Me neither."

"Okay. You're in charge for now. It's your arrest. What are we going to do?"

"Hmm, yeah." Billy Ray said. He got out of the car, hitched at his belt nervously, turned and stared across the street, thinking. After a bit, he turned to face Leroy. It was darker than when they drove up. The porch lights of the mobile home office came on.

He asked Wilson, "Will your camera take pictures in this light?"

Wilson stared out the window. "Won't be worth a shit, frankly."

"Okay, we'll leave the car lights on, Leroy. Park with the lights angling on the front porch. Leave the motor running."

Leroy shrugged. "Okay. I sure as hell hope you know what you're doing."

"It's going to be fine," Billy Ray said.

"Okay," Billy Ray said poking his head through the car's window. "Park it like I said and follow me. We'll spread out. I'll stand to the left of the porch. You stay right. I'll tell him he's under arrest and we'll have to play it by ear after that. Who knows what the son of a bitch will do?"

"What about me?" Wilson asked.

"You stand this side of the car so you'll have a good angle to take pictures of me and the guy we're arresting, Charlie Howard." He waved toward the place he wanted Wilson to stand.

"Damn, this is something else! Son of a bitch. I'm having fun!" Wilson said.

"Yeah. I hope it stays that way," Leroy said, then asked, "How we gonna get him to come out, Billy Ray?"

"Leave that to me."

"It's yours," Leroy said.

He told Leroy where to park the car.

Leroy parked as told, got out and stood facing the right side of the porch, thirty yards away. Wilson stood on the left side of the car with his camera behind Leroy. From where he stood, he could pivot left and right to get shots of Billy Ray and Leroy as well as Charlie Howard as the arrest developed.

Billy Ray hurried to his position on the left side of the porch, also about thirty yards from the door to the office, his twenty two automatic gripped firmly in his hand.

Leroy wished he hadn't brought it, but didn't say anything. They were about to confront a man who'd shot another man and if Billy Ray were somehow right, the man had also killed two old people with a club. He might need the twenty two if things got rough.

Wilson got to his knees and focused on the office porch. Then, he waited.

Both men watched Billy Ray take out his phone and punch in telephone numbers. Leroy, closer than Wilson was to Billy Ray, heard him say, "Let me speak to Charlie." The lady working at the desk shrugged and said something to Charlie who picked up the other phone.

"Charlie, I was passing and I saw one of your men – I think - get out of a car and collapse in the parking lot. Left the lights on. I thought you ought to know." He immediately punched off before Charlie could say anything.

They saw Charlie look out the window before rushing for the door. He came onto the porch and was on the first step of the stairs down when Billy Ray shouted out, "Charlie, we're from the Marshalltown Sheriff's office. We're here to arrest you for the murders of Earnest and Bessie Walters and for killing Scooter Todd."

Leroy cringed when he heard the reference to the Walters. They were not named in the warrant.

Charlie stopped mid-step and turned to where Billy Ray stood with his twenty two leveled at him. "Hands up." Billy shouted and fired a shot. The bullet grazed Charlie's head but did little damage. He dropped to his knees and began firing the Glock he'd yanked from his belt-holster. The first shot hit Billy Ray in the chest and knocked him down but he was wearing a flack-jacket so it only stunned him.

Wilson began taking pictures when Charlie came out the door and continued flashing.

Once Charlie began firing, Leroy opened up with his Glock. The first shot hit Charlie just above his hip, knocking him on his side. He cursed and groaned. But, he still leveled his gun and shot back. His shot hit Leroy in the stomach. Leroy got a bit lucky because the bullet hit his belt buckle first and shattered. Nevertheless, it dropped him to his knees. He continued firing wobbly and managed to hit Charlie in the left arm.

Wilson moved around to get better shots.

Billy Ray fired again, drawing a rapid fire response from Charlie. One shot hit Billy Ray in the flack-jacket but a second hit him in the arm. He fell but held onto his automatic rifle.

On the other side of the parking area, the pain got too much for Leroy. He dropped his gun as he rolled over and grabbed at his stomach.

"I'm hurt, Billy Ray. Call for a damn ambulance."

Charlie did about the same thing. He shouted, "Okay. You got me. I'm not shooting anymore. Need a doctor. Throwing my gun out." He threw his Glock to one side of the porch.

Leroy got to his knees. "He's quitting, Billy Ray."

But Billy Ray ignored what both men said and continued firing his twenty two. He wanted Charlie dead. Most of the shots went wild because Billy Ray couldn't hold the gun steady with his injured arm. The shots plowed into the side of the office. A couple ripped up splinters from the porch where Charlie rolled back and forth to stay clear of the shots. He cursed when Billy Ray kept shooting. Inside, the secretary began dialing presumably to call for help after the first shot.

About a couple of minutes later, the sirens reached them.

Two police cars rolled up, sirens blaring, and red lights flashing. Four officers jumped out of the cars and stood behind their doors. One shouted, "Throw down your weapons!"

Wilson got all that as well.

Though in pain and pressing his hand to his stomach where Charlie's bullet shattered, Leroy managed to shout, "We're from the Marshalltown Sheriff's department, here to serve an arrest warrant on Charlie Howard for murder."

At that time, Billy Ray staggered up and said, "I cautioned Charlie Howard that we were here to take him in for the murder of Scooter Todd and to ask him about the murders of Earnest and Bessie Walters. When I said that, he started shooting at me with his automatic. Hit me in the chest. We had no choice but to return fire. We figured he was trying to escape when he heard me call the Walters names."

Wilson got close and took a shot of Billy Ray talking to the other officers, blood running down his arm.

Leroy looked at Billy Ray, dumbfounded. What the hell. We shot first. You shot first. What the fuck am I going to do? He figured his ass was on the line. He had no choice but to go along. It was their word against the word of a guy who'd killed once, and if Billy Ray were to be believed, maybe he'd killed three times. I wonder if Wilson heard what Billy Ray said before he started shooting? I don't know whether to ask or let Billy Ray coach him. Son of a bitch!

"We're taking all three of you to the hospital for treatment," one of the officers said. "I'll talk to my supervisor about what we should do next. Let me see that warrant you were talking about," he asked Leroy.

Leroy walked, moaning from the pain and bent over, to their car, got the warrant and handed it to him. He studied it briefly and handed it back. "Only names Scooter Todd."

"I didn't hear it all, but my deputy, Billy Ray, told Mr. Howard we wanted to question him about the Walters. That just came up. We found out where Mr. Howard was working and figured we should bring him in on the other murders. We had no idea he'd start shooting when the Walters' names were mentioned." Son of a bitch. I'm lying through my teeth. I may be driving a truck for a living after this. I sure as hell hope Billy Ray wins the election. That's the only way, I'll keep my job.

The officer asked Wilson, "You have anything you want to add?"

"No sir, I'm with the Marshalltown Press. I just came for the story." He showed him a press card.

"Okay," the officer said.

Leroy breathed a sigh of relief.

The officer grumped and walked away. The three wounded men were loaded into the ambulance which took them to the hospital for treatment. Charlie's secretary watched from the porch until the officer questioned her. She only heard the shooting and none of the verbal exchanges between the men.

In response to the officer's questions about the shooting, she said, "I don't know one gun from another. So, there's nothing I can tell you about that."

Everyone left.

*****

The officer's superior listened to the man's report and said, "I don't think we have a choice. They had a warrant and apparently Charlie started firing when the one deputy, Billy Ray something … told him they wanted to talk. Only a guilty man fires first. Send him to Marshalltown as soon as the doctors give their okay. I'm gonna call the sheriff down there first though."

He got Sheriff Tolar at home and told him what had happened.

"What? That warrant expired last year."

"The one I saw had been renewed … a week or so ago."

"Couldn't have. All renewals have to come through me. Hell, usually. Somebody else might have done it. Should be in the file. I'll check it in the morning when I get in."

"Till you get it squared away, I'm sending Howard to you as soon as the doctor releases him. Okay? He's your problem till you get that warrant looked at."

"Okay. I'll do what I have to do."

The next morning early, Charlie Howard was driven to Marshalltown where he was taken to the country jail and put into a cell.

Leroy and Billy Ray were driven to Marshalltown by Wilson in their car. Neither man was believed seriously enough injured to have to spend any more time in the hospital.

# Chapter 29

The sheriff pulled the file and found no document authorizing an extension of the warrant. He asked his secretary who said she'd seen Billy Ray in the file room but didn't know what he was doing. Later, she told one of her friends, it was like steam coming out of the sheriff's ears.

He called Leroy and Billy Ray into his office.

"Okay, Billy Ray, why the hell did you take it on yourself to extend an expired arrest warrant. That damn warrant you served had expired last year. Nobody had extended it. You were seen in the file room. YOU altered it. I'm firing you ass for cause right now!"

"I didn't, sheriff. I didn't. I looked at it and saw it was outstanding so I decided to serve it."

"How'd you know where he was?"

"Uh, somebody who knows Julia Howard said she saw a letter that had his address on it."

"Leroy? What do you know about this?"

"Nothing, sheriff. Billy Ray showed the warrant to me and said we should serve it. It was still good as far as I could see."

"Get out of my office, both of you! Neither of you is worth spit!"

Billy Ray looked back at the door and said, "Enjoy that chair for a little while longer, sheriff. It's gonna be mine in a few days!" He laughed.

*****

The newspaper story came out that afternoon with a page full of photos. The story, backed by photos, lauded the efforts of the sheriff's department to keep after Charlie Howard until Billy Ray bravely confronted him in a shoot-out.

While wounded, the story continued, both men continued to trade shots with the Charlie Howard until the accused surrendered. The television crew followed up with a filmed version of the story, giving Billy Ray complete credit for the arrest.

The sheriff called the DA and asked what he should do. The DA left a message for the judge. It would be the next day before the judge told them to get a full release from Howard and transport him home.

"Make damn sure he gives up all rights in exchange for you dismissing all charges against him," he told the DA.

It was done.

Of course, right away, Billy Ray was telling the newspaper and television news how the sheriff had "once again" released a known criminal for technical reasons. At the end of the day, Billy Ray was three points ahead of the sheriff in the polls.

The election was eight days away.

*****

Caleb had a full day's work that day, four trucks, all with odd problems. The last one was at Odom's which he finished up around six. He had to rebuild a part for that one.

As he was finishing, the chief walked in. "Caleb," he said. "I was driving home and saw the light. Figured it was you."

"Yeah. Just wrapping it up," he said. "How's it going?"

The chief asked if he'd heard about the Charlie Howard arrest for shooting Scooter Todd and on suspicion of killing the Walters. He had and was aware that Billy Ray was making hay out of the story.

"You know Charlie was released don't you?" the chief asked.

"No, I didn't. Why?"

He explained about the defective warrant, the mutual release and how Billy Ray was blaming the sheriff, the DA and the judge for once again letting criminals go because they were too lazy to prosecute.

Of course, there was no real evidence to even support any connection of Charlie Howard with the Walter's murders. Besides, a quick call by the DA found that Charlie had been in New York at the time the Walters were murdered.

"Be damned," Caleb said. "No, I hadn't heard that. A warrant that wasn't a warrant. An arrest that was invalid and a charge that no longer existed." It reminded him what Glow had said about all that glitters not being gold.

The chief said goodbye and went home.

Caleb closed the shop and drove to his new home, his old family home. He was thinking all the way home however about Glow's enigmatic comment.

"I have to think broadly," he told himself and began rehashing all he'd heard about the Walter's murders. By the time he'd reached home, he had an idea. It wasn't much, but since he gave Glow credit for never saying anything that wasn't important, it was worth telling the sheriff.

So, he called the number he'd been given for the sheriff.

"Yeah," the sheriff answered in his usual gravel coated voice. "Sheriff Todd. It better be good calling me at home."

Caleb told him who he was and said, "I had a thought for you, on the Walter's murders. Might not be worth a hill of beans, but here it is."

Not wishing to have the sheriff hang up on him or worse, he didn't tell him how the thought came about, from the Glow that had been with him since he'd arrived in Marshalltown. Instead, he said, "You know the woman who sold the coin in Mobile? Rough looking, nobody knew?"

He did.

"What if it wasn't a woman, but a man dressed to look like one." That'd sure as hell fit with what Glow was saying, in broad terms.

"So."

"You said the woman probably sold the other coins to a foreign collector. I assume for cash. Well, about that time, Hugo gave Red some money, he said was from his sister's estate to get their catalogue business up and running. I think his sister died of cancer."

"Yeah. I hope this has a point, Caleb. I'm nursing a beer."

"I hope it does too. What I'm suggesting - the point - is this." He asked the sheriff to check and see how much of an estate the sister had. Also, check to see how much money he gave Red for the business. If the two amounts didn't match, he should search Hugo's apartment for a wig and lipstick. "I'm thinking the sister didn't have much money. If that's the case, assuming Hugo gave Red a fairly big amount, it had to come from someplace else. Like from the sale of Earnest's coin collection."

"You're suggesting Hugo might have killed them for the coins? And sold them?"

"I'm betting his fingerprints were found in their house. He had done work for them so he didn't have to worry about fingerprints. I'm also betting his sister had chemo and had to wear a wig, the same wig Hugo might have worn as a disguise, I'm hoping you'll find it in Hugo's apartment. Put that wig and the amount of money he invested in Red's business together and you'll have a decent case against him for murder."

"He did take a bullet for Red. I suppose you have to really like somebody to do that. Maybe like 'em enough to kill for 'em. Well, Caleb, I first thought you were full of shit when you started talking, but by the time you'd finished, I thought you were making good sense. We've had no luck with the case. Not a bit. Your theory looks pretty damn good. I'll get on it tonight."

"Good luck."

"Uh, I don't guess you have any numbers to go with what you've been suggesting?"

"No. Sorry, sheriff. Strictly guess work on my part." *And Glow's hints. But, I'll keep that to myself.*

"Well, I reckon I'll have to rattle a cage or two in New Orleans to see if I get anything." Hugo's sister lived in New Orleans.

And, he did, that same night. With the election only a few days away, he knew he was the one that needed to pull a rabbit out of the hat to win. He also called the DA and asked for his help. Legally, he figured the DA might have strings he could pull a lot faster than he could.

*****

Caleb went about working on the house. He'd pretty much had it in livable condition. As he worked, he became aware of the yellow-orange dot floating around him.

"Ah, you're here," he said.

Glow replied, "I am. I was impressed how you'd let your free will deduce that the Hugo guy might have done the killing. Even if he didn't, I think it was a good piece of deduction."

"Are you saying I've sent the sheriff off on a wild goose chase?"

"No indeed. I'm just congratulating you for some good thinking. You'll know by the morning if you were close."

"Damnit Glow, whatever you are, I won't sleep thinking about it now."

"Well, I think you should get a good night's sleep."

"I'm going to take that statement as a good sign."

"Take it any way you like, Caleb. You're still my project."

"I hope that's a good thing. What can you say about Julie?"

"She's a lovely lady. Deserved better than the man she married, but he was competent. Good business man. Kind of had some bad luck shooting that guy over the gambling debt. I guess it worked out okay for him … and for her. He's getting married," Glow said.

"I … I hope she will be too."

"Ah, who knows? Got free will involved in that."

*Yeah. Her free will mostly. My free will is clear.*

With that, Glow diminished to nothing.

Caleb took a shower and went to bed. In spite of what Glow had said to reassure him, he still had difficulty sleeping.

*****

The next morning Caleb had calls from two repair shops in town for electrical problems their resident electrical mechanics couldn't solve. He promised to take a look and had both trucks on the road before noon.

Bonnie Fae called mid-morning to invite him to dinner. That pleased him. They always had great food but the real joy he felt came from knowing he'd see Julia. Both seemed to take pride in only putting the most delicious dishes on the table and both always seemed glad to see him.

She didn't say and he didn't ask if Red would be there. Having heard nothing from the sheriff, he wasn't sure if his theory of the night before was valid of just a piece of fanciful guesswork.

*Hell, for all I know, Red was the murderer. No, makes more sense for Hugo to be the one with the club, if either man was involved.* He cautioned himself that what he'd told the sheriff was as much guesswork as anything else.

*I'm easily confused, he told himself. My wife had two children by another man and convinced me they were mine. And, she never loved me.* However, he had to admit that he'd never loved her either. The marriage had been a total sham. But, as he looked around the house, he knew he owed her a debt of gratitude for saving the house.

*And, now, for the first time in my life, I think I've met somebody I can love. Hell, I do love her. And, I know she loves me. I can see it in her eyes. I just have to see if I can put together a life for us.*

By the end of the day, nobody had called about Hugo and he was reluctant to call and ask. "Hell," he said to himself, "My name is probably mud at the sheriff's office for embarrassing him. He might have already resigned."

He spent the rest of the afternoon moving everything else from the cave into his new home. He dismantled the lights and generator and radio and left them in the back of the cave. Leaving, he pulled the vines and briars over the trail and the mouth of the cave to conceal it from strangers stumbling past.

He also did some more thinking about how he was going to make a secure living. Jumping from one shop to another around town, when they had work, didn't seem secure enough to enter a serious relationship. His thoughts jelled with putting together the "traveling" van to make repairs all over still seemed good. He could work from his house.

*I love Julie. I love her. I feel warm when I get close to her. I want to reach out and hug her, kiss her. I want her with me all the time. But, I have to be able to make a living. Even if she's doing okay in her business, it's still my job to make a living.*

It was what his dad had taught him and he had no doubt that he had been right.

He did more thinking about how he could get a more stable business going and decided he was on the right track. He'd sleep on it and re-visit it the next morning, over coffee.

*****

He parked and rang the front door bell that evening. Julie answered and kissed him on the lips. He responded with a kiss of his own and almost asked if she wanted to see the progress he'd made getting his house ready for living, but didn't.

Bonnie Fae brought him a beer, in a frosted glass. He'd said how much he liked beer in a frosted glass and she remembered. She and Julie had tea.

Julie asked, "Have you heard the news?"

282

"No. What news?"

"About the sheriff?"

*I hope he didn't resign.*

"Tell me."

"He solved Earnest and Bessie's murders. It was Hugo. They found a wig in his apartment. Also lipstick. They had figured he'd dressed like a woman to sell Earnest's coin collection in Mobile. They found one coin also. The last one. They think he sold the others to a foreign collector for around a hundred thousand dollars."

"A hundred thousand! Wow! What'd he do with it?" He knew, or figured he knew, but wanted to make sure.

Julie looked down, embarrassed. "Well, I hate to say, but he gave it to Red for the catalogue business with Amazon that we'd started. I don't know what's going to come of that. Red may have to give it back. Trouble is, he doesn't have it. He spent it getting the business up and running."

She went on to say that Hugo had said the money came from his sister's house in New Orleans, but when they investigated, they found the house had been mortgaged to its value to pay for her medical treatment before she died.

"Hugo denied killing the guy from New York, but the sheriff's investigators, with some help from the New Orleans police department, think they can link Hugo to the guy's last hours. They found his body in Lake Pontchartrain."

"Has he confessed?" Caleb asked. He didn't figure Red would get implicated by Hugo, even if he had been part of it, but was curious.

"Not to killing the guy from New York but kind of to killing the Walters," Julia said. "He said Red needed money and he did what he had to do. The DA said it was just a matter of time before they got everything out of him."

"What a shock! Anything else?"

Bonnie Fae said, "Hugo did say that he'd thrown the club he'd killed them with in the front yard by the ditch. He hadn't taken anything but the coin collection, none of the junk jewelry Billy Ray and Leroy found in the junk yard."

"I imagine the sheriff asked them about that. They tried to frame me with that."

"Oh, he did. The sheriff did," Bonnie Fae said. "Leroy talked his head off. Said he saw Billy Ray stuff something in his pocket the day they were investigating inside the house. Also saw him pick something up by the ditch and put it in the trunk of the car."

Julie added, "The sheriff had a news conference this afternoon and told the whole story. The newspaper and television station ran it as their lead story."

Bonnie Fae added, "Don't forget the arrest of Charlie, Julie. And, how Billy Ray tried to work that. Leroy said Billy Ray started shooting before Charlie did. That newspaper reporter told that."

"Be damned. I can't say I'm the least bit sorry that Billy Ray got nabbed. He deserved it. What'd he come up with as an answer?" Caleb asked.

Bonnie Fae laughed. "He didn't blame it on you ... at first anyway. He hemmed and hawed but those reporters wouldn't let it go. They were onto him by then. So, he finally admitted that he may have misunderstood what Charlie said when he told him he was under arrest. He was sure Charlie cursed him and reached for his Glock. That's why he started shooting. Leroy said he heard everything and what Billy Ray was saying just wasn't true."

"So, Leroy finally stood up and told the truth. He's been covering for Billy Ray the whole time. I don't imagine the polls will show Billy Ray with a lead over the sheriff tomorrow," Caleb said.

"People the reporters interviewed all said they'd never vote for Billy Ray for anything," Julie said. "There's some talk that he may withdraw from the race."

"He should," Bonnie Fae said.

"The sheriff terminated him as of this afternoon so he's no longer a deputy," Bonnie Fae added. "The reporters asked if the sheriff was going to press charges."

"You know what Billy Ray said then?" Julie asked.

"What?"

"That's when he got around to blaming it all on you. After you'd molested his son, he became confused and made stupid mistakes. Used bad judgment."

Caleb laughed. "I guess he did."

"I imagine they'll be after an interview from you tomorrow," Julie said.

"I'll be ready. What'd the sheriff say about pressing charges? Billy Ray should spend time behind bars for all he's done."

Julie answered, "The sheriff said he was turning his file over to the DA. The DA will make a decision about what to do with Billy Ray and Leroy."

"Poor Leroy. I know he must have considered Billy Ray a kind of friend." Caleb recalled what Leroy had told him about Billy Ray's high school days, how he'd been bullied and abused.

Bonnie Fae and Julie shrugged. If they knew the story, they weren't telling it. So, Caleb let it drop.

# Chapter 30

Dinner that night with Julia and Bonnie Fae was great for Caleb, and made all the better by the news he'd heard about Billy Ray. And, the dessert, bread pudding with decaffeinated coffee, was *out of this world.*

Julie walked him to the door. Bonnie Fae, as had become her habit, said goodbye in the dining room. He was glad she understood.

Caleb held her close and kissed her softly at first, then with more intensity. Julie responded. Both were reluctant to turn loose of each other.

"I love you, Julie," he said, looking into her eyes.

"I love you, Caleb. I never thought I'd love again," she said. "You swept me away the first time your eyes met mine."

"I felt the same way. You know something, I just came down here to die," he said. "Now, I'm so glad I didn't."

She drew back. "I kind of thought something was the matter. You are so capable. I wondered why you were walking up and down the road working for food. Mama thought so too. She was afraid you had a disease or something."

He laughed and said, "No disease like you would imagine, but I'll tell you about it one day. It was more a disease of our culture." I wonder what Glow would say about that? It sounds like something he'd say.

"But, if I hadn't tried to work for food, I wouldn't have met you." He knew he had Glow to thank for it, but felt that was a secret he'd better keep to himself.

"I was coming out to see you in the morning. See what all you've done. What you need to do, if anything," she said. "We could have coffee … and talk."

He agreed, but read more into what she had said. The coffee suggestion was okay. Also the talk, but … he knew there'd be more.

Driving home, he figured his solution, the one he'd been kicking around in his thoughts on how to make a living was a good one. He'd get a van, like he'd been thinking, maybe one from the junk yard that he could get to run and put his name and phone number on the side, along with some kind of logo about the business. He'd either scrounge or buy the equipment he'd need and install it in the van.

He'd consult with repair shops on their difficult electrical problems and after a diagnosis and recommendation, if the local repairman couldn't fix it, he'd do it. He'd advertise up and down the southern part of the state, where driving wouldn't be a problem.

He'd use an answering machine to take calls when he was otherwise engaged. There'd be no need to hire anybody to help. *Keep my overhead low.*

There'd have to be the usual business arrangement with credit cards. Everybody paid with credit cards, well most people did anyway. By the time he was driving into his driveway, he'd reached a number of decisions and had a number of questions that might impact those decisions.

He'd give the business a year. If it took off, he could ask Julie to marry him.

*Hmm, maybe I'll ask her ahead and tell her my plan. A one year wait might not be bad. She'd be able to get to know me. Hopefully, she'd still be willing after the year.*

*I don't know what impact Hugo's misdeeds will have on her catalogue business, but she can continue it at least through Red's craft's store.*

She had been selling all she crafted and now with the other ladies doing some crafting, she could offer her art pieces in other stores around the state. Maybe he could help her with that.

He wondered what impact, if any, Hugo's jailing will have on Red's business. If the Walter's heirs, their two girls, demand the money back, would Red have to cough it up or could he just give them Hugo's investment. Could he cough it up?

*I'm glad it's not my problem.*

*****

He pulled into his driveway and went inside. Even though he'd had a beer at Julie's, he wanted another one, well a glass of beer anyway, on the porch before he turned in.

He sat in a rocker on the back porch and looked into the night. The moon was almost full and covered the pasture and pond in a silver sheen. The birds and night creatures were calling to one another. A huge raccoon raced across the back yard as he sipped his beer.

"Well, you've become domesticated," Glow said as it appeared in the adjacent rocker. "You looked comfortable so I thought I'd join you. The rocker doesn't work for me however." The orange glow jiggled a bit like Glow was laughing.

"I have a new life. Well, almost. Thanks to you. You more or less guided me."

"I didn't. I just encouraged you to use your free will and you did. Now, all you need is for Julie to use hers."

"Uh, huh. I've been thinking about that."

"I know. Your traveling business. It should work. You're well qualified."

Caleb thanked it.

"I note that you left your bag of hemlock in the cave."

"The bag was my way out of my past life. I thought it was over."

"Good thing Billy Ray's boy needed saving."

Caleb laughed. "Yeah. Thanks. And, thanks for sending me down the road to work for food."

Glow again bobbed up and down, like it was chuckling. "A man of your talents and skills doing common labor, but it got you going."

"It did."

"Good night," Glow said and disappeared.

Caleb finished his beer and went to bed. And, he slept well, at peace with himself, something that had eluded him for years.

The next morning, as he had breakfast and coffee, he turned on the radio he'd bought for the house. The announcer was saying, "Now, Billy Ray Johnson. You've been relieved of your duties as a sheriff's deputy. You may be facing criminal charges and yet, you've just said you intend continuing your campaign to be sheriff. How can you possibly do that?"

Billy Ray said, "I have done nothing wrong. I served an outstanding warrant and was shot by a man wanted for murder. I brought him in and the sheriff, like he always does when he has to work, let him go. I was almost killed as was my deputy, Leroy, and the sheriff just let the man go. When I saw that, I knew I had to campaign on. Let the people decide my future. I have nothing to hide. I want to be your sheriff. I know I'll do a good job. Just disregard what the sheriff is saying. What would you expect the man to say? He's just trying to cover his behind for being a bad sheriff all these years."

"You said your boy had been molested by Caleb Stanley and it made you depressed to the point where you might not have been thinking clearly."

"I did, but let me clarify that. I never said or did anything wrong. The depression just drove me to be more intense about bringing him in … about bringing in all criminals. And, every time I did, the sheriff let 'em go. It's time to let the sheriff go. Elect me and I'll make sure he's gone."

The reporter thanked him.

"Be damned," Caleb said. "Old Billy Ray isn't going quietly into that dark night."

He heard a car door slam outside and assumed it was Julie. He went to the front door about the time the bell was ringing. It wasn't Julie but a newspaper reporter and photographer. He wanted to ask questions about the charges Billy Ray had been making.

Caleb invited him into the kitchen. They sat at the table for the interview. Caleb explained how he'd come into contact with Billy Ray, all about rescuing his son from being snake bit and how there was absolutely no evidence that the boy had been molested in any way.

"He thought I hit him with a rock but I was asleep when it happened. No way could I have hit him. And, that was verified. He accused me of killing the Walters and that turned out to be completely false. The evidence he used was planted and there is some proof that he probably planted it."

"We reported on that at the time," the reporter said.

Caleb thought a moment before saying, "You probably don't know it, but Billy Ray had a hard childhood. He was bullied by boys and girls alike because he was short and not strong enough to participate in sports. You should check that out. I think because of that, he attacks people like me as his way of getting even for what had happened to him when he was in school."

He didn't like disclosing what Leroy had told him, but he didn't like Billy Ray continuing his attacks either. So, he figured it was time to go on the offensive.

And, indeed, when the story came out that afternoon, it contained comments from some of his teachers and class mates that supported what Caleb had said. One of his class mates said, "I was surprised that Billy Ray was ever employed as a deputy sheriff. We all thought he was a nut case. He blamed the coaches for not making any teams. That was a lot of bull. He just didn't make it. Lots of others didn't either and they didn't act like he did. He went to practices and laughed and made fun of us when we did anything wrong. He was bullying us, not the other way around. At the games, he always cheered for the other team. We had a talk with him and asked him to stop. He toned it down."

Another class mate had similar comments but added, "He's been chasing around after Julie Howard. His wife found out about it and left him. Last week."

*Goes to show, Caleb thought, you always need to get both sides of a story.*

Of course, Billy Ray laughed at what the classmates said and claimed all were backers of the sheriff.

The next car door he heard was Julie's. That one brought a smile to his face.

He showed her all he'd done since she and Bonnie Fae had visited. "I need to get furniture for the living room one of these days," he said. "Right now though, I don't expect visitors so I don't need any."

They had coffee. She talked about Red's problem. "The Walter's daughters hired a lawyer who demanded that Red refund the money Hugo had given him for the business. Red's lawyer advised him to do it but Red doesn't have the money."

"What's he going to do?"

"He's thinking about it. Right now, it's a friendly exchange between lawyers. They haven't set any dates for doing anything. Red's in a stew though. His lawyer thinks he might negotiate with them to take an investment in the catalogue business in exchange for the money. But, Red doesn't like the idea of having strangers looking over our shoulders so he may try to sell something."

"Glad it's not me," Caleb said. He had an idea he wanted to show her, how he wanted to re-do the master bathroom to bring it up to date.

She liked what he had in mind. "Two lavs are always a blessing for a husband and wife." She looked at him and smiled. Their eyes stayed locked together. He pulled her close and kissed her.

Sometime later, he pulled her close again and told her his plans for a business. "I want to marry you Julie. But, I'm old fashioned and want to support my family. So, if you say yes, can we stay engaged for a while to see how my business goes?"

She squeezed him hard, looked into his eyes and said, "Yes. I would marry you tomorrow. I want to, but I understand what you're saying."

"I want us to spend as much time together as we can though. Would you mind staying with me here part of the time? I'll fix you a work shop in the garage."

She wouldn't mind at all.

He felt like his heart skipped a beat when she agreed with what he'd said.

*****

The election for sheriff and other local officials was held the next day. As most had expected, the sheriff won in a landslide.

Afterwards, the sheriff and the DA made a joint announcement about Billy Ray and Leroy. The sheriff let the DA do the telling.

"The sheriff and I have looked at all the facts surrounding what Billy Ray and Leroy did. Charlie Howard says he won't press charges if we dismiss all charges against him. The judge says I can do that with prejudice so he'll be free. He's getting re-married in a few days. In light of that, and because no one was seriously injured by all the things Billy Ray and Leroy did ... let me interject that Mr. Stanley is in complete agreement with what I'm saying. Anyway, we are not going to file charges against either man. Neither man is now associated with the sheriff's department and neither will be rehired."

The local newspaper ran a story that included an editorial comment, "Billy Ray campaigned on the theme that the sheriff was soft on criminals. I imagine today he's celebrating that fact that the sheriff was soft on his and Leroy's crimes."

*****

Julia told Caleb that Red had decided to pay the Walters' daughters all the money that Hugo had given him, $100,000, and had put everything he owned, except the truck stop, on the market. As soon as he had a firm offer for anything that'd enable him to pay Hugo's investment, he'd take what was left off the market.

Caleb spent the night thinking about it, then the next morning, called McNally and authorized him to make an offer on the building that housed the restaurant and the craft's store. He'd offer ninety thousand dollars, cash, but would settle for one hundred thousand. Red was asking a hundred and fifty thousand but business was business as far as Caleb was concerned. And, he'd never warmed up to Red, especially after the night they had dinner together at Julie's home. He'd been borderline rude.

A few days later, Caleb owned the building. The first thing he did was install Bonnie Fae as the manager of the restaurant. Julie could manage the craft's store. She wanted to divide the store into stalls which she would rent to other ladies who created crafts.

And, in the meantime, Caleb pursued his consulting business. He bought a used van and outfitted it the way he'd planned. And, he began advertising.

After the dust had settled, he was traveling all over south Mississippi, diagnosing vehicles with complex electrical problems.

And, after six months, he asked Julie if she was still willing to marry him. She kissed him and said, "Of course, I do! When?"

They were married within the week.

*****

The day before the wedding, Caleb sat on his back porch and drank a glass of wine. Julie was inside. As he did, Glow suddenly appeared.

"I thought you'd been recalled," he said.

Glow replied, "I have but I wanted to say goodbye. You were a good project, Caleb. I picked you because your ideas and views on life ran counter to the permissive culture that is undermining the progress mankind had made over the years. There are others like you. It is my belief that over time, you can reverse the galloping drift towards the permissive lack of discipline that has your culture by the throat."

"Our destruction?"

"Yes. I think your free will, and the free will of others like you, has a shot at saving your culture and extending the progress you've made."

"I hope you're right."

"As you know, I'm rarely wrong."

With that, Glow lifted out of the rocker and streaked away. Julie came through the door just as the orange streak swept across the sky.

"A comet," she said and pointed. "An omen of good luck for us, Caleb."

Caleb smiled. "Yes. It is." *It saved my life and led me to you.*

He stood and took her in his arms. "I love you Julie."

"I love you Caleb."

And, in his thoughts, he heard the words, "The End. I'm going home, Caleb! I'm going home!" Glow's final statement.

The End

Made in the USA
San Bernardino, CA
30 June 2020